Other Works

As T. Kingfisher

Nine Goblins
Toad Words & Other Stories
The Seventh Bride
The Raven & The Reindeer
Bryony & Roses
Jackalope Wives & Other Stories
Summer in Orcus
Clockwork Boys

Coming in 2019:
The Twisted Ones

As Ursula Vernon

From Sofawolf Press:

Black Dogs Duology
House of Diamond
Mountain of Iron

Digger Series
Digger Omnibus Edition

It Made Sense At The Time

For kids:

Dragonbreath Series
Hamster Princess Series
Castle Hangnail
Nurk: The Strange Surprising Adventures of a Somewhat Brave Shrew
Comics Squad: Recess!
Funny Girl

THE WONDER ENGINE

Book Two of THE CLOCKTAUR WAR

By T. Kingfisher

Argyll Productions
Dallas, Texas

The Wonder Engine
Production copyright Argyll Productions © 2018

Published by Argyll Productions
Dallas, Texas
www.argyllproductions.com

ISBN 978-1-61450-417-7

First Edition Hardcover, March 2018

Typeset in Adobe Garamond Pro and Starship Regular.

For Andrea and her long-suffering canine compatriot, Nemo

PROLOGUE

Slate is a thief who specialized in stealing, forging, and planting paperwork. When she is arrested for treason, she finds herself part of a suicide mission with Brenner the assassin and the disgraced paladin Caliban, once a demonslayer, now host to the dead remains of the demon which sent him on a murderous rampage and shattered his world.

Their goal is both simple and nearly impossible. Find a way to stop the Clockwork Boys, the massive, alien ivory creatures from Anuket City wreaking ruin upon the countryside. Should they stray from their mission, crude magical tattoos will devour them. Fail and the Anuket City forces will kill them.

Accompanied by the brilliant but sheltered scholar, Learned Edmund, the trio evaded a squad of Clockwork Boys, only to be captured by rune, murderous deer-people led by an ancient demon. Slate, never the most likely of heroes, somehow rescued her friends and made an unlikely ally—a gnole, a small, peculiar badger-creature named Grimehug.

In their flight from the deer-people, they discovered a wonder-engine, a strange, cryptic device that none of them were able to use. Learned Edmund knew of other such devices, but the expert is Brother Amadai, a vanished scholar of his brotherhood, last seen in Anuket City.

Anuket City is where the Clockwork Boys originate. It is also the place where Slate herself lived until she angered the wrong people and had to flee.

Now Slate and her friends have reached Anuket City, and what lies within its clockwork gates will prove more terrible than anything they could have anticipated…

CHAPTER 1

The first thing they saw when they got into Anuket City was a corpse.

The body of a gnole swung ghoulishly from a lamppost, head cocked at an impossible angle, paws dangling limply. A crowd had gathered beneath the unfortunate creature, but they were already starting to disperse when the five of them and the string of mules rode through the city gates.

"My god!" said Learned Edmund, his fingers flicking in a benediction.

Its coat of rags had been ripped off, and somehow that seemed the saddest thing to Slate. The body underneath was scrawny and hunched, the ribs straining visibly against the skin. It had a stub of a tail, and the thick badger stripes along its head ran down its back, clear to the base of the spine.

"Why would they do this?" asked Caliban. He looked around. "Why didn't the Watch stop this?"

"Maybe it was a criminal," said Brenner.

Strangely it was Grimehug who seemed the least bothered by the sight. "It happens. Some gnole gets in the wrong place, wrong time, humans get crazy, string some gnole up, you know?" He shrugged.

"This happens frequently?" asked Caliban.

"Often enough, big man."

"And you stay here anyway?"

"Where else is a gnole gonna go?" He spread his hands, rags flapping. "Humans here, wild boars over there. Maybe a clocktaur steps on a gnole. Maybe a gnole starves. Something bad everywhere a gnole goes."

"Something should be done," insisted Caliban.

"One crusade at a time, paladin," said Brenner. "Let's find somewhere to stay."

It rapidly became obvious that Anuket City was different from the Dowager's capitol, and not just because it was a city-state instead of merely a city.

No one tried to stop them from entering the city. The guards looked bored.

"I expected it to be harder to get in," murmured Caliban.

"Why would it?" asked Slate. "They want you to come in and spend as much money as possible."

"They're at *war*."

"Which means the other city needs to worry about keeping *them* out. The war's happening miles away and there are no human soldiers from this side. Most of the citizens probably don't even notice it's happening."

"Still," said Caliban.

They were less than twenty feet from the entrance to the city when a woman walked by, her eyes vague and distant, surrounded by a cloud of hummingbirds on tiny jeweled leashes. They darted around her in bright, erratic zig-zags, occasionally hovering to sip nectar from flowers in her hair. Her face was beautiful, but as she passed them, they saw her pupils vastly dilated and her mouth slack.

"You see why no one noticed us," said Slate.

"This place is weird," said Brenner, as he watched the hummingbird woman leave.

Slate glanced over at her companions. In another city, they might indeed look strange, if not individually then certainly as a group.

Brenner was wiry and slouched a lot, which made him look shorter than he actually was. He had long, ragged dark hair and shaggy eyebrows. You could easily overlook Brenner in a crowd, which was useful for someone who killed people for a living.

There was no overlooking former Knight-Champion Caliban. He did not slouch. He was tall, blond, and had the sort of face that people stamped on coins and immortalized in marble. He wore leather and chain armor and an undyed tabard that was, it had to be said, much the worse for wear. (It had been pelted with owl pellets approximately an hour earlier.) The massive sword on his back was made for killing demons. It looked very impressive, since hardly anyone realized that most demons possessed farm animals.

Caliban caught her look and gave her a quizzical smile. Slate shrugged at him and looked away. That smile haunted her, at least during the brief periods of time when she didn't want to bash his head in with a brick for being so relentlessly knightly.

Slate herself would have been overlooked even if she weren't standing next to Caliban. Dark brown hair, medium brown skin, colorless clothes. She had worked for thirty years to become invisible and most days she managed it very well indeed. In her line of work, it did not pay to stand out.

All three of them shared one physical trait in common. On their left arms, painted teeth sunk into the skin, was a crude tattoo of a scowling face.

Slate scratched absently at hers. The tattoo had had very strong opinions about her rescue of the other night. It had torn a jagged line across her bicep that had scabbed over now, but Slate knew that it would leave a scar.

Which hardly matters, does it? None of us expect to survive this experience. Well, no one but Learned Edmund…

The designated survivor was a slender, pleasant-faced young scholar. He wore the ink-stained robes of a dedicate of the Many-Armed God, which would attract respect and dread in equal measure. Respect, because the Many-Armed God only took the most brilliant scholars in His temples. Dread because they were also notoriously difficult to work with.

And then, of course, there was Grimehug, the gnole. She'd pulled him out of a village of murderous deer-people and he had adopted her in turn. Slate wondered if the odd little badger-creature would stick around, or if he would vanish into the city now that they had returned.

She rather hoped he'd stay. She'd gotten used to having him asleep at the foot of her bedroll. He was warm and solid and didn't wake up when she had an allergy attack in the middle of the night, which gave him points over her ex-husband.

Still, Anuket City is where Grimehug lives. He's coming home.
I suppose, when you think about it, so am I.

For Slate, the memories coming back were a strange mixture. She was oddly proud of the strangeness of the city—she had lived here for seven years, she had survived—but under that was a gnawing sense of fear.

They were all still here.

Boss Horsehead, still here. The Shadow Market, still here.

All the old chickens, looking for a place to roost.

"Well," she said. "Well." She adjusted her hat, pulling it low over her eyes. No sense being obvious. No sense being too obviously disguised, either. Her greatest asset was that nobody in their right mind had ever expected her to come back. "Welcome to Anuket City."

CHAPTER 2

They left the horses at a stable just outside of town. Slate was in no way sad to see hers go. It seemed unlikely that she would see the horse again.

Hopefully it'll find someone who doesn't sit on it like a sack of wet bricks.

"Good riddance," muttered Brenner. "Never getting on one of those beasts again."

"How do you propose to leave the city, then?" asked Caliban, amused. "Assuming we do?"

"On a sedan chair carried by voluptuous maidens."

"Voluptuous maidens with very strong backs," said Slate.

"Best kind, darlin'."

Learned Edmund made a small sound of moral pain.

Finding an inn proved more problematic than the stable. There were plenty of inns and plenty of vacancies, but one of their number wasn't welcome.

"No gnoles," said the innkeeper.

"He's with us."

"No gnoles."

Slate dropped another coin on the counter. "I said, he's with us."

"I *said*, no gnoles."

Three more coins hit the counter.

"Look, lady," said the innkeeper, sounding tired rather than annoyed, "you can stack coins to the rafters, and the answer is still no. It's a health issue. No lepers, no public privies, and no gnoles!"

"What? Why not?" Slate's hand went out to rest on Grimehug's head.

"They carry werkblight." He frowned over the counter. "I hope you wash your hands after you touch that one."

"Werkblight? What's werkblight?"

"Goddamn, you're not from around here." The innkeeper made shooing gestures. "It's a disease. You'll know it when you see it, believe me."

"Sorry," said Slate. "I did live here once, but that was five, six years ago."

"Just missed them, then," said the innkeeper. "Lucky you. Little blighters were everywhere one day, and the werkblight broke out not long after. Now get out of here, and take your gnole with you."

"Jerk," muttered Slate.

"*Do* you carry werkblight?" asked Brenner, once they were back out on the street.

"Brenner!"

"What? You'd rather I didn't ask?"

Grimehug grinned. "Good question, dark man. Don't think so. Don't know. Gnoles don't get sick from it. Never touch werkblight though, leave that for grave-gnoles."

"What does it look like, this werkblight?" asked Learned Edmund. "Is it anything like the blight back in the capitol?"

"Don't know. Never seen your blight." Grimehug shrugged. "Stay in Anuket City, you'll see werkblight soon enough. Don't be touching it."

They tried three more inns. None of them would take gnoles for any amount of money, and one threw her out for even suggesting it.

After that, she stopped asking. Instead she called a halt on the street, in a square lined with statues. She and Brenner stood under a battered statue of a winged lion, and put their heads together. Their fingers flickered in small, descriptive gestures that Caliban couldn't even begin to follow.

"Backdoor?"

"Too much traffic."

"Balcony?"

"Garden."

"With drainpipes."

"Doable."

The two separated, nodded to each other, and Slate turned to the other three.

"Wait here." She spun on her heel.

"But—"

He was too late. Brenner had already melted into the crowd. Caliban tried to keep his eyes on Slate and lost her within a dozen heartbeats. The square was fairly crowded at this time of day, but it was still uncanny.

Priest and paladin were left standing under the lion statue. The gnole plopped down at their feet.

"Well," said Learned Edmund. "I suppose we wait."

"I suppose we do." Caliban had an intense desire for a hot bath. This did not mean anything in and of itself, because Caliban had wanted a hot bath for weeks now. It was just that there was a chance he might actually get one.

"Big city," said Learned Edmund.

"Very."

The lion statue sat up on its haunches and lifted a paw with a creak. Caliban jerked back, startled.

"Twelve…oh….clock…" rasped the lion, in a deep, mechanical voice. "And…all's…all's…all's…"

Grimehug reached out and smacked it upside the head.

"All's well!" said the lion, and flapped its wings twice. It settled back on the pedestal with a grinding sound.

"They do it regular, every hour," said the gnole. "You get used to it."

All over the square, the other statues were repeating variations on this statement, with various mechanical movements. A griffin raised and lowered its crest, a horse pawed at the air, and something went badly wrong with a statue of a mermaid, causing her to slap herself across the face with her own tail. Clunking noises and a badly chipped nose indicated that this probably wasn't the first time.

"I wonder what they do if all's not well," murmured Learned Edmund.

"They don't do nothing." Grimehug yawned. "Seen 'em shout "All's well!" when the square's on fire."

"What an odd city."

The crowd parted briefly to let a rider through. His steed was horse-shaped and horse-sized, but appeared to be made of wrought iron. Elegant curlicues defined the shape of cheek and eye and the flow of mane, while complicated shafts and gears moved inside the iron frame. It crossed the square, walking sedately, sparks flashing under its hooves.

"Flash bastards. Not supposed to ride them in the square," said Grimehug, disgusted. "Tear up the street, those hooves."

They waited.

Learned Edmund leaned back and studied the sky. "Do you think they will find something?"

"It's what they're good at. Cities…all this…" Caliban shook his head. He understood cities, but he did not wear them like a skin the way that Slate and Brenner did.

"I will confess that on the journey here, I had begun to worry about their competence."

"The horses, yes." Watching Slate and Brenner adapt to riding horses had been an education. "I think they're very competent, in their own field."

Learned Edmund nodded. He took a deep breath and said, with the air of a man determined to be fair at all costs, "I misjudged Mistress Slate. I did not realize that a woman would be capable of such heroism."

Caliban pinched the bridge of his nose and told himself that the scholar was trying his best. The Many-Armed God, who Learned Edmund followed, was known for producing brilliant, sheltered scholars, all of whom were sworn to celibacy and most of whom had not seen a woman since they were dedicated to the temple at the age of five.

"But Mistress Slate is not typical, I expect."

The paladin barked a laugh. "Typical! I no longer know what is typical of anyone. But I have generally found that women are capable of great heroism. At least as great as men." He thought of the nuns who had raised him and added, "And they frequently make less fuss over it."

Learned Edmund was clearly skeptical. "Well," he said. "I have met very few, of course."

"You might try meeting more."

"The Many-Armed God teaches us to avoid distractions."

15

Caliban had a brief, vivid memory of one of the older nuns saying: "Maybe their god could use one of those arms to pull his followers' heads out of their own asses!"

He missed nuns. You always knew where you stood with nuns.

He reminded himself that Learned Edmund had come a long way in a few weeks.

"You might consider how much knowledge you're missing by avoiding them."

Learned Edmund's nostrils flared. "I will think on it," he said finally. Caliban rubbed his temples and thought uncharitable thoughts.

Grimehug glanced over at him, ears half-cocked. He could not read the gnole's expressions well, but he thought it was amusement, and something else as well.

He did not quite trust Grimehug, and yet he found himself being grateful.

There had been a moment, in that flight from the rune, when Caliban had almost forgotten himself. When Slate had been limping and he had tried to be her crutch, the way he would have for Learned Edmund or Brenner or anyone else.

He had slid his shoulder under her arm and she had pressed against his side, breast and hip and thigh. And her face had been too close and he could smell her suddenly, under the sweat and the blood and the tang of pine needles. And his stupid body, still dazed by the rune-demon's attempt at seduction, had roused again.

For a half-dozen heartbeats, he'd imagined taking her right there, up against a tree, and both their wounds be damned. Hard and fast until she cried out his name and he forgot that there had ever been a demon that wore her face.

Then Grimehug had pulled at him and said, "Too tall, big man. Let a gnole try," and Slate had slipped off his shoulder and braced herself on the little badger-creature instead.

The gnole had given him a look as they traded places. Just a brief one, with his lip curled up over one fang. Not a threatening look, but Caliban had a strange, unsettled feeling that Grimehug had known exactly what he was thinking.

It had been like a splash of cold water. No. Of course not. Even if Brenner and Grimehug hadn't been standing *right there*, his hands were still covered in the old shaman's blood. For the love of the Dreaming God, how could he, even for a moment, have imagined doing that?

"Sorry?" said Learned Edmund. "I didn't catch that."

"Beg pardon?"

"You said something about Mistress Slate."

Caliban shook his head. "Sorry. Wool-gathering."

He glanced at Grimehug, and saw that the gnole was watching him again, thinking gods-knew-what behind those yellow eyes.

Caliban could feel a headache coming on.

Even had they been in private and somewhat less blood-covered, Caliban suspected that he'd blown his chance with Slate sometime earlier. She had rescued him and then he had rescued her, and it should have worked out somehow, but instead he'd opened his damn mouth and started babbling nonsense about the strong protecting the weak.

The memory made him cringe. He couldn't even blame the demon. That had been purely human stupidity, nothing more.

Frankly, after that little display, it was a miracle Slate had come back to rescue him from the rune at all.

Well, you had Brenner with you. She was probably rescuing him.

Brenner, who was ruthless and sarcastic and killed people for a living and who made no bones of the fact that he didn't trust Caliban any farther than he could throw the paladin in full armor.

Brenner, who had been Slate's lover once, and definitely wouldn't mind filling that position again.

And if I had an ounce of sense, I'd get out of his way. She is my commander and my liege and that is all that I have any right to ask of anyone.

...I do not seem to have much sense.

The way that they had spoken together, almost with their own private language, filled him with gnawing envy. Brenner understood that part of Slate's life in a way that the paladin never could.

Envy is a terrible emotion for a paladin. Nearly as bad as pride.

"Twisting your own whiskers, big man," said Grimehug.

Caliban opened his eyes. "Hmm?"

"You. Thinking. Smells like whisker twisting."

"I suppose I am."

"Humans don't have whiskers," said Learned Edmund. "Does this denote a painful act?"

Grimehug gave him a dubious look. "Hurts, yeah. But a gnole does it sometimes anyway. Knows a gnole should stop, but keeps twisting. You know?"

"I know," said Caliban. "Believe me, I know."

"Thought you might, big man."

Forty-five minutes and a subjective eternity later, Slate and Brenner returned. "This way," said Slate.

The inn she had found was expensive and exclusive, and there was no question about them taking gnoles. But it was expensive enough to have a garden courtyard and the rooms had balconies, and that meant that a gnole could scurry up a drainpipe and over the railing into Slate's room.

The three men had a suite across the hall, with a sitting room, and they hurried the gnole across while Caliban stood guard in the hall.

"Whoa!" said Grimehug, turning in a circle in the middle of the room. "Swank! Other gnoles gonna be crazy jealous."

"Well, what do we do now?" asked Brenner, dropping sideways into a chair in front of the fire. "Grab someone and say, 'Hey, which way to the secret clockwork factory?'"

"Not much of a secret, dark man," said Grimehug, and grinned. "Go to the Clockwork District, all the clockwork you need."

"Can we have a bath first?" asked Caliban plaintively.

"And cigarettes," said Brenner.

"And laundry," said Learned Edmund.

"Fine, fine." Slate waved her hands. "God forbid our suicide mission take precedence over clean underwear…"

They regrouped two hours later. Caliban was still slightly damp. Brenner was smoking a post-dinner cigarette with the intense concentration he usually reserved for killing people.

"Everyone's fed?" said Slate. "Nobody's starving or filthy or has bugs in their socks?"

"You're not wearing socks," Caliban pointed out.

Slate wiggled her bare toes at him. "I have one pair that is not more hole than sock. They are taking a well-deserved rest. They are heroes of the sock world."

Caliban put his fist over his heart in tribute.

"Furthermore, I did not get to take a bath, because apparently all the hot water was bespoke by *someone* in the room across the hall from me."

He had the decency to look embarrassed.

"All right," said Slate. She sat down on a footstool opposite Grimehug. "Now. Now that we are not in the woods, being chased by demon-deer or savage vegetables—tell me everything you know about the Clockwork Boys."

"For you, sure, Crazy Slate." The gnole sat down on her foot and gave her a canine grin. "Not much, maybe. Never heard 'em called that. Clocktaurs, here." He wrinkled his nose. "Come out of the big warehouse downtown…"

CHAPTER 3

What they managed to piece together, through careful questioning, was both less than Slate had hoped and a great deal more than they had known before.

Clocktaurs emerged, fully formed, from a warehouse in the Clockwork District. It was a huge building, the biggest in the city. Bigger than the Senate building. (Anuket City was nominally a representative democracy, in much the same way that Slate was nominally a taxpayer.) Grimehug had never been inside, and could not tell them anything about the contents. Nor could he explain how the clocktaurs were made.

"Nothing going in," he said. "Not ivory, steel, nothing. Not parts. Just people, going in and out. And garbage."

They could elicit no details as to the garbage. "Just garbage. Trash, you know. Rag-and-bone. Some gnole takes it out. Grave-gnoles, too."

"Could you find those gnoles and ask?"

Grimehug wrinkled his nose. "Rag-and-bone gnole, sure, yeah. Not touching grave-gnoles. Not getting in *smelling* distance of grave-gnoles. You don't either, if you're smart, Crazy Slate."

Once every few days—three and some change, Grimehug wasn't clear on exact times—a clocktaur ambled out of a door in the warehouse and into the street.

"Big damn door," said Grimehug. "Little damn street. Gnole has to go along and make sure nothing gets hung up, you know?"

"The…clocktaur…might get hung up?" asked Learned Edmund.

"Street might get hung up on the clocktaur, book man."

The clocktaur walked to the old parade ground, escorted by gnoles. As far as Slate could tell, the gnoles just hung around waiting for the clocktaurs to come out. Once they reached the old parade ground, someone would give them a few copper coins.

"A guard?" asked Caliban. "The clocktaur's keeper?"

"Merchants paying for it, not army. Army never pays a gnole anything." Grimehug made a rude gesture, presumably in the army's direction. "Merchant, he says 'Keep people out of clocktaur's way, keep doors shut so clocktaur doesn't knock them down, move the trash cans.' Merchants, they pay a gnole, fetch and carry, keep clocktaurs from knocking down city. Bad for business."

Apparently you couldn't steer a clocktaur. You could just get things out of its way. The merchants must have realized that it was better to pay gnoles to clear the way than to pick up after—and they were gnoles, so if a couple got squashed by a clocktaur now and then, who cared?

Slate realized that her nails were pressed into her palms. She stared at them like they didn't belong to her.

"But nobody questions it?" asked Caliban, baffled. "Those huge, awful things—they don't ask what's going on?"

"They wouldn't," said Slate slowly. "Not here…"

In this city full of artificial marvels—iron horses and clockwork statues—the clocktaurs, astonishingly, had gone largely unnoticed. People knew that they existed, but assumed that some artificer had made them. They were fighting for Anuket City, after all, and the fighting was furthermore happening a long way away, so other than making sure that the streets were clear when they went by, no one thought much about it.

Slate, who had once left the capitol for Anuket City, could understand that. Artificers here were viewed as basically harmless geniuses. Their creations might explode or trample you, sure, but they were just as likely to fall apart or trip over their own feet.

And the artificers were good for business. People came from hundreds of miles around to buy their creations.

She could understand how, in this city, alone in all the world, you could quietly create an army of clocktaurs, and nobody would pay all that much attention.

"As long as they don't tear up the street or smash the trash cans, people don't care," she said.

"They're eight feet tall!" said Brenner.

"Ten," said Grimehug.

"Ten, then. I didn't take a tape measure to the ones we saw."

The clocktaurs would stand in the parade ground, unmoving, like statues.

"Dare," added Grimehug. "Climb a clocktaur. Impress the mates. A clocktaur doesn't move." He grinned, showing all his badger-like teeth.

And then one day, when there were thirty clocktaurs—enough to form a column three wide and ten deep—guards would throw open the big gates by the parade ground and the column would march out. Not on the trade road, where they'd upset the ox-carts and make a fuss, but the old army road.

"It hooks up to the trade road on the other side of Archenhold," said Slate. "That's how they're getting up as far as we encountered them." She slumped back in her chair, rolled upside down, and put her feet over the back of the chair.

"Think there's anything left of Archenhold?" asked Caliban.

"I think they probably saw the first column go by and suddenly realized that Anuket City was their dearest friend in the world."

The last few columns—most likely including the one they had seen—had been accompanied by several gnoles.

"Too smart for a gnole's own good," said Grimehug, sounding annoyed. "Thought maybe there'd be more money at the end. Couple gnoles go out with the columns most times. Go wherever they're going. Safer. Nothing attacks clocktaurs."

Brenner gave a humorless laugh.

"Me and some buddies, we went out with them this time. Move more things out of the way, maybe get paid, yeah?" He curled his lip back. "Then a gnole falls down, gets stepped on. Clocktaurs don't care. So a gnole tries to help. Couldn't. Clocktaurs kept going. Me, got lost, get found by crazy rune. Know how that ended, yeah?"

"Yeah," said Slate. She squeezed his shoulder. It hadn't occurred to her, with everything else, that Grimehug had lost friends recently.

Caliban cleared his throat. "It's a cheap way to fight a war."

Slate glanced up at him.

"You send an army of clocktaurs down toward a city and tell them to destroy everything in their path. Then you send a message to the city saying, 'Surrender, or we do it again.' And then you do it again."

"And again," said Learned Edmund, "and again. And once one city surrenders, you send them out to the next one. Eventually, governments will surrender just to keep from being razed to the ground."

"I don't know how they plan to administer their conquered cities, though," said Caliban, shaking his head. "Unless they set up regional governors and have them send tribute back...It'd be extortion, not empire."

"That sounds about right," said Slate. "Extortion and very generous trade deals. As long as they control the clocktaurs, the Senate can pull in tribute hand over fist."

"It's a very short-sighted way to govern," said Caliban sternly. "And it wouldn't last for long. If everyone rebelled at once—"

"Yeah, but the first city that does gets thirty clocktaurs in their teeth. Who wants to risk that?"

"But once they do risk it..."

Slate nodded at him from her upside-down vantage. "Then they pull the clocktaurs back to the city and cut off trade to their attackers. And bet that they've got more money than the other guy does."

They sat in silence for a while.

"Well. I know the old parade ground," Slate said finally. "It was right by the edge of the city. There was nothing out there but farmland and the knackers, though. The Clockwork District must be new."

"Here when I got here, Crazy Slate."

As near as they could pin down, that had been three years ago, although gnoles had been trickling into the city probably just as Slate was leaving it. Gnoles lived in family bands, which could grow, in a congenial city, into a good-sized warren. They had started in Emmet and seemed to be spreading west and south, leaving whenever over-crowding forced some of them on.

Grimehug himself had been wandering around a town called Grymm's Hollow when word had come that there was work in Anuket City.

"Never liked Grymm's Hollow," he said. "Snakes in all the gutters. Good eating on a snake, but a big one, he thinks good eating on a gnole. So came here, me."

"Which is sociologically interesting," said Learned Edmund, leaning back, "but not particularly relevant to the Clockwork Boys. Although it probably means that the capitol will see gnoles soon—"

"Some gnoles gone already," said Grimehug, yawning. "Not many."

"I haven't seen any," Brenner said.

"If some gnoles don't want to be seen, dark man, you won't see them. More going soon, I guess."

"Assuming it's not wiped out by clocktaurs first."

There didn't seem to be anything to say to that.

"Any idea where to start looking for your scholar friend?" asked Slate.

Learned Edmund sighed. "I'll make inquiries in the Artificer's Quarter. There is one Ashes Magnus there, who corresponds with my temple. A truly original thinker. I hope he may know where to begin."

"What about the codes in the journal?"

"They fall in two parts. The first cipher is easy. All the servants of the Many-Armed God know it. The second one..." He shook his head. "I need the key, and it is not in this journal. He must have written it down somewhere."

"Must he?" asked Slate.

Learned Edmund looked puzzled, as if she had asked something nonsensical. "Of course. You always write down the key to a cipher, or what if the knowledge is lost?"

"What if you don't care if it's lost?"

"Then," said the dedicate severely, "you are *not* a servant of the Many-Armed God!"

"...I'm sorry I asked."

"Our work is cut out for us," said Caliban, obviously trying to smooth the moment over.

"I'm going to go take my own bath," said Slate. "And then I'm going to sleep in a real bed. And then—well, I guess if Grimehug here is willing, we'll go find a clocktaur."

By the time she finished drying off, the gnole was stretched out full length at the foot of the bed, snoring. The contrast of dirty rags and clean linens was striking.

Oh, well, as long as he's on top *of the sheets...* Slate shrugged out of her clothes. Her modesty did not extend to a sleeping gnole.

She slid under the sheets. Grimehug grumbled and made room for her feet. The bed was cool and crisp and soft, and all of Slate's fears could not keep her from sinking immediately into sleep.

CHAPTER 4

Slate dreamed.

Initially it was nothing much, just the fragmented and absurd world of dreams. She was walking through a house with too many rooms, looking for something. The house was made of her mother's chambers in the brothel and Slate's first apartment and the academy where she had taken lessons and for some odd reason, the stable of the inn they had stayed at the third or fourth night on the road.

She opened a door at random, and found a closet stuffed with trumpets and rune. She closed it. She opened another door, and found another door behind it. She opened that one.

She fell out into the Shadow Market, flat on her face, and looked up to find Boss Horsehead staring down at her.

"You crossed me," said Horsehead, looming over her, impossibly large, the size of a giant. "No one crosses me." Slate reached for a knife, but she was stuck to the floor, she couldn't move, and Horsehead was picking her up by the shoulders and she was being swung aloft, with a clank of chains, into one of the crow cages over the Shadow Market.

She was bolted to the bars, weighed down with chains. The crows circled her, shrieking.

One landed on each shoulder, and they spoke to each other over her head, in gabbling gnolespeech. Slate asked them to repeat themselves, very politely, but they buffeted her face with their wings. She opened her mouth to scream, and feathers slid down her throat and filled her chest, and then she could not scream, but only cough…

"Slate! *Slate!* For God's sake, wake up!"

Someone was shaking her. She woke up, sucked in a great ragged breath, and began to cough violently. Whoever had woken her pounded her on the back while she choked and spluttered, saying something, but she was coughing too loudly to hear.

"Breathe," instructed the person pounding her back. "Breathe. In and out. Easy."

After a minor eternity, she was able to breathe again. Her chest ached and her throat felt raw. He was holding her chin tilted back at an angle that left her airway clear, the sort of practiced gesture she'd expect from a healer.

She groaned and scrubbed at her face.

When she moved her hands, a handkerchief was dangling in front of her, and that was how she realized who had woken her.

"Caliban?"

The knight sat on the edge of the bed, illuminated by a sliver of gaslight through the window. He was holding her up with an arm around her shoulders and he looked distinctly rumpled, but his voice was as calm as ever.

"Grimehug came for me. He said you were choking, and he couldn't wake you up."

She took the handkerchief and wiped at her face. Her cheeks felt hot. "I feel like I've been dragged by a horse."

"Another allergy fit? You're not sneezing…"

"No, no. More of a night terror, I think." She smiled weakly. "When you've got lungs as overactive as mine, it all gets tied together. Thank you for waking me up."

"Your enemies are my enemies, remember? Knight, liege lord?"

"Oh, *that.*"

"What was it?"

"What was what?"

"The night terror."

"Oh—I—" Slate waved a hand, hoping she hadn't talked too much in her sleep. "Nothing. Someone I knew once."

"Are you sure?"

He was using the voice on her. The paladin's voice, calm and patient and absurdly trustworthy. Slate wasn't sure if she resented that or not.

She should tell him about the crow cage. If she told him, she would probably feel better.

If she told him, she'd have to think about Horsehead.

And at that point, three things occurred to Slate more or less simultaneously.

The first was that she was naked, except for a sheet that had mostly fallen off while she was coughing. The second was that Caliban was still holding her up. His arm lay across her bare back. His hand was very warm and he was running his thumb across the point of her shoulder without seeming to realize it.

The third, unfortunately, was that with her hair hanging in sweaty strands and her face red and damp and her nose swollen, she was probably about as attractive as an injured mudskipper.

She hadn't yet worked out whether the third one negated the first two, when Grimehug bounced up on the bed, and that tipped the balance. Caliban jerked his arm away as if stung, and Slate pulled the sheet up to her chin with a faint sigh.

Oh, well, probably for the best. Am I even allowed to nail a knight sworn in my service? Is that fraternizing?

Would he be doing it because he wanted to, or under orders? Does that fall into duty to one's liege?

Have I even forgiven him for calling me weak? He did apologize, but then he swore fealty to me like an idiot, and I don't know if I've forgiven him for that, either.

No. No. This is too complicated. Entirely too complicated. Stick to the mission. I don't have time *for this.*

"You feeling better, Crazy Slate?"

"Yeah." She reached out a hand and ruffled his fur. "Thanks, Grimehug."

"Glad to help, crazy lady." Apparently deciding that the evening's entertainment had ended, the gnole plopped down at the foot of the bed and stretched out again.

"I should go," said Caliban.

She nodded. "Sorry to wake you."

"I owed you a midnight waking," he said, a bit dryly. "And at least you didn't try to stab me."

"You could go out and come in again and I could have a knife ready, if it would make you feel better."

He rose. He was wearing a pair of trousers and not much else. Slate didn't know whether to bless Grimehug or boot him out into the hall.

God, the knight was stupidly beautiful. She'd seen him without a shirt on before, but usually only in passing, as he shrugged into different clothes. Not with dim blue moonlight lying across his skin, highlighting the muscles from his shoulders down his arms.

She could see white scars slashed across his chest and she wanted to drag her fingers over each one and feel the way the texture changed from skin to scar and back again.

"If you need me again—" he began.

No, no. Being weak again. Paladins don't take advantage of the weak, even if the weak bloody well wish they would.

Shoulders like a goddamn ox and a brain to match.

"I know where you sleep," said Slate ominously.

"Yes, and don't think that doesn't scare me." He nodded to the gnole. "Come get me again, Grimehug, if you need to."

The door closed.

Slate dropped back to the mattress with a groan. *Four months in a jail cell.* No one *should look that good after four months in a jail cell. The Dreaming God has impeccable standards.*

Why couldn't he look like…like Brenner, say? I'd have jumped his bones weeks ago if he looked like a human and not a damn piece of statuary.

"Grimehug?"

"Yeah, Crazy Slate?"

"Why'd you get Caliban?"

"Couldn't wake you up. You were choking bad."

"No, I know, but—why him? Why not one of the others?"

There was a long silence from the foot of the bed.

"Think maybe a gnole won't answer that, Crazy Slate."

"What? Why not?"

Grimehug shrugged. She felt the gesture ripple across her feet. "Humans all crazy, Crazy Slate. You crazier than most. Humans can't smell. Leave it alone, maybe."

"Huh," said Slate. *I better not push him—we need his help too bad to bully him over something like this.*

Still, she wondered. Despite the limited vocabulary, she suspected Grimehug knew a lot more than he let on, and she wondered what exactly he'd been thinking.

CHAPTER 5

"I don't like this," said Caliban. "There ought to be guards."

Grimehug gave him a look over one ragged shoulder. "Clocktaurs don't need guards, big man."

"Yeah," said Slate, "they're ten feet tall and made out of…whatever that stuff is. What would they need guards for?"

"To stop people like us," said Caliban.

Brenner laughed at that.

Slate shook her head. "This is a bad neighborhood. They'd need to guard the guards."

Learned Edmund looked around worriedly.

They were in the Old City, near the parade grounds. Grimehug assured them that this was the route that the clocktaurs took out of the Clockwork District.

And it was, quite clearly, a bad neighborhood. There were rats in the gutters—not skulking, but strolling around as if they had a right to be there. Garbage piled up in the alleys. The houses were run-down and crammed tightly together. Caliban did not see a single gnole.

Also, Brenner looked more comfortable than he'd been for days.

"Some gnoles here," said Grimehug, when asked. "Not worth being seen. Some gnole pokes his head up, maybe some gnole gets his throat slit for fun, eh?"

Learned Edmund shuddered.

They crowded into an alley. It was near dusk and the shadows were getting thick. Caliban ran into a garbage bin and cursed.

"I'd tell you to be quiet," said Brenner, taking a long drag off his cigarette, "but we actually don't want to startle anyone. So try to clank louder, will you?"

"Ha ha."

The paladin was flanking Slate, one step behind. It reminded him of the first time they had walked together, in the halls of the palace, with Caliban ragged and battered, in too-loose clothes and a season's growth of beard.

He expected that few people would recognize him as the same man. Slate looked exactly the same, though, her face still as mobile and expressive.

He couldn't remember now if she had always been bad at hiding her feelings, or if he had gotten better at reading them.

Last night, it had been blatantly obvious that her night terror was actually about something real and present and probably about to crash on all their heads. Caliban would have found this rather alarming, except that he'd had his arm around her naked shoulders and concentrating on the fact that she was lying to him was the only thing that kept him from making a fool of himself right there.

Well, that and Grimehug.

It was very difficult to seduce a woman in front of a gnole. There was something about them that was the very opposite of romantic. Probably the smell of wet dog.

Which was for the best. *The strong do not take advantage of the weak. Or the…errm…the equally strong who happen to be having a moment of weakness. As the case may be.*

…and if I'd said any of that out loud, she'd probably have shoved me out a window in full armor. So really, *it's for the best.*

The alley opened onto a narrow street. It was dark and the few unbroken windows were not lit. Slate frowned.

"That's a bad neighborhood," she said, jerking a thumb over her shoulder the way they had come, "but this street used to be the border. It was always pretty lively. There's even some nice houses on the other side. What happened?"

"Three guesses," said Brenner, "and they all start with clockwork." Caliban sighed.

They waited. The shadows got longer and melted together.

"How long until the clocktaur comes?" asked Slate quietly.

Grimehug shrugged. "Usually come out around now. Sometimes sooner, sometimes later."

"I imagine we'll hear it coming," said Learned Edmund.

They did not wait long.

Thump. Thump. Thump.

"There's your clocktaur, Crazy Slate."

Slate put a handkerchief to her face pre-emptively.

The windows rattled as the thumping grew closer.

Caliban put his hand on his sword. It was a useless gesture and he knew it, but his body felt better for it, even if his mind did not.

The clocktaur came into view at the end of the street.

Two gnoles were jogging along in front of it. Grimehug leaned out of the alley mouth and waved cheerfully. One of the gnoles waved back.

"Eh! Grimehug!"

"Eh! Cobble!"

Brenner made a brief, abortive move forward. Slate put a shoulder in front of him. "It probably knows we're here," she hissed. "The point is that right now it doesn't *care*."

"But—"

"I'm not sneezing."

Brenner subsided.

The clocktaur pulled alongside the alley.

It was one thing to see them marching and know the beasts were tall—it was another to see it pass a dozen feet away. The clocktaur's blunt head was even with the bottom of the second-story windows. Caliban could see gears on it, turning, all of them the color of old ivory and none of them doing anything he understood. He heard Slate draw a breath and hold it and go very still.

And then it was past them. It stomped on down the street, accompanied by the gnoles. Caliban was amazed that the stones did not shatter under the thing's feet.

It did not turn its head or acknowledge their existence. It did not acknowledge anything's existence. When it reached the end of the street and turned, it seemed to be following a pre-ordained path. The gnoles scampered out of its way.

The five of them stood in silence for a moment, broken by the sound of Learned Edmund opening his notebook.

"It can't *work*," he muttered, sounding distressed. "Those gears shouldn't *do* that. It moves like a beast, not like a mechanism. How did anyone ever *make* that?"

No one had an answer. The scholar scribbled a few notes before closing his notebook again. "Too dark to write," he muttered. "We should go back."

"I wonder if they heal?" mused Caliban. "Beasts heal. Mechanisms don't."

Grimehug shook his head. "Seen one bash into another one once. Walked into each other. One got a chunk knocked off it. Could tell that one by the hole 'til they all marched out."

"That's useful," said Learned Edmund. "Thank you, Grimehug."

"How's the smell?" asked Brenner in an undertone.

Slate wiped her nose. "Not bad. A little rosemary, but that's all."

"Oh, well," said Learned Edmund, sounding a bit more cheerful. "If I may venture a hypothesis?"

"Venture at will."

"It would seem that your—mmm—talent is perhaps a form of weak precognition? It is warning you about things that may be dangerous. Since this clocktaur is not dangerous to you, the effects are significantly weakened."

"Could be," Slate admitted. "Though it's not always about danger." She shot Caliban a look he couldn't read. "Still, I'm not complaining…"

She leaned out of the alley mouth and looked in the direction that the clocktaur had gone. "Well, at least we know why that street's empty now. Can't imagine you'd want that walking by every—"

"'scuse me, darlin'," said Brenner quietly, "but we've got friends."

They all turned.

There were men in the alley. They did not look friendly. Caliban could see at least four, and one of them had a rather large knife out.

"See, I knew this was a bad neighborhood," said Slate, to no one in particular.

"This is a poor idea, gentlemen," said Caliban. "You should leave."

The footpads did not look impressed.

"We are capable of defending ourselves," he added.

If possible, they looked even less impressed. Brenner snickered.

"You want to try?" asked Caliban over his shoulder.

"Sure." Brenner raised his voice. "Sod off, you bastards, and we won't kill you."

One of the footpads spat.

Caliban felt mildly gratified by Brenner's failure, right up until the first man charged.

Damn it. Damn it. Damn it.

There were too many of them. His sword was absolutely useless in an alley this narrow and he didn't have a shield. On the other hand, he was wearing chainmail and a rather thick cloak. Cloth bound up knives remarkably well. And it didn't look like a very good knife to begin with.

For lack of anything better to do, Caliban pushed Slate behind him and punched the footpad in the face with a mailed fist.

The man staggered back. Either he hadn't been expecting resistance, or he hadn't been expecting quite so *much* of it.

Caliban darted a glance behind him. *I have to stay between them and the others...*

"Can we talk about this, gentlemen?" asked Slate, from somewhere in the vicinity of Caliban's left elbow. "I'm sure no one wants this to turn ugly—"

The first footpad pulled his hands away from his nose, which was streaming blood. "Ob show you ubly!" His compatriot made short stabbing motions with his knife.

Slate sighed.

"Now?" asked Brenner quietly.

"Fine."

And then Brenner moved.

Caliban didn't even see it happen. It didn't look like he was doing *anything.* Brenner just walked forward, very calmly, and lifted both hands.

Both footpads clutched their throats and fell against the walls of the alley.

The cause of this appeared to be a pair of knives stuck into their necks.

One made a valiant effort to stab Brenner on the way down. Brenner leaned to one side and looked at the next pair of footpads in the alley.

"Well?" he said.

The sounds of running footsteps died away. Grimehug sat down and scratched.

"Amateurs," muttered Brenner.

"I will admit it. I am impressed," said Caliban.

The assassin shrugged. "It's easier when they stand close together like that. They get in each other's way more than yours."

Learned Edmund sketched signs in the air—blessings or requests for mercy, Caliban couldn't say. His skin looked gray.

"Well," said Caliban. "This has been…educational. I suppose we should report this attack to the—Slate!"

"What?"

"Are you going through their pockets?"

"I'll wash my hands." She held up a single coin and scowled. "They *must* have been hard up. Hardly worth rolling."

"We could sell their boots," said Brenner.

"A gnole knows a good place for boots," offered Grimehug.

"We are not selling *anyone's* boots," said Caliban. "We are informing the guards—"

"Oh, the hell we are," said Slate. "Have you forgotten what we're doing here?"

There was a brief pause.

"…yes," said Caliban. "I had, actually. All right." He hastily signed benedictions over the men's bodies. "Let's go home, shall we? Unless there's something else you think we can learn?"

He inclined his head toward Slate.

She's in charge. Don't take command just because you're used to it. This is her world, not yours.

"I think we've learned quite enough," said Slate. She wrinkled her nose. "Good job, Brenner."

The assassin shrugged, but there was a glint of pleasure in his eyes.

"I suppose now that we've seen one, we need to figure out how they're made." Slate glanced over her shoulder, in the direction the clocktaur had gone.

"All come out of the Clockwork District," said Grimehug. "You want a clocktaur, that's where you go."

CHAPTER 6

As they walked back toward the inn, Slate fell back a few steps. Caliban immediately dropped back to flank her.

"Is this how you treat your liege?" she murmured.

He was silent for a moment. Then, "No, I forget myself. But you should probably be used to that by now."

She glanced back at him, amused. He was smiling and it sent a familiar jolt through her.

Dammit. No. Down, girl. This is not the time.

"Do you plan to walk behind me like this forever?"

"Would that be a problem?"

"Frankly, yes." She scowled. "I have worked very hard to be invisible. You are *very* visible."

"I could attempt to disguise myself."

He said it entirely earnestly. Slate remembered his suggestion of a disguise in the capitol. Had it only been a few weeks ago? She looked at him again. Still six feet tall, almost obnoxiously beautiful, armed to the teeth, wearing a *white cloak*, for the love of the gods…okay, they could maybe fix the cloak, but as to the rest…

She pinched the bridge of her nose. It would be like disguising a war-horse as a donkey. Theoretically possible, but…

"Caliban, there is no earthly reason for someone like me to have a bodyguard that looks like you."

He looked at her with total non-comprehension. "Like me?"

"Militant," Slate said. *Why couldn't you look a little less like a damn statue?*

"I could try to look less militant."

She gave him a skeptical look. "Uh-huh. Caliban, I am not a priestess. I am not a nun. I most *definitely* do not want to be mistaken for a Senator. If you follow me around like this, people will assume that I must be either a wealthy merchant or a courtesan. The first will get me robbed and the second will get me propositioned."

"I will not allow either," he said.

"Caliban…" She placed a hand in the middle of his chest and shoved. He moved slightly less than a quarter inch.

"*Or* you could go walk up ahead and hover over Learned Edmund and then you can be a temple guard for a dedicate and I can be a secretary acolyte-type that no one notices."

He was quite good at the inscrutable paladin look, but she could see wheels turning behind it.

"Very well," he said finally. "My liege."

"Oh, don't start," she muttered, and glared at his back as he went to guard Learned Edmund.

The perfect gentle knight. She had a strong urge to kick him in the shins.

Which would do precisely nothing and he'd look confused at me. And then probably offer to take his shin armor off so I could try again without hurting my foot.

He glanced back, a faint line of worry between his eyebrows, which smoothed out as soon as he saw that she was still there.

I will not feel gooey inside, she instructed herself. *I won't. And I most certainly will not think about kissing that line. I will go back to thinking about kicking him in the shins.*

She had absolutely no desire to kiss his shins. Shins were a distinctly specialized interest in Slate's experience.

This line of thought got her most of the way back to the inn before her mind wandered again.

Stupid paladins.

And stupid forgers who want them…

Getting into the Clockwork District was easier said than done, at least for anyone that wasn't three feet tall and covered in rags.

They tried—delicately—to approach by five different streets, and there was a guard post and a gate at each one. (Well, for a value of "delicate." Brenner and Slate drifted through the shadows, and Caliban stood on the corner looking as subtle as a siege engine. Learned Edmund, on the other hand, had gone to the library.)

It didn't matter anyway. While the main streets were full of people, the crowds vanished on the streets leading to the Clockwork District. Any guard who wanted to look would see all three of them.

Each gate had a short rectangle cut in it. Gnoles streamed in and out, unbothered by the guards.

It's a *cat-flap*. They've got cat-flaps for the gnoles on the gates. *Dear god.*

After trying all five streets—and getting some suspicious glances from the guards—they regrouped in a courtyard café off the main square. Slate ordered tea, backed her chair into a corner, and pulled her hat brim down.

"This isn't going to work," she said. "We can't get close and they've cleared a gap between the walls and the houses. There's not even a blade of grass there, not that it would do us any good if there were."

"Can you go over the rooftops?" asked Caliban. "At least enough to look?"

"Not in broad daylight," said Brenner. "And if we get caught, there is a certain lack of plausible deniability. I'd rather wait until we don't have a choice."

"High ground, then," said Caliban, drumming his fingers on the table.

"Eh?"

"We take the high ground and spy out the land."

Slate stared off into space, stirring her tea.

"There's a church—" she began.

Brenner gave her a genuinely shocked look.

"—Not *that* church! A cathedral! A real one. *Still* a real one, I mean."

Caliban looked from one to the other. "What am I missing?"

Brenner said nothing. Slate hunched one shoulder. "Nothing important. Not very important. But—well, if somebody mentions the Grey Church to you, I wouldn't count on popping in for a sermon, all right?"

Caliban considered this. "Is this an…underworld thing?"

"Yes," said Brenner.

"No," said Slate, at the same time.

"Well, maybe," said Brenner. He leaned back and folded his arms.

"It doesn't matter," said Slate. "Not relevant. Hopefully nobody'll have to have any dealings with the Grey Church and no one will do anything stupid and no one will end up in a crow cage—"

Brenner kicked her under the table.

"So, a real cathedral!" Slate said hurriedly. "Bell-towers! Good view! Stained glass! Dedicated to the Forge God, but I can't imagine that they wouldn't let a dedicate of the Many-Armed God and a paladin of the Dreaming God in for a private tour."

"I'm not in service to the Dreaming God any more."

"And we're not in service to any god at the moment. What does that have to do with anything?" asked Brenner.

Caliban's eyebrows rose.

And then he smiled. It was, for a paladin, a very wicked smile.

"Well," he said. "I expect we'll be able to work something out."

CHAPTER 7

"I'm going to kill him," said Brenner.

"Oh, I don't know." Slate surveyed the assassin. "Acolyte's robes are very...*you*, somehow."

He flashed her an obscene gesture.

"And didn't you dress up like a monk once to get at that bishop? I seem to remember something about that..."

"They wore brown. Brown is okay."

Acolytes of the Many-Armed God wore green. Brenner looked like a large, lethal shrubbery.

"Just remember you're under a vow of silence," said Learned Edmund. "I shudder to think of the damage to our order's reputation otherwise."

Slate was surprised at how accommodating Learned Edmund was about disguising Brenner as a member of the priesthood. She would have expected him to be more of a stickler about such things.

But he had actually laughed. "The Many-Armed God knows his own," he said. "And his scholars have done worse things in pursuit of knowledge, though we do not speak of it a great deal."

"Does this mean my genitals are going to fall off?" asked Brenner.

"Women of the world, rejoice!" said Caliban, coming back into the room.

"Don't you two start now," warned Slate. "We have to get into the church between services."

They made their way across the city, more or less without incident. ("Don't *lurk*, Brenner. You're an acolyte. Acolytes look worried all the time. Like they're afraid they'll do something the gods will disapprove of.")

At the door of the cathedral of the Forge God, Caliban took a deep breath and became a Knight-Champion.

Slate would have given her ears to know how he did it. One minute he was Caliban, who always looked as if he were beating himself up internally for something, and who always carried a handkerchief.

The next minute he was about an inch taller and seemed to be standing in a brighter light than everything else around him. Even his shoulders looked broader.

Slate was quite sure that he was still wearing rather battered armor and a disgracefully grubby cloak, but he seemed to be…shining?

Why did we even bother dressing up? Nobody's going to notice us at all.

Nobody did.

A Knight-Champion of the Dreaming God walked into the cathedral. Two lay-brothers saw him and shot to their feet. One ran to find a priest and the other approached, babbling.

"Blessings be upon you—oh—oh—we weren't expecting anyone—so sorry—blessings—can we help you, sir?"

Slate was used to, "Can we help you?" translating as, "If you make me get up, I will have you drawn and quartered." She'd never heard it mean, "I will throw myself off a building if it will make your day better, sir."

"I am an escort for the Learned Edmund, dedicate of the Many-Armed God," said Caliban. (Which, Slate thought, was entirely true, which was probably why the voice came out so marvelously effectively.)

"I am fascinated by religious architecture. Specifically bell-towers," said Learned Edmund. "You have a marvelous example here of pre-Assignation architecture, and I am hoping to examine it more closely."

"I am certain that will not be a problem, sir!" said the lay brother.

"I am certain that will not be a problem, sir!" said the priest, when he arrived.

"I am certain that will not be a problem, sir, and we are furthermore very very honored to assist the Knight-Champion in any way that he may require!" said the deacon, when he arrived.

Brenner said something under his breath and Slate stomped on his foot.

"You can assist me best by assisting the dedicate," said Caliban graciously. "My secretary, here, will take any required notes." He waved a hand at Slate.

"Of course! If you are sure—the bell tower has not been remodeled in some time, you understand—the pigeons have—well—" He kept up a stream of apologies all the way to the door of the bell tower, which he unlocked from a key ring on his belt.

"It is quite all right," said Learned Edmund. "I am interested in the original architecture, you understand. And I am quite used to pigeons."

"Oh, well, if you're sure…"

The door to the bell tower opened. There were approximately four hundred stairs in it.

"He can't do it in full armor," said Brenner in Slate's ear.

"Bet you a copper?"

The deacon looked in their direction. Slate immediately busied herself with her papers. Brenner tried to look like someone under a vow of silence.

Caliban, disgraced former paladin, might have balked at four hundred stairs in full armor, but Caliban, Knight-Champion, never faltered. In fact, he went first.

"Do you assign guards to the towers?" he asked the deacon, who was panting and trying to keep up.

"No—oh—ho—not—usually—nobody—"

"Demons have been known to fly," said the Knight-Champion sternly. He gazed out of one of the arrow slits as if expecting an attack at any moment. The deacon slumped against the wall, panting. Slate toiled up the stairs after them. Her legs were starting to feel like that first day on horseback.

"Should—we—assign—will see to it—"

"You know your own defenses best, of course," said Caliban, in a voice that indicated the exact opposite.

The deacon held up a hand. When he had caught his breath, he said "It's only—there's no—demons—in Anuket City."

Slate saw the Knight-Champion mask waver for a fraction of a second. The line between Caliban's eyes lengthened, and then it smoothed away.

"A fortunate land," he said to the deacon. "Not all lands are so blessed."

They reached the top of the stairs. The deacon collapsed. Even Brenner was gasping. Learned Edmund had come up more slowly, ostensibly making tracings of the carvings around the arrow slits. Caliban had a faint sheen of sweat on his forehead but that was all.

Slate wrote *You owe me a copper* on a scrap of paper and showed it to Brenner. He struggled over the words, lips moving, then scowled.

Learned Edmund went to work. This mostly involved wandering around the bell tower, gazing up at the bells and murmuring to himself. The deacon trailed after him, shooting occasional worried glances at Caliban, as if he might be called to account for not knowing the answer to the dedicate's questions.

Slate sidled over to the paladin and whispered, "How are you not dying right now?"

"Pure willpower. I think I ruptured something on the last flight of stairs."

"Poor baby." She suppressed a grin. It was nice to know that the Knight-Champion thing was mostly on the outside.

She went to the window and gazed out over the city.

Her smile faded. The Clockwork District was immediately obvious.

Anuket City had, when she left, been roughly circular. But now, on the far side, there was a jagged new spur sticking out. An enormous roof reared out of the ground, like a beetle shell, and clapboard buildings had gone up around it.

"Forgive me, deacon," she said, as he passed, "but when I lived here some years ago, that was a river bluff, was it not?"

"Oh, yes," said the deacon. "A few years, now. They were mining, I believe. Apparently they found something, because it's been roofed over. Archaeological ruins, they say, of great historical value. They moved the army barracks, and there was some grumbling, but you know the Senate is always very interested in preserving history—"

"A fine body of men," said Slate, with a straight face.

"Very much so, very much so. Always very generous to the church." He hurried after Learned Edmund.

Caliban joined her. "Anything?"

"No obvious approaches." She made a quick sketch of the streets. "I see two ways. The rooftops aren't clear—too much space between. Probably so the clocktaurs can move around, and they can get the carts in, but it's not helping us much either. The road to the old parade ground has to go through the old city, that's why they need the gnoles, but the warehouse itself..." She shook her head.

"What's the best way?"

"By the river. Maybe." She chewed a thumbnail. "Problem is, they'll *know* it's the best approach..."

Caliban gave Learned Edmund a meaningful look. The dedicate closed his book.

"Thank you so much for the tour, deacon," he said, with absolute sincerity. "I don't think you have any idea just how helpful it's been."

CHAPTER 8

They sat around in the larger of the two rooms in the inn and stared at the walls. Grimehug snored at Slate's feet.

"Archaeology," said Learned Edmund.

"River approach," said Slate.

"We're screwed," said Brenner.

Caliban cleaned his armor. It didn't help, but it didn't hurt either, and was at least as useful as staring at the wall.

"Suppose they did find an archaeological site," said Slate finally. "Could they have found something in it?"

"Like what?" asked Learned Edmund.

"Oh...I don't know...an army of clocktaurs?"

The dedicate tapped his pen against his lips. "It's possible, I suppose. I would have said that none of the ancients had such things... but someone made the wonder-engines, after all. An army of clocktaurs, underground?" He shook his head slowly. "Possible."

Glum silence reigned.

"Look on the bright side," said Brenner finally.

"There's a bright side?"

"That would mean there's a limited supply." He tipped his hand back and forth. "Say they're down there, and they found a way to wake 'em up. What stops us from going in and waking up a few of our own?"

"I don't know," said Slate. "Maybe the fact that we don't know how to do it?"

"Details. Somebody will have written it down. If the Senate's in on this—and they'd have to be, wouldn't they?—surely they'll have at least three or four guys who know how to do it, in case one falls down a privy shaft in the middle of the night. Bureaucracy thrives on redundancy."

"We're getting ahead of ourselves," said Learned Edmund. "They may still be making the clocktaurs, or growing them. This is pure speculation. Perhaps the site had an ore they need, and they invented a tale of archaeology as a cover for their operations."

"True," said Slate slowly, "but I think Brenner may be right, as far as it goes. Somebody knows how to make them, or at least how to wake them up. And surely they must have written it down somewhere."

"It could be kept on site," said Caliban.

"It could," acknowledged Slate, "but show me a clandestine operation without leaks, and I'll show you one where everybody involved is dead."

"*We're* a clandestine operation," said Caliban.

There was an awkward silence.

"And I won't swear that the Captain of the Guard, or the Dowager, or Grimehug here isn't going to talk about it," said Slate.

Grimehug opened one eye and said, "Not telling anybody, Crazy Slate. Nobody listens to a gnole, 'cept other gnoles." He adjusted his rags. "'sides, Crazy Slate, got a warm place to sleep, plenty of food. Living the good life now."

"Thanks, Grimehug," said Slate. "You're a prince among gnoles."

"Gnoles got no princes. No kings, either. Too much trouble."

"There's a certain amount of wisdom to that," said Learned Edmund. "I wonder if anyone has written a book on gnole culture?"

"Human words," said Grimehug. "Human books, book man. Not gnole words."

"A good project for you when this is all over," said Caliban. He stared at the elbow guard in his hands. "No demons in Anuket City. That can't be right, can it?"

"I never heard of any," admitted Slate, "but it wasn't like I was paying attention. Does it matter?"

"I don't know."

Brenner, who had been silent for some time, said, "The building's not looking promising. We might get in once, but I don't think we'll get in twice. Too risky." He leaned forward. "But I'm thinking—if we can find out who the officials involved are, we can send Slate to their private offices. See if we can't turn something up. Then when it does come time to break into the warehouse, we won't be going in blind."

"You think they'll leave a big folder lying around that says "Care And Feeding Of Clocktaurs" on it?" asked Learned Edmund dubiously.

Caliban laughed. "People leave idiotic things lying around," he said. "Even I can tell you that much. I've gone into houses after demons and seen things out in plain sight…" He shook his head.

Slate smiled at him. "He's not lying. You'd be amazed the things I've found. Everybody assumes that people act sensibly and lock everything up in a safe. But they don't. I've found stacks of love letters shoved in the nightstand where the maid could read them."

"Fair enough," said Learned Edmund.

"The problem, as I see it," said Caliban, "is in learning who's in charge. I could try to find out, in my position as Knight-Champion—"

"Which would be about as subtle as a siege engine," said Brenner. "And maybe word'll get back to them that somebody is asking about clocktaurs, and maybe they *will* start locking stuff in a safe."

"Mind you, I *can* break into a safe," said Slate. "But extra guards are a little more difficult to work around."

"I can ask among the artificers," volunteered Learned Edmund. He smiled sheepishly. "People expect scholars to be overly-interested in things. I don't think it will be remarked. And Brother Amadai was working on something related, so it is only natural that I try to find out what."

Slate nodded slowly. "You may be right." She thought of the artificers she had known, years ago—yes, Learned Edmund would fit right into that company. The hard part might be getting him back out again.

"How do you know he was working on something related?" asked Brenner.

Learned Edmund blinked at him. "The last correspondence," he said. "We couldn't read half of it. It had been water-damaged and his handwriting was never good to begin with. But it had a drawing of a clocktaur from multiple angles."

Slate sighed. "With our luck, he included simple directions on how to stop them, and that was what got damaged." She drummed her fingers on her boot. "There's another way to find things out. There are people who know how everything fits together. Who works for who, where they live, what they do. They make it their business to know."

"Do you think they would know where Brother Amadai has gone?"

"They might. We just have to find them, and pay the right price."

"*Can* you find them?" asked Learned Edmund.

"All too easily," muttered Slate.

"And they won't talk to anyone else about your questions?" asked Caliban.

Brenner smiled faintly. "Only if someone else pays them even more."

CHAPTER 9

While the thieves descended into the city's underworld, the Knight-Champion escorted the scholar of the Many-Armed God to the Artificer's Quarter.

It was a strange neighborhood in the old part of the city. The buildings leaned together, sometimes touching over the top of the street. The impression was of walking under dozens of ramshackle bridges.

Everywhere he looked, Caliban saw clockwork. Doors did not swing, they ratcheted open. A display window crawled with oiled brass insects. One of the teapots at an outdoor café had climbed up the side of the building and clung there, exhaling steam.

"I hardly know where to start," murmured Learned Edmund. "My temple provided me with a name, but no address."

"We'll start with the name," said Caliban.

"He signs all his correspondence as 'Ashes Magnus.' My temple orders multiple copies of all his treatises. So many artificers do not keep good notes, and Master Magnus writes everything down. And indexes it correctly, too. A good index is a thing to treasure."

Caliban went over to the café. A waiter had emerged with a broom and was trying to knock the teapot off the wall.

He returned to Learned Edmund a moment later, trying to hide a smile. "This way," he said.

"You've gotten an address?"

"Oh, yes. Ashes Magnus is very well known here."

"It is gratifying," said Learned Edmund. "The world is often sorely unappreciative of quality indexing."

Caliban led him down the street. Behind them, the waiter succeeded in knocking the teapot to the ground and shoved it into a wicker cage. It whistled irritably.

There were so many marvels that it was hard to know where to look. Half of them didn't work, but Caliban had to admire the minds that could even conceive of the idea. Who would have thought to build a balcony on rails that moved around the building to take advantage of the sun? Even if it kept ramming itself into the building next door.

They passed a stable full of clockwork horses. One didn't have a head, and a disgusted looking artificer had an arm jammed down the stump of the neck, rummaging around inside.

"I confess," said Learned Edmund, "I find such things…disturbing. They seem to contradict the natural order. At least with mules, one knows where one stands."

"Usually in mule droppings."

"Well, yes. Still."

Caliban eyed the clockwork horses thoughtfully. They were bound to be expensive—Slate undoubtedly knew to the penny just *how* expensive—but there was something appealing about them. For one thing, they probably didn't ever get possessed. Demons couldn't do much with unliving things. The memory of the demon-haunted draft horse chasing him around the field was still entirely too fresh.

His own demon lay very quiet. The magic of Anuket City was all in machines. It was a strange kind of relief.

He led Learned Edmund down the street, sidestepping some kind of mechanical golem. It had rusted in place and there were flyers plastered to it. A bird was nesting in its open mouth.

"There is an odd consolation in knowing that these devices don't always work—" Learned Edmund began.

"Look out!" somebody shouted from overhead.

Caliban's immediate reaction was to throw himself over Learned Edmund. The scholar squawked in alarm.

Something exploded several feet over Caliban's head. "Crap!" yelled the voice from above.

Debris rained around them. Caliban was suddenly glad he'd come dressed as the Knight-Champion. His shoulder guards took most of the damage. Something small hit him on the back of the skull and he winced.

"Sorry…" came from above them.

Caliban straightened, one hand going to his sword. People didn't usually yell apologies while they were trying to kill you. It made it difficult to know how to retaliate.

A door slammed open, and a skinny young boy came out. He was wearing thick smoked-glass goggles and enormous leather gloves. "Sorry! It went the wrong direction. It wasn't supposed to go out the window…"

"Was it supposed to explode?" asked Learned Edmund.

"Oh, definitely. That part went well." The boy pounced on some of the remains. Bits of metal shell were smoking in the gutter.

"Just be more careful next time," said Caliban, sighing.

"Yes, sir. Sorry, sir. Um, your cloak's on fire."

"So it is."

The boy went back into the building. Caliban extinguished his cloak. It was now gray with black-edged holes.

"You were saying, about the devices not always working…?"

Learned Edmund shook his head, his eyes wide. "And Mistress Slate lived in this city?"

"For some years, apparently."

"Goodness. And she survived!"

Barely, if you listen to the things she's not saying. And I would guess it wasn't the artificers that were the threat.

The storefront belonging to Ashes Magnus was narrow and discreetly marked. The wooden door had burn marks around the bottom.

There was a door knocker in the shape of a dragonfly. When Learned Edmund lifted his hand to it, the wings thrummed against the door—*tap-tap, tap-tap, tap-tap.*

A moment later, the door opened with the silence of impeccably oiled hinges.

The front room was small and had a high wooden counter. There were no mechanical devices visible inside, except for a single, elegant clock.

Caliban had been to tailors with storefronts like this. The results were usually wonderfully well-fitted clothing and an extraordinary bill.

There was a woman behind the counter. A great deal of woman, in fact.

She was very large—not just fat, but with a large frame under it. Standing, she would have been easily as tall as Caliban. She had gigantic forearms with slender wrists and scarred, nimble fingers.

"Can I help you, gentlemen?"

"I am seeking Ashes Magnus," said Learned Edmund.

"Well, you've found her," said the woman. Her eyes travelled over the pair of them. She gave Caliban an appreciative up-and-down, which he was weak enough to enjoy.

Learned Edmund gaped at her. "Ashes...*Magnus?*"

"That's what the sign on the door says. What do you need?"

The waiter at the café had said, "Sure, she's three streets down and one over." Caliban had been waiting for this moment, and it did not disappoint.

"I...that is..." The scholar held his satchel in front of him like a shield.

"This is Learned Edmund," said Caliban, taking pity on him. "A scholar in the service of the Many-Armed God."

Ashes tilted her head. "They do buy my monographs."

"*You* wrote *Reflections on Interchangeable Gear Construction?*"

"Volumes One through Five. Forgive Volume Four, the engraver didn't know his ass from a hole in the ground." She eyed Learned Edmund. "Why?"

"He is," said Caliban, "a great admirer of your indexes."

The artificer's expression thawed somewhat. "Really? No one *ever* appreciates a good index."

Caliban looked over at Learned Edmund. *Come on,* he urged internally, *you can do it...*

The scholar took a deep breath and squared his shoulders. "Indexes," he said determinedly, "are essential to the proper functioning of a civilized society."

Ashes slapped the top of the counter. "There, you see? A man after my own heart. I *am* sorry about Volume Four. How can I help you?"

Learned Edmund walked forward and offered his hand. "It is an honor to meet you, madam."

They shook. Caliban bowed, and turned to the door. "I'll return in a few hours, shall I?"

Learned Edmund nodded, distracted. Ashes pushed her stool back. "So what brings you to Anuket City?"

"My order has lost contact with one of our scholars who was working here in the city…"

Caliban let himself out.

CHAPTER 10

Someone knocked on the door to the suite.

Caliban opened it and saw Slate, who was apparently dressed as a Chadori tribeswoman. A veil covered her face to the eyes, and a band of cloth covered her hair. Her boots had been replaced by broad, shapeless shoes trimmed with tassels. She had black robes, black gloves, and looked like a stray bit of extremely modest shadow.

"Ah—hmm," said Caliban.

"It's me! Slate!"

"Yes, I know."

The only visible bits of her scowled. "Damn. So much for my disguise."

I would know you anywhere. I would recognize you at the bottom of a mineshaft on a moonless light, if I were deaf and blind.

This is not the sort of thing you can say out loud. Caliban was a little surprised that he'd even thought it.

He settled for, "It's probably fine."

"It'll do," said Brenner, peering around the doorframe at her. "Just try not to sneeze."

"If I sneeze in this outfit, I'll fall down. These shoes were designed by an evil genius." She focused past him. "How'd it go with the artificers, Learned Edmund?"

The scholar set aside his stack of notes. "Amazing. Simply amazing." He ran a hand through his hair. "Mistress Magnus has an incredibly tidy mind." He shook his head. "She showed me her workshop. I'm going back tomorrow. What she is working on will revolutionize the way we create complex machinery."

"He's been like this all afternoon," whispered Caliban.

"Damn. No one ever tells *me* I've got a tidy mind."

"It's tidier than mine," said Brenner.

"Yes, but yours is full of spiders."

The assassin looked absurdly flattered by this.

"Did you learn anything about the you-know-whats?" Slate asked.

"The you-know—oh!" Learned Edmund shook his head. "I didn't want to ask right away. It might look suspicious. Though I cannot believe that Mistress Magnus holds to anything but the highest ethical standards…"

Slate watched the dedicate sing the praises of Ashes Magnus for a few moments, then leaned over to Caliban and whispered, "An afternoon of that *would* be a bit much."

"You have *no* idea. I believe he has fallen passionately in love with her indexes."

"Did you find anything about your lost scholar?" asked Slate.

Learned Edmund paused in his raptures. "Mistress Magnus said that she'll look into it. No one's heard from him in some time, but that happens fairly frequently with scholars."

"He probably tripped and fell into an index," whispered Caliban. Slate made a strangled noise.

"Beg pardon?" said Learned Edmund.

"Nothing. Allergies." Slate twitched a veil into place. "Well, I'm glad you and this Magnus person are getting along. Hopefully it'll lead somewhere. The less time I have to spend in the Shadow Market, the happier I'll be."

"Are you sure you want to do this?" asked Caliban. The flimsiness of her disguise worried him. If *he* could see through it…

The robes were very loose when she stood upright, but when she folded her arms and stood on one leg—as she was currently doing—things pulled more tightly around her body. He always thought of Slate as small, probably because she was so much shorter than he was, but was occasionally reminded that she was rather more generous through breast and hip than one normally saw.

He understood perfectly well why she wore shapeless clothes. It just baffled him sometimes that people didn't notice her anyway.

"Plenty of people dressed like Chadori in the Shadow Market," said Brenner. "People dress like this when they don't want to be recognized and we all…um…"

"Maintain a polite fiction," said Slate. "I'm told genuine Chadori think it's hilarious. Apparently only old women dress like this, so you get assassins wandering around dressed up as somebody's spinster aunt."

Caliban did not believe for a moment that anyone would mistake Slate for someone's spinster aunt.

"She won't stand out, believe it or not," said Brenner. "It's...ah...a courtesy. You don't try to figure out who someone is in the robes and they don't try to figure out who *you* are when *you* wear them."

"And this works?"

"...more or less."

"And you'll find the people you need to talk to in this place?"

Brenner and Slate exchanged a glance.

"Eventually," said Slate. "We'll find the people who know the people who know who we should talk to. And we will pay them a little and then we will pay someone else a little more and by gradual stages, we'll get to the people who know what's going on." She took off a glove and wiggled her fingers, grimacing. "Seven years ago, I could have just walked up to Blind Molly and said, "Okay, give me the dirt," but times change."

"She might recognize you?"

"She's a little bit dead, actually."

"Ah."

Brenner slipped under Caliban's arm, and into the hallway. "I'm ready. Shall we?"

"Right. Yes." She tried to adjust her veils again and dropped her glove. Caliban picked it up and handed it back.

Her fingers, when they touched his, were cold as ice. He looked up, startled.

It was impossible to see her expression under the veils, but there were lines around her eyes that Caliban didn't like at all.

He wanted to hold her hand between his until the heat of his fingers warmed her.

He wanted to say *Don't go.*

He wanted to say *Let me come with you.*

He said, "Be careful…my liege." The tattoo on his arm throbbed like a burn.

She took a deep breath and let it out. "Wish us luck," she said, nodding to the knight and the scholar.

"Dreaming God go with you," said Caliban.

Learned Edmund looked up long enough to sign a benediction. "Good luck."

They went down the hall, twin shadows, dark and dark, gliding like oil. Caliban heard Brenner say something. He could not make out the words, but it made Slate laugh.

His hand twinged, and he looked at it, vaguely surprised, as if it belonged to some other person. He was holding onto the doorframe so hard that his knuckles had gone white.

"Worried for them?" asked Learned Edmund.

For her, anyway. He dropped his hand.

"Yes," the paladin said.

CHAPTER 11

It was a long evening. Learned Edmund read and muttered and scribbled notes. Caliban helped Grimehug down the rain gutter and the gnole went off on some errand of his own, humming tunelessly to himself.

Caliban did sword forms until his arms ached. Then he did a few more.

Learned Edmund continued to write. The scratching of the pen across the page scraped on Caliban's nerves.

It's not his fault. It's good that he is usefully occupied, not sitting here fretting like I am. And nothing will happen. Slate will be fine. Slate is with—well, she'll probably be fine, anyway.

He went out and got food from a vendor selling some variety of spiced meat on a stick. Learned Edmund thanked him and went back to scrawling notes.

She is fine. They are fine. Even if someone from her old life recognizes her, there is no reason to think they will be hostile.

This would have been a more convincing line of argument if Caliban had any idea what Slate had done to make enemies.

Surely she couldn't have turned the entire *underworld against her...*

He could still feel how cold her hands had been.

He took a bath. The hot water soothed his muscles and did nothing at all to soothe his mind.

They won't recognize her.

Brenner will take care of her.

He grimaced at the thought.

Finally, for lack of anything better to do, he leaned his head back against the rim of the tub and prayed.

There were several long-form prayers that temple paladins learned. Caliban knew them all backwards and forward. He recited each one carefully, forming the words in the dark place behind his eyes, letting each word die away into silence.

There was no heat, no light, no sense of divine presence. Caliban no longer expected one. Perhaps the words were still enough.

I can do nothing more. Dreaming God have mercy.
Bring Slate back to me. Please.

He knew it was the wrong prayer. He knew he should not dare to ask for such a thing.

My brothers and sisters whom I killed, forgive me. I should have made my life into a penance for my sin against you. I should not be…I should not have allowed myself to feel what I do for Slate…

But he had and here he was and he was afraid.

His demon was quiet inside his head. It had never cared for prayer, but it had been small and silent since the encounter with the rune-demon in the Vagrant Hills. He did not know if it had been frightened or exhausted.

He did not want to be grateful to the rune-demon, but the absence was welcome. And yet, he could not keep from poking at it, like a tooth that should hurt. It had been his constant companion for too many months. He did not trust its silence.

The water cooled around him. Eventually, there were no more prayers. He felt hollowed out, balanced between dread and resignation.

If the water got cold, it would stop being soothing and start to carry old memories. Caliban sighed, opened his eyes and found himself looking into Grimehug's badger-like face.

"Hey, big man," said the gnole.

"Hey, Grimehug. Did Learned Edmund let you back in?"

Grimehug dipped his head in a nod. "Yeah, yeah. Want to tell you that Crazy Slate's coming back. With dark man."

Caliban sagged with relief, then grabbed for a towel. "You were watching her?"

"Some gnole watches, yeah. Bad place, big man. People go in, don't always come out, you know?"

"I know."

Grimehug nodded. "Scared," he added. "Good to be scared, though. Scary stuff."

With this cryptic utterance, the gnole went back into the shared room of the suite. Caliban hurried into his clothes and followed.

The door opened a few minutes later and Slate came through it, limping badly.

"Good lord! Are you hurt?" Caliban leapt to his feet.

"It's these shoes," she growled, going to the sitting area and dropping gracelessly into a chair. Her voice was rough, as if she'd been crying or inhaling smoke. Brenner followed, closing the door behind her. "Apparently this cobbler believes Chadori women have eight toes and no heels." She pulled her veil and hood off, revealing a disgruntled expression.

"Did you learn anything?" Learned Edmund asked, setting his notes aside.

"Mmm. Some." Slate yanked the hated shoes off and laid a foot across her lap. "I'm going to have a blister the size of a goddamn grape." She began kneading her calf with a grimace. "Right. This is a tricky business. People are wary of discussing military matters. We're skirting the edge of treason."

"They're *criminals*," said Caliban.

"Well, yes. But the clocktaurs are fighting for Anuket City, and these are Anuket City thieves."

"You're telling me most of the thieves are patriots?" Caliban didn't bother to keep the disbelief out of his voice.

Brenner looked up from rolling a cigarette. "My dear paladin, you won't find anyone who cares more about a country than its underworld. If the wolves eat all our sheep, where are we going to get mutton?"

Caliban snorted. He would probably have had more to say on that particular topic, but his eyes were fixed on Slate, who was pounding on her calf muscles with a knuckle and making terrible grimaces of agony and relief.

He had a sudden urge to go over and kneel before her and run his hands over the offending muscles until they loosened.

It was chivalrous, surely. He'd be helping a maiden in distress. One's motives couldn't get any purer than that.

He didn't dare do it because he wasn't sure he'd stop at the knee.

No. No. Even such thoughts are dangerous.

Brenner was saying something. Caliban tore his eyes away.

"Is there anyone whose loyalties can be bought?" he asked.

There was a hiss of pain behind him. "Ahhhsonofabitch…what is *wrong* with those shoes?"

"Everyone's loyalties can be bought," said Brenner. "But we don't necessarily have the money to buy them. Our budget's large, but not infinite, and we're potentially asking them to sell out a sizeable portion of the Anuket City military-industrial complex with this."

"So where does that leave us?" asked Learned Edmund.

"We got one lead," said Slate. Having beaten one leg into submission, she draped it over the arm of the chair and started on the other one. Caliban glanced over and quickly looked away, directly into the teeth of Brenner's grin. It was not an entirely pleasant expression.

If he doesn't know what I'm thinking, he's at least got a suspicion.

"Indeed," said the assassin smoothly, "we had one lead." He glanced at Slate.

She hunched up a shoulder. "Go ahead, Brenner."

"The war effort was dreamed up by a group of Senators…or possibly praetors…"

"Both," said Slate. "And a couple of Consuls, too."

"Right. Whole bunch of them. Stupid way to run a city."

"Representative democracy is considered one of the most enlightened—"

"Later, Edmund."

Brenner lit his cigarette. "So apparently part of the government always wanted war, which wasn't very popular in these parts because that involves spending more money on the army and merchants hate to spend money on things like armies. Then the clocktaurs turned up and suddenly the Senate falls in line with this idea to send them against people."

"This was a few years back," added Slate. She jammed her thumbs into her calf and wiggled. "Everybody was happy to talk about *that*. No secret to it."

"So who wanted a war?" asked Caliban thoughtfully.

"Or who saw profit in backing the people who did?" Slate dropped her foot back to the floor and glared at her knees as if they had offended her.

"What sort of profit?"

Slate spread her hands. "This is barely more than a guess—people were only hinting—but I suspect the Senate is paying a lot of money to somebody for the Clockwork Boys. Suppose somebody knew they had an army on their hands…they might consider it worthwhile to invest in a pack of Senators willing to pay for that army."

They sat in silence, digesting that.

"They bought Senators so that the Senators could turn around and buy their army from them?"

"Gotta spend money to make money," said Brenner.

"You think it's the same person," said Caliban. "Or people."

"I'd be very surprised if it wasn't."

"So if we can figure out who that person is…"

"We may know who to kill," said Brenner. "Or at least where to start killing." He stubbed out his cigarette.

Learned Edmund looked a bit green.

"It seems like this sort of person would not be easy to find," said Caliban.

"Ah, but that's the lead!" Slate raised her finger. Since she had flipped around in the chair and was now hanging, head down, with her legs over the back, this was perhaps not as effective a gesture as it could be. "Anuket politics are miserable and there's no reason to assume that just because you've bought a bunch of Senators, you're in charge of the Clockwork Boys. People buy politicians all the time. You aren't anybody until you own a Senator. But the important bit here is *who was behind the excavation that turned up the Clockwork Boys in the first place?*"

"You think the people behind that excavation are responsible?" said Caliban.

"They'd almost have to be, wouldn't they? They're the ones in charge of the clocktaurs, they're the ones who figured out how to use them, so why wouldn't they—or one of their backers—be the one doing the using?"

"A scholar might have worked it out," said Learned Edmund. "For knowledge's sake."

"Your missing Brother Amadai, for example? Yes. But I doubt he dug up the whole thing single-handed. How rich is the Many-Armed God?"

Learned Edmund looked blank.

"It is perhaps safe to say that they are more rich in knowledge than in gold," said Caliban.

"Right, so if he was involved, I think it's safe to say somebody else was holding the purse-strings, and they used his scholarship for their own ends."

Learned Edmund pinched the bridge of his nose and looked suddenly rather older than nineteen.

"We'll keep going back," said Slate. "Assuming I can walk. This sort of thing takes a few days—we have to let it be known that we're interested in information, but not seem desperate." She stood up, tested her footing, and scowled. The black robes flapped around her like wings.

"Is that safe?" asked Learned Edmund. "If there is a chance you'll be recognized…"

"I'll keep wearing the damn veils." She turned and advanced on Caliban. "You!"

"Yes?"

"Give me your socks."

"The ones I'm wearing?"

"A clean pair, if you've got them."

"You want my *socks?*" Caliban would have laid down his life for Slate, probably with a sense of relief, but a man's socks…that was asking a lot.

She glared at him. "Look, a man with an endless supply of clean handkerchiefs has got to have extra socks. If I don't pad these boots, I'm going to have a permanent limp by the end of the week."

"I…suppose…"

A few minutes later, a heavily veiled woman carrying her boots and wearing a thick pair of wool socks padded out into the hall. She appeared to be limping on both feet simultaneously.

"That was my last pair that didn't have holes in them," said Caliban mournfully.

Brenner slapped him on the back. "Chivalry sucks, huh?"

CHAPTER 12

Slate lay in bed with a gnole on her aching feet and stared at the ceiling.

It was made of pressed tin tile with an elaborate pattern of curling vines. With the lamp off and the shutters open, she could make out just enough of the pattern to let her eyes and mind wander.

She'd gone to the Shadow Market.

She was still alive.

How 'bout that?

On some level, Slate realized, she had been expecting to die tonight.

She hadn't felt terror. Terror was dropping out of a smokehole onto a homicidal deer-person, or huddling in the woods with the Clockwork Boys marching down the road a hundred yards away.

This was something else, something grey and drab and inevitable. This was a horror that she walked toward with her eyes open.

She thought she'd been doing well. She'd walked out of the inn and joked with Brenner and told herself that no one could recognize her under the veils and then they'd turned down the street toward the entrance to the Shadow Market and she had only barely had time to rip her veil down.

Brenner watched her heave her guts into the gutter without comment.

When she was done, he said, "Better?"

Slate nodded.

He asked no questions.

They walked the rest of the way down the street. They did not try to hide. There were eyes on them and trying to hide would only make those eyes sharper and more interested.

At the boarded-up door of a church, Slate stopped.

She went up the broad steps with Brenner behind her, and she touched the door with one gloved hand.

The gatekeeper opened the door. There were no passwords, no counter-signs, no secret knocks. If you knew the Shadow Market existed, you were allowed in. It was as simple as that.

They went inside. The hallway was short and unlit, the sort of generic hallway you might find in an inn or a whorehouse or a government building. Slate was vaguely aware that she was shaking.

Learned Edmund wouldn't have noticed. Caliban would have tried to comfort her and probably said something horribly stupid in the process. Brenner's eyes flicked over her and he offered neither comfort nor comment, which was itself strangely comforting.

They stepped through the doorway at the end and the Shadow Market lay spread before them.

In many cities, there are places where the underworld elements gather together. Business is transacted. Questionable services are offered for sale.

In many cities, these places are raided and shut down as soon as they are discovered.

In Anuket City, where all things are for sale, the Shadow Market was protected by unwritten truce. The guards did not go there. The Senate was officially unaware of its existence. (It was rumored that the rulers of the Shadow Market paid a great deal for this consideration.) In return, the Shadow Market stayed where it was. Neighborhoods did not become dens of crime, open-air markets did not deal in black-market goods, and criminal acts did not become common on street corners.

It was a strange system, but it worked.

The result was a vast underground flea market where one could buy drugs, whores, bodyguards, weapons, poisons, slaves, or a hundred other things banned by law.

Slate stood on the steps of the Grey Church, looking down, and part of her said, *I'm going to die*, and a part that she had never suspected said, *I'm home*.

The feeling of homecoming was so strong and so unexpected that for a moment it felt like joy and crowded out the dread. She looked down on the rows of stalls and awnings and her feet turned automatically toward her old spot.

Three rows down, on the left hand side. She'd had a counter and cabinets full of parchment. Waxes, seals, rows of ink bottles—the tools of the forger's trade. She would cook books, too, although that was trickier stuff and Slate usually needed to take the books home with her.

She'd made enough to pay her share of protection money, so that she could arrive in the evening and be sure that her goods would still be where she left them. She'd been good at it. Over the years, the work had turned from forging permits and licenses to complicated accounting. She would take a single commission and spend three weeks hiding thousands of dollars worth of funds, and make enough to live on for the next four months.

In the Dowager's city, her dark skin had set her apart—not much, not a great deal, but enough. People like her were everywhere, but they were mostly found in the docks and the labor yards. Eyes slid over her without seeing her.

We were never anathema. We were simply invisible. And Mother cut all ties with her family long before I was born, because she could not bear to be invisible.

Perhaps it would have been different if Slate's mother had been different. Perhaps Slate would not have felt such a strong need to flee from under that particular shadow. Perhaps she would not have married badly and run from it and landed here instead.

And perhaps I would have stayed home and become a courtesan and gotten knifed by a jealous lover by now. Past is past.

When Slate came to Anuket City, she found a place where a hundred races came together and no one was extraordinary. In the upper city, she worked very hard to become invisible again.

In the Shadow Market, though…

Everyone was alone and everyone else watched you carefully, in case you had a knife. You fought your way to the top, or you broke and crawled home to die.

She'd earned her place and held it, right up until the end.

For a long, dizzying moment, standing on the steps of the Grey Church, it was as if the intervening years had never happened, as if this were another day at work like any other day.

Chains creaked, and Slate's eyes lifted.

There were five crow cages hanging over the Shadow Market, from the rafters of the ancient church.

There's five.

But there's only supposed to be four.

Where did the fifth one come from?

Seven years of history crashed down on her. Adrenaline stroked cool chemical fingers down her spine.

They added a fifth one.

Just for me…

Lying in bed, hours later, Slate was able to snort at herself. Probably there had just been too many bodies one day, and Boss Horsehead had ordered another one hauled up. It had nothing to do with her. She'd probably been gone for years by the time it went up.

At that moment, though, it had seemed to fill the entire world. Her ears rang and the crowd noises faded away and there were five crow cages and there was Slate and—

Brenner said, in her ear, "Not a good time, darlin'."

She inhaled too sharply, almost gagging, and let him steer her aside with a hand on her elbow.

Not now. Later. Slate pushed down the panic and the memory, aware that she would pay for it later. That was fine. Once she was safely back in the hotel, she could do anything she had to do—weep, scream, throw a chair at Caliban's head.

He'd probably even bring me the chair.

She laughed soundlessly behind the veil, teeth bared. It felt almost like screaming and the panic retreated.

Later. It was a promise to herself.

"Better?" asked Brenner again. There was a look in his eyes that Slate knew. He did not want to have to ask again.

"Better," she said. "Let's go."

They went through the Shadow Market together, she and Brenner, two more carrion crows in the gathered flock. Brenner asked the questions and she showed him who to ask. No sense letting anyone hear her voice if they could help it. No sense letting anyone see her face.

People watched them. People watched everyone. Slate watched them back. There were new faces and old. The ratty-eyed little man with the knives. Sparrow, Blind Molly's daughter. Rumor had it that she'd killed her mother to take her place. The wonderworker who could spell locks. She knew them all, albeit some only by reputation.

But Slate didn't know the old woman with the glass eye who gave her such a peculiar look, or the cringing giant, or the man with the ferret.

Well. They say you can't ever go home again.

The relief of familiarity faded and the dread crept back. When they had learned everything they could for one night, and turned to leave, she had to keep from running up the steps of the church, like a child fleeing the basement one step ahead of monsters.

But they left.

And no one stopped them.

They walked home. They doubled back on their trail and split up through a building and came together again. If they were being followed, it was by highly skilled trackers indeed.

In the hall of the inn, Brenner turned to her, scowled, and then put his arms very carefully around her.

Slate was not expecting that. Even less was she expecting to bury her face in his shoulder and give a single ragged sob.

"Darlin'," said Brenner after a moment. He smelled, as he usually did, of leather and tobacco smoke. "Do you feel like lying to me?"

"No?"

"Then I won't ask what the problem is." He shook his head and let her go with exaggerated care. "You do good work. Even when you're so scared you're puking in corners. But you better handle this or I'm going to have to handle it for you."

"I don't think you can murder your way out of this for me," said Slate.

"Darlin', you'd be amazed what I can murder my way out of." He kissed her forehead gently, as a friend might, then stepped back and let her lead the way into the suite to report.

Afterward, Slate went into the bedroom and locked the door and curled up in bed with the blankets over her. Then she screamed, very quietly, into her pillow.

Caliban came and knocked on the door—it had to be Caliban, nobody else had a tread like a bull moose and a knock that sounded like an apology—and she ignored him and eventually he went away again.

When she was calm again—or could fake it convincingly—she got up and opened the door. Grimehug came in a few minutes later and curled up on the bed.

And it was over.

And she was still alive.

For another day, at least.

CHAPTER 13

Brenner slipped around a corner.

He was skulking. It was a good skulk. There was an art to it, and Brenner was a master. You kept your cloak around you and your hood up and you put your feet down quick and quiet and you looked over your shoulder every few seconds—

The side of his head encountered an armored wall and rebounded. He clapped a hand to his ear and hissed.

Unfortunately, some people just didn't get into the spirit of the thing.

"Going somewhere?" Caliban asked. He only had a few inches on Brenner, but he glared down them quite effectively.

The assassin made frantic shushing gestures, still rubbing his ear. "Keep your voice down! Someone'll hear you!"

"Perhaps you should explain what you're doing," the knight said, a bit more quietly.

"What, here? In an alley?"

"Unless you'd like to go back to the inn…"

"Hmm." Brenner frowned and scanned the street. There was no one suspicious, except an anonymous gnole, who was doing a pretty good skulk itself.

"Why'd you follow me, anyway?"

Caliban rolled his eyes. "You were watching the corridor like a hawk while that servant girl was lugging bath water to Slate's room. As soon as the splashing started, you bolted. It was a little suspicious."

"Mmm." Brenner frowned. "Okay. You have to swear not to tell Slate anything."

"Why not?"

"Because I don't want her to know what I'm doing, obviously."

An expression of disgust passed briefly over the knight's face. "You're not going to a brothel, are you?"

"What? No!"

"That's a relief."

"You think I have to pay for that sort of thing?"

"I wouldn't presume to speculate."

"I'm an assassin."

"So you say."

"We ooze danger."

"Indeed."

"Women love that."

"How nice."

"Now, if you wanted me to find *you* a brothel—"

"Moving *right* along…" grated Caliban.

"Right, right." Brenner glanced around again. The gnole had found an exciting bit of trash in the gutter and was squeaking happily over it.

"Okay. How much do you know about why our Slate left Anuket City?"

Caliban frowned. "Very little. She got into some trouble with some people, and it worries her, but that's about it."

Brenner sighed and turned his attention to the cobbles between his boots. "Damn. I was hoping she'd let something slip."

"Why, what do you know? You've known her for years."

"Not much more, unfortunately. Our Slate is quick with the insults, but not so much with the personal history." He spread his hands. "Generally I respect that—this is not a line of work where people pry—but not when my life is on the line."

"I see." Caliban's frown deepened. "What do you know?"

"She showed up in the capitol a few years back, fresh from Anuket City, and said she couldn't ever go back. Of course, the best laid plans…" He made a sweeping gesture that took in both of them, the street, and the inn on the corner. "The person she pissed off is apparently named Boss Horsehead, and that's quite literally all I know. And I only know that much because I happened to overhear a woman say, 'Boss Horsehead sends his regards,' right before she tried to put a dagger in Slate's guts."

Caliban blinked. "What happened to her?"

"I slit her throat. *Obviously.*"

"Good."

"Our Slate was *very* grateful afterward."

Caliban did not rise to this very obvious bait, but Brenner saw the lines around his eyes tighten almost imperceptibly and counted it as victory.

"Our Slate's not telling us everything," he continued, "and by that I mean she's not telling us *anything*. She won't let me ask around about him, and when I ask her, I get the death glare."

"I can't imagine she'd do anything to endanger us—"

"No, no," Brenner glanced around for listeners. "But she's far from infallible, our Slate, and I'm getting a feeling that maybe this is a bad place for a blind spot. Near as I can tell, this Horsehead person runs half the underworld. That might mean he's either involved with the clocktaurs or knows who is."

"I see." Caliban did. "So—what? You're going out somewhere—"

"The Grey Church."

"—to this Grey Church place to see what you can find out about this Boss Horsehead person without her?"

"Exactly."

"It's a good plan."

"Thanks."

"I'm coming with you."

"Like hell you are!"

"Do you think I don't know how to act around thieves and ruffians?"

"The fact that you even use a word like 'ruffians' is not filling me with confidence, no."

The knight folded his arms. "I can always go back to the inn and ask Slate outright."

"Fine. Fine. Just…fine." Brenner pinched the bridge of his nose. "I can't believe I'm doing this. Slate wouldn't do this. Slate would hurt me if I even suggested doing this."

"Digging into her past affairs?"

"No, taking a paladin into the Shadow Market. The digging she'd chalk up to understandable paranoia." He let his hand drop and looked the knight over. "Do you have a cloak?"

"Yes."

"Maybe you should get it to throw it over the armor—"

"It's white. Some idiot thought he was being funny."

Shame flitted briefly over Brenner's face, but found itself in unfamiliar surroundings and didn't settle. "Oh, right. Forget the cloak. Just…err…could you at least slouch a little?"

Caliban slouched. It didn't go well.

It was a measure of Brenner's concern about their situation that he didn't abandon the whole idea immediately. Instead, he closed his eyes briefly and raked a hand through his hair. "If anyone asks, you're a mercenary."

"Very well."

"A *mute* mercenary."

"Don't push your luck."

"I'm already pushing it to the breaking point taking you to the Shadow Market." He ran a hand over his face again. "I must be nuts."

They walked down the street together. Brenner didn't bother skulking. There wasn't much point, with the knight clomping down the sidewalk beside him like a draft horse.

If Slate ever got wind of this…no, it didn't bear thinking about.

He chalked it up alongside the other things that Slate should never, ever get wind of. There were plenty of them by now.

The streets of Anuket City were nearly deserted in the mist. Brenner pulled the hood of his cloak up again. Caliban got damper and damper, until his hair hung in lank strings over his forehead, which helped a little. In bad light, he might look almost disreputable.

The Grey Church loomed out of the mist, the spires gleaming wetly overhead. Brenner halted.

"Now, remember," he muttered. "Keep your mouth shut, and don't do anything noble. Bad things are going to be happening here, and you are going to let them keep happening. You are not going to intervene, you are not going to protect anyone, you are not going to stop to help women or pets or small children. Do you understand?"

"I understand."

"Are you sure?"

"Yes."

Brenner sighed. "If you breathe so much as a word to Slate…"

"I won't."

"Okay. One last thing. Give me your money."

"I beg your pardon?" said Caliban.

"Give me all your money. C'mon, hurry up, I don't want anyone to see us…" He scanned the street. It was a lousy night out. The mist was turning into rain, and the flagstones glittered.

"Are you *mugging* me?" asked Caliban incredulously.

"Dammit, I'll give it back. But you look like a pickpocket's dreams come true. They'll pick you clean before you've gone ten feet. But if you don't have anything to steal, they'll assume you're hiding it really well, and leave you alone."

"And they won't try to steal from you?"

"Don't be ridiculous."

Whatever Caliban was looking for in the other man's face, he either found it or decided not to bother. The knight slid his belt pouch off and handed it over. It clinked softly as Brenner made it vanish somewhere about his person.

The assassin glanced around, crossed the street quickly, and knocked on the door of the Church. He could hear the knight's footsteps coming up the steps behind him.

The door opened a crack, and the gatekeeper looked out.

The man's eyes flicked from Brenner to Caliban, briefly back to Brenner, back to Caliban, where they stayed for quite some time, then finally over to Brenner again. The gatekeeper raised his eyebrows in mute eloquence.

"He's with me," Brenner said.

The eyes flicked again. The eyebrows went even higher.

"Really."

The gatekeeper shrugged. Presumably it did not pay to inquire too much in his line of work. He opened the door.

Brenner ghosted through. Caliban started to bow to the gatekeeper, caught himself, and followed.

CHAPTER 14

Caliban was in over his head, and he was willing to admit it.

When Brenner and Slate had discussed the Shadow Market—very reluctantly, in Slate's case—he'd pictured it set in an ordinary church, like the small rural buildings he had visited by the hundreds when they sent him out demonslaying. Because of that, he'd pictured something of a certain scale. Even a fairly large church would only hold a dozen or so merchants in the main sanctuary and perhaps a few more in the nave and the side chapels.

He hadn't pictured a vaulted cathedral, sunken down into the ground and opening up into bays and galleries and catacombs on every side. It was twice the size of the Forge God's cathedral. It was larger than the Temple of the Dreaming God in the capitol, and the Shadow Market filled it to overflowing.

There was a crowd swirling across the floor, between the stalls, but it was like no crowd he had ever encountered. It didn't move right. It didn't *sound* right. It hissed when it should have roared, and this bothered him a great deal, because he had previously thought that all crowds behaved more or less the same way.

He lifted his eyes to the great stained glass window, and the crow cages hung like chandeliers. There were five of them. Crows with broad, stunted wings perched on the iron bars of four, while the last hung empty, the door open and askew.

He wondered if there was an exit somewhere near the roof for the birds, or if they lived their entire lives in the Grey Church, feeding on dropped food.

Something twitched in one of the crow cages. The paladin looked away. Apparently the crows had at least one other source of food.

This is not my world.

It was definitely Brenner's world. The assassin glided down the steps and into the crowd without so much as a pause.

Don't stand here. If you stand here above the crowd, you'll make a big fat target out of yourself.

He plunged after Brenner.

The assassin had stopped at one of the first booths, in front of heaped piles of fabric. He glanced up at Caliban, then back down at the table. "Mmm…here."

Money changed hands.

"What is—"

"Put this on," said Brenner, and then, in an undertone, "and keep your mouth shut, remember?"

Caliban slung the cloak around himself. It was too large, and badly frayed, but it covered most of his armor, which was undoubtedly the point, and it was an indeterminate shade of gray-green.

"Better," the assassin said grudgingly.

"Now what do we do?" asked Caliban, in an undertone.

"We're going to go buy someone a drink."

There was a bar in the Shadow Market, or at least there was a place that had tables and something resembling alcohol. "Bar" was perhaps too kind. This place might aspire to "dive" if it was cleaned up a bit.

They had to walk down one of the side corridors of the Grey Church to get there, a rough-hewn area that looked as if the builders had expanded into the old church catacombs. Possibly they had—there were odd little niches in the walls. One had a shrine to the Masked God in it. Caliban glanced at it as they passed, unsure whether he was comforted to see a religion or depressed to see that particular one.

Along the way they passed two sex acts, a beating, and a robbery in progress. Caliban wanted to intervene in at least three of them. He kept his eyes locked on the back of Brenner's neck instead.

It was an odd echo of his trip with Slate—a thousand years ago, it felt like—through the market in the capitol. The ceiling was high and distant, but he had no fear of falling into the sky.

I'm afraid I might fall into the abyss instead.

They reached the bar. There was no sign, but the sounds of mugs clinking and someone laughing came through the blanket that served as a door.

Caliban had always believed that he had been in some very shady establishments, particularly for a Knight-Champion. Even paladins go slumming occasionally. Surely nothing in the Shadow Market could surprise him.

The magnitude of his former naiveté astonished him.

This place had boxes instead of chairs and the beer appeared to be made entirely of dregs. The bar was made of unfinished wooden boards thrown over sawhorses. There were bodies in the corners, and not all of them looked like they were merely asleep.

"Now what?" Brenner would let him talk if he didn't move his lips.

"Now we sit here and wait for a prostitute."

Caliban stared morosely into his beer. "I thought we were avoiding brothels."

"Freelance prostitution is regulated by pimps. Pimps pay protection money to gangs. Gangs report to crime lords. Do I have to explain the entire crime food chain to you? We have to start at the bottom."

Caliban glanced around the room, then back down into his beer. "I'd say we're there."

"See, this is why I never take you anywhere."

They sat in stony silence for a while. Caliban stopped even pretending to drink whatever the stuff in the mug was.

"Okay," murmured Brenner, barely moving his lips, "We've got a mark. Try not to lose your head."

The woman who wove her way toward their table had probably been lovely at one point, but had been worn down to a kind of haggard prettiness. Her clothing left little to the imagination, but Caliban found the deep lines scored around her eyes more unsettling than the amount of flesh on display.

Brenner, however, held out an arm and grinned like a shark when she sat down next to him. "Hello there, darlin'."

"Don't think I've seen you boys here before," she purred.

"It's been a while, darlin'. My friend's new in town. Thought I'd bring him around…show him the sights…"

The downward direction of his eyes left no doubt as to what sights he'd meant. Caliban stared into the middle distance and prayed for death.

The prostitute leaned forward across the table. "Really?"

Anyone's death. Brenner's would do.

Brenner kicked him under the table. Caliban transferred his gaze to the prostitute and tried to look politely interested.

"Your friend doesn't say much."

"He's the strong silent type."

Caliban grunted.

"I can appreciate that in a man," she said, smiling, and slid across the crates until her hip pressed against his.

I am going to need to bathe in boiling water.

Brenner's grin seemed to stretch beyond the confines of his face. The prostitute ran a sharp-nailed hand down Caliban's thigh.

I'll burn these clothes. On the end of a stick. Without touching them.

"You're a big one, aren't you?" she murmured.

Sweet Dreaming God, do people actually say *that?* Caliban took a recklessly large swallow of the awful beer.

"So tell me, darlin'," Brenner said, with a purr of his own, "what's new in town since I've been away?"

"Well, that depends. How long've you been away?"

"Oh, coupla years now…"

The prostitute apparently decided her current approach wasn't working, and ran a fingertip over the rim of his ear instead. He jerked, startled, and tried to cover it with more beer. She chuckled.

I'm going to have to burn this ear, too.

Brenner had the beatific expression of a man whose dreams have all come true.

"Well, let me think…" She rattled off a string of names and relationships that made no sense at all to Caliban, but Brenner nodded gravely and made appropriate exclamations. "Really? Oh, you're kidding me, darlin'… He did not!"

Granted, it was probably easier for the assassin to concentrate. He didn't have fingers curling up the back of his neck with professional ease.

Two baths. Ten baths.

"…then the Old Crows got wiped out by the Black Friars a year or two ago, practically a war in the underground. Got very hot down here, let me tell you."

It was getting fairly hot somewhere else as well. Even if he found the prostitute more sad than attractive and the surroundings repellant—well, it had been a long time. Caliban didn't know if he should be deeply disgusted with himself or resigned to the fact that flesh was only flesh, and it could only take so much.

The last woman to touch you was a demon. The last one before that was…was…

Dreaming God, I can't actually remember.

He tried to take another slug of beer and discovered that his mug was empty, and thus, to his unutterable relief, he could get up and get another.

"Excuse me," he muttered, getting hastily to his feet and making his way to the bar.

Once there, he remembered that he had no money. "On his tab," he muttered, jerking a thumb at Brenner. The bartender, a grim man in a stained apron, nodded silently.

He returned to the table as slowly as possible, holding the awful beer in front of him like a shield.

There was a shriek of metal from above. A few heads turned.

One of the crow cages was being raised. The others swayed and jangled on their chains.

It was dim in the Grey Church, but Caliban could tell that the empty cage was no longer empty.

The figure inside was slumped, unconscious, or dead.

Caliban measured the distance as best he could from the ground. Twenty yards, perhaps, across the Shadow Market to the chains that raised and lowered the cages.

And then what? You fight and you die and no one gets saved.

He forced himself to look down. This wasn't his world.

"Still keeping up the old crow cages, I see," he heard Brenner say pleasantly.

"Oh, yeah, wouldn't be the Grey Church without 'em. Boss Horsehead's very fond of his crow cages, y'know."

A predatory light gleamed briefly in the assassin's eyes. "Ah, yes. Boss Horsehead's still…?" He made a kind of vague gesture with one hand that could have meant anything.

"Oh, yeah, yeah. They keep waiting for him to die, but he'll outlive all of us."

Caliban sat down partway around the table from her, hoping to gain a reprieve, but she scooted up next to him immediately. He stifled a sigh.

She brightened. "Oh! If you've been out for a few years, maybe you missed it. Did you know Boss Horsehead was going to get married?"

"I vaguely recall something about that right before I left…" Butter wouldn't have melted in Brenner's mouth.

Someone seemed to be drinking Caliban's beer at a shocking rate. He wasn't sure why, since it did not improve at all upon repeated exposure.

"Oh, yes!" She rubbed her hands together. This was sufficiently juicy to make her forget Caliban, which made him very happy.

"He was going to get married to this very posh lay-dy—*very* upper crust, born with a silver spoon up her ass—"

I could excuse myself to go to the privies. But then I might actually find the privies. Given what the rest of the place looks like, I don't think I dare.

"No!" said Brenner. "You don't say!"

"And her family! So high in the instep, you'd think their shit didn't stink!" She fanned herself. "But they'd been running low on money, and Boss Horsehead thought maybe he'd like to marry into high society—"

"We're not good enough for him?" asked Brenner, grinning.

You'd never know that he's never heard of most of these people in his life. Damn. Caliban was impressed despite himself.

"I know, right?" The prostitute laughed out loud. "But—this is the best bit—" She lowered her voice and looked around. "Only not so loud, 'cos he's still touchy about it. She wanted a big church wedding, right? Full temple, bells, carriages—and he gets there, and pulls out the marriage license to give the priest—"

Caliban had a sudden premonition. He met Brenner's eyes, and knew the assassin felt it too.

"And it's a warrant for Horsehead's arrest! For human trafficking and—" she had to slap the table a few times to get her breath back, "—*bestiality!*"

Oh Slate, Slate, you never do anything by half measures, do you?

Brenner let out a low whistle. "He *never!*"

"Hell of a scandal." She sat back and wiped her eyes. "Priest nearly had a heart attack. Wedding cancelled right away, o' course, and the bride went off to a nunnery. They think it was Coney, who ran the Black Friars, hired it done. He's dead now, rest his soul, but they never did catch who did the actual papers."

"He must have had some suspicion," said Brenner.

She shrugged. "Ah, well. People said it was Grey Hemlock, but Boss Horsehead's been seen with her since, so it couldn't have been. He'd have killed whoever it was." She leaned in closer. "Between you and me and your friend here, I say it was Mistress Slate. She ain't been seen around here since it happened, and Johnny the Hand, who was rookery-master over in River's End, says that he never knew anybody else could've forged it so well."

"You don't say!" said Brenner.

She grinned and leaned back. "I do say. And she dropped outta sight right then, and a good thing for her, too. Boss Horsehead ever catches who done it, he'll put 'em in the highest crow cage and take their eyes out himself."

CHAPTER 15

"Well," said Brenner.

"Well," said Caliban.

"That's a helluva thing."

"Bestiality, no less."

The two men were sitting on a low stone wall, well away from the Grey Church. Neither of them could think of anything to say. Possibly there were so many things to say that it was hard to know where to start.

"You paid the girl, I assume?" asked Caliban finally.

"Yeah, and not very chivalrous of you to pretend to get sick and run off to the privies, *might I add.*"

"Who says I was pretending? That beer was an affront to decency."

"*And* left me with the tab."

"Which you paid with *my* money."

This seemed to pretty well thrash out the argument. They sat in silence.

Brenner started to laugh, softly, and shook his head. "Stole the marriage license! Dear god. Great big brass ones, our Slate. Who'd have thought?"

"You can see why this Horsehead gentleman is not inclined to forgive."

"Yeah, money's one thing, but public humiliation is forever." Brenner drummed his heels against the wall. "I hope it paid well. He gets his hands on her now, it's going to be...ugly."

"He'll get to her over my dead body," said Caliban, with no humor at all.

"You say that as if you think it'll stop him." Brenner pinched the bridge of his nose. "Damn. From what I'm hearing, he could field enough warm bodies to bury us both."

Caliban stood up. "Well. I suppose we should go and speak to Slate. I wish she'd told us. Clearly it is not safe for her to walk about alone, even disguised."

"Clearly," said Brenner. "And I just can't wait to hear what she has to say about it…"

What Slate had to say about it came with a lot of obscenities, but boiled down to one major point.

"You took him to the Grey Church?!"

"Under protest," Brenner said, raising his hands. "And anyway, my behavior isn't the really interesting bit here—"

"He's a paladin!"

"You're wanted by a crime lord!" said Caliban.

"Not that it's any of your business," snapped Slate. "And that was years ago! He's probably forgotten."

"Oh no," said Brenner. "Dearie, dearie me, *no.* You don't forget being jilted at the altar because you just handed the priest a warrant for your arrest on the charges of horse-buggering."

"Sheep-buggering," muttered Slate. Caliban could see a grin fighting to get out. "The warrant was very specific. And you still shouldn't have taken a paladin down there."

"I am curious," said Learned Edmund, "as to how you actually managed it. There are seals on a warrant, as I understand it, and those are kept entirely by the judiciary." He steepled his fingers. "Even assuming that the entire thing was prepared in advance, you would still need access to the seals—"

Slate's grin broke through, and she beamed at Edmund. "*Thank you.* I have been waiting for *five years* for somebody to appreciate that."

"You didn't just lift one?" asked Brenner.

"They keep closer track of those things than the Crown Jewels. The gods themselves couldn't get at one. No, I had to steal some arrest warrants and make copies based on the seals, which is not easy. I had to get this filler—they make it out of quicksilver, nasty stuff—and pour it in. And the only place to get the filler is the barbers—they use it on bad teeth—and since they use such small quantities, I had to break into every barber shop in the city to lift it. And we didn't have much time because the wedding was a rush job, so I was doing three barber shops a night for a couple days, and then you get the imprint and harden it off—and it takes real silver, let me add—and then I spent two days making practice seals to get the hang of it." She lifted her chin. "As thievery goes, that was pretty much my *magnum opus.*"

"Very impressive," said Learned Edmund. "One could wish such genius was directed to more…deserving…channels, but nevertheless…"

"Oh, he deserved every bit of it, I assure you."

Caliban leaned back in his chair. Watching her pace around the room, explaining the heist, he couldn't help but admire the expressiveness of her gestures. She told the story with both hands.

She's still not beautiful. I think I may be half in love with her, and I still wouldn't call her beautiful. And it doesn't seem to matter at all.

He had known a fair number of beauties, and he could not remember enjoying the way one told a story half so much.

I just wish Brenner wasn't also watching her in quite that way.

When she finally reached the end and flopped down on a footstool, the paladin stirred.

"Well. I never had any doubts about your skill, but if I had…" He spread his hands. "However, that's really not the most important issue, is it?"

Slate wrinkled her nose. "I probably took a year off my life, fooling with quicksilver like that!"

"Yeah, and if Boss Horsehead catches you, he'll take all the rest of the years off for you," said Brenner. "He wants to put you in a *crow cage.*"

Slate turned a little too fast. "He has to catch me first!"

Her voice was too loud for the small space. She scowled fiercely into the silence.

"Brenner makes a valid point," said Caliban. "You shouldn't go out alone. If someone recognizes you—"

Slate's eyes narrowed.

Uh-oh.

Don't say "It's for your own good." Don't say it. Don't.

Among the many skills paladins required was the ability to convince people to evacuate dangerous areas.

86

This was sometimes difficult. People were reluctant to admit that, say, the ancestral family farm was now an open portal to hell. There were phrases you used and phrases you very much learned to avoid.

Saying "It's for your own good" pretty much guaranteed that no one was going anywhere.

"Really, it's for your own good," said Brenner.

Damn it all to hell...

"It's for *all* our goods," said Caliban hurriedly. "We can't do this without you, Slate. If we have to steal somebody's notes about how the Clockwork Boys work..."

"I am hardly equipped to climb up rain gutters," said Learned Edmund earnestly.

She exhaled. "I'm not sure when exactly this became a democracy!"

"Ah..." Caliban looked down at his hands. She had a very valid point. But then, so did he.

"I suppose you plan to follow me around? Clanking?"

"Ah, don't worry about it," said Brenner. "You know I'm always here for you, darlin'..."

Slate curled one corner of her lip. "I'll take Grimehug with me," she said. She met Caliban's eyes. "Will that be good enough for you, Mister Knight-Champion?"

Better the gnole than the assassin... He inclined his head.

"Then I'm going to bed. Unless you're afraid the trip down the hallway would be too dangerous?"

Caliban knew better than to touch that one, and was glad to see that Brenner did too.

CHAPTER 16

Slate was half-expecting the knock on the door, and hadn't bothered taking off her boots. She sat on the bed and glared at the man in the entryway.

"Come to apologize?" she asked. "Or do paladins not do that?"

Caliban shifted on his feet. "I'm sorry," he said. "I still don't think you should go out alone, but you are the one in charge."

"A fact that you seem to forget when it's convenient for you," she snapped. "I can't imagine that you'd be mother-henning over Brenner, if he'd managed to piss off Boss Horsehead."

"I wouldn't care as much if he ended up on a crow-cage. Not like you," said Caliban quietly.

The statement seemed to hang in the air and make a space around itself. Slate felt her stomach turn over.

Oh, this is very sensible. I'm getting all woogly because he just said he doesn't want to see me pecked to death by crows. How romantic.

He made the situation worse by the fact he was standing in the exact spot where lamplight from the hall made a halo of his hair, and Slate knew he wasn't doing it deliberately, but it infuriated her nonetheless. She had a strong urge to kiss him, and then perhaps beat him about the head and shoulders with his own sword.

She struggled back to the conversation. "Fine. I'll accept that you might be right. I *may* be in more danger than the rest of you, and my skills *may* be harder to replace." *A good commander listens to people when they're right. Even if it pisses her off. Right. I'm being good about this. Dammit.*

She was just feeling pleased with her own resolution when—predictably—Caliban said something stupid and she lost her temper again.

"You should have told us that you were at risk."

Slate threw her hands in the air. "Oh, like you've been so forthcoming? Forgive me if I'm not rushing to tell everyone all about my past! Hell, I still don't know how you wound up with a demon in your head, but am I lecturing you about it?"

She folded her arms and glared at him.

And now he'll point out that it doesn't matter if he ends up dead because he's not terribly essential now that he got us to Anuket City and he'll probably be right. Dammit. I don't want to be essential.

Caliban took a deep breath, let it out, then closed the door. He stood clasping his hands behind his back. He stared at the floor.

Oh god, he's at parade rest again. Why is this my life? Slate rubbed a hand over her face.

"Pride," said Caliban.

He seemed to be waiting for a response. Slate said, "Err, what?"

"Pride," said Caliban. "It's a sin. In my case, a mortal one."

"…okay?"

He lifted his eyes to her face. "No. I have not been forthcoming. It is not a story that reflects well on me."

Slate sighed. She was tired and her feet hurt and she was about to learn something that was undoubtedly going to be unpleasant.

She couldn't do the voice, but there were still things a decent person could do. *Even if I'm not a paladin.*

She moved her aching feet to one side and said, "Sit down."

"I—"

"It's a liege…order…thing."

He sat.

"All right. Let's hear it."

"When you fight a demon," said Caliban, "if it's in an animal, you kill it. If it's a person, you bind it and take them back to the temple for exorcism, if you can." He studied the floor again. "If you can't bind it, you kill them. Paladins on the temple's errands are immune from murder charges, did you know that?"

"Ah," said Slate. "That explains why they didn't…"

"Hang me? Yes. Technically I was still on duty, so killing ten people was legal for me." He made the bitterest sound she'd ever heard from a human throat.

Slate dragged her aching feet cross-legged and put her chin in her hand.

"That said…there are times when we bend the rules a little."

Is he expecting me to gasp with shock?

"If someone is very young or very frail, we will try to exorcise the demon there, if we can. Exorcism is hard and it is not made easier by dragging them fifty miles in chains."

Slate, who had been dragged approximately two hundred yards in chains some weeks earlier, could see how difficult it might be. *And that was inside the Dowager's palace, and they took them off as soon as I agreed to go on this wild goose chase. Yeesh.*

He said nothing for a few moments. Slate finally said "And…?"

Caliban looked up at the ceiling. His voice became flat and detached, like a man making a report to a superior officer. *Which, I guess, he is.*

"Exorcisms are always done in pairs. It's a formality. Usually a formality. You bind and then you exorcise. If the demon comes unbound and jumps and finds a foothold in the one doing the exorcism, the second priest—or paladin—is supposed to catch it. That never happens, though. Once bound, a demon becomes obedient."

Slate nodded. "Not a formality this time, huh?"

Caliban shook his head. "I had done dozens of bindings by now, you understand. Mostly of animals, but still. It wasn't hard. My heart was pure. Demons trembled at my name."

He didn't say it like he was boasting. He didn't say it sarcastically. He said it like it was true.

Slate had surprisingly little trouble believing him.

"And then I had a case of an infant possessed. The mother was begging me to save it. The infant…well, the priestess I was working with had broken her leg the week before and I was a long day's ride from anywhere. Demons aren't easy on their hosts, and it was half-dead already. I thought there was little chance I'd get it to the temple alive, and less that it could survive the exorcism, but if I did the rite right there…" He put his head in his hands.

"Didn't work?"

"Oh, it worked," said Caliban. "It worked beautifully. I breathed life back into that half-dead child and the demon went back to hell with a will and I felt smug with a job well done. And then the one that had been in the mother jumped, while my soul was wide-open and I was wallowing in my own pride."

Slate winced.

He dropped his hands. In a more normal voice, he added, "I still don't really know how the demon did it. They can pass very well for human if the human hosting them agrees to it, but they *hate* being near each other. I think it must have caught and bound the first one to bait the trap—it was smart. And very strong." He snorted. "That's the temple's judgment, not mine, incidentally. It took three priests and four tries to kill it, and they couldn't get it all. You know all the rest."

"You were trying to do the right thing," said Slate.

He sighed again. "No. Self-justification doesn't survive an exorcism. I was trying to be a hero, and convinced that I was more righteous than other paladins before me. That I was holy enough to break the rules. And I should probably have told you all that the first day."

"Well," said Slate. "Neither of us was at our best."

"There's that."

She scratched the back of her neck irritably. *And now I suppose I have to do something gracious, having learned an object lesson about the dangers of arrogance. Damn him, anyway. And it was all entirely earnest and entirely true, that's the worst of it.*

That was the trouble with genuinely honorable people. You just couldn't get any traction at all.

"So…that's when you had your crisis of faith?" she asked, to buy time.

"My what?" He looked so blank that it left Slate feeling nonplussed, as if she had misunderstood something vital.

"You said, back when we met, that you thought your god had abandoned you…?"

"Yes," said Caliban. "But that's…no. A crisis of faith is what you have when you're a teenager and wonder if the gods even exist. Or you're a middle-aged priest and you question the teachings of your religion and the problem of suffering and how futile everything seems. Something like that. Me, I kill demons."

"Well, la-di-*dah*," muttered Slate.

He actually smiled. "It's remarkably straightforward. The Dreaming God is not a terribly prescriptive god. Very few commandments. We don't even go in for prophets very much. We just try to stop demons before they can do too much harm."

"There are worse philosophies, I guess."

"I cannot question the existence of the Dreaming God. I felt His presence for many years. It is only by His grace that we humans can bind demons at all."

"So when you say He abandoned you...?"

The smile faded. "Exactly that. It seems that He will not or cannot share a soul with a demon."

"He won't?" Slate was starting to feel like the stupid one in this conversation, as if she were trying to have a conversation about machinery with Learned Edmund that started with, 'So, gears, do you know they exist?'

"I am uniquely qualified to comment, and no. I have not felt His presence since the demon took me."

He sounded so calm about it. Somehow that made it worse.

"But all that praying you do..."

Caliban shook his head. "Prayer is for the one who prays. It would be a monstrous arrogance to think that my prayers might sway the heart of a god."

Much more of this, and he's going to start apologizing to the gods in front of me. I can't take it.

He's also not going to leave until he gets an answer.

She glared at him. He sat there, hands folded, apparently willing to sit in silence until the end of the world, if that was what his liege required of him.

God's stripes, as Grimehug would say.

"I can't swear that I won't have to follow some leads on my own," she said finally, "but—when possible—I will take an escort. Grimehug or Brenner or you."

Caliban nodded. He seemed relieved to change the subject. "Grimehug is a good choice. I doubt he will be noticed, and he can at least bring us word."

He stood to leave, reaching for the door. She should have left it there. She *knew* that she should leave it there. But—

"Not Brenner, eh?"

Caliban would not meet her eyes.

Slate waited.

"I don't like the way he looks at you."

Slate raised her eyebrows. Was this jealousy, or something less? "I may not look like my mother," she said mildly, "but men do look at me occasionally."

Caliban shook his head, lifted a hand. "Not like that. It's not... normal."

Her eyebrows climbed higher. "What, does one of his eyes pop out or something?"

"I'm serious."

"Trying to keep me from doing something I'll regret again?"

Caliban flinched.

After a moment, he said, "Madam—*Slate*—if you don't trust me as a knight, then trust me as a man. We recognize these things in each other. The way he looks at you has no love in it, and too much hunger."

Her laughter came out in a short, painful bark. "Well, there's little enough love in Brenner, that's true." *Lust, yes. Even passion, if memory serves. But there's not much call for assassins who can love.*

Caliban sighed, and his shoulders slumped. "Forget I said anything. It's not my place." He turned away.

"No—wait—" She reached out and caught his forearm, and he halted. "I'm sorry. You're just trying to look out for me. You may even be right that I should have told you all about Horsehead. Fine. But I don't know what else I can say—we need Brenner for this. You know we do."

He nodded slowly, looking down at the hand on his arm. She let him go.

"Besides," she said, trying to make light of it, "there's no crime in looking."

"No," said Caliban. He raised his eyes to meet hers. "I'm glad."

His were very dark in the candlelight and very deep and there was a great deal of hunger in them. And something more than that.

He left the room before she could think of anything to say.

Slate stared at the door long after it had closed behind him.

She didn't know if she should laugh or burst into tears. And she had no idea what, if anything, to do about it.

CHAPTER 17

Slate was watching gnoles.

She sat cross-legged on the roof of the inn, in the shadow of one of the chimneys. Grimehug was not with her, but that was because the inn would have gotten very upset if there was a gnole on the roof.

It was a perfectly good reason and she would tell Caliban that if he tried to lecture her about it.

Am I being petty? It's possible I'm being petty.

Serve him right for...for looking at me like that! And then stomping off to go brood somewhere. Goddamn paladins.

She wouldn't have been half so annoyed if he hadn't had a valid point about the risks.

How dare he tell me about his awful past at a particularly relevant moment? The nerve of the man!

Slate grinned sourly to herself.

Gnoles moved through the streets below, small, rag-wrapped figures. They mostly stayed out of the way of the humans, keeping to alleys and shadows—but they didn't *hide*.

Slate had to admire the technique.

The gnoles weren't doing anything to avoid being seen. Instead, they were moving like they belonged there, going somewhere, doing some small, vital, probably disgusting task.

For someone who staked her life on being overlooked, it was like watching masters at work. In the Dowager's city, being short and female and dark-skinned made people's eyes slide over you, but it was nothing compared to the gnoles.

Being invisible nearly drove me mad, until I learned to use it to rob people blind. I wonder how the gnoles manage. Do they ever wish that they weren't invisible?

They weren't human. She had to remind herself of that. Perhaps the gnoles did not care what humans thought, because they weren't invisible to each other.

Rag-and-bone gnoles. Grave-gnoles. There's some kind of class system, to hear Grimehug talk, even if they don't have kings. But regardless, they're all doing nasty little jobs that humans don't really want to do.

And nobody looks too closely at them.

And I bet nobody knows how many there are.

Over the course of an hour, Slate counted several dozen. Probably she counted a few twice, but still, there were lots of gnoles out, even relatively early in the morning.

There could be thousands in the city. I'd be a little surprised if there weren't.

She didn't wonder what they were eating. She'd already seen a gnole pounce on an unwary pigeon and scurry off with it.

I bet the rat population is way down. And the feral dogs and the feral cats...

Good thing Grimehug's on our side.

Slate picked at a loose thread on the side of her trouser leg.

Assuming...of course...that he is on our side. But no. There's no way you'd plant somebody in the middle of a rune village in the Vagrant Hills to try to throw spies off the track. He's told us too much, and we've verified most of what he's said.

I suppose he could still decide to sell us out. He worked for the merchants, after all. It could be in his best interest to keep the clocktaurs around.

He seems pretty bitter about them, though. Particularly since they left his friend to die, and the rune caught him.

A ragged pair of gnoles crossed the square across from the inn. They were dressed more drably than Grimehug, in grays and browns.

Rag-and-bone gnoles, I think...

The rag-and-bone gnoles dug in the gutters, moving out of the way if a human came near. They reminded Slate of crows settling on something dead.

Nothing wrong with that. Be a much nastier world if not for crows.

Come to think of it, the city did seem cleaner than it had when she'd lived here...

Of course. You don't have to pay gnoles what you pay humans. The Senate probably loved that. The Merchant's Guild, too. The city gets cleaned up and you can cut an entire segment of the payroll...and they'll eat the rats and the cats and the rest of the vermin. Who wouldn't *want* gnoles?

She chewed on her thumbnail. Innkeepers, apparently.

Do they really carry werkblight? Wouldn't I have it by now?

But I saw blight in the Dowager's city, too. If it's the same thing, where did it come from?

The rag-and-bone gnoles finished their sweep of the gutters and scurried away down an alley.

Grimehug had said something about gnoles in the capitol, so it was possible. They'd found no pattern to the deaths in the capitol, but they also hadn't been looking for gnoles. Nobody knew they existed.

They'd just be some ratty little critters living in alleys by the docks... nobody'd pay much attention down there...half the merchants do business in Anuket anyway, so they'd be used to seeing them...

More gnoles, in brighter clothing, moved through the square. Three of them laughed together, then split apart and went three separate ways. A man went through on one of the wrought-iron artifact horses and nearly ran over one, not looking, not seeing.

No, it can't be gnoles. If they were the ones carrying werkblight, every-body in Anuket City would have it by now. The guards by the factory would have it. The Merchant's Guild would have thrown them all out. I don't care what the innkeepers think, there's gnoles everywhere.

A knot of white-clad gnoles entered the square.

Slate sat up, interested.

They were dragging a dog-cart behind them. Two gnoles were pulling it along and two more walked behind the cart—and people *saw* them.

Humans drew back when they approached. The rider on the artifact horse turned his steed sharply and went down another street.

They halted outside a small building and waited. Their wrappings were pale, marred with dust and darker things.

Are they wearing burial shrouds?

What did Grimehug say? Rag-and-bone gnoles, job gnoles, grave-gnoles...

There was no mistaking which these were.

One of the grave-gnoles tapped on the door and waited.

Someone wailed from inside the house. A woman came to the door and held it open. Slate was too far away to make out her expression, but the set of her body was grim.

The two grave-gnoles went silently into the house.

The square emptied entirely of humans. Even the other gnoles pulled back into the alleyways.

The door opened again. The grave-gnoles carried a bundle between them, wrapped in blankets.

Slate didn't have to be on ground level. There was only one thing that was ever that shape.

The grave-gnoles loaded the body into the dog-cart and pulled it away.

After a few minutes, the square began to fill up again, but Slate wasn't around to see them, because she was hurrying over the rooftops in hot pursuit.

CHAPTER 18

The grave-gnoles could not take the narrowest alleys, because of the dog-cart, so their path across the city was a roundabout one. Slate disliked the rooftops in daylight. People didn't look up much, but when they did, they tended to point.

Still, there were a couple of chimney sweeps about, and even a few gnoles raiding pigeon nests. The sweeps eyed her oddly. The gnoles ignored her.

She kept an eye on the dog-cart, although she had a sudden suspicion that she knew where it was going.

They passed into the Old City. The buildings got shorter and the roof tiles changed underfoot. Slate had to pick her way carefully, dividing her attention between her footing and the grave-gnoles.

They turned once—twice—and then Slate pulled up short. She dropped to a crouch and watched the cart rumble away through the streets.

The grave-gnoles were taking the corpse into the Clockwork District. Slate closed her eyes and listened intently—was that the sound of the gate being opened?

They're taking the bodies into the factory there. Nobody's paying attention, because they're grave-gnoles and people don't look at them.

They look at the other gnoles and don't see them. They see *the grave-gnoles so they don't* look *at them.*

This was troubling, as much for what it said about humans as about the fact that corpses were regularly being dragged into the Clockwork District and *no one was paying attention.*

Slate chewed on her thumbnail and then Brenner popped up next to her and she let out a squawk.

"Didn't you just promise not to go out without an escort?"

"I didn't go *out*. I went *up*."

"I'm sure that'll be a consolation when you're dead."

"Shut up, Brenner."

"I will not. For once, the paladin and I agree on something." He dropped to his heels next to her and began rolling a cigarette. "Well, anyway, what'd you find?"

"Not sure yet. Something, maybe. Let's go back to the inn."

"What'll you give me not to tell the paladin you're wandering around unsupervised?"

"I won't push you off the roof."

"Aww."

"He's not in charge here."

"Really? After all that time in your room last night…"

Oh, so that's what this is about. Slate stifled a sigh.

"Tell me, darlin', is he calling his god's name or yours when he—"

"Brenner."

The assassin grinned like a shark.

Slate groaned. "He was confessing his sins, if you must know."

"For paladins, that's practically foreplay."

Slate didn't want to laugh, but she did anyway, and immediately felt unkind. Brenner looked more smug than usual.

They made their way back across the rooftops. Slate glanced over her shoulder in the direction of the Clockwork District several times.

What's going on in there? What could they possibly be doing?

Brenner started to say something and Slate held up a hand. He dipped his head in acknowledgement. They proceeded along the roofline in silence, while Slate's mind added things up like a column of figures and came out with results that didn't seem remotely possible.

It can't be all the bodies. People want to bury their dead…if they can afford it…

In a city this size, there are lots of people who can't afford it. And the grave-gnoles just take the bodies away, no questions asked…Have they taken the place of the pauper's grave?

What about murder victims, though? What does the Watch think of the grave-gnoles, I wonder? Are they glad they're taking away bodies or…?

Slate shook her head. That was one group she wasn't going to get to ask.

I suppose we could send Caliban over in full regalia...no, I'd rather not come to their attention at all, if we can avoid it. You don't forget Mister Knight-Champion in a hurry, and not when he's asking weird questions about where the dead bodies go.

Still, suppose the gnolls have pushed out the men with the body carts. Wouldn't those people kick up a fuss?

Brenner started to say something and Slate held up a hand. "Thinking," she said. He nodded.

What if the corpsetakers did kick up a fuss? They're the lowest of the low. They make their living looting the dead and selling the bodies to the resurrection men. The Watch and the Senate both would probably be ecstatic to see them replaced by small, polite creatures that don't talk to humans much.

They reached the square with the inn and dropped down into an alley.

On the house that the grave-gnoles had entered, there was a sign. It was boldly stylized—a black circle with a droplet inside, like blood.

Now isn't that interesting...

"Go in without me," said Slate. She glanced over her shoulder at the notice. "I want to talk to the innkeeper."

"And get the paladin all up in arms? I'll wait."

Slate gritted her teeth. "Fine..."

She went into the inn by the front door, while Brenner lounged against the fountain outside, flicking bits of ash into the water.

The innkeeper looked up. "Can I help you, miss?"

"Excuse me..." said Slate. "There's an odd sign on a building across the way—a black circle with a red drop in the middle—"

"Werkblight," said the innkeeper. "Three-day quarantine."

"Only three days?" asked Slate, surprised. Blight was treated much more harshly in the capitol.

"You want it to run longer? Three days is plenty," said the innkeeper. "If you've got it, you'll likely die in half a day or so, and if you aren't going to get it there's no sense sitting around with a pile of corpses. It used to be a week, but you'd get people running out of food and water and coming out. Didn't seem to matter much."

"Do they know what causes it?" asked Slate.

The other woman shrugged. "People say the gnoles carry it, but there's people who work with 'em every day and never get it—and merchants who walk through the gates and fall down dead with it two hours later. Me, I think it's a curse of the gods for our impure living."

"And the grave-gnoles take them away?" asked Slate, who could see a conversational pit looming before her and was hoping to avoid it.

"Yep. They don't let people touch 'em. Graveyards won't take werk-blight corpses. The gnoles take 'em off somewhere, dump 'em in a pit or something. Burn 'em, maybe."

"You don't know?"

The woman gave her a defensive look. "Not my job. I'm sure the city pays the little blighters to take care of it proper."

Slate thanked the woman and fled to the relative haven of their rooms.

Caliban pulled the door open. The paladin looked distracted. He didn't even say anything about the fact that Brenner had come in five minutes before she did.

"What's happening?" asked Slate. The line between his eyes was worrying her.

He ran a hand over his face. "Learned Edmund has discovered something."

Slate glanced past him, to where the scholar was sitting. "He's back early."

"I pleaded a headache to Mistress Magnus," said Learned Edmund, putting his face in his hands. "Oh, I'm a fool."

Slate raised her eyebrows and glanced at Caliban. The paladin shook his head marginally.

"I should have guessed immediately. I should have guessed the moment we saw them. No, I should have guessed before it. That was why Brother Amadai was drawing them."

"Are *we* going to have to guess?" asked Slate acerbically.

Learned Edmund gave her a woeful look. "All I had to do was ask Mistress Magnus. It wasn't a secret. It's not any kind of secret among the artificers. *Why* didn't I see it before?"

"Animal, vegetable, or mineral?" asked Slate.

"Is it bigger than a breadbox?" asked Brenner.

Caliban sighed and intervened. "Learned Edmund, we are all of us blind sometimes. It is our lot as humans. Please tell us what you have learned."

Brenner rolled his eyes and shot Slate a look. Slate put her chin in her hand.

Well, I suppose paladins know how to talk to priests…

Learned Edmund sat up straight in the chair. "Yes. You're right, of course. My pride is the least injury here." He took a deep breath. "The clocktaurs. They're coming out of a wonder-engine."

"Like that thing in the field?" asked Brenner.

The scholar nodded. "Exactly like. They unearthed it some years ago. The artificers are very dismissive of the clocktaurs. They are not made by modern skill, but by some engineering of the ancients."

Slate could see this all too easily. The artificers were prickly and often protective of their secrets. Having superior killing machines produced in great quantity by unskilled means would certainly gall them.

Feed materials in, get a clocktaur out—and no one has to get paid. Oh, the artificers would be furious…I can't believe that none of the Dowager's spies ever thought to ask one.

Of course, if they thought the artificers were making the things, perhaps it didn't occur to them to ask. You don't walk up to the enemy and say, "Excuse me, how are you doing that?"

Unless you're poor dumb brilliant Learned Edmund, who just assumes that of course someone will tell you if you ask politely. And it turns out he's right.

"A wonder-engine," said Caliban. The paladin dropped into a chair, looking exhausted. "How in the Dreaming God's name do we fight *that?*"

"You're sure that this woman you're talking to is telling the truth?" asked Brenner. "You can trust her?"

"Of course," said Learned Edmund, looking surprised that anyone would ask.

"It makes sense," said Slate. "That weird ivory stuff they're made out of…it looks a lot like the stuff the wonder-engine was made from, doesn't it? And you're getting things out that *shouldn't* work, but do."

The scholar nodded to her. "Completely correct. They are feeding something into it—I know not what—and getting out clocktaurs."

Slate felt her heart sink. The column of figures had all been tallied, and there, at the bottom, was something she didn't like at all.

No matter how many times she added it up, though, it didn't change.

"I've got a pretty good idea what they're using," she said.

Every eye turned to her. On the floor, Grimehug let out the thinnest thread of a whine.

"They're feeding it werkblight corpses."

CHAPTER 19

"How in hell do we dismantle a wonder-engine?" asked Caliban.

Several hours had passed. Caliban had gone off, taken a hot bath, and come back. Everyone was still repeating variations on this question, mostly to thin air. This time, unusually, Learned Edmund answered.

"I don't think we do," he said. "They're not indestructible, but they're awfully close. When Carex mercenaries sacked the city-state of Romanga, the wonder-engine took almost no damage."

"They take the Clockwork Boys apart by dropping them into pits and smashing them apart with sledgehammers," said Caliban. "At least, that's the way they were doing it before I was—well."

Rain beat at the windowpanes. Brenner poked up the fire and Grimehug grumbled on the hearthrug.

"Boiling," said Slate. "Boiling works pretty well, but it's hard to get the things to hold still long enough. Hot oil slows them down a bit. Could we heat the wonder-engine?"

Learned Edmund lifted his hands, baffled. "We could try. One was damaged in the Great Fire of Halting—although they never learned what it does, so it's possible that it still works."

"The Great Fire went on for six days," said Caliban, "and killed hundreds, if not thousands."

"I suppose we could try setting the Clockwork District on fire," said Brenner. "Although they're right by the river, so they might put it out more quickly. I'm not sure how we'd arrange a sustained fire *around* the wonder-engine…"

"Ahem," said Caliban. "I said, 'killed hundreds, if not thousands.'"

"Yes, I heard."

"That doesn't bother you?"

"Do you think it would bother the Dowager?" asked Brenner.

"It would bother *me*," said Caliban.

"Yes, but I could kill you and then no one would be bothered."

Slate rubbed a hand over her face. "Gentlemen—"

Learned Edmund said "Before anyone sets anything on fire, perhaps we should attempt to ascertain whether we are, indeed, correct in our assumptions. We have only Mistress Slate's observations about the grave-gnoles. And while I trust Mistress Magnus's information, she has not, herself, seen the wonder-engine."

"I'd love to be wrong," said Slate. "Truly!" She drummed her fingers on her knee. "But it makes sense. If you steal corpses, people notice. People don't like it when Grandma goes missing. But if Grandma had werkblight, nobody expects to see her again. They're just glad that somebody took her away where she won't infect anybody else."

"You think the people behind the clocktaurs are spreading the werkblight?" asked Brenner.

All three of them stared at him.

"What? If I wanted a lot of corpses nobody'd miss, I'd start a plague too."

"Such a crime would be considered monstrous by all known authorities," said Caliban.

"Yeah, the people generating unstoppable giant killing machines are probably real concerned about that."

"As no one knows how the werkblight is spread, it seems unlikely that it is deliberate," said Learned Edmund. "What gain would there be in killing those people in the town that we passed, when there would be no access to the bodies?"

"The Blight's been around here for a few years," said Slate. "The Clockwork Boys didn't show up until later. I'm thinking maybe the people who needed bodies just got lucky. And clever."

"It is quite possible that the exact manner of death does not matter," said Learned Edmund. "The grave-gnoles are taking the werkblight corpses because those are what they are supposed to take. If they took a corpse that did not have werkblight, it might work just as well."

"That makes more sense," said Slate. She felt a sudden relief, although she couldn't have said why. "If wonder-engines are really from the ancients, then they'd have wanted to feed them something that they'd have on hand. Everybody says werkblight's new."

"Or an old disease that has re-emerged," said Learned Edmund. "They do that, sometimes. There's a monograph about the summer fevers that—"

Slate moaned and dropped her head again.

"Perhaps another time," said Caliban.

"Look," said Brenner, "that bit doesn't matter, does it? We can't very well choke off their supply of corpses."

"Can we?" asked Caliban.

The assassin gave him a sidelong look. "My job is making more corpses. The only way I could make *less* is if I retired early."

"You could always take holy orders," said Caliban.

Brenner snorted. "Your body count's probably higher than mine, paladin. And I didn't have priests to hold them down for me—"

"Enough."

Slate wasn't surprised that she'd said it, but she was a little surprised at how much it sounded like an order.

Caliban actually snapped to attention. Brenner rolled his eyes and put both of his hands ostentatiously over his mouth.

Much more of this and I'll get used to giving orders. Perish the thought. Still, if it keeps them from each other's throats…

She attempted to drag the conversation back to a useful direction. "I suppose what we need now is to talk to a grave-gnole."

"Oh, as to that…" Learned Edumund sat up, looking more cheerful than he had in hours. "The gnole culture is really quite fascinating."

On the floor, Grimehug rolled his eyes.

"Ah?" asked Slate.

"Indeed. They have a very complex caste system, did you know? Grimehug is a job-gnole, which makes him socially inferior to a hunt-gnole or a garden-gnole—"

Grimehug curled his lip back to show one fang. "Strong words, book man."

"No offense intended, Grimehug. *Inferior* is meant without censure. Indeed, I find the notion that your society honors food producers to be marvelous."

"All right, then."

"Would you prefer to explain it? You are certainly the expert, and I do not wish to presume to speak for your people."

The gnole threw Slate a look of tolerant amusement. "You go ahead, book man. Humans explain better to other humans. A gnole will speak up if a human gets it wrong."

"Thank you, Grimehug. Please do, I don't wish to perpetrate any misunderstandings." He cleared his throat. "Now, as I was saying, Grimehug here, is, however, socially superior to a junk-gnole, a rag-and-bone gnole, and a grave-gnole. And because he's a job-gnole, he speaks our language much better than most of his contemporaries. Among humans, he'd be considered a skilled negotiator."

Somewhat mollified by this, Grimehug stretched out and closed his eyes again.

"The grave-gnoles are the lowest caste. They handle the dead, particularly plague victims. I get the feeling that grave-gnoles are a relatively new development in gnole society. Most of the words for them are borrowed human words, not gnole words, whereas *job-gnole* is actually a translation of—oh, I don't know if I can explain it! 'One who sees that things are accomplished,' maybe."

Grimehug grunted. "Close enough."

"This is riveting," said Brenner, in a not-very-riveted tone, "but does it get us any closer to the factory?"

"Patience, Brenner." Learned Edmund held up a hand. "If Mistress Slate is correct about the fuel for the clocktaur wonder-engine—and I must say, it makes a dreadful kind of sense—then the logical people to contact are, indeed, the grave-gnoles."

Grimehug scowled. The fur on the back of his neck spiked up.

"If Grimehug here is prevented by social convention from contacting a grave-gnole—"

"God's stripes," muttered Grimehug. "Ever *smelled* a grave-gnole, book man?"

"Well, no. But please correct me if I am wrong, Grimehug, but can you speak to a rag-and-bone gnole on our behalf?"

"Oh, sure." Grimehug's fur smoothed. "Rag-and-bone gnole is no problem."

"And could a rag-and-bone gnole speak to a grave-gnole?"

Grimehug shrugged. "Suppose. If some gnole wanted to. None of *my* business."

Slate went down on one knee. "Grimehug, would you be willing to find us a rag-and-bone gnole to talk to? One who could ask a grave-gnole questions for us."

The gnole drew his lips down, revealing his fangs. "Asking a lot, Crazy Slate."

"I know." She rubbed her bicep. The tattoo had been quiet since they reached the city. Apparently it thought she was trying her best.

He considered for a moment. Then he looked over her shoulder at Learned Edmund. "Want something, book man."

"Anything I can do, Grimehug," said Learned Edmund.

"Writing down stuff about gnoles," said Grimehug. "Book about gnoles, maybe?"

"I'd like to write a book about your people. I don't think anyone has."

"Nobody has," said Grimehug. "Lots of human books. No gnole books. You write a book about gnoles, yeah? Well, a gnole wants to know what's in it, first. Humans say a lot of things. Want to make sure they say the right things about gnoles."

Learned Edmund nodded. "That is very fair, Grimehug. In fact, I will write a letter to my brothers at the Temple of the Many-Armed God stating that a monograph on gnoles is long overdue and that you are to be consulted, in case something happens to us here. Will that satisfy you?"

Grimehug nodded. He glanced up at Slate. "Book man's word good, Crazy Slate?"

"Word's good," said Slate. "Better than my word, probably."

"Then a gnole finds you a rag-and-bone gnole," said Grimehug. He walked to the balcony and opened the glass doors. They heard the rattling as he swung himself down the drainpipe.

"Got off lightly," said Brenner, shutting the doors against the rain. "I'd think he'd want more."

"On the contrary," said Learned Edmund. "Wanting control over the way his people are represented—that's a very large thing. And a very sophisticated one."

"Grimehug's no fool," said Slate. "And the gnoles are everywhere, have you noticed? There's probably as many gnoles as humans in this city, and they're controlling some pretty vital services. It's a little unsettling."

"As long as he's on our side," said Brenner.

"Some days I don't know if *we're* even on our side," said Slate.

"It's not as easy as just writing down things," said Learned Edmund. "The gnoles have no written language. As near as I can tell, each word's meaning changes based on the posture of the speaker. Have you noticed how Grimehug moves his ears? To him, that literally changes the nature of the words he's speaking."

"Huh?" said Brenner.

Learned Edmund sighed and sat back. "Take—oh—*crazy*. You know he says that a lot?"

"I'd noticed," said Slate dryly.

"Yes, well. The thing is that in gnolespeech, he'd be saying twenty different words. The vocal component is only part of it. The rest is in the ears and the whiskers and the posture and maybe some other things I don't know how to ask about. But because we only recognize the spoken word, we don't understand all the nuance."

He picked up a sheet of parchment from the table. "I started trying to write down all the meanings the other night. He told me as many as he could. Actually, he told me I was crazy trying to write it all down, but with ears up and whiskers forward, which means 'doing something silly,' and I think there might have been another nuance that I didn't catch that said he was going to humor me. And a word that means so far in love that your behavior is irrational, and a word that means drunk or intoxicated on drugs. And when he says 'Humans are crazy,' that's *another* word that means 'doing things that make no sense to gnoles but presumably make sense to humans.' But when he calls you Crazy Slate, *that* means that he thinks you're brave but—ah—not sensibly so—"

"Completely nuts," said Brenner.

"That's the impression I got, yes," admitted Learned Edmund. "It's a compliment, sort of, but also a warning to other people that you don't always act in your own best interest."

Slate rubbed her hand over her face. Naturally Grimehug was warning other gnoles against her. That was only sensible.

"Ironically, the word for insanity is something else entirely," said Learned Edmund. "I had to explain what I meant. We went in circles around the concepts of unpredictable behavior, because he kept saying that the mentally ill were usually predictable, so *crazy* was the wrong set of words to use."

"This is all fascinating," said Slate, "but be honest. Is Grimehug only here to keep an eye on us?"

The scholar looked sheepish. "Not *only*. He is genuinely fond of you. But he's not—ermm—completely altruistic, I don't think. The word he uses for you means that people in your vicinity might get hurt."

Brenner laughed. Learned Edmund gave him a nettled look. "Meanwhile, the word he uses for Brenner here means that Brenner hurts people deliberately."

"It's a living," said Brenner, not at all ruffled. "But what's the point of all this?"

"The point is that Grimehug's vocabulary is probably twice the size of yours," said Learned Edmund. "And I've got no idea how to write it down and I don't think a human could ever really learn to speak it at all."

"Speaking of people with large vocabularies," said Slate, "did you find anything else out about your lost scholar?"

"Oh." Learned Edmund's enthusiasm faded. "Brother Amadai's workshop is gone. I asked if the people using it knew where he had gone. They said no, that he had stopped paying the rent and left everything behind."

Slate winced. "Did his notes get lost? It seemed like, from what you said, he'd be the one most likely to know how to destroy a wonder engine."

"Thankfully, no," said Learned Edmund. "The artificers take that sort of thing very seriously. All his research notes were taken to the Guild archives."

"So they're there now? In these archives?"

Learned Edmund nodded. "I hope, as a fellow dedicate of the Many-Armed God, that they will allow me access to them."

"Well, if they don't, there are other ways."

He looked puzzled.

"You want paper stolen, our Slate's a gem," said Brenner.

"Stealing from a *library?*" said Learned Edmund in horror.

"It's a living," echoed Slate. She stood up. "I'm taking a nap. Seems like all we can do now is wait."

CHAPTER 20

Wait they did, until long after dark. Caliban lit the oil lamps. Learned Edmund scribbled in his notebook. Slate didn't know whether he was writing about wonder-engines or the social habits of gnoles or the personal dynamics of four tired, worried humans with a terrible secret. It didn't seem to matter much. She tried not to sigh.

Caliban took down the padded jerkin that he wore under his armor and began mending a tear in it. Slate looked over at the tiny, exact stitches and shook her head, bemused.

"You should have told me you could sew."

He glanced up at her. "Fighting demons is hard on your clothes. And paladins don't inspire confidence when they're wearing rags."

"I've got at least three shirts with holes in them."

He heaved a sigh. "Bring them here…"

"Are you taking requests?" asked Brenner.

Caliban pinched the bridge of his nose. "Why did I admit to anything?"

Slate returned with an armful of clothes. Caliban picked up the shirt she had been wearing when she dropped onto the rune and wrinkled his nose. "I am a paladin, not a resurrectionist. This shirt is dead."

"I liked that shirt."

"I can give it last rites. That's as far as I'll go."

"Fine, fine…"

She curled up in a chair and watched as he set to work on the surviving shirts with needle and thread.

Caliban's hands had been one of the first things she had studied when she had found him in the prison cell so many weeks ago. He had set his hands on the bars next to hers. His fingers were covered in small white defensive scars. Hers, much smaller, were stained with ink and mottled with marks from engraver's acid.

At the time, her chief concern about his hands had been whether he would try to snap her neck through the bars.

Now she watched his hands moving over the fabric and could imagine all too easily what they would feel like on her skin.

Being weak again. Dammit, Caliban, why did you have to go and say all those stupid things?

And why do you have to be so goddamn pretty?

He looked up at her and smiled. She scowled at him.

"Am I using the wrong color thread?"

"What? Oh. No, it's fine. It's...it's the waiting." She gestured vaguely toward the window. *Which is not a complete lie, anyway.*

His expression cleared. "Ah. I understand, believe me."

He bent his head over the fabric again and Slate thought dark thoughts behind her eyes.

Eventually there was a scrabbling at the drainpipe. Brenner vanished and a minute later, he and Grimehug came over the railing. He straightened his rags and looked up at them. "Found a gnole," he said. "Will talk with you, book man, and Crazy Slate." He glanced between Caliban and Brenner. "Not you, big man, or you, dark man. Smell too much like death. Scare a gnole away."

"You don't expect us to let them go alone!" said Caliban.

"Down, boy," said Slate, annoyed. "We're coming, Grimehug. Let me go get my robes on."

Caliban tried to give her a meaningful look. Slate smiled pleasantly, refusing to take any meaning from it.

She made it as far as her room when he caught up with her. "Slate—"

"If you're going to talk, help me get this boot on."

He dropped to one knee and held the boot open, a gesture as practiced as a sword drill. Slate shook her head, amused. *Of course. How many years do paladins spend as squires before they kit them out with armor?*

"This could be a trap," said Caliban.

"Yep," said Slate. She handed him the other boot.

"You shouldn't go alone."

"Nope."

"It could be terribly dangerous."

"Yep."

He paused, still holding the second boot. Slate wiggled her toes at him. She was wearing his extra socks.

His lips twisted. "You're going anyway, aren't you?"

"Yep."

"Am I being an arrogant jackass again?"

"You're right on the edge."

He sighed.

"I'll be with Grimehug," she said, relenting. "And I'll protect Learned Edmund—as much as one can, anyhow. And if it were Brenner going, not me, we wouldn't be having this conversation."

He bowed his head and put on her other boot.

When he pulled her to her feet, there was a brief moment where their bodies pressed together, Slate's shoulder against his chest and her right thigh against his left. They both paused for a half-second too long, then sprang apart.

I am too old for this, thought Slate. Caliban had his typical inscrutable paladin absolutely-nothing-going-on-here-ma'am expression. *I am thirty years old, for god's sake. I should kick his feet out from under him and sit on his chest and tell him "Look, I saved your armor-plated ass from the rune so don't give me any crap about the strong and the weak. I don't see you getting any better offers."*

I should.

Not right now, though.

"Are you all right?" asked Caliban.

"It's these damn shoes," muttered Slate.

CHAPTER 21

The night was wet with drizzle. Anuket City did not get a rainy season as such, but it got a damp season and they were in the middle of it. Puddles shone along the cobblestones and gurgled into the storm drains.

Grimehug was waiting for them in the alley. "This way, Crazy Slate. You too, book man."

They followed him into the alley, through twists and turns. The trash cans here were tight together, and even Slate had to go sidewise. "Doesn't matter if he wanted to come or not," muttered Slate, "we'd never have fit Caliban down here."

Learned Edmund nodded. "I suspect these ways are used mostly by gnoles."

Grimehug glanced over his shoulders. "Suspect correct, book man. Humans leave alleys too big, waste space. A gnole fits."

"A human doesn't," muttered Slate, turning sideways and sucking in her breath.

A gnole scrabbled out from underneath a wooden bin. She seemed to be mostly eyes, and her badger-like stripes were huge on her small face.

"This gnole is named Sweet Lily," announced Grimehug.

Learned Edmund bowed. Slate, for lack of anything better to do, bowed as well.

"A gnole meets you," said Sweet Lily. Her accent was much thicker than Grimehug's. "Is well." She ducked her head and her ears.

"This gnole has found a grave-gnole," Grimehug added, his lip curled as if smelling something disgusting. "This gnole is a good gnole, though."

"We are very grateful for the help," said Learned Edmund.

"Not going to be grateful for the smell," muttered Grimehug.

Sweet Lily led them onward into…*what?* wondered Slate. *The Gnole Quarter? Do they have their own quarter now?*

Given the enormous number of gnoles that had settled into the city since she left, perhaps so.

A tiny alley nearby led to an equally tiny courtyard. In it, wrapped in ragged shrouds, sat a grave-gnole.

The courtyard itself was full of garbage, bits of old wooden packing crates and broken ends of chairs. It looked like a place where people threw things away. The grave-gnole fit among them very well.

Sweet Lily went up to the gnole and began chattering to it animatedly. Grimehug's ears were flat back.

Learned Edmund crouched down in front of the grave-gnole. Slate could not read any expression on its face, but she remembered what the dedicate had said about the gnole language. Undoubtedly there were volumes being spoken in the twitch of whiskers and the positions of their ears.

"Do you understand this language?" Learned Edmund asked the grave-gnole.

The grave-gnole did not take its eyes off him, but it leaned over and spoke to Sweet Lily.

"A gnole says a gnole understands," she said. "But a gnole hears better than a gnole speaks. This gnole will speak their words."

Learned Edmund nodded. He continued to address the grave-gnole, and Slate gave him points for that.

"Do they have a name I may call them?"

Grimehug snorted. Slate felt embarrassed. She liked Grimehug, not to mention the small matter of him being the key to figuring out the clocktaurs, but his casual loathing of the grave-gnoles was more than a little troubling.

They are not human, she reminded herself. *I should not judge them on human terms. There may be reasons that I won't understand.*

And even if Grimehug's just being an ass, he's the only lead we've got, so this really isn't the time.

The grave-gnole's name was silent. It seemed to be a long exhaled breath and a hand passed over top of another hand. Learned Edmund looked helplessly at Slate, who shrugged just as helplessly back.

"Please ask—" he attempted the grave-gnole's name—" about where they take the werkblight corpses…"

They tried. They really did. The problem was that while Sweet Lily spoke the trade language reasonably well, their questions required a very specialized vocabulary. The gnolespeech had no words for 'wonder-engine' and 'roof access' was mostly a matter of pointing and mime. Learned Edmund tried to ask about possible controls for the clocktaurs and received two sets of blank looks from Sweet Lily and the grave-gnole alike.

Grimehug finally groaned and stationed himself next to Sweet Lily. "This gnole will translate for a rag-and-bone gnole," he said. "*Not* for a grave-gnole. Ask your questions, book-man."

This made things go a great deal more smoothly. It was blatantly obvious that the grave-gnole was listening to Grimehug, but Sweet Lily dutifully repeated what he said to the grave-gnole, then repeated what the grave-gnole said back.

Slate was glad that Brenner wasn't here to see this. He would not have been diplomatic.

The grave-gnoles learned where bodies were from other gnoles. The other gnoles didn't exactly address them, as near as Slate could tell, they would merely mention loudly, to thin air, that a plague death had occurred, and the grave-gnoles would go and get the body. The bodies were placed in the carts and taken through the gnole-sized doors in the Clockwork District. The doors were about two years old. Before that, they would wait outside the door for someone to notice them. How did they know where to take the corpses? A deal had been made several years ago. Humans had dealt with the bodies before, but humans didn't want to do it now. Humans caught werkblight. Gnoles didn't. Humans paid the grave-gnoles to take the werkblight corpses away.

What humans had made the deal? The grave-gnole didn't know. Other humans. With other grave-gnoles. Now the bargain was in place. No one asked about it.

Slate thought of the innkeeper saying *Not my job*. "Like the knack-ermen. Nobody bothers to ask who first hired them to take dead horses away. They're just glad that somebody's doing it before it starts to stink."

Grimehug paused in translation long enough to nod to her. "Like that, Crazy Slate. Yes."

Was there a way in? There was the way the grave-gnoles went. Another way? There was the human way. Many guards. The grave-gnole—Slate was thinking of this one as Breath-swipe, which she knew was a tragically human approximation—did not know how many guards. Many.

"Is more than ten," said Sweet Lily. "Is…probably not one hundred."

Once the gnoles went through the door with the bodies, they passed through an open courtyard. There were guards on top of the roof. There were none down at the ground. Guards didn't want werk-blight. There was a big building in the middle. Breath-swipe thought it was like the buildings that humans made to put their things in, not to live in.

"A warehouse?" said Slate.

Grimehug, Sweet Lily, and Breath-swipe had a three-way conversation for a moment before Grimehug agreed. Yes. Something like a warehouse.

The grave-gnoles went into the warehouse. There was a room and they dumped the bodies from the carts there. Then they went through another door and a human gave them money. Then they left.

Were there guards in the room with the corpses? No. There were not. No one guards the dead.

"Another grave-gnole takes the bodies somewhere," said Grimehug. "From the room where a grave-gnole drops them. This grave-gnole says that grave-gnole says there is a…" He looked to Sweet Lily, barked a question.

"Hole," said Sweet Lily. "Or is a…long hole?"

"Trench," said Grimehug. "Metal trench?" He shrugged at Slate and Learned Edmund.

"A chute of some kind, perhaps," said Learned Edmund.

"Maybe, book man. Inside of warehouse is big, goes down. Thing in it. No words for thing at bottom. No, some words. Stupid words." Grimehug's lips curled up and he growled something, almost directly at the grave-gnole. Breath-swipe stared at the ground, not speaking.

"Please tell us what they're saying, Grimehug," said Slate. She was getting very uncomfortable with his treatment of the grave-gnole, but she didn't dare alienate their only source of information.

Grimehug groaned. "Metal spiderwebs. Bone or clay thing. Bone tails hooked together."

"The wonder-engine," said Learned Edmund. "It's all right. They—" he attempted the grave-gnole's name again "—can't be expected to have words for that. Most human languages don't."

"Humans can't smell," muttered Grimehug.

That seemed to end the interview. Slate looked to Grimehug. "I'd pay an informant," she said. "Can I pay the grave-gnole?"

"Do whatever you want, Crazy Slate." He looked surly, then unbent a bit. "Pay Sweet Lily, though. A rag-and-bone gnole did good work."

Slate pulled out the same amount she had paid Sparrow in the Grey Church and held it out to Sweet Lily. "Sweet Lily, what is fair to pay this grave-gnole?"

Sweet Lily plucked the coins neatly out of her palm. "A rag-and-bone gnole pays this grave-gnole," she said, and turned to the grave-gnole. Money exchanged hands, though Slate couldn't see how much.

Sweet Lily said something in gnole-speech to Breath-swipe. They looked up, startled, then glanced at Slate, then back to Sweet Lily.

She leaned in and swiped her tongue across the grave-gnole's muzzle. Grimehug grunted, but didn't protest. The grave-gnole's ears went up and forward and they seemed to stand up a bit taller.

Then Sweet Lily turned away and led the humans back out of the Gnole Quarter.

"A gnole didn't need to go that far," muttered Grimehug.

"Is rag-and-bone gnole business, not job-gnole business," snapped Sweet Lily, the angriest Slate had heard her speak.

Grimehug accepted this rebuff with a grunt. After a moment, he leaned over and groomed Sweet Lily's ears. She made a small, grumpy purr.

"Grimehug..." said Slate.

He cocked his ear at her.

"Your people go along with the clocktaurs to see where they're going, don't they? It's not actually to make money."

Grimehug's ears flicked sharply, then he gave her a rueful grin. "Big damn clocktaurs, a gnole likes to know, hey? Maybe some gnoles don't want to go to the wrong place, get squashed in a human war just when a gnole's getting comfortable."

Slate nodded.

"A gnole doesn't complain about the money, though."

"A gnole wouldn't," said Slate dryly.

There was a logical extension to this, too. She knew it perfectly well. Grimehug was staying with them for reasons that had nothing to do with, as Grimehug claimed, how swanky the inn was.

We're paying quite a lot of money to the gnoles. It's worth their time. But they're also watching to see what we do. Grimehug's…if not a spy, at least an informant.

The only thing that she was sure of was that Grimehug was working for himself, or perhaps the gnoles, not for the government of Anuket City.

Because if he wasn't, we'd all be rotting in a cell by now.

"Grimehug?"

"Yeah?"

"You know we're trying to stop the clocktaurs."

"Yeah."

"Your people make money on the clocktaurs."

Grimehug paused. Light glittered off his dark eyes. "Don't twist whiskers too hard, Crazy Slate," he said. "Grave gnoles make money on clocktaurs. Rag-and-bone gnoles don't make any. Job gnoles don't make much." He tilted a hand back and forth. "Clocktaurs wreck a city, maybe no gnole makes any money."

Does that mean they won't get in our way?

They haven't so far. They're helping us.

Are the grave gnoles making too much money compared to the higher castes? Do they want to return the system to normal?

"Relax, Crazy Slate," said Grimehug, reaching up and patting her arm. "A gnole's your friend. A gnole tells you if a human's about to do something a gnole won't like, hey?"

And with that, she had to be content.

The humans entered the inn and climbed the stairs, the gnoles dispersed, and Slate was left wondering if they had learned anything, or everything, or nothing at all.

CHAPTER 22

When they returned, Caliban was alone in the main room of their suite, surrounded by bits of mail and plate.

"What happened here?" said Slate. "It looks like an explosion in an armor factory."

"I was cleaning my armor."

"If you do that too much, you'll go blind. Where's Brenner?"

"He went out."

Slate's eyes narrowed. "Following us?"

"He said not."

She dropped into a chair. Learned Edmund held the window open for Grimehug. Sweet Lily had returned to the hotel as well, but had declined to climb up a drainpipe to join them.

"How come you let him go out without an escort?"

"So far as I am aware, no one wants to hang *him* from a crow cage."

"Give it time," said Slate. "Brenner's talented like that."

Learned Edmund took out a sheet of foolscap. "I have to write this down while it is fresh in my mind," he said. "Mistress Slate, will you stay until I have finished, so that you may check over my writings?"

"Sure." Slate made a mental note to find Ashes Magnus and shake her hand. She couldn't imagine the dedicate of a month ago asking Slate to read his notes.

Caliban knelt down in front of her. Slate had a horrible fear that he was about to apologize for something, or start *my liege*-ing at her, but instead he untied her boots.

"I take back everything mean I've said about you recently," she said, as he pulled them off.

"What, all of it?"

"Well, the bits where I swore, anyway."

He gazed at her socks, formerly his. "I'm not getting these back, am I?"

"Not until I'm done with the shoes."

Grimehug stretched out on the floor in his badgerskin-rug pose. Caliban went back to fixing his chainmail, which involved pliers. Learned Edmund's pen scratched across the paper.

It was warm and oddly peaceful. Slate curled up in the chair with her legs over the arm and felt herself drifting. She watched Caliban bent over the heap of metal in his lap, his hands busy with individual links. The oil lamp cast warm golden light over the side of his face. Slate watched his brows furrow and smooth, over and over, as he fitted tiny lengths of wire into the mail links and used a pair of tongs to force them closed.

I just confirmed that the gnoles are dragging corpses into a warehouse, probably to be turned into rampaging killing machines. I've probably figured out a way into the warehouse, and it's nasty. And I...seem to be falling asleep...

She woke when Brenner came through the door. Someone had tucked a blanket over her. Probably no need to ask who.

"Where've you been?" she asked, sitting up and yawning.

"I can see you've been worrying yourself sick about it."

She yawned again. "It was a worry-nap. You selling us out to the enemy?"

"I tried, but nobody's got enough money." He dropped into another chair. "No, I was investigating the river approach."

"And?"

"We're not getting in that way. It's built out over the river. Big metal grates down into the water, and I mean *big*. It'd be hours of treading water with a hacksaw to get through them, and I don't know if we'd even be in the damn building at that point, or if we'd still have layers of floor to go through."

Caliban let out a sigh that almost sounded like relief.

Probably worried about sinking in all that armor...

"And the walls?" he asked.

"Unless you got a siege engine you're not using, it's not gonna happen."

Slate groaned. "How thoughtless of them."

She drummed her fingers on her thigh. There was an obvious way in, but she didn't like it at all.

Brenner met her eyes across the room. He was probably thinking the same thing.

"You thinking what I'm thinking, darlin'?"

"You know I am."

"Think we can get the gnoles to go along with it?"

"Let's see if we can figure something else out," she said. "Which I suppose means back to the Grey Church for us."

Caliban winced, but didn't object. Slate limped into the hall and her bedroom, to find that Grimehug had already beaten her there.

There are no demons in Anuket City.

The words had been rolling around Caliban's mind, popping up at odd intervals, like a fragment of poetry or a line from a song. He could not get them out of his head.

There are no demons in Anuket City.

There had to be. Sooner or later, there were demons *everywhere*.

He leaned his head back against the rim of the bathtub and tried to clear his mind. Hot water helped him think. Always had, ever since he had been very young and living on his father's farm. It was strange, stony, largely useless ground, but it had natural hot springs, and Caliban could always go and sit in the hot water and think.

He had been the youngest of four brothers. His mother died not long after bearing him. He grew up learning to take a beating and to keep his temper so he didn't take a bigger one. In that part of the country, a child sent to the temple meant a year of not paying taxes, and when he was nine years old and the harvest worse than usual, Caliban was tithed, or sold, or whatever you wanted to call it.

The Forge God had been set to take him, ironically enough. But a visiting champion of the Dreaming God had been at that god's temple and she had looked at him with cold gray eyes and informed the temple that she would be taking him instead. The Forge God's priests hadn't thought it was worth fighting over a skinny nine-year-old of no particular merit, and had sent him along with only token haggling.

In the Dreaming God's temple, Caliban had blossomed. Given enough food for the first time in his life, he shot up taller than any of his brothers and filled out broader. Fearing neither pain nor farm animals, as it turned out, went a long way towards making one useful as a demonslayer. The year he turned seventeen, the Dreaming God poured into his soul like hot metal and forged him into a weapon.

The god picked only the good, the calm, the just. After a few years in the Dreaming God's service, Caliban suspected that He also only picked the uncomplicated.

Knight-Champions lived almost sybaritic lives, by some standards. It was part of the bargain that no one ever talked about. You had clean clothes and soft beds and good food. You were sought after by men and women (and Caliban had had both in his time). You were lionized and praised and admired. In return, you trained with the sword every day and you were sent out over and over again, to fight things that gripped your soul like oily smoke and licked your heart with black metal tongues.

Demons tried to tempt you. It was their nature. If you desired power or knowledge or any one of a hundred complex desires, the demons had a foothold to work on you. So the ranks of the Knight-Champions were swelled by those who wanted nothing more than to be useful, to be appreciated, to kill demons, to have hot water and decent food and a warm bed at the end of the day.

Because you had everything you desired, you were very hard to tempt. So you tried to kill the demons and the demons tried to kill you and most days you won and one day they'd win instead. There weren't that many old Knight-Champions. Less than half of the people that Caliban had trained with as a novice were still alive.

On the other hand, you did get hot water. And they didn't begrudge you any of it.

He sank a little deeper into the tub, which wasn't very deep at all. It simply wasn't large enough to accommodate his frame. (Slate could probably have swum laps in it.)

Well, it was likely for the best. Caliban could no longer bear to have his face submerged. Even a hot towel while he shaved made him twitchy. He could not remember the exorcisms clearly, but his body remembered enough.

Mostly he remembered the cold. The hot water helped with that.

There had been times, in the prison cell, when he thought that he would never be warm again. Even now, there seemed to be a core of ice in his bones that woke sometimes and sent chill fingers outward through his flesh.

There are no demons in Anuket City.

There had to be. It didn't make sense for there not to be. Demons were attracted to humanity the way that wolves were attracted to sheep. Presumably they'd be just as interested in gnoles.

Why weren't there any demons here?

Was something keeping them out? Driving them away? He hadn't felt anything, but his demon was keeping a very low profile these days, as if the incident with the rune-demon had traumatized it. Caliban was *not* complaining about that.

It would be a good thing, if there were no demons. *Oh Dreaming God! It would be a glorious thing. A place on earth where they don't need me. Someplace that I knew would be safe.*

The idea was incredibly seductive, the embodiment of all that the Dreaming God's temple worked for…and apparently traveling with Brenner and Slate and their suspicious minds had rubbed off on him, because all Caliban could think was:

But if the demons aren't here, where are *they?*

"Politics," said Slate. "I *hate* politics."

"Doesn't everyone?" said Caliban.

"Presumably politicians enjoy it," said Learned Edmund.

"I don't even know why we're bothering," said Slate. Her voice was somewhat muffled because she was lying facedown on the floor, where she had collapsed dramatically a few minutes earlier.

Brenner came in, nudged her with his boot, and said, "Are you dead?"

"Yes. I am dead."

"Can I have your stuff?"

"None of it will fit you. Except maybe these boots."

"I take it," said Caliban, setting aside the bit of chain he'd been working on, "that this last round did not go well."

"It went great," said Slate, propping her head up in her hands. "We're actually getting somewhere. It's just where we're getting is useless."

"Oh?"

"The Senators who started the war aren't even in charge any more," said Slate darkly.

Caliban raised an eyebrow. "They aren't?"

"No. Two of them turned up dead and a couple retired."

"Turned up dead?"

Slate flapped a hand at him. "Don't get sidetracked on that. Senators turn up dead all the time. It's one of the acceptable forms of retirement here."

"My god."

"Yeah, don't go into politics in Anuket City unless you like power enough to die for it. Anyway, the point is that those people we were trying to find, who wanted a war?"

"Yes?"

"Somebody found them first."

Caliban digested this. "Is that good?"

"Hell if I know."

"So if they're dead…why is there still a war?"

Slate collapsed facedown on the floor again. "Politics," she said. "It doesn't make any sense. People do the stupidest shit and you want to scream that it's against their own interests and you never know if they're playing some deep game you don't know about or if they're really just that stupid. Right now, I think we're having a war because we've already got a war, so we might as well keep it."

Caliban nodded slowly. "They have paid most of the costs already, have they not? And the people who have learned to profit from the war will wish to continue."

"Yeah. I mean, all the war is costing them is clocktaurs. And trade with the Dowager's city, which is probably why at least one of the two turned up dead. And meanwhile everybody else is being very, very nice to Anuket City, so for all I know, it's still profitable. Hell, not having Archenhold threatening to secede every ten minutes might be worth it all by itself."

"Wars are harder to stop than to start," said Learned Edmund cautiously.

Slate pointed at him without lifting her head. "Also, what he said."

Brenner lit a cigarette and stared into the smoke. "So the problem, then…"

"Yeah." Slate sighed into the floor. "Yeah. Now who the hell are we supposed to kill?"

CHAPTER 23

Caliban was about as subtle as a warhorse in an apothecary shop, a fact that he was well aware of. If he hadn't been aware of it, Brenner would have told him. He discarded the notion of a disguise at once. If he wandered around looking suspicious and asking questions about demons, people were bound to notice.

Instead he mended the burn marks in his cloak, straightened his back, and swept out as the Knight-Champion of the Dreaming God, slayer of demons, who obviously had a pressing interest in demonic activity. He simply hoped that nobody recognized him as any specific Knight-Champion who might have been incarcerated recently for possession and mass murder.

It was a very strange city. He couldn't help but compare the streets to the broad, tree-lined avenues of the capitol. Anuket City looked old, as if it had grown up on the ruins of a dozen other cities, which it had picked apart and built with or occasionally carted off for scrap. Ancient stones formed foundations for modern-looking brick. Streets meandered and twisted back on themselves, or dead-ended into walls. Humble tenement buildings sported monstrous gargoyles from earlier incarnations as churches and cathedrals.

There were people of every possible nation, different races in different clothes. Caliban saw Chadori tribesmen (who were presumably genuine, unlike Slate) dark-skinned soldiers and merchant princes, great red-haired barbarians…every version of humanity imaginable. Even a minotaur, hooves clicking on the stones, and Caliban would have sworn you never saw them this far from the ocean.

He got lost immediately, but that didn't bother him. He was looking for temples in general, not any one in particular, and the city did not disappoint. There were temples to most of the major sects, and tiny cloisters dedicated to gods he'd never heard of.

He asked the same questions at every temple. Were there any reports of demons? How long since there had been any? Really. Fascinating, thank you.

Drop a coin in the alms box, go to the next temple, repeat.

After the third one, he started to get increasingly uneasy.

There simply weren't any demons. No one had heard of one for years. The bishop of the Forge God had been right. Wherever the demons were, it wasn't in Anuket City.

"Well, there were reports of one when I had just come here," said an olive-skinned person at the Temple of the White Rat. They had long hair and thin, elegant hands. "But it was actually a child with the falling sickness. You know how superstitious people can be."

"Was the child all right?"

The priest made a maybe-yes-maybe-no gesture with their right hand. "Taken to the healers before anyone could do anything foolish in the name of exorcism. I'm afraid I don't know much more than that."

"Thank you," said Caliban, dropping a coin in the alms box.

The fifth or sixth temple was a tiny hole in the wall and he'd have walked right by it, except that the priestess there wolf-whistled at him.

"Look at you!" she said cheerfully. She was even shorter than Slate, very round, with a shaved head and enormous silver earrings. "Dreaming God always did know how to pick 'em. We don't see too many of your kind out here, paladin."

He bowed to her, very deeply indeed. "Our loss, clearly, Sister."

"Ha! Sit down a spell, or are you off to smite something?" She patted the rug next to her.

"I fear I am at a loss for things to smite," he said, taking the opening, and sat down opposite her. "In fact, it seems that there are no demons anywhere in Anuket City to be found."

She had heavy eyelids, but the eyes under them were sharp as adder's tongues. "That's a good thing, isn't it?"

"Is it?"

"Seems like it should be, doesn't it?"

"You tell me."

She grinned. She had a gold tooth on the right side. Caliban could smell divinity clinging to her like expensive tobacco or cheap wine.

If he'd been about ten years younger and not half out of his mind over Slate, he would have been rather attracted to her. A woman like that would drink you down to the dregs and leave you half-dead in the gutter with a smile on your face. There was a great deal to be said for that.

As it was, even if he had been completely available, he was a little afraid she might break him in two. So he simply enjoyed the warmth of the divine that radiated off her. Even if it was not his god, it had been a long time since he felt such a power. Certainly no priest in the city that he had yet met had it.

Goddess, he thought. Not one he knew. He could taste salt and herbs and a strange, astringent tang, like leather.

"Somethin' weird about it, isn't there?" she admitted. There was a brazier in front of her and she poked the coals with a thin rod. "City this size ought to be bringing 'em in. You'd expect some body-jumping murders, maybe somebody floating over the fountains screamin' in devil-tongues, eh?"

"I would," he admitted.

The power in the room was growing. Each time she poked the coals in the brazier, they seemed to pulse and the power grew deeper.

"Strange. And none of the other temples troubling themselves to notice. That's strange too, don't you think?"

"Yessss..." said Caliban. The word stretched out longer than he intended, with much more venom. Until that moment, he hadn't even realized that he was angry.

Why didn't anyone pay attention? Why didn't they tell us that they'd found a place without demons? We could have studied it—learned from it—found the cause! Instead they all just ignored it, as if we had all poured out our blood for a mild annoyance!

The priestess looked at him for a moment, her heavy-lidded eyes lowering even farther. Then she reached out her hand and offered it to him, palm up.

He inhaled sharply.

"Your god's a hard one, paladin, for all He doesn't lay out many commands. Mine's a bit kinder. Knows how to say thank you."

"I..."

"Come on. I'm not old, but I'm not getting younger." She snapped her fingers.

She didn't even need the voice. Caliban had spent a lifetime obeying nuns. He could no more have disobeyed than fly.

His hands were shaking as he removed his gauntlets. He eyed them as if they belonged to someone else.

He held out his hand and she turned hers and gripped his wrist, her palm across his pulse. Her eyes locked with his.

The power of her goddess surrounded him and ripped his breath out of his lungs.

She was an old, fierce thing, a thing of high places and the hearts of beasts. Her children would walk sure-footed in the dark. Her priests knew the taste of loneliness, and, knowing it, had put their boots on its neck.

The places in Caliban's soul that had been empty for too long cried out in anguish. He wanted those places burned away, filled with the certainty of divinity, wanted it like an addict wanted the drug that destroyed them.

Yes. Please. *Please, some god take me. Any god. I was made to be a sword in someone's hand. It is all that I know. It is the only thing I'm good for. Please...*

The dead demon shrieked, but Caliban barely heard.

Her lips curled up at the corners. "I never saw the need for paladins of My own. But *my*, what lovely, broken creatures you are..."

It occurred to Caliban, as he fought for breath, that he was no longer sitting opposite a mortal.

Her eyes were full of wolves and shadows, snow and thornlight. She would have him go to empty places and hold them against those who would destroy them. When he fell at last, ravens would carry bits of his flesh away on black wings and make one final use of his sacrifice.

The strength of his own desire to serve shocked him. His god had abandoned him. He had made his peace with that.

He had not quite realized that he would crawl on his knees to any other god that would take him.

Please. Please! Take me—use me—make me useful again—give me meaning again—

"Ah..." She said, with real regret. "No, paladin, you're not for Me. Shame. I'd take you if I could. You're too good a weapon to leave lying around unclaimed. But you were made to answer to one hand only, and it isn't Mine."

She released his wrist. Caliban nearly cried out in pain. The power melted away like a handful of ashes, and he was mortal again and his soul was still so much less than it had been and...

...and someone was pushing a teacup into his hand.

The heavy-eyed priestess had gotten up and returned. He didn't think that much time had passed, and yet here she was, carrying tea, looking as tired as he felt.

"Drink it," she said. "It isn't poison. Didn't expect to be an avatar today myself, but that's what I get for not eating breakfast."

He drank. The goddess had not been evil, whatever else she had been. He did not fear poison.

Their hands met as she took the empty cup, and he felt only skin heat and the warmth of a distant divinity, not the raging bonfire of a god in mortal flesh.

"Do I pass her test, then?" he asked hoarsely. Fairly sure that he hadn't passed it, whatever it was. In the end, he hadn't been the one who chose.

"Heh!" The priestess grinned. "That wasn't a test—or if it was, it wasn't a test of *you*. But I meant what I said. She knows how to thank someone who's given up everything to keep the rest of us safe. So by way of Her gratitude, I tell you this: the demons are being pulled in by a mechanism somewhere in the city. Have been for some time."

"Someone's made a device that traps demons?" said Caliban.

"It seems so. One of these mad artificers, perhaps. Perhaps something else. She does not know. She does not pretend to be all-seeing. But the demons that come into the city go very quiet. If they jump from their host, they don't land into another one." She scowled. "I've pushed my fellows at the other temples to investigate, but no one listens to me. They tell me to go back to the hills and wilderness, that I'm jumping at shadows. Even the sweet ones say that if there is such a device, well, we're all the better for it, aren't we?"

She leaned over and spat.

"Thank you," said Caliban. He was still kneeling. He drew his sword and set the point to the floor, forehead pressed against the cross-guard, an obeisance made to one's liege and the highest of one's order.

The priestess sighed. "Ah, She's right. Damn shame. You'd have been welcome, brother."

"I'm sorry," said Caliban, and meant it. "Will you give me your blessing?"

She smiled and tapped two fingers on his shoulder. "You already have Hers."

"I'd rather have yours," said Caliban, and meant that, too.

CHAPTER 24

He found his way back to the inn easily, as if the complicated city had unwrapped itself. Perhaps the blessing of the priestess of the wild goddess had something to do with that, or perhaps his feet knew the way, once he stopped thinking that he knew where he was going.

Something was trapping demons. *A mechanism. From the artificers? Or Learned Edmund's wonder-engine?*

It was possible that it had nothing to do with anything. It was possible that he had stumbled into a second, minor mystery, of interest to no one but a paladin of the Dreaming God.

Caliban entertained this notion for about five seconds, then discarded it.

He was not one of those people who believed that there were no coincidences. There were plenty of coincidences. They frequently worked out badly, but they happened.

But you did not grow up in a temple without learning to see the hands of the gods at work.

The gods work through mortals. We are their tools. They have used mortals to make the world into this shape.

What shape is it? What are They hoping to achieve?

Where do They wish me to strike?

All he had ever been was a sword in the hands of a god. He knew no other way. If a god would not wield him, then very well, he would have to wield himself and hope to do Their will regardless.

The priestess had said one thing more to him before he left. She had risen to her feet and said, "Listen. I say this as a mortal to another mortal."

He leaned down to hear her. She was almost whispering, as if whispering would hide her words from the gods.

"Be careful, paladin," she whispered. "The hole in your heart is very large. Be careful what you allow to fill it."

Slate looked up at him as he came back into the main room of the inn. "Do I have to make *you* swear not to clank off anywhere by yourself?"

For a moment, he could not think of an answer. The priestess was tangled in his head with her goddess, and the hole in his soul was tangled up with Slate, who was draped over her chair as if she had no bones.

"What?" said Slate, as he stared at her. "Do I have something in my teeth?"

"Uh…"

Rescue came from an unexpected quarter. "Easy, darlin', the man's walking like he just took a set of brass knuckles to the face. What happened to you?"

"Heh…" Caliban dropped into a chair. "Brass knuckles. Yes. That's about what it feels like." He stared at his hands for a moment, pulled off a gauntlet. It seemed like the priestess's touch should have left a mark, but it hadn't. "I met a goddess."

"Well, these things happen," said Slate. "Except, wait, no, they *don't*. What the hell? Why'd you meet a goddess?"

"Which goddess?" said Learned Edmund, finally glancing up from his notes.

"I don't know," admitted Caliban. "I mean, I know—I'd know Her again—anywhere—but I don't know what she's called. A goddess of wilderness and lonely places."

"Inzaa, perhaps," said Learned Edmund, his gaze returning to the page before him. "Sometimes folded into a triple goddess figure. The hunting crone. Not sure what She would be doing in a city, though."

"Cities are often lonely places," said Caliban.

He didn't mean to use the voice, but the words tolled out with the ring of prophecy. Learned Edmund did look up at that.

"God's stripes," muttered Grimehug. "You pick up gods like a gnole picks up fleas, big man."

"I think She tried to recruit me. No, I know She did. It didn't work. I would have—well. It didn't work. She wanted to tell me about the demons, but…" He raised his hands helplessly, let them fall.

"What *about* the demons?" asked Slate.

"Something's catching them," he said. He repeated what the goddess had told him.

"Somebody putting you out of a job?" said Brenner.

"God, if only!" said Caliban, with more passion than he intended.

"What, you don't like chopping demons out of peasants?"

"Shut up, Brenner," said Slate. "Are you thinking they might get your demon out?"

Caliban's head snapped up so fast that he heard his vertebrae crackle.

"…so you weren't thinking that," said Slate. "All right."

He hadn't been. It honestly hadn't even occurred to him.

"It—it doesn't work like that," he said haltingly. "Demons jump between those they possess or are driven out by a stronger demon or they are bound and they choose to go back to hell. But they choose to leave. You could force a bound demon to possess someone else, but once they're dead they're…well." He spread his hands helplessly. "Dead demons don't leave. The rune-demon seemed to think that it could take the dead one's place, but it was not a bargain that I wished to make."

"Might have been interesting," drawled Brenner.

"I'd rather not go on another killing spree, if it's all the same to you."

"Aw, but—"

"Shut *up*, Brenner. Do you think the demons are related to the Clockwork Boys?"

Caliban rubbed his sternum. It felt as if the goddess had reached inside and touched a hollow place underneath his breastbone. He could still feel Her fingers on his heart. "Yes. And no, I don't have any proof. But the Dreaming God's paladins are the only ones who can catch demons. It's what we *are*."

"Not the only ones," said Learned Edmund absently, still looking at the page in front of him.

"What?"

"Oh." He blinked over at Caliban. "The Many-Armed God's dedicates made a study of it, a few years ago. One of them did, anyway." He frowned. "I can't recall which one…the folio was bound in red leather…"

Caliban was used to Learned Edmund's digressions by now. "How long ago?"

"Oh, only a century or so, I think."

"Practically current," murmured Slate.

Learned Edmund tapped his stylus on the table thoughtfully. "He determined that binding a demon is a skill possessed by individual humans, with the backing of a god to provide the power. The Dreaming God, of course, selects among those individuals for his Knight-Champions, but presumably there are others not emotionally suited for such work who still possess the talent involved."

Caliban considered this for a moment. "All right…" he said slowly. "I suppose that is more or less what the temple teaches, if you look at it sideways. But those other individuals, if they exist, still couldn't bind a demon without a god's help."

Learned Edmund steepled his fingers. "Unless they found another source of power."

"Like what?"

"Maybe like a wonder-engine," said Slate.

CHAPTER 25

"I still can't believe we're breaking into a library," said Learned Edmund.

"You make it sound like we're robbing graves," said Slate. "It's not like we're stealing for the fun of it. We're taking notes that they should have given you anyway."

This distracted Learned Edmund nicely. "I cannot believe they did not hand Brother Amadai's writings to me! A fellow dedicate! Those works belong to the Many-Armed God!"

"And He'll be happy to have them back," said Slate cheerfully. "We just have to go get them for Him."

Learned Edmund gave her a level look. "I am fully aware what you are doing, Mistress Slate," he said.

"Am I wrong?"

"…no."

"All right then."

They entered the great Hall of Artificers. It had once been an extraordinary building, full of marble pillars, high ceilings, and clean lines. Now it was dimmed with soot and bits of clockwork clung like tree-mushrooms to the pillars. A spidery thing ratcheted up and down one pillar, clinging by two legs, while a disgruntled trio of men stood underneath, glaring up at it.

"The library is through here," murmured Learned Edmund, pointing to a set of double doors in the corner. A large sign on the door read: NO STEAM OR EXPLOSIVE DEVICES IN THE STACKS.

A man looked up at them as they entered. "Learned Edmund," he said. "Again. And…?"

"My scribe," said Learned Edmund.

The man pursed his lips, looking from one to the other. He clearly knew full well that the dedicates of the Many-Armed God were not fond of women.

"I read seven languages," Slate lied smoothly, "and am sworn to celibacy. The god has graciously allowed me to transcribe the words of his dedicates."

The man rolled his eyes but gestured them onward. "You may remove nothing," he said. "Return volumes here, and *we* will place them back on the shelves."

Slate bowed and followed after Learned Edmund.

"*Do* you read seven languages?" whispered the dedicate.

"Hell no. Two well, and I guess I can get by in the third one. Fortunately, everybody uses the same numerals and almost everybody does their accounts in one of the trade languages."

Learned Edmund shook his head and smiled. "I…well. All right. Brother Amadai's records aren't here, though."

"Where did they go when you asked?"

"Through a door back here." He led her to the back of the stacks, where a door was set unobtrusively in the wall.

Slate glanced around and tried the door. It was unlocked. She nodded to herself.

"We need to kill time for an hour or so," she said.

"We are in a marvelous library," said Learned Edmund. "I do not think that will be a problem."

While Edmund lost himself in rapturous indexing, Slate kept an eye on the librarians. The one at the front desk was bored. Another one roamed the stacks, replacing books, scrolls, and portfolios of paper.

After a few moments, she approached the man at the front desk. "Pardon, but are there privies here?"

He jerked a thumb out the door, toward the main hall. Slate went out, found them—they had comfortable wooden seats, which was nice—and then returned.

She went out again about forty minutes later, smiling awkwardly at the man at the desk, and returned.

After the fourth or fifth time in two hours, he no longer seemed to be noticing her. He didn't question it, though. Slate thought, not for the first time, that men had no real idea about the bladder capacity of women.

Or maybe he thinks it's that time of month. Either way.

"Leave in ten minutes," she murmured to Learned Edmund.

"But—"

"Trust me. I'll be fine. He's not counting how often I go in and out. But if you're here, it'll remind them that I'm supposed to be here too. I'll find my own way out."

He looked at her over his glasses. "Mistress Slate, be *careful*."

She grinned. "Don't worry. I'll be turning your bowels to water again before you know it." She reached for the door handle, opened it soundlessly, and slipped inside.

Slate had been in the Artificer's Guild Library Archives twice before, although it had been years ago. She was pleased to see that they hadn't changed anything much. There was still a narrow corridor lit by lamps, the chimneys tall and covered with screens to prevent soot from escaping.

She walked briskly down the hallway, feeling in her element for the first time in months. This, she understood. Monstrous living siege engines, dead demons, live demons, politics of war…those were all above her paygrade, and if she'd had her way, they would have stayed there.

Breaking into libraries and digging through the files, though…

She'd always liked the Guild Library. The Guild itself could be a bunch of hidebound, backbiting, condescending bastards, but the Library was *organized*. Everything that came in was indexed and the index itself was neat, legible, and once you understood the system, easily navigated.

If you were trying to lift something from the archives, this was a glorious gift. Slate had once had to pull files from the corresponding guild library in the Dowager's city, and had been horrified to discover that this was not a universal trait. She had spent six days breaking in through a skylight every evening and trying to decipher the archivist's idiosyncratic system of organization. By the end, she had been sorely tempted to have Brenner murder the man as a service to both thieves and accountants the world over.

The archives were kept locked, which inconvenienced Slate for the space of about two minutes. She slid a lockpick out of her sleeve and popped the tumblers by feel, one ear pressed to the door.

She didn't hear anyone inside, but that didn't necessarily mean anything.

The lock clicked open.

She listened for another minute, then opened the door and slipped through, closing it silently behind her.

The archives appeared to be empty, but Slate didn't trust appearances. She ducked down one of the rows of bookcases and waited.

Nothing happened. No one came and demanded to know what she was doing.

Slate listened for footsteps, turning pages, breathing...anything to indicate human presence.

Silence.

Well, every artificer I've ever known was a night owl. I'm beating the rush.

She stood up, brushed herself off, and went back toward the door.

And there it stood in all its glory, chained to the pedestal, same as it had been a decade earlier—the index.

Learned Edmund may have been on to something. A good index is a thing of beauty.

There were two parts to the book, one organized by the date of acquisition, one by author. Slate wasn't certain of the exact date that Brother Amadai's effects had come into the hands of the Artificer's Guild. She tried the name instead.

To her moderate annoyance, Amadai had been a frequent contributor to the archives. There were multiple numbers after his name, each of which corresponded to a place on the shelves. Most had an "L" prefix, indicating that they were in the main library itself.

Those must be published monographs. You figure that dead men don't contribute too many books, so I probably want the last entry by his name...

The last number indicated a position in one of the smaller rooms off to one side. Slate had to pop another lock, although this one was so perfunctory as to be almost insulting to her talents.

Her heart sank a little at the sight of the room. Bookcases ran to the ceiling and boxes full of loose papers spilled out over the edges.

Index, don't fail me now...

Scraps of paper were haphazardly applied to the outsides of boxes and many had fallen to the floor. The archivist with the militant organizational skills seemed to have let things slide in this room.

Slate sighed and rolled up her sleeves.

And this is why people like Brenner will never replace people like me...

It took nearly two hours. Slate had to stop once and hide as people came into the archives, but they had no business in that particular room and did not seem to even notice that the main door was unlocked.

She tucked herself into a gap in a bookcase and sat in silence, waiting.

Her mind wandered after awhile, as the people in the main room showed no sign of leaving. Questions for Sparrow about the excavation of the wonder-engines. Questions for Grimehug about gnoles. Really cutting things to say to Brenner. *Can never have enough of those, really...*

Her nose itched. She dug out a handkerchief and prayed that she wouldn't sneeze.

It was one of Caliban's, of course. She wondered where they went to when she lost them.

She didn't mean to keep losing them. They just sort of vanished. Probably there was a trail of misplaced handkerchiefs stretching clear back to the Dowager's city.

Great shoulders. Always has a handkerchief. Gods above, if he would just make a damn move...

She wasn't going to make the first move. Not after he'd rejected her last time.

Shit, maybe I really should just roll Brenner again. Mooning around after a paladin like this can't be healthy.

Working with the assassin in the Grey Church had brought back memories. Not always good ones, but oddly comfortable ones. They had worked well together. Still did, when the occasion demanded it.

She remembered one job in particular. She'd been crouched down, working a lock with intense concentration. A tricky five tumbler job and she'd broken two picks on it before getting the fifth one popped.

She had straightened up, turned around, and found Brenner lowering a corpse to the ground behind her.

"Brenner!"

"You were busy, darlin'."

"You could have said something!"

His teeth had flashed in the shadows. "Locks are your job. Killing's mine. Figured I'd let you get on with it." And he'd swept past her, through the door she'd just opened, knives at the ready, doing his job.

Not that he was ever bad with locks, but he also never had a problem admitting I was better. Which is a rare enough virtue in the world, even if it is attached to Brenner.

The main door closed as the archivists left again. Slate listened for a few minutes to make sure that all of them had gone, then crawled out of her hiding spot.

Let me see…where was I…

She narrowed it down to what she thought was the right shelf, pulled out a paper from a box, read the name, and put it back. *Not that one…not this one…interesting theory on artesian wells, but no…aha! This handwriting looks familiar…*

Victory!

She had stared at Brother Amadai's particular cramped and crooked handwriting long enough to recognize it. The box was full of loose papers, scattered notes, and several journals.

Any which of might be critical. I'm going to have to take the whole damnable box.

Slate stifled a sigh. She hadn't really expected any better.

She pulled the box free and lugged it out into the main archive room.

All right. Now I just have to go out the window onto the second floor roof…

She went up a bookcase like a ladder, setting the box down on a shelf, going up to the next, and pulling it up to her level. It was inconvenient, but nothing she wasn't used to.

The windows were kept tightly shuttered to keep light from getting in and fading the ink. Slate unlocked the shutters, swung them open… and stopped.

Huh. Those bars weren't there last time.

She tapped her fingernail against her teeth, thinking.

She knew from experience that there was no other way out of this room, unless there was some kind of secret door. Slate had no interest in digging around looking for that sort of thing—they weren't as common as people seemed to think, and in a building run by artificers, the odds were pretty good it would explode anyway.

If it had been one or two books, she could have hidden them under her robes, but thirty pounds of assorted paper was going to be a bit more difficult to deal with.

Well.

Needs must...

Slate did not love books the way that some people did, but she respected them. If she was going to do this, she wanted to use something no one would miss.

She climbed back down, lugging her box, and flipped through the index. *All right, what have we got to work with...*

Slate ran her finger down the page and found something that looked promising. *Anatomical drawings of chickens, first and second drafts. I suspect the world will limp along without these.*

She located the box. There was a completed monograph on top, covered in dust. Slate removed the monograph, set it on the shelf, and hefted the box in her arms.

She could just carry the two boxes, one under each arm. One of the oil lamps was a little more difficult. She had push the door open with her foot.

Now, let's not mix up which box is which...

She reached the main library, slipped through the door, and set both boxes down. No one was in sight.

Brother Amadai's notes went on the bottom of a nearby shelf. Slate took a deep breath and upended the oil lamp onto the chicken drawings.

They caught with a satisfying whoosh. She dropped the oil lamp into the box, took a deep breath, snatched up Amadai's box and bellowed *"Fire!"* at the top of her lungs.

CHAPTER 26

It was regrettably hard to climb a drainpipe carrying a box of papers. Slate resigned herself to using the door like a respectable person.

How galling.

She could at least use the back door. She slouched through the courtyard of the inn, past the potted plants, trying to be as invisible as possible.

Not that anyone here cares, but it's the principle of the thing...

"Ugh," said a female voice in the scullery, carrying through the open door. "Where's my hot water?"

"Went up to the bronze suite again," answered another woman's voice from deeper in the inn.

"Again?"

"They called for another bath."

Slate, who was in the copper suite across from the bronze, hid a smirk behind the box.

"For the pretty knight, was it?" The scullery maid laughed. "Well, I won't begrudge that one."

"Pretty with the armor off, too," said the keeper of the hot water.

"Oh, you never did!"

Slate, who had been past the scullery and on her way to the back entrance to the inn proper, found herself stopping and examining a potted plant with great interest.

"No," admitted Hot Water. "Walked in to ask if he needed anything else, that's all."

"I can imagine what else you thought he needed," said Scullery.

I'm jealous, thought Slate, examining the hard knot in her gut as if it belonged to someone else. *How about that?*

"Can't blame a girl for trying. Last knight came through here was sixty years old and looked like he'd swallowed a fish."

"Ah, get on with you..." More laughter and a splash and something Slate didn't quite catch.

Slate picked up the box again and hurried through the door.

147

I've got no right to be jealous. I offered once, he turned me down, and we've been dancing around each other like idiots ever since.

Besides, you're not the only woman in a twenty-mile radius any longer. There's no reason someone who looks like that would be interested in a cranky forger who looks like me when he had a city full of options available.

Anyway, she only looked. I said myself there's no crime in looking.

This was all entirely logical and true and she repeated it to herself several times on the way up the stairs and then Caliban opened the door and she snarled "Don't you take *enough* baths?"

He said, "Uh?" His hair was still damp and plastered against his forehead. Then chivalry took over and he grabbed the box she was balancing. "Did you walk the whole way from the Artificer's Guild with this?"

"Don't be ridiculous. I took a carriage to the main square and then walked around the block in the other direction so the driver wouldn't know where I went. It was only about two blocks, not thirty."

He set the box down on the table. No one else was in the main room of the suite. "Learned Edmund will be glad of the notes, I am certain."

Slate glared at him.

"Is something wrong?" he said, and then, somewhat worriedly "... my liege?"

I am being ridiculous. And I am taking it out on Caliban. Which is unfair and also unsportsmanlike.

If I kicked him, he'd apologize for getting in the way of my foot.

She exhaled. She was thirty years old, for the love of all the gods. She knew better. She was acting like a teenager.

"No. I just..."

She trailed off because there was nothing she could think of to say.

Hell, if I kissed him, he'd probably apologize for getting in the way of my lips.

That might be an interesting apology.

They stared at each other across the room for so long that Caliban's worried look faded and was replaced by something else entirely. He stepped away from the table.

Five steps across the room. Three for him, because his legs are longer. And then I'd be close enough to...to...

...to remember that I'm too bloody short to reach any higher than his collarbone.

He took one of those steps forward, then another.

The strong taking advantage of the weak. Shouldn't we be worrying about that?

Caliban was not looking at her as if she were weak.

Slate felt her breath come a bit faster and she tilted her head up so she could meet his eyes. She wondered if her face was as easy to read as his.

His lips parted and she thought *Please, gods, don't let him say something stupid that I'll have to kick him for,* and then Learned Edmund opened the door and said, "Mistress Slate! You succeeded! I prayed for you but I was afraid..."

Caliban appeared to suddenly recall an urgent appointment on the other side of the room.

"Yes," said Slate, "I got a box of Amadai's notes. I hope those are the right ones, because they're definitely not gonna let me back into the guild hall."

Learned Edmund looked suddenly worried. "Mistress Slate! You didn't damage the archives!?"

"Nothing anyone will miss," said Slate. "And they weren't very good chicken drawings."

Learned Edmund's eyes went wide.

"Look, I wouldn't just burn things at random."

"Mistress Slate!"

Slate rolled her eyes. "They put it out immediately. I made sure there wasn't anything nearby that could catch. And I charged out screaming fire at the top of my lungs with the box under my arm."

"But the *damage*—"

Slate could feel her irritation returning. "Learned Edmund, it's the Artificer's Guild. They can deal with fire better than anyone else in this city. That's why the whole place is made of stone. I wouldn't set a fire in a library if I thought there was any kind of chance that it would do more than singe a few bricks. I'm not a *monster*."

"But—"

"And now we have Brother Amadai's notes."

That silenced him.

Slate lifted her head and saw Caliban watching her across the room.

"Are you going to lecture me about taking risks alone?"

Paladins were not known for their sense of self-preservation, but this one still had sense enough to step back from the brink. "Under the circumstances, I don't see how you could have done otherwise. Though if I had known, I would have gone with you to wait outside the hall."

Slate, more than ready to fight someone at this point, narrowed her eyes.

"I could have carried the box," he said.

Slate threw her hands in the air and stalked out.

Damn the man. And damn Learned Edmund for coming in before I could climb him like a drainpipe and see what he thought of that.

CHAPTER 27

"I need your help," said Caliban.

Slate looked up at him from her seat on the floor. "Oh? Need a document changed, or just practicing your looming?"

"Am I looming?"

"Quite effectively, yes."

He crouched down next to her.

"Still looming," she said. "Though not as badly."

She looked faintly amused. Caliban was glad to see that she was no longer aggravated with him over…whatever it had been.

Although she was also not looking at him with naked hunger in her eyes.

Probably for the best. I have demons to chase down, not…not…

"I'm not sure if I can make myself any shorter without lying on the floor," he said.

Subtle.

Slate lifted one eyebrow very slowly and said "Well, that *would* be interesting…"

He cleared his throat. *Down, boy. You are working.*

"I need documents located. I am looking for records on demonic possession. I read well enough, but for actually searching a library…" He spread his hands. "Although we probably won't need to risk burning this one."

Slate laughed. "Learned Edmund is undoubtedly better than I am at locating records, although…" She looked over at the dedicate, who had Amadai's notes piled around him.

"He seems busy," said Caliban.

"There's so much here…" said Learned Edmund, not looking up. He turned the papers helplessly in his hands. "All his notes. Notes on *everything.*"

"That's what you wanted, isn't it?" said Slate. "Can you crack the codes?"

"Yes! The codes are simple! He wrote the key in the front of the journals—it's all there—" He waved his hands.

"Hardly important," said Slate, amused. "The key to everything we've been trying to learn, that's all."

"But the pages aren't organized, and they're barely readable and I don't know what parts I should be trying to figure out, and…there's just so *much*…"

"Very busy," said Caliban.

"So he is." Slate scrambled to her feet. "Well, let's see what I can turn up for you."

Five minutes later she re-entered the room, wearing the ink-stained cassock of the nameless secretary. "All right," she said as they left the inn. "You walk in front of me, remember?"

"I don't know where we're going," said Caliban, holding the front door open.

Slate rubbed a hand over her face and sighed. "Tell me what you want and we'll figure it out."

"Records on demonic possession," he said, falling in step with her. "Historical, anyway. I want to see when demons stopped appearing in Anuket City."

She drew her eyebrows down and chewed on her lower lip. Caliban watched her face and very nearly ran into a lightpost.

"Careful!"

"It's fine," he said. "Jumped out at me, that's all."

"Yeah, well, I didn't survive that whole stupid trip from home for you to get knocked out by a post."

She screwed her face up in thought again. "There wouldn't be religious records, would there? You don't have a temple here."

"No. A fact which now strikes me as more than a little peculiar."

"Hmm…"

They crossed a pedestrian bridge over the Falsefall River. Caliban walked on the inside, not looking into the cold water.

"If somebody murders somebody and doesn't do anything weird, there's no way to know if it's demons, right? Without one of you people around?"

152

"So long as they limit themselves to normal human behavior, yes." Caliban dipped his head, resigned to elite Knight-Champions of the Dreaming God having been relegated to "you people."

"Right." Slate turned sharply at the foot of the bridge. "We're going toward the stockyards. Now you lead."

He took his place a step ahead of her. His training tried to rebel and he squelched it firmly.

You will make less trouble for her if you walk ahead. We do not need more trouble.

His overheated imagination attempted to point out that if there was trouble, he might conceivably dispatch said trouble, save Slate, sweep her off her feet, and…

And she would tell me to put her down and try to steal their boots to sell. Let it go.

Their destination helped. Stockyards were not romantic in any way.

"Is there any particular reason we are going to go see cows milling around?"

"Yes," said Slate. "But we're not going to the actual cows. Turn here."

The stockyards, like the tanners and the knackers and all the other smelly, unpleasant parts of city life, were downriver from the main city, on the opposite side of town from the peculiar river bluff where the grave-gnoles went every day. A broad, well-lit street ran parallel to the river, with the counting houses and mercantiles that served the docks on one side, and the similar houses that served the stockyards and other land-based businesses on the other.

Merchants and men of business walked back and forth here, with messengers darting between them like minnows. Caliban felt extremely out of place. Knight-Champions did not end up in counting houses unless someone inside was possessed.

Slate, on the other hand, was in her element. He could tell by the way her eyes widened with interest, the way her gaze flicked back and forth between buildings.

"Will you look at that window…" she murmured, mostly to herself. "Window boxes! They're footholds are what they are. I could be in some of those file cabinets and gone again and probably water the geraniums on the way out."

"You're enjoying this," said Caliban, amused.

"What? Oh! Yes, a little." She grinned sheepishly. "Well. You know how it is."

"I'm not sure I do."

"Oh, come now…" She cocked an eyebrow at him. "If somebody's got a levitating cow that needs the demon chopped out of it, you can't tell me that you don't enjoy…oh, maybe not the chopping bit, but having done it, anyway."

Caliban considered this. "It's not really enjoyable work. But knowing you did a good job and the world's a little better…yes, all right. I understand that."

"Well, there you go then. We're not that different. Only swap out 'crooked accounting' for 'levitating cow.'"

"Yes, those are certainly very similar."

"See? We're practically twins."

She poked him in the ribs while he was still shaking his head. "Over there. Livestock Historical Society."

"A what?"

"They keep the studbooks for the horses and the cows and everything. Very important. They also keep records about diseases, breeding, droughts, prices of grain…" She steered him toward the door.

"And you think they'll know about demons?"

"I think they'll have a record on every levitating cow in a hundred miles."

Caliban smiled down at her. "That's honestly rather brilliant."

"I have the occasional moment."

"More than just occasional," he said.

He knew there was too much warmth in his voice when she flushed. Probably most people couldn't have seen it, as dark as her skin was, but he could see the minute change in her color. She glanced away, embarrassed, and he…regretted nothing, actually.

Oh, I should be careful…or something…but…

Without Brenner's watchdog presence, he felt free.

We have an assassin for a chaperone. Is it any wonder things are strange between us?

"Come on, then," said Slate. "Let's go see what the studbooks say."

They emerged from the Livestock Historical Society three hours later. The sun had begun to sink and the sky was turning hazy violet, lit with red from underneath from the lights of the city.

"Well," said Slate. "Huh."

Caliban nodded.

"Not a single levitating cow in all of Anuket City's records."

"Lots in Archenhold, though," said Caliban. "And in the outlying farmlands."

"What does that mean?"

Caliban shook his head. "I have no idea."

They walked slowly back in the direction of the inn. Merchants going home streamed past them, jostled in the other direction by merchants only starting the day's work. A place like Anuket City never truly slept.

"So there's never been demons," said Slate slowly. "But we know they have records of demons from outside the immediate area."

"Which implies that whatever is trapping them has been here as long as the records have been kept," said Caliban.

Slate gnawed on her lower lip. "And we know they're being trapped, not just driven away?"

"I do not believe that the goddess I spoke to would lie."

She groaned. "From anyone else, that would be *such* a weird statement…"

He raised an eyebrow at her. "Do you not believe me?"

It had not occurred to Caliban that she might not believe him. It certainly hadn't occurred to him how desperately he would *need* her to believe him. If she doubted the gods, she doubted the very core of his being.

He could see her thinking about it, read the conflict in the way her eyes met his, the furrowed eyebrows. In a way, it was comforting, because when she sighed and said, "No, I believe you," he knew that she was not lying. Reluctant, but not lying.

"It sounds nuts," she added. "But you're *you*. And if you're delusional, you're certainly pulling it off well."

That startled a laugh out of him. "Truly a heartfelt endorsement."

"Don't push your luck."

They paused at the bridge. Slate leaned on the railing. Caliban steeled himself, looking over the water instead of at it.

The oil lamps had been lit along the bridge. Insects swirled around the lights and nighthawks had come to catch them. The air was full of their high-pitched, nasal calls.

Slate shivered and rubbed her arms. The acolyte robes were more notable for their drabness than their warmth.

Caliban instinctively slung his cloak off his shoulders and started to reach toward her.

"Caliban…" She gave him an exasperated look. "Knights do not give their cloaks to acolytes."

"The decent ones should."

She pinched the bridge of her nose.

"Are knights allowed to do this?" he asked, daring to step closer and put his arm around her so that the cloak covered them both.

Slate stood very still. Caliban could feel the tension in her shoulders. He had a sense of everything balancing on edge.

One moment. I will wait one moment, and if she steps away, so will I.

Then she sighed and leaned against him. "Only one of them," she said.

CHAPTER 28

They returned to the inn walking exactly as a knight and an acolyte should. Caliban led and Slate followed, a pace back, invisible as she wished to be.

He still didn't like it, but it was probably for the best that she couldn't see the helpless smile plastered across his face.

He could still feel the weight of her body against his. For once he could be sure that she had been there because she wished to be, not because she couldn't stand up or couldn't get onto her horse by herself.

He wanted to dance around and laugh hysterically and howl at the moon. He wanted to kiss Slate passionately and yell to random passersby, "She probably doesn't hate me!"

He did not do any of these things, because for one thing, he was approaching forty and more importantly, Slate would probably roll her eyes and then punch him as high as she could reach.

He had not dared to do more than stand with his arm around her for several minutes. He had a sense that the connection between them was fragile enough that one wrong word would shatter it.

And let's be honest, I say a lot of wrong words.

When she finally straightened and grumbled something about how they should probably go back to the inn, he let her go. But he looked down at her and whatever she saw in his eyes made her flush again and shove her hair out of her face with the hand that wasn't trapped between them.

That was enough. For now, it was enough.

They went back to the inn. Learned Edmund looked up when they came in, looked past Caliban, and said "Mistress Slate..."

"Hmm?" She padded over to him.

"Can you decipher this?"

Slate picked up the sheet of paper he handed her and stared at it for a bit, her head tilting to one side. "Ah...uh...huh. Brother Amadai's handwriting is something else, isn't it?"

"That is an understatement so vast as to border on inaccuracy."

Slate snorted, clearly only half-listening. "One of your cascading codes?"

"I can't even tell. The code does not require such dismal handwriting."

"Is this about the wonder-engine?"

"I have no idea," said Learned Edmund. He leaned his forehead against the heel of his hand. "It might be. It might be a recipe for boiled cabbages. Nothing is organized. I am going old before my time looking at these."

"You're *nineteen*."

"Each of these pages is taking a month off my life."

"When you get to the bottom of the box, you'll still be younger than I am."

He sighed. "Were your investigations successful?"

"I guess." She waved vaguely at Caliban. "You talk. I'll see if I can write this out in readable language."

Caliban outlined what they had learned about the occurrences of levitating cattle in Anuket City and environs.

"Hmm." Learned Edmund tapped the table. "If it is, indeed, the wonder-engine trapping them, then that would make sense. The wonder-engines have been here for a very long time, since the ancient civilizations passed."

"I thought they had to be activated in some fashion," said Caliban. "By putting something in."

Learned Edmund shrugged. "Possibly? But we do not know if they have passive effects on the environment either. It is possible that it has been quietly collecting demons for—how long has Anuket City been here, Mistress Slate?"

"Probably a good thousand years," said Slate. "They just didn't call it that beforehand. It's not like the Dowager's city where somebody went and planted a flag and said, 'Here I shall build my city!'"

"Jon Wedoff," said Learned Edmund absently. "The great general. He said in his memoirs that he was tired of fighting in places that were less defensible than nearby trees, and that he would build a city that could hold out until the army invading died of old age."

"Pity he didn't figure on the Clockwork Boys."

158

The dedicate nodded. "Though I suspect that had he *not* made such a city, the Dowager's city would have been overrun long ago."

"And had not some genius a few thousand years ago decided to build a wonder-engine, we wouldn't be overrun now," said Slate, with some asperity. "We're living with decisions made by people so long dead we can't even piss on their bones."

She put the page down. "I don't think this one's going to be helpful. I could be wrong, but he seems to have burned his left hand and is using different treatments on each finger to see which one works the best. I'm not seeing code markers."

Learned Edmund looked up, eyes narrowing. "You've cracked the code?"

"It's not as hard as you people think it is. I can't read it, but I can at least see where it starts and ends."

Learned Edmund groaned. "If only there was an index!"

"We can't all be Ashes Magnus." Slate sat down across from him. "I'll help, though. If you want me to sort out the ones that obviously aren't related, maybe we can narrow things down."

"That would be an enormous help, Mistress Slate."

Brenner draped his arm over her shoulder. "That would be an enormous help *tomorrow*," he said. "Darlin', we got a date with your informant tonight. That Sparrow woman."

"Oh, her. Right." Slate sighed. She rather liked Sparrow, but she also suspected that Sparrow worked very hard to make herself likable. It was a useful trait if you were a person who bought and sold information. Still, with Blind Molly gone, Sparrow was supposed to be the next best thing…and she *didn't* know Slate on sight, which was a great benefit for all involved.

"Is it dangerous?" asked Caliban.

"Yes," said Slate simply. "For us and her. We've been doing a dance for a week where we both hint around what information we might want and what we might have and how much we might be willing to pay for it. And then we both retreat to our opposite corners and wait to see if the whole thing was a trap and a bunch of angry men with clubs are about to land on our heads."

"How unpleasant," said Learned Edmund.

"It's not my favorite activity," Slate admitted. "But with the information from Ashes Magnus, we were able to skip asking a lot of stupid questions. Now we're down to *who owns the clocktaurs, no, really?* and *who's paying for all this?*" She spread her hands. "I'm not saying it'll help in the long run, but if there's one or two key individuals running the show, we've got targets and then Brenner's magic fingers can do the rest."

Brenner cracked his knuckles in a suitably murderous fashion.

"Must we really assassinate people?" asked Learned Edmund, a bit sadly.

"Well, it's that or this ink chews my arm off, so forgive me if I'm feeling a little expedient."

"Oh." Learned Edmund stared at the page. "Yes. I had forgotten."

"We hadn't," said Slate, and suspected that she spoke for all of them.

CHAPTER 29

Sparrow smiled when she saw Slate. "You're back," she said.

"I said I would be."

"Yeah, but you know how it is. Everybody says things." She beckoned Slate into her stall. It was separated from the rest of the Shadow Market by heavy curtains which muffled sound. The milling crowd became a distant background noise, like water flowing over stones.

"So the people you're asking about…" said Sparrow, sitting down at a low table. Slate sat across from her. "The ones with an interest in archaeology?"

"Mm-hmm."

"Big names, some of them."

"Doesn't surprise me."

Sparrow quietly took a slip of paper from beneath the table and passed it across the table. Slate unfolded it.

Keep your face absolutely still. Keep it still. Don't give her information to sell to someone else.

Three names she knew. Two names she didn't. One surprised her.

The three familiar names were merchant houses. Their presence was honestly not particularly significant. They were silent backers of nearly every politician in the city, giving money to make certain that their particular business interests were never encroached. She'd have been surprised if they *weren't* on the list.

She tapped one of the unfamiliar names and raised an eyebrow at Sparrow.

"Former head of the Courtesan's Guild," said Sparrow. "She spread a lot of money around."

"Didn't think archaeology was her style."

Sparrow shrugged. "Doubt it is anymore. New one got elected last year. She's been acting like Horsehead's personal piggy-bank ever since."

Slate worked very hard not to grit her teeth. "Boss Horsehead," she said. "He's not on the list."

"Don't think he cares about archaeology much. He wanted power, not artifacts."

"Didn't figure Horsehead for a war-monger," said Slate.

"He ain't much of one. Didn't so much back the war as he was backin' the people who backed it, if you know what I mean," said Sparrow. She glanced at the curtain as if expecting eavesdroppers. "Horsehead always wanted to be a Senator. He wanted to marry into it, but when *that* went south—"

Slate hoped that the other woman didn't see her wince.

"—he had to get to it another way. So he started bankrolling Senators. They needed money and he had it." Sparrow scratched herself vigorously, reminding Slate vaguely of Grimehug. "They all know he holds the purse strings. Sooner or later he'll call it on in."

Slate nodded. "And the...err...the clocktaurs?"

Sparrow shook her head. "Dunno. That place is locked up tighter than a nun's ass. They ain't answering to Horsehead, I know that."

Slate raised an eyebrow.

Sparrow laughed. "Come on, if Horsehead had an army, he wouldn't waste it on a different town. He'd point it at the Senate and make hisself Boss of the whole damn place."

Slate laughed at that, shortly. "You're right there. Thanks, Sparrow." She dropped a handful of coins in the jar.

"No worries. Those things give me the willies." She shuddered theatrically.

"You and me both..."

"What I've always wondered," said Sparrow, as Slate rose to her feet, "is how they're giving them orders. They never send anybody out but a handful of gnoles, and you can't tell me *they're* doin' it. Unless they are."

"You don't know?" asked Slate.

"Nah. Not my business. Not my business why you care, either," said Sparrow, leaning back. "Big damn things stomping through the city, no reason not to wonder. Been turning all the traffic on its ear ever since they dug 'em up."

Slate was glad that the Chadori veil hid most of her face.

She had no real memory of leaving Sparrow's stall. She must have said the correct things. She walked through the crowd with her head down, looking for Brenner. Her nose was itching abominably under her veil and she didn't dare lift it to scratch. She kept smelling something, but whether it was rosemary or one of the various smells from the Shadow Market was anyone's guess.

Brother Amadai.

He had been the last name on the list.

What is a scholar of the Many-Armed God doing mixed up in this? And where is he now?

Learned Edmund had been on the right track. The box of notes she'd pulled out of the Guild might be the answer to everything…if they could just figure out how to read them.

I've been obsessing over Boss Horsehead because he wants me dead, and what does he matter? He just wants power. He doesn't control the clocktaurs. If we get rid of him, the Senators are still going to have an army. I might feel better, the world might be a better place afterwards, but it's not gonna help with the war.

Her tattoo twinged. She gritted her teeth.

Amadai dug up the clocktaurs and then he vanished. The Artificer's Guild locked up his notes. Why?

Did he vanish because the other people involved decided he was inconvenient?

What did he know?

Slate caught a glimpse of Brenner's profile in the crowd and made toward it. She started to lift a hand to wave to him.

An arm went around her neck.

She was not surprised. That was the bit that got her. A cool wash of dread filled her body, but she was not at all surprised.

On some level, she'd been waiting for this all along.

"Little Miss Slate," crooned a voice in her ear. "We know it's you."

There was a knifeblade just pricking her back, above the kidneys. Slate wasn't worried. If her attacker meant to kill her, she'd already be dead. She pulled at the arm, but that was reflex, her body fighting back.

Sparrow must have guessed, and saw the chance at a really big payoff.
Damn.

Damn, damn, damn.

She saw Brenner look over. For a moment she was afraid he'd run to the rescue, and then he did a fast fade into the crowd.

Well, obviously. It's not like he's a paladin.

"Horsehead wants to see you," whispered the voice.

The crowd was making room. No one was looking at them. When things like this happened in the Shadow Market, people made a point not to see it.

"Fine," hissed Slate. "Let's get it over with."

The voice laughed.

Someone pulled a bag over her head, and Slate's world got dark and hot and unpleasant.

Her last thought, as her assailant slung her over his shoulder, was to hope that Learned Edmund would eventually think of the question that they'd all been too blind to ask.

CHAPTER 30

There was a loud pounding on the door. It was not a knock. It sounded like the door was about to come off.

"The guards?" Learned Edmund asked, pulling his book against his chest as if to defend it.

"I don't know." Caliban drew his sword. Friendly people did not knock like that.

The pounding came again, a frantic hammering, someone determined to take down the door if it didn't answer to normal means.

The Knight-Champion caught the doorknob and flung it open, the point of his sword level with an intruder's chest.

It was Brenner.

The assassin ducked under the point of the sword and came up on Caliban's other side like a black eel. The paladin recoiled, startled, and heedless of the steel in his hand, Brenner reached out and caught his shoulders in a grip like iron.

"It's Slate," Brenner gasped. "She's been taken."

"Boss Horsehead?"

"Who else?"

"What is he going to do to her?" asked Caliban. His voice was very calm, and he was taking the time to put his armor on only because Brenner flatly insisted on it.

The assassin raked a hand through his hair. "Oh, he'll kill her. Eventually."

"Is she dead now, then?" He was calm, calm. He had never been so calm.

If she is dead, I will take this city apart stone by stone.

"No. He's not a rash man. He'll want to know why she's here."

"Will she tell him?"

"I don't think she'll have much choice."

Learned Edmund made a ragged sound from where he sat on the bed. "You mean he'll torture her?"

"Probably not to death," Brenner assured him, never taking his eyes off Caliban, who was sliding his hands into his gauntlets. "He'll want enough left to make an example of."

The gauntlets clenched convulsively into fists. "What sort of example?" said Caliban softly.

Brenner backed up until his spine touched the wall. For a moment, Caliban thought the assassin might break and run. Almost, it was amusing.

"What sort of example, Brenner?"

"He'll hang her from the rafters of the Grey Church. That's what the cages are for."

"I see." The paladin shrugged into the sword harness. He was calm, so very calm. He reached out a hand and caught Brenner calmly under the chin. "Show me where this man lives."

Brenner's throat worked against the gauntlet as the assassin swallowed. "You can't just walk up there and kill him!"

"Show me, Brenner."

"What about the mission?"

"Ngha, ha, rhea-rhea-ha!"

There was a little silence. Caliban licked his lips. The demon voice had burned his throat, and the creature roiling in his soul didn't feel much like a corpse at all.

Brenner's eyes flashed. For a moment, Caliban almost expected the assassin to answer him back in a demon's voice of his own.

"All right," said Brenner, human-voiced and very calm. "All right. Let go and step back, paladin."

Caliban looked down and saw the knife. The point lay against his belly. One good thrust and he'd die by inches.

He loosened his fingers.

The assassin pried the offending hand away from his throat and made his knife disappear. "Listen to me, Caliban. We can't storm his mansion, because that's stupid. She's not going to be there. Nobody tortures people at home. It ruins the carpets."

"Where will she be?"

"I don't *know!* He's got to have a place for this sort of work."

"Gnoles will find out," said Grimehug. "Gnoles saw Crazy Slate get taken, they know she's a gnole-friend. Came and told me."

All three humans stared at him. Grimehug shrugged. "Gnoles're crazy, maybe, but we're not *stupid*."

"Who knows?" said Caliban. "Who can tell us?"

"When gnoles knows, gnoles come, big man," said Grimehug. He looked up at Caliban, oddly fearless, as if the paladin had not had his hand around Brenner's throat bare moments before. "Gnoles can't follow below the church. But gnoles will watch."

"It's not soon enough," said Caliban. "He could kill her. He could be killing her now."

Brenner shook his head. "He'll hang her in the crow cage first. She made a fool of him, and he'll make an example of her."

"So she'll be there," said Caliban. "She could be there right now. We can get her out."

"And we can all die in the Grey Church," snapped Brenner. "There's at least fifty guards and probably two hundred people who will join in a brawl just for fun. And they've got crossbows, so even if we get the cage down, she'd be a pincushion before she hit the floor. Dammit, paladin, stop acting like an armor-plated idiot and *think!*"

"*Nghaai!*"

Brenner sighed, took off his gloves, and slapped him across the face with them.

Caliban blinked.

"Are you...are you challenging me to a duel?"

"No," said Brenner. "Because that would be *stupid*. Just like you're being stupid *right now*."

"Listen to the dark man, big man," said Grimehug. "You think Crazy Slate wants to watch you die?"

Caliban blinked again. Then—"All right. All right. Not the crow cages, unless there's no other way."

They did not take Slate immediately to the cage. She hadn't expected it, really. Instead she was slung over someone's shoulder and carried, uncomfortably, through the Grey Church.

Her hearing was muffled inside the sack, but she didn't hear any uproar. Well, she hadn't expected that, either. If the enforcers grabbed someone, you didn't raise a fuss. That was a good way to get your own head shoved into a sack, or failing that, just be stabbed for interfering.

They left the large, echoing reaches of the church and entered an enclosed tunnel. Her heart sank a little, which was impressive, since she would have sworn that her heart was already somewhere in the vicinity of her borrowed socks.

Several twists, several turns. Slate got very tired of the shoulder that was rammed into her side. She didn't fight, because fighting would just get her hit, so she breathed shallowly and lay like dead weight, waiting.

A door slammed, then another. Her world lurched as her captors dropped her roughly into a chair. Someone yanked her hands around behind her and tied them with what felt like a strip of cloth.

At least they don't have rope lying around the room. That's good, right?

They pulled the sack off her head. She knew that was less good, even as she gasped fresh air.

If they don't care if I see them, then they're going to kill me.

Well, it's not like that's a surprise.

With the sack off her head, she could see that she was in a small room hung with oil lamps. It was reasonably clean, with several chairs and a table. It was the sort of room where people conducted private meetings, if they could afford to pay for such privacy, instead of relying on the noise of a crowd to keep them anonymous.

Horsehead, of course, would have no trouble paying for such a room.

If Slate had been innocent, she might have blustered or demanded to know what they meant by kidnapping her and dragging her into the back tunnels of the Grey Church. As it was, she said nothing. What was there to say? She knew why she was there, they knew why she was there, and the less talking she did, the less chance someone was going to smack her around for not showing proper respect.

Instead she waited in silence. So did the guard.

Horsehead did not show up immediately. He was a busy man.

I suppose it's nice that he didn't drop everything to come deal with me? Maybe?

I know I'm going in a crow cage. I suppose now it's just a matter of how many body parts I'm missing before I go.

...way to stay positive, there.

The door opened. Slate's stomach lurched, but it was a tall, thin man that Slate recognized from years ago. One of the old enforcers. He'd come up in the world a bit, judging by his clothes.

"Yeah, that's her," he said to the guard. And: "What the hell'd you come back for, Slate?"

Slate shrugged. "Seemed like a good idea, Marez."

Marez shook his head. "It wasn't," he said.

"Getting that impression, yeah."

"The boss has wanted your guts on a plate since you ditched town. You know he's gonna hang you from the rafters."

Slate shrugged again. "Looks like it."

Marez sighed. "What a waste," he said. "You were a helluva forger."

"Don't suppose the boss is looking for a forger?" said Slate hopefully. "Willing to let bygones be bygones?"

Marez snorted. "Yeah, right."

"Worth a shot," said Slate.

The enforcer shook his head and turned away. "I'll tell him you're here."

"No rush."

An hour or two passed. Slate had to go to the bathroom, but she doubted that the guard would be sympathetic. She considered the merits of simply pissing herself, but Horsehead would probably think it was terror. Also, there was a slim chance that if she waited, she might be able to get some on him.

It wasn't like he was going to kill her *less* dead for being agreeable.

169

The door opened again. The man in the doorway was large, broad in the shoulders and thick through the middle. He had thin, silver-shot hair and his hands were studded with rings. One of them, most prominent, had a horse's profile picked out in gemstones.

He'd aged in the years since Slate had seen him last, but there was no mistaking his identity.

"You," said Boss Horsehead. "You, at last."

CHAPTER 31

"Why are you even here?" said Horsehead. "I never figured you for an idiot."

Slate shrugged. "Ah, you know…"

He struck her across the side of the head. Slate's head rang, and when it stopped ringing, her ear felt very hot.

Oh, lovely…

"Last I heard, you were holed up in the Dowager's city. I sent a couple assassins, for all the good it did me."

Keep him talking…if he's talking, he's not killing you…

"Good help is hard to find," said Slate. She'd only known about one assassin. Brenner had killed her, which had actually led to Slate falling into his arms in gratitude.

Another mistake I can lay at Horsehead's feet. So that's nice, anyway.

He leaned over her. He didn't have to lean, he was already a lot bigger than she was, but he did it anyway. "Someone paying you to come back?"

The tattoo clamped down, which was exactly what she didn't need right now.

Slate rolled her eyes. "I was in the capitol, yeah. But you're sending legions of bloody clocktaurs at it, if you hadn't noticed. Figured the safest place to be was back here. At least they're all pointed the other way."

Boss Horsehead snorted. His breath smelled like his last meal, which had apparently been heavily spiced. "Those damn things." He shook his head. "Still, if they drove you back here, at least they finally did me some good."

"And here I figured you'd be war profiteering off 'em."

Horsehead hit her again, not as hard. Slate got the feeling it was more of a reflex than actual malice. This did not make her ear feel any better.

"Bad for business," he said. "But I tell you what's good for business, hey?"

Slate felt her stomach sink.

"Showing people what happens when they cross me."

Well, I didn't think he was going to let bygones be bygones…

"I'm going to put you in the crow cage," said Horsehead. He grinned at her, and his teeth were immaculate, made of ivory by the finest artificers. "I'm going to give you one night to see the entire Shadow Market staring at you."

He leaned forward then and put his hands on the back of her chair, on either side of her neck. Slate wanted to be the sort of person who spit in his face. She discovered, somewhat gloomily, that she was not.

Let him rant. Let him rave. As long as I'm in the cage and not dead, there's still a chance.

"And then," Boss Horsehead said, "I'm going to cut out your eyes."

"We have to make sure she isn't dead," said Caliban. "If she's in a crow cage, we'll know right away."

"At the moment, I don't trust you not to run berserk," said Brenner.

Caliban found the wretched cloak that he'd worn before and threw it over his armor. "I am going to the Grey Church with or without you."

Brenner swore under his breath. "You are going to make me old before my time, paladin."

"As Slate is fond of telling us, we're probably not going to live that long."

"Speak for yourself," muttered Brenner, and followed him out the door into the street.

Slate sat in the bottom of the crow cage with metal digging into her skin. The cages weren't made for comfort. The rivets were heavy, the edges unfiled, and they tore threads out of her clothes when she moved.

She was unbound. That was funny. Hilarious, even. Boss Horsehead wasn't worried about her getting out. They'd left her most of her clothes, minus the veil—and after checking for knives, they'd left her the damnable boots.

That was arguably a form of torture, but presumably Horsehead didn't know that.

Horsehead knew that she wasn't going anywhere. If she somehow picked the lock and climbed up the chain holding the crow cage, she would hit a baffle, and then she would be clinging to the chain until her arms tired. Possibly someone would shoot at her, but possibly not. It might be more amusing to them if she fell.

A prisoner had managed to get out of the cage once, which was why the baffles were in place. The man had opened the door with a concealed lockpick and climbed and clung and looked around.

A roar had gone up from the floor then, and everyone had stopped and turned and watched.

The prisoner nodded once, to himself, and then he took two steps and dove headfirst at the ground, like a swimmer entering deep water. He died instantly, which no doubt he had intended, rather than rot in the crow cage until thirst and hopelessness claimed him.

Slate wondered if she would have that kind of courage.

She knew that the denizens of the Shadow Market were staring at her. They had watched with interest as she had been hauled aloft. She could catch a few words up here, and her name had gone out through the crowd like ripples in water.

Slate. Slate. Mistress Slate. Horsehead caught her. He said he would. Slate. It's Slate. She'll rot in that cage until the crows eat her. It's Mistress Slate...

And then it had stopped and everyone had gone back about their business. A five-minute wonder, that's what her life was worth.

She sat with her back to one of the bars and the rivets jabbing her, watching the crowd swirl beneath her.

Every few hours someone else would come in and look up and she would hear her name again, spreading through the new crowd, like an echo.

She was going to die. She had managed to have hope right up until they slammed the crow cage door, and then it had run out of her like water from a broken cup. Despair had rushed in instead—*hello old friend, I'd forgotten you for a little while, so nice to see you again.*

In a way, she was grateful that she had spent so long waiting to die. It gave her a kind of bleak strength. She could sit and look down on the Market and she did not cry or scream or sob. She simply sat.

Pride, Caliban said. *Pride was his sin.*

Was this pride, then? Not wanting to break down in full view of people who remembered her name?

She thought briefly of Caliban—not her friend, but *Lord* Caliban, Knight-Champion of the Dreaming God. They said that he had asked for nothing at his trial, that he had stood silently while the charges were read and the names recited. That he had asked neither for mercy or forgiveness, that he knew he deserved neither.

Was this the same kind of pride he had at the end? The very last kind, the pride that where all you had left was that you did not wish a crowd to see you break?

She should have asked him. Gods, she had wasted so much time when she could have asked the important questions—said the important things—kicked his damn stubborn-ass feet out from under him and showed him that the weak could take down the strong if they had the right bit of leverage.

Something teased at her nostrils. It smelled almost like rosemary.

Caliban?

No, surely not. Probably just the memory. Or magic or danger or the end of the world or any of the useless things her gift tried to warn her about.

Brenner wouldn't be stupid enough to bring the paladin back here. Not now.

Surely not.

She leaned back in the crow-cage, very carefully, so as not to set it swinging.

The rosemary struck her hard.

Dammit, she thought, pinching the bridge of her nose, *dammit, dammit.* She was too proud to cry, but no amount of pride in the world could stop her allergies.

Slate sneezed violently into her sleeve and wiped at her watering eyes.

There was a figure in the crowd below her.

She knew him instantly. The ridiculous cloak over him was hardly a disguise at all—but maybe she would have known him anywhere.

Caliban looked up at her and she looked down at him.

Brenner was right behind him, hand locked on the paladin's shoulder.

Good. *Good. Keep him from doing anything stupid. You can't get me out. You can't. No one gets out and lives. You'll just get killed, and I'll still be rotting in this crow-cage, except that I will have had to watch you die.*

She didn't even dare acknowledge him, in case Boss Horsehead's men were watching for her associates.

But she lifted two fingers to her lips, seemingly at random, and hoped like hell he took her meaning.

Go. Get out of here. Figure out how to kill the Clockwork Boys before that damn tattoo eats you.

I was probably in love with you, or would have been if any of us had any chance of living.

He had one hand on the hilt of his sword. He dug with the other in his pocket, then held something up, against his chest, where no one else could see it over the crowd.

It was a handkerchief.

Of course.

She rolled over and put her arm over her head, so that she would not have to see him walk away, and so that the Shadow Market did not see her cry.

CHAPTER 32

As the hours ticked by, Slate's fatalism began to desert her. The cold knot in her gut began to widen into a clawing panic.

I'm going to cut out your eyes.

She imagined it, all too vividly, Boss Horsehead's look of concentration and the knife coming at her, the point the last thing she saw, the last thing she would ever see...

After that, even if she lived, even if Horsehead dropped dead of apoplexy five minutes later, her old life was done.

I'm a forger. I make my money by my eyes and my hands. What will I do if he takes my eyes?

There were thieves who could make a living without their eyes. Slate wasn't one of them.

What will I have left? Earning my money on my back, while I try to find someone to take a blind apprentice?

If she could find a partner to work with, locks weren't picked with your eyes, but with your fingertips and your ears. There was no great amount of money in it, but it was better than being a whore, particularly when she lacked the beauty or charm to be a courtesan. She could find a fence, maybe, who needed a cracksman...not here in Anuket City, obviously, but perhaps in the capital...

Caliban would see me home, she thought bleakly, *and I wouldn't be able to see him looking at me with pity.* It was the coldest sort of comfort. Slate had been given her life and she had always known that she'd have to give it back someday. But her livelihood—she'd earned that. Skill was the one thing that she'd had that no one could take away.

Brenner, maybe? Brenner was adequate with locks but not terribly gifted. If she could get him stealing files, and hire a clerk to read them to her, possibly between the two of them they could manage something...

Oh, it's all stupid anyway. Here I am worrying how I'll earn my bread, when I'm going to die of thirst in this cage in the next few days.

She shifted her position again, trying to get blood back into her feet, and gazed across the Shadow Market as if it were the last thing she would see.

"For the love of god, will you stop pacing?" snapped Brenner.

"I can pace or I can begin knocking down walls. Your choice."

"This won't help our Slate."

"Then bring me something to kill that *will* help."

Grimehug planted himself in Caliban's way. "Gnoles looking," he said. "Gnoles working as fast as they can."

"I know." Caliban turned on his heel and did another tight circuit of the room, feeling as if he were in a crow-cage himself.

Brenner had had to half-drag him out of the Church. Every moment of thirty years of training was screaming to do *something*—climb to a higher point and get to the chain somehow, or kill the guards, or maybe just kill everyone.

"Come on," hissed Brenner in his ear. The assassin's fingers dug into his upper arm. "We've got to leave. This isn't helping anyone."

Caliban shook his head. Leave? How was he supposed to leave?

"You're very close to making a scene. They will notice. And they will take it out on her."

A shard of ice slid into his heart, as Brenner had no doubt intended.

"We have to do something," he said to Brenner, as much a plea as an order.

"We will," said the assassin, as if to a very small child. "I promise. Now come with me."

Caliban cast a last, anguished glance over his shoulder and followed.

"What is our plan?" he asked, when they were safely away from the Shadow Market.

"Horsehead has special plans for our Slate," said Brenner. "He'll take her down from the cage, and take her somewhere that he can cut out her eyes in peace."

Caliban's fingers closed convulsively on the hilt of his sword.

"Will. You. Calm. Down?" snarled the assassin. "I'm not supposed to be the reliable one here! I'm supposed to be the one who stabs people for money, and this lovesick bullshit of yours is seriously cramping my style!"

Caliban turned his head away, not trusting himself to answer.

"The plan is still good. The gnoles will know where they take her. Then we'll go there. Wherever that is."

"What if we can't get in?"

"They won't keep me out," said Brenner simply.

"You said we couldn't storm a mansion."

"We can't, and we won't have to. You don't shit where you eat. Horsehead will take her someplace that he can torture her. Places like that, nobody watches who goes in and out, and nobody pays attention to the screaming." He jerked his chin to the demon-killing sword. "And that's where you and I go to work."

Caliban nodded.

He didn't want to say it. The thought made his chest ache as if the demon were clawing through it. But he had been a Knight-Champion and he had done terrible things with his eyes open, so he said it anyway.

"What if we don't succeed?"

Brenner met his eyes and squared his shoulders. "Then I have a crossbow. And if I'm still alive, I will go to the Grey Church and shoot her out of the crow cage when they put her back."

Learned Edmund inhaled sharply. "Surely that won't be necessary!"

Assassin and paladin both ignored him.

"Thank you," said Caliban, almost inaudibly.

And then, because he could do nothing else, he began to pace.

Twenty minutes ago word had come from the gnoles that Slate had been taken down from the cage. Caliban was so keyed up that, when someone tapped at the window, he nearly put his fist through the wall.

Brenner gave him a disgusted look and opened the window. Another gnole, so small and ragged that it looked to be all eyes and stripes, slipped inside.

It spoke to Grimehug in a rapid gabble of gnolespeech. Grimehug answered, and nodded to the humans. The newcomer peered shyly up at them, wringing its paws together.

"This gnole knows," said Grimehug.

Caliban went down to one knee in front of the newcomer. "Tell me where they took Slate."

The little gnole shot Grimehug a worried look. Even kneeling, the paladin loomed over the newcomer. Its nostrils worked, and its ears were flat against its head.

What does it smell on me? Does it smell the demon or only human desperation?

It doesn't have to smell anything, it can probably see that I'm a wreck. Collect yourself. You were a Knight-Champion once, act like it!

"Please, little one," said Caliban, dredging up the paladin's voice from somewhere. Low, that was it, low and calm and kind. "She is our friend. Please help us find her."

"This gnole is named Sweet Lily," said Grimehug.

"Of course it is," muttered Brenner.

"This gnole spoke to book-man and Crazy Slate before. This gnole remembered."

Caliban took a deep breath. "Sweet Lily—if you know…"

The gnole's ears came up, but her nostrils still twitched. "Warehouse," she said softly. "Warehouse to the south. Lots of roads. Lots of guards. Gnoles still watching it, sent a gnole back."

"Can you show us where it is?" asked Caliban. *Calm, calm…*

"Show you, yes." Another look at Grimehug. "A gnole not going inside, though."

"You don't have to go inside. Just show us where it is. Thank you." The paladin rose. "We'll leave immediately."

"You understand—" said Brenner, reaching out and grabbing Caliban's wrist. "If we do this, it's over. No help from the Grey Church. We're putting ourselves completely in the hands of Magnus and the gnoles."

"Get out of my way, Brenner."

"We'll have a hard time even going out to get *food* without getting killed on the street."

Caliban's hand closed on the hilt of his sword. "And if you don't shut up and come with me, you'll get killed in this room, right now."

"Whoa, now." Brenner lifted his hands. "I'm not saying we leave our Slate. I just wanna make sure we're clear on this."

"We're clear. Stop talking."

"I want to come too," said Learned Edmund from the doorway.

Caliban stiffened. "Learned Edmund—this is no task for a scholar—"

"You have two men and a handful of gnoles to storm some gutter citadel. If I come, maybe I can help."

Sweet Lily scooted over to Learned Edmund, apparently remembering him.

"If you come, maybe the whole mission ends right here." The knight felt a sudden jab as his tattoo bit down. "I can't let you."

Learned Edmund ignored him, and went down on his knee in front of Sweet Lily. "Lily?"

"Yeah, book man?"

"These are all my notes on the Clockwork Boys. Will you remember that?"

"Yeah!"

"If anything happens, will you take them to Ashes Magnus, in the Artificer's Quarter? Do you know where that is? They will reward you for it."

Lily worried at her lower lip with her fangs. "Some gnole knows. A gnole can do that."

"What good will that do?" Brenner demanded.

Learned Edmund had already pulled out a sheet of parchment and a pen. "She will send them on to my Temple. They do not get involved in wars, but they will not deny the request of a dead brother. They'll get my notes to the Dowager's people, somehow or other."

It took less than five minutes to write the note. Caliban paced like a caged tiger, chafing at the delay. Their guide hid behind Grimehug, chattering in unhappy gnolespeech.

"What's she saying?" Caliban asked.

"Saying you smell like someone's death, big man. Hoping it's not ours."

"It won't be," said Caliban. "Someone's, though."

CHAPTER 33

Slate was taken down from the cage and reintroduced to her old friend, the sack.

As little as she liked the crow cage, the grind of chains as her cage was lowered shattered what was left of her nerve. She was almost grateful for the sack on her head. At least she didn't have to worry that people could see she was terrified.

She knew on some level that people who kept cool in the face of death still ultimately ended up dead. She just would have liked to think of herself as cool and calm and sardonic to the end, instead of sobbing and wetting herself in terror.

Oh well. My self-respect wasn't worth much to begin with. I suppose it'll be worth even less by the time they're done with me.

The guards carried her outside. She could tell by the sudden wash of cool, humid air and the sounds. Then she was dropped into a carriage and then, a few minutes later, when the carriage had stopped, carried into a building.

The room she found herself in, when they had tied her to yet another chair and removed the sack, was larger than the last one. It was also clean, but in the fashion of a room that can be easily sluiced down to get the bloodstains off the walls.

That was a happy thought. I'm so glad I had it.

The door opened again. The guards went out. Another man came in.

Her torturer introduced himself politely.

Slate had absolutely no illusions about her ability to withstand torture. If anyone so much as pointed a sharp object at her, she'd sing like a robin in springtime.

Sure, she might try to hold off spilling her guts—might even resist for a good thirty seconds—but there was just no way. Slate's allergies were legendary. Foremost among them was an allergy to pain.

Sorry, guys. Sorry, Caliban. We're not all tragic heroes. Some of us are just tragic.

The only problem was that she didn't think she knew very much that Horsehead would care about. They had to know that the Dowager would be trying to stop the Clockwork Boys—as state secrets went, it wasn't exactly a surprise. Slate didn't know anything about troop movements or plans, and the big mystery of how the Clockwork Boys were made was unlikely to impress the boss, who presumably knew anyway.

The only information she had that anyone would care about were the identities of her cohorts. That probably wouldn't be enough to buy her a quick death. The boss was *really* sore over that bestiality warrant.

He might not even ask me any questions. He might just move straight to the pointy bits.

She hoped her friends had had the good sense to relocate as soon as she'd been caught.

And if not, I suppose my guilt can keep me company while I'm hanging over the Grey Church in a crow's cage.

Heck, the man probably wouldn't even believe anyone was stupid enough to try an assault on the clocktaur factory with only four people and a pack of gnoles. Maybe if she was lucky, he'd kill her trying to extract information about the army that she really *ought* to have.

Which spares me losing my eyes, anyway. For what that's worth.

Her only consolation was that she'd bitten her fingernails so short, they'd have a devil of a time pulling them out.

As consolations went, she'd had better.

Ironically, she actually knew where she was. It would have been nice if it was because of her highly trained senses, keeping track of the sounds of the carriage wheels on the cobbles and the echoes of the time-keeping statues, but it wasn't. Horsehead's repurposed lumberyard was simply one of the worst kept secrets of the Shadow Market. She'd even come here a time or two, under her own power, to deliver forged confessions for signing.

Only once when the boss was…ah…*playing*…however. After that, she'd steered clear.

*If he wasn't such a rat bastard, I wouldn't have taken the gig. Still,
somebody had to keep that poor girl out of his clutches.*

You do one good deed…

And here she was, tied to a chair, with a very unpleasant man
getting ready to soften her up.

The torturer waved a device under her nose. It was silver and had
pointy pinchy bits, several serrated holes, and a spring. Slate hadn't the
faintest idea what it might do and was afraid to find out.

"Are you going to talk?" he asked.

"Almost certainly," Slate said, eyeing the device. It was the sort of
object confined in kitchen drawers and liberated once a year to make
chutney. She could easily imagine it doing vague but unfortunate
things to various orifices, or appendages, or both simultaneously.

"Now," said the torturer calmly. "I am going to hurt you. Then I'm
going to ask you a question. If you don't answer it, I'm going to hurt
you again."

"You know, I'm pretty sure I'm going to tell you everything I know,
so we could just skip to that part and avoid the hurting altogether."

He cracked her upside the head with the silver thing. Slate yelped.

Well, that was actually sort of anticlimactic, even if it did hurt.

"Ow! Goddamnit, I said I was going to talk!"

Her head hurt, and there was something tickling the back of her
neck, which probably meant she was bleeding from the scalp. The
pointy bits had been sharp. Someone was very serious about their
chutney.

"Does your *mother* know you do this for a living?"

"You're starting to annoy me, lady."

Slate did a brief mental calculation of whether annoying one's
torturer was a bad idea, or whether you were going to get tortured
anyway and you might as well go out on a defiant note, and decided
to err on the side of caution. "Sorry. I babble when I'm nervous. I'm
very nervous right now. You probably guessed that. Hey, did I already
mention that I'd tell you everything you want to know?"

The torturer folded his arms and frowned down his nose at her.
"Was someone in here before me to soften you up?"

"No, I'm very soft to begin with." She considered. "I don't suppose there's any chance I could seduce you out of this? I mean, not to be insulting, I'm sure you're a man of principle, just figured I'd ask, in case you were a *lonely* man of principle—"

"I'm married."

"I'm sure she's lovely." Slate sighed. She rolled her shoulders. Her elbows were getting stiff from being locked behind her, and the back of her neck had started to itch dreadfully, which was almost worse than the sting in her scalp.

He smacked the silver widget into his palm. *Horse chestnut peeler, maybe?* Slate tried scrunching her neck back and scratching the back of her head on the chair, which didn't help at all.

"So are you going to ask me any questions, or are you just gonna smack me with your candied apricot shucker or whatever the heck that thing's supposed to be?"

"I'll have you know, lady, this is a—"

The true identity of the mystery widget remained a mystery, because the door opened again, and one of the flunkies came and murmured something to the torturer.

"Hmmph. No cockroaches? And the eggs are rotten? Very well." He turned back to Slate. "I shall return momentarily."

"Take your time."

He set the widget down on the table in front of her, where she couldn't help but stare at it.

"You might consider…thinking things over. Like your cooperation."

"I already offered to tell you anything I know!"

The door slammed.

Slate, who had a pretty good understanding of the criminal mind— you didn't hang around Brenner for long and not pick things up—was pretty sure that they were waiting on the boss to show up. This was *his* petty vengeance, after all, and he'd want to watch. Otherwise, the efficient man with his cactus descaler would have reduced her to a weeping heap.

There was also almost certainly nothing planned involving either cockroaches or fresh eggs. They were under orders to wait, and were simply letting her stew in her own imagination while they did.

"Joke's on you, you bastards," she muttered. "I'm an accountant. I don't *have* an imagination."

Although I would have liked to know what that thing actually was. Not knowing is going to drive me nuts.

So there she sat, tied to a chair in the middle of a mostly empty room, her wrists and ankles tightly bound, with blood leaking slowly down the back of her neck.

It was, Slate reflected, the first thing that had gone right all goddamn day.

CHAPTER 34

The warehouse stood in an abandoned lumber yard. There were stacks of wood everywhere, to provide a desultory amount of cover for the other activities in the building. If one looked closely, one might discover that most of the lumber had warped, splintered, or quietly disintegrated into piles of dry rot, but by the time one got that far, guards were already looking closely back.

"Three guards," said Grimehug. "Three that a gnole can smell."

"Is there a back entrance?" asked Brenner.

"Probably," said Caliban, unsheathing his sword and walking into the open.

"Aaaaand you're an idiot," said Brenner.

Caliban broke into a run.

"He's an idiot," said Brenner to Learned Edmund, sighting down his crossbow.

"He seems to be very concerned," said the dedicate, pushing his glasses higher up on his nose. "I hope that he does not do anything terribly fool—"

Click.

Thrum.

The archer on the roof fell over the side of the building to the ground. Brenner began cranking the bow back to reload it.

"See why Crazy Slate likes you, dark man," said Grimehug. He gave Brenner a thoughtful look. "See why she's scared of you, too." Brenner grinned like a shark.

The first guard, who had been looking at Caliban in disbelief, turned and looked at the dead body, apparently quite surprised. He turned back, apparently realizing that a lunatic with a sword was really honest-to-god charging him on a quiet night in the middle of the warehouse district.

To his credit, he did try to block. It went badly. Caliban swung his sword and something awful happened in the vicinity of the guard's head.

Learned Edmund let out a squeak and put his hand over his mouth.

Another crossbow bolt came out of the darkness, missed Caliban by a quarter of an inch, and slammed into the ground.

Caliban flattened himself against the side of the building. Brenner finished cranking his own weapon back and shot that archer, with substantially better aim. The body fell backwards onto the roof.

And then everything was quiet.

"You should be dead," hissed Brenner. "You should be so dead! You don't just charge people like that! My god! *How* are you not dead?"

"They're used to gang warfare," said Caliban calmly. "And the watch, and I assume they've bought them off. They don't expect Knight-Champions to charge them waving a sword."

He cleaned his sword off on the dead man's tunic. "They aren't armored for it," he added. "You really need a shield against people like me. Or a pike. Pikes are good. The farther away you keep me, the better."

"You're insane," said Brenner. "Just—just—*gahh!*" He waved his arms in the air a few times, shaking his head. "There were *archers!*"

"Yes, and you shot them."

"They could have shot you first!"

"I had faith in you."

"Gaaaaah!"

"Also I went along the side of the building. It made me significantly more difficult to hit. They had to come up to the edge to shoot down, and I assumed that would give you a clearer shot."

Brenner folded his arms and looked sullenly furious.

"Would you like to open the door?" asked Caliban.

"What, you're not going to just bash it down?"

"I could if you like, but I thought you'd like to feel useful."

Brenner said something under his breath. Caliban thought it was probably just as well he didn't catch it.

Two minutes later, they were inside Boss Horsehead's private playground.

By dint of half an hour of intense wiggling, Slate had gotten a foot loose.

It was the shoes, the wonderful, amazing, badly fitting Chadori shoes. The ropes had been tight, but the shoes had not, the socks padding them had been pushed down with a lot of toe flexing, and Slate had thrashed and kicked and chewed on her lower lip and felt blisters break and yelped and swore and finally gotten her foot out.

Bless you, gods of footwear. I will make sacrifices at your temple if I live through this. Bless you, Chadori cobblers. You are saints among men.

The second one was a lot easier, because she could help it along with the other foot.

Once she had both feet loose, she scooted her hips as far forward in the chair as her shoulder joints would allow, reached out with her toes, and started trying to grab the widget.

There were several more guards. They all looked extremely surprised. None of them were heavily armored, particularly around the head and neck, which meant that none of them survived more than a few seconds under Brenner's daggers.

"Do you ever miss?" asked Caliban.

"All the time. I missed that last guy."

"You put a dagger in his eye."

"Yes, but I was aiming for the *other* eye."

All the guards were strung out throughout the outer hallways, in the way of men who expect theft much more than they expect, for example, two extremely angry men with bladed weapons to come charging through, killing anyone they run across.

Learned Edmund threw up.

They waited for a moment while the dedicate retched. Grimehug held him upright, looking bemused, or at least something that Caliban thought was bemusement. It was hard to tell with Grimehug.

"Please don't kill this next one," said Caliban, as they rounded a corner.

"What? Really?"

The next one was a short, rat-faced fellow with a drawn dagger. He let out a shout, which would probably alert someone, and started to run away.

"Back of the knee, Brenner."

"You just don't appreciate the work that goes into this," said Brenner angrily. "Daggers in knees? Seriously? It's very difficult when they move like that!"

Thrum.

The crossbow bolt took the running man in the calf and dropped him to the ground.

"Which is why I use the crossbow for that," the assassin continued.

The rat-faced man dropped to the ground, screaming and clutching his leg.

Caliban picked him up, slammed him against a wall, and said "Is Boss Horsehead here?"

"No!" shrieked the man. "No, no, my leg! *My leg!* I'm going to die!"

"It can't be that bad," muttered Brenner. "I didn't have time to crank it back hardly at all."

"Horsehead," said Caliban, bouncing the back of his head off the wall again.

"Ngghh! No! He was supposed to come later—he hasn't yet—my leg! My fucking leg!"

"And where does he keep his prisoners?"

"Pris...wha...my leg..."

He fainted. Caliban dropped him.

"You gonna kill that?"

"No," said Caliban. "He's a paid thug and he's not in my way any more." He began to lope down the corridor, sword out.

"Paladins," muttered Brenner bitterly, and followed.

Slate was having a long day.

She'd gotten the widget in her toes, she'd flipped it into her lap and between her thighs, she had wiggled it, with some awkward posterior action and a lot of widget holes, around to the back and had managed to get one of the pointy bits wedged against her bound wrists.

After that, it was just a lot of painful sawing.

There was another painful jab in her wrist. She winced.

Her great fear was that she'd push too vigorously or at the wrong angle and shove the widget onto the floor. Then she'd be sunk. There was no way to manage without the widget, even with her feet free. If she tried to flip over the back of the chair, she'd rip both arms out of the socket.

Her wrists must look like chutney. The blood was making them slippery, which was a mixed blessing.

At least they were giving her plenty of time. No one had even looked in on her. That was actually kind of odd.

Slate sawed harder.

CHAPTER 35

"I suppose you want me to not kill the next one, too," said Brenner nastily.

"That would be most helpful, yes."

"I was being sarcastic."

"I wasn't."

The assassin let out a growl of frustration.

Caliban was wondering if there would even *be* another guard. The center of the building was almost empty. They'd opened a few unlocked doors and found a broom closet, a privy, and two completely empty rooms that probably hadn't been used since the place had been a lumberyard.

It was a trifle awkward, when you were carrying an enormous sword and out for blood, to discover that you'd raided a building which didn't have that many people in it.

"I don't think they were expecting us," he said.

Brenner did not dignify this with a response.

"Or else there's just…no one here…"

The assassin sighed. "Why would there be anyone? We're raiding a building with a couple of outer guards. They've got no reason to expect anyone to be coming here. You said it yourself, they expect gang warfare and the watch, not people charging them with swords."

"I assumed once we got inside, Boss Horsehead would have more guards."

"I don't think he's even here yet," said Brenner. "He travels with an entourage, but why bother paying for a bunch of men to stand around when he's not here?"

"What about Slate? Shouldn't someone be guarding her?"

"Meaning absolutely no disrespect for our Slate, but I don't think you need a dozen men for that."

Caliban frowned. "So that's everybody, then?"

"Not by a long shot," said Brenner. "Horsehead's probably having a nice dinner, maybe some wine, to warm up for torturing an old enemy.

Once he shows up and sees what we did to his front door…well, I'd as soon not be around for that."

"I was hoping to kill him."

"Go ahead. Slate and I will watch. From a very long way away. Possibly the next district."

"Assuming we can find—hey! You there!"

A man was walking down the hall, wearing a vague, distracted expression and tightening a pair of rawhide gloves. He looked up, puzzled.

"What are you doing h—"

Brenner threw a knife. It hit the man in the sternum and quivered upright.

The man stared at the knife. He seemed very concerned about it, as anyone would be. It had not penetrated particularly deeply, but having a knife sprout from one's chest tends to narrow one's focus.

"Brenner!"

"What? I didn't kill him."

"You could have!"

"Pfff, not with all those ribs. Throwing knives at people's ribs is stupid. That's why I like eyes. Even if you miss, there's still a knife in their face and it scares the crap out've them."

The man poked the knife cautiously with his finger. It was apparently held in mostly by his clothes, because it fell out and clattered on the floor.

"What the devil…?"

By this point Caliban had reached him. He picked him up by the neck.

The man stopped worrying about the knife.

"Where is Slate?"

"Gnnrrkk…"

"You have to move your thumb or they can't talk when you do that," advised Brenner, lounging against the wall.

Caliban adjusted his thumb and banged the back of the man's head against the wall. "Slate," he said. "Don't make me ask again."

"Who…"

"The woman who was brought here."

"Torture… room…."

Brenner winced. "See, that was the wrong answer."

Caliban lifted the man up several inches off the floor. "Has she been tortured?"

"Ngghkk…nggh…"

"Thumb," said Brenner wearily. Caliban muttered to himself and changed his grip.

"Barely…didn't…" He rolled his eyes wildly, apparently not sure what he could say that wouldn't involve being killed in short order.

"*Where* is the torture room?"

"There," the man gurgled hopefully. "Door…?"

Caliban punched the man between the eyes with a mailed fist, which dropped him to the ground, unconscious or dead. The paladin looked around wildly, spotting a heavy door set in the wall. Brenner was already sprinting toward it.

The assassin had always been faster, which was why Brenner was the first one who charged through the door, and thus, the one that Slate brained over the head with a table leg.

"Gaaah!" The assassin dropped, clutching at his skull.

Caliban skidded inside the room, nearly trampled Brenner, and saw Slate.

She looked like hell. The back of her head was matted with blood, her forearms were red to the elbow, and she had a table leg in one hand and an indescribable metal device in the other.

She was alive.

He hadn't thought—hadn't allowed himself to think—that she might be alive. He had expected, every moment, to find a body, some broken husk, all that was left after the torturers were through. He hadn't dared to hope, because hope might destroy him.

"Brenner? Shit!" She dropped the table leg.

Caliban stepped over the prone assassin.

"Caliban? What are you doing h—?"

He didn't think. He hadn't planned to do it. He hadn't planned anything at all.

So it was a complete surprise to both of them when he took another step forward, caught her up, and pulled her so close that neither of them could breathe.

"Wha—" she began, and he locked his mouth over hers.

This is madness. This is dangerous. This is really stupid to be doing right now, there are guards, you're insane, you have a dead demon in you, you're both covered in blood—

He didn't care. She was alive and whole and in his arms.

Does she *care? She's just been tortured, you idiot, and you come in here and manhandle her. How chivalrous is that?*

That shot told. He lifted his mouth away. Someone was gasping for air. Maybe it was him.

"Ahem," said Brenner, from the floor.

"I'm sorry—" he started to say.

Slate grabbed his hair, nearly clipping his ear with the widget, and yanked him back down.

No, no, this is madness, this is not safe…

Slate's lips opened under his. Her free hand slid up the back of his neck.

Any objections his mind might have been marshalling drowned under sensation. Her mouth was soft and hot and her body molded against his until expectation and coherent thought drowned as well.

"Sure," said Brenner bitterly. "Don't mind *me*. *I've* just been hit on the head."

There is only so long that you can press yourself against a man wearing chainmail, particularly when he has a naked sword in one hand and you have an automatic fish strainer. Slate finally had to disengage, panting for breath.

She let her head fall back, smacked her injured scalp, and winced. He'd managed to back her against the wall. That had been some kiss.

She thought she could probably even get to like the faint scent of rosemary that surrounded him.

"You're alive," the paladin said hoarsely, burying his face in her shoulder. He had to bend quite a way down to do it, but Slate didn't mind.

"Apparently so."

"I was sure you'd be dead."

"Surprise?"

He stepped back, letting her go. Slate could see all the practical reasons for doing so, and let him, not without reluctance. His body was almost feverishly warm. The world felt cold in comparison.

"Why'd you hit me?" Brenner wanted to know, rubbing his skull.

"I didn't know it was you! I was planning on hitting the next person coming through the door, because I thought they'd come back to torture me."

"Did they torture you?" asked Caliban, catching her arm. He held up her bloody wrist. "I'll kill them."

He sounded very matter-of-fact about it. The sky was blue, the night was dark, he was going to kill them. It was an alarming sort of voice, but Slate approved wholeheartedly of the sentiment.

"Actually, I did that myself cutting the ropes with my abalone peeler here." She waved the widget.

Brenner's eyes widened. "Do you know what that *is?*"

"No! Do you? It's not a horse castrator, is it?"

"No, it's…actually, probably better you don't know." He rubbed at his skull and gave her a reproachful look.

She grabbed his shoulder. "Sorry, Brenner."

He met her eyes. She hoped he could read the apology there, for more than merely whacking him over the head.

"Hmmph. Well, as long as you're safe, darlin'…" He straightened. "Now, then, we still have to get out of here."

"Harder than getting in, maybe," said Grimehug. "But don't got to kill people twice, so that's something, dark man."

"Pardon," said Learned Edmund from outside the doorway, "but I believe there are more people coming?"

"You brought *him?*" said Slate. "What were you *thinking?*"

"He wouldn't stay at the hotel, darlin'."

"Paladins in the Grey Church, priests here…Brenner, you've really got to learn to say no."

"What? Why is this my fault?"

196

"Because obviously when I'm not here, you're the sensible one."

"But I don't want to be the sensible one," said the assassin plaintively. "I want to be the one who kills people and gets paid a lot of money."

Slate would have had something to say about that, but Caliban picked her up around the middle and carried her bodily into the hall.

"I see I'm not walking now."

"Your feet are covered in blood."

"It was the boots. If I'd known you were staging a rescue, I'd just have stayed tied up and left more of my blood on the inside. Take the left corridor."

"Eh?"

"Left. It goes to the old delivery entrance. Gods willing, it'll have fewer guards."

"How do you know that?"

"Obviously because I've made deliveries here before."

Three men rushed into the end of the hall, shouting.

"Darlin', I thought you said—"

"I said fewer! Not none!"

Caliban put her down. She was somewhat relieved by that. Being carried by a man in armor, even one who had kissed you like you were his last hope of heaven, was not a terribly comfortable experience.

Grimehug settled into his accustomed spot as her crutch. He rolled an eye up at her. There was a splatter of blood across his stripes.

"Glad you're alive, Crazy Slate. Called you right, though."

"Yeah, I think you did. You don't happen to have a knife on you, do you? They took mine."

Brenner reached back without speaking and handed her a dagger. It was still warm from the previous owner, who was lying on the ground. Certain vital parts appeared to no longer be connected to other vital parts.

"Thanks, Brenner."

"What are friends for?"

CHAPTER 36

Ashes Magnus opened her door, looked at the motley crew, and sighed. "One night only," she said. "After that, you're going to a safehouse down the way. And if anybody breaks anything looking for you, I'm billing the Many-Armed God. *With interest.*"

"We haven't met," said Slate, "but I have a strong desire to be your friend."

She was walking more or less under her own power, supported by Grimehug on one side and Sweet Lily on the other. Caliban was hovering behind her anxiously.

There had been a moment of discussion about how exactly she was going to leave the warehouse. Caliban was all set to go back to carrying her the entire way, until Brenner pointed out that he only had three knives left and a large man with a sword would be extremely useful for clearing hallways.

Grimehug and Slate had solved the matter by stomping ahead, like a mismatched team in a three-legged race, and Caliban had stopped hovering and gone back to guarding.

Someone had apparently figured out that something strange was happening at the warehouse and Boss Horsehead's men were filling the streets, but none of them were well-organized and none of them paid attention to gnoles. Grimehug had led three of the four humans into the narrow gnole tunnels and away. (In Caliban's case, this had been more than a little difficult, and at one point they had to dismantle part of a wall to fit him through, but they had managed.)

Brenner had simply melted away into the shadows and then reappeared on the other side.

"Wasn't hard," he said. "They're all tripping over each other's backsides. I put a bolt in a couple of them, just to stir up some confusion."

Once in the Artificer's Quarter, it was easier. People were used to seeing bloody, confused people in the street. Learned Edmund began talking very loudly about what they had learned from a hypothetical explosion, and anyone who had looked up rolled their eyes and looked away again.

Ashes Magnus was very calm about having fugitives in the house.

"Not the first time," she said. "Probably not going to be the last, either. Usually it's from people who blew up something that they shouldn't."

"Do you want to know what we did?"

"*Hell* no."

Slate grinned. "Artificer Magnus—"

"Ashes," said the artificer. "And you're Slate and the pretty one's Caliban and that boy who thinks he's clever is Brenner and if anyone asks, I've never met any of you."

"How much will that cost?" asked Slate.

Magnus laughed. "You've paid already. Brother Amadai's notes. Learned Edmund brought me what he had, and now I'm afraid you're stuck with me. At least until we get the rest of them deciphered."

"Do you think they'll be helpful?" asked Slate.

"Helpful or not, they're *fascinating*. That man was a genius. Not your garden-variety genius either. You can't throw a brick without hitting one of those around here. Amadai had something else. He was *bent*."

She said this with deep admiration. Slate nodded, then winced.

Learned Edmund tutted over the back of her head. "It's not deep," he said. "It just bled a lot because of where it is. I don't think I need to sew it."

"Just clean it out," said Slate. She sat at Magnus's kitchen table and stretched her arms out in front of her. Her wrists were raw from rope burns.

"No tendon damage. Lucky you. I've got a salve for that," said Magnus, and dropped a jar on the table.

Caliban looked at her battered hands and thought, *I did not kill enough of them.*

Slate tried to open the jar, scowled at the lid, and he reached out and took it away from her.

The salve smelled of honey and onions. Caliban dipped his fingers into it and took Slate's hands between his.

She stared at their hands. So did he. As if in a dream—*am I doing this? truly?*—he rubbed the salve over her wrists, across her palms. Her hands were so small compared to his. Both of them scarred, though, hers with acid blotches and his from swords.

Her pulse was beating under his fingertips, but she sat as still as a statue. The calluses on her palms were small, hard knots. The skin on her wrists was very soft.

Am I hurting her? Is this pain? Is she afraid?

Was I too late?

She had not kissed him like a man who was too late, but perhaps it had only been the rescue and the relief and if Brenner had moved faster—and ducked more quickly—it would have been the assassin instead.

He had finished salving her wounds minutes ago, and he realized that he was still staring at their joined hands. Hers lay cupped inside his fingers, and his thumb lay across her palm.

He looked up, finally. Her usually expressive face was blank, as if she were concentrating on something so hard that she had retreated from her own flesh.

"Did I hurt you?" he asked.

"No," she said, almost inaudibly. "No, it's fine."

"Ah!" said Learned Edmund cheerfully. "Thank you, Caliban. Quick treatment of scrapes will prevent scarring."

They both jumped guiltily. Caliban dropped her hands and she drew them back against her body.

"God of architects," muttered Ashes Magnus, rolling her eyes.

Learned Edmund looked puzzled. In the corner, Grimehug began to whistle, sounding like a tea-kettle that could carry a tune.

Slate excused herself and went to the privies. When she returned, somewhat cleaned up, Caliban hadn't moved at all.

"I should go to bed," said Slate. "Ashes, thank you for your hospitality."

"Go, go." The artificer made shooing motions. "*Try* to get some rest."

Slate walked away, down the hall. She looked over her shoulder once, then resolutely looked away.

Caliban stared after her.

A heavy fist landed on the table and made them all jump. "Young man," said Ashes severely, "if you do not go after that woman, you are too stupid to be allowed to live."

Learned Edmund's puzzled look deepened.

Improbably, after all that long and wretched night, Caliban found that he was laughing.

"Grimehug—"

"Staying out here tonight, big man," said the gnole cheerfully. "In case a gnole needs to find me."

They are humoring me. Dreaming God help us all.

He rose to his feet and looked at Ashes Magnus. "I am probably too stupid to be allowed to live," he admitted, and he bowed very deeply to her, as if she were the head of his own order.

"Well," sniffed Ashes, to his retreating back, "at least you admit it."

CHAPTER 37

He caught up with Slate in front of her door. It was not a long hallway. She must have walked very slowly.

They stood in the hall and looked at each other. The silence quickly passed uncomfortable and moved into downright painful.

"I'm sorry," said Caliban finally. "I shouldn't have—"

"Oh, for god's sake," said Slate bitterly, "don't you *ever* get tired of beating yourself up?"

He sagged. *I'm doing this wrong. Again.*

"Look," she said, opening the door to her room, "I have had a hell of a night, and I'm going to bed. If you want to be strong and noble and miserable, do it in your own room."

He lifted his eyes from the floor. Her back was to him, and as he watched, the lines of her back softened just a little.

"However," she said quietly, not looking at him, "if you're as shook up and scared as I am, and you would like to be shook up and scared together…well, you know where to find me."

The door clicked shut behind her.

Caliban didn't know how long he stood in the hallway. The door was made of knotted pine, and the grain swam in front of his eyes, resolving into round-eyed faces, like little owls. He could hear the wooden floor creaking as Slate moved inside her room.

He had been strong all his life. He had been strong until the demon had come, and strength no longer mattered, and then when he was broken, he had kept on trying to be strong because he didn't know what else to do.

Perhaps he'd come at last to a place where strength no longer availed him. Perhaps it was time to try something else.

The pine owls boggled at him.

He lifted a hand to the door.

Slate yanked it open and clenched her fist in his tabard.

"I think," he said hoarsely, "that I've had enough of being strong."

"Good enough," she said, and pulled him inside.

Slate had had fantasies about this moment, god help her. She'd wondered what he'd say. *You're beautiful. I want you. I've waited for this.*

Probably not, *I love you,* but, *Take me now* would have been fine.

Given how her life was going, she had been somewhat resigned to, *We're about to die, wanna go out screwing?* although in her fantasy, she'd been the one talking, and all he had to say was, *Yes.*

Knowing Caliban, though, it was probably going to be, *I'm sorry.*

"I don't want to hurt you," he said, staring down at her wrists.

Well, she'd figured it was going to be something *like* that.

"I don't know what they might have done—"

"Very little, apart from whacking me on the head and scaring the hell out of me. I mostly did this to myself getting loose."

"Are you certain you…"

Oh, hell with it. If you wait for him to talk himself into it, you'll both die of old age.

She turned and took his face in both hands and kissed him, with a great deal of pent-up passion and no small amount of pent-up rage.

By the time she finished, his breathing was ragged and he was standing with his knees locked, like a horse that had run too far, too fast. He had both hands clamped around her back and she wanted to melt against him like—*damn, like a thing that melts, who cares, this is not the time to worry about specific melting things—*

There was, unfortunately, a small impediment.

"Take off this goddamn armor," Slate rasped, stepping back. "I don't know how to do the buckles."

He did, as if it were an order, flinging it aside. She had never seen him so careless with his equipment. Only the demon-slaying sword escaped, handled with automatic reverence, and then he was standing there, bare chested.

God*damn,* he was pretty. It was practically offensive.

She did what she had wanted to do for a long time, and ran her hands over his arms. There were so many scars and they snaked around, over and under. She tracked one that ran over his shoulder, down his chest, where something had apparently tried to slice him open and hadn't quite succeeded.

He shivered. "Slate..." he said, catching her hands. "Slate, I am not sure I can do this right."

She raised an eyebrow at that. "Really? It's pretty straightforward." She glanced down and added "I could be wrong, but it doesn't look like there's going to be a problem."

Caliban stared at her and then started to laugh. He raised her hands to his lips. "I meant that I wanted to make this perfect."

His breath on her fingers was going to drive her nearly as mad as his voice.

"We'll go for perfect next time," she said, and dragged him down beside her.

It would not go down as one of history's great acts of love, but it got the job done. They managed well enough.

When he entered her, they both gasped. It had been a long time. He pulled her head against his shoulder and moved, slowly, then harder, until in what seemed like no time at all, she was crying his name in his neck while her body bucked and she fell over the edge, into a moment that caught like pain.

"Shhh," he said. "I've got you. It's all right. It's all..."

And then he shuddered even more deeply inside her and whatever he was saying turned into her name, and then into no words at all.

And as far as Slate was concerned, that was nearly perfect enough.

Caliban insisted on making the bed afterward. Slate let him tuck the blankets in around her and fought the urge to giggle hysterically.

"It's more comfortable this way," he said.

"If you say so..."

He sat on the edge of the bed, fingers laced with hers. "Do you want me to stay?"

"Yes."

"I might...the demon might speak. You know that."

"Yeah, I've heard it already."

He lifted her hand and kissed each knuckle. "It's a little different when...well."

Slate shook her head and pulled back the blanket. "Get in bed. We'll manage."

He was large and warm and reassuringly solid. Lying with her back against him was like putting her back to a wall. *Not safe. None of us are safe. But maybe in a more defensible position.*

She laughed to herself at that.

"Do I want to know?" asked Caliban.

"Probably not."

"All right, then." He wrapped his arms around her and she felt him sigh against her hair.

"Mmm?"

"I had planned to take my time," he said, almost plaintively.

"Tomorrow," she said. "When I'm not half-dead and stinking of onion salve."

He laughed softly. "Tomorrow. Then I'm going to sleep now. There's less chance I'll say something stupid and you'll make me sleep in the hall."

She started laughing again, but it turned into a yawn, and then another one, and then she slept.

This is happening. That actually happened.

He had dozed and awoken and dozed again with Slate still in his arms and when he finally woke for good, she was still there. His hand was still cradled between her breasts and he could feel her heartbeat against his palm.

She was alive. Not in a crow cage. Not dead in Horsehead's torture chamber. Alive. Unharmed...or, well. Bloodied but unbowed. Which was Slate all over.

She's alive and I am allowed to touch her like this.

He wanted to run his hands over her body and learn all the places he hadn't yet. He wanted to kiss her between the shoulderblades and set his lips in the hollow of her throat. He wanted to drive into her body until he drove out even the memory of fear.

I am a fool. I should have done this weeks ago.

He had wasted so much time. He could have been inside her every night, woken with her in his arms every morning. He would have been there when she woke with night terrors and he could have driven them away.

It was a night terror that had woken him. Something like that, anyway. Slate had jerked in his arms and mumbled something that sounded less frightened than angry.

A night irritation, perhaps?

"Slate…"

She twitched again. Memories of the crow cage? Something worse?

"It's just a dream," he said in her ear. "I've got you."

And it worked. She sighed and the tension went out of her body. Caliban held her and thought, *There is a person in this world who feels safe in my arms.*

It felt like grace.

He knew that he should feel guilt, if anything. This was hardly a proper penance for his sins. But the only remorse he could summon was that they had not done this sooner, and that it had been over so quickly once they finally had.

Next time. Next time I will go slow and savor every moment. Next time…

Caliban's lips twisted. Well…unless Brenner stabs me first.

As if the thought had summoned him, the door banged open, and the assassin stood framed in the doorway.

"Wakey wake—"

He stopped. His eyes moved from the paladin's face to Slate's, down the length of their bodies.

Caliban couldn't help himself. He slid his hand down possessively over Slate's hip and stared the other man full in the face.

Mine.

It was an entirely primitive response and Slate would undoubtedly have said something sarcastic and he regretted none of it.

Mine.

Brenner nodded slowly to himself. Caliban braced himself to throw himself over Slate and take a dagger to the shoulder if that was what was required. He wasn't sure if he could get to his sword before Brenner got to him, but he could damn well try.

The assassin put both hands on the doorframe with exaggerated care. "We're moving to the safehouse," he said. "I suggest you two get dressed."

And he closed the door and walked away.

CHAPTER 38

"Did someone come in?" yawned Slate, stretching.

"Brenner."

"Oh," said Slate, in a rather different tone, and sat up.

"Is that a problem?" asked Caliban. He could feel shards of ice settling in his chest. *What if she made a mistake? What if it wasn't really me she wanted...?*

"Rejecting a man who slits throats for a living is always a problem," said Slate dryly. "But I dumped him and we've worked together fine since, so I'm not that worried."

"Is he in love with you?"

She snorted. "Love's not in his vocabulary. We're friends, by which he means he respects my talents and nobody's paid him money to kill me."

She stretched. This did things to her body that Caliban watched with great appreciation. "What did he want, anyway?"

"We're moving to a safehouse," said Caliban. "We should probably get dressed."

"Ugh."

He folded his arms around her and put his face against her neck. "Why did we wait so long to do this?"

"'Cos we're stupid."

He snorted. "I seem to recall being the one who said most of the stupid things."

"Yes, well. I was being polite." Slate yawned again. "No rest for the wicked, though."

He released her, not without reluctance. She rolled out of bed and began pulling on clothes. Her bruises were beginning to turn spectacularly violet, and Caliban winced looking at them.

"I need to wash," Slate muttered. "I think I've still got torture gunk on me."

"I'm sorry I didn't—"

"You came and got me. If anything, I'm sorry I was careless enough to get caught."

"You don't need to apologize for that!"

"Then neither do you."

"Slate—"

She held up her hand. "Are you going to say something stupid again?"

He considered this. "Quite possibly?"

"Is it about sex?"

"I didn't hurt you, did I?"

She rolled her eyes. "Put your pants on. I've been beat up by better men than Boss Horsehead." She rubbed the back of her neck and grimaced. "Honestly, sitting in that damn cage for half the night was much worse. I'm going to have a crick in my neck for the next week."

Caliban cleared his throat. "I could rub that for you?"

"See, now that wasn't stupid. Say more things like that."

"I'll do my best....my liege."

"Gahhh!"

Five minutes later, Caliban sat at Magnus's table. Learned Edmund was the only one there, poring over Brother Amadai's notes.

Slate emerged from the bathing chamber a few minutes later, slightly damp, and sat down beside the paladin on the bench.

Caliban glanced around then began to rub the knotted muscle at the base of Slate's neck. He wasn't sure why he felt an urge to hide—it wasn't as if Magnus and Grimehug didn't know already, and Brenner certainly did now. Still. Force of habit, perhaps.

Slate, apparently untroubled by such concerns, made a small, pleased noise and lowered her chin.

Learned Edmund didn't even seem to notice. He beamed at them both. "Mistress Magnus and Brenner are securing our transport. It should be only a few minutes, I hope. Apparently this building is in the Gnole Quarter."

"In the Gnole Quarter," said Brenner, strolling in, "and hidden inside one of their dens. It's a hideout for failed artificers."

Caliban fought the urge to snatch his fingers away from Slate's skin. He met Brenner's eyes. "Failed how?"

"Only one real way to fail here," said Slate, leaning back against him. "Blow up the wrong thing…place…person, or fail to blow them up."

"Could they not simply make a device that did not function? Would that not count as a failure?" asked Learned Edmund.

"You're new in town, aren't you? Blowing up is how everything here fails."

"Oh."

"The gnoles have extracted our gear from the hotel," said Brenner. "Too dangerous to go back for the horses, though." He did not sound as if this pained him much.

"Darn," said Slate.

Caliban sighed. He'd rather liked his horse.

"And my mules?" asked Learned Edmund.

"I'm sure they'll be sold to a very nice drover who only uses them on holy days," said Brenner.

Learned Edmund signed a small, sad benediction.

"And we've found our way into the factory," said Brenner. "You won't like it."

Slate sighed heavily. "Well, I figured it was inevitable."

"You know it is, darlin'."

"For those of us who aren't able to read minds," said Caliban, "what method is that?"

"The grave-gnoles," said Slate.

"Got in it one." The assassin tipped a finger at Slate. "We're riding in with the body carts."

Caliban grunted. The thought was…*horrifying, actually, if I'm being honest.*

But the alternative was apparently going in by water, and that would be infinitely worse. The cold water dragging at him, closing over his head, over and over…

"Oh well," said Slate. "Not the first time that I've disguised myself as a corpse."

There was a pause while everyone in the room absorbed this statement.

"What? How else was I getting into that mortuary? They had locks and guards and dogs. I stained everything with dye like I had the witch-pox, so they didn't want to touch me and I was able to sneak out later and get into the files. You would not believe how many times they were selling a single grave. It was nasty."

Before Caliban could think of anything to say to that, Ashes Magnus leaned in the door. "Your carriage awaits, gentlefolk."

The carriage was a wagon apparently full of crates, with a canvas tarp thrown over it. It had pulled up behind Ashes Magnus's workshop.

There was an opening in the center, between the crates. They all piled into it. Magnus pushed a crate to block the view of anyone watching. Slate heard her footsteps as she walked past the boards, then the creak as she climbed up onto the wagon seat and gave the driver directions.

It took a moment to settle themselves. Slate leaned back against Caliban. He felt a flash of surprise, then wrapped his arms around her. This too, it seemed, he was allowed.

Brenner studiously ignored them both.

"Do you think he's trustworthy?" murmured Slate, jerking her head in the direction of the driver.

The assassin studied the wall of crates. "If he isn't, I've got a gap here. I can get a crossbow bolt into his kidneys if he tries anything funny."

"I can hear you," said the driver.

"Then everybody's on the same page, aren't they?" said Ashes Magnus.

"Your friends get ruder every time, Magnus."

"Yes, but they pay more every time, too."

"There's that."

The wagon creaked and rattled through the streets. Learned Edmund clutched the box of Brother Amadai's notes to his chest.

Caliban rested his chin on top of Slate's head. *We are likely going to die soon. It is wrong to feel this gloriously happy.*

He feared for Slate, of course. He feared for them all. And yet... and yet...

I clearly do not believe that the gods will be so unkind as to separate us.

He knew that was foolishness. The gods would sacrifice Their followers without a second thought to achieve Their ends.

But Slate's back was warm against his chest and her hair smelled like soap. Last night she had smelled like sweat and sex and she had cried out his name as if he had been the only other creature in the world.

I will not fail again. I will not fail her. If I have learned nothing else, surely I have learned enough not to fail at this.

The ride to the safehouse did not last nearly long enough, so far as Caliban was concerned.

When they finally unloaded, they were in the Gnole Quarter. The driver accepted his money, did not look at them, and drove away.

"Is he reliable?" asked Slate.

"I've no idea," said Ashes. "Which is why we're walking from here to the actual safehouse."

Slate grinned. "You are a woman after my own heart, Mistress Magnus. And I hear you appreciate indexes, as well."

Ashes looped her arm through Slate's and whispered something to her that made the forger laugh out loud. The two of them strolled off together, followed closely by Learned Edmund.

Caliban looked at Brenner. Brenner looked at Caliban.

"Lead the way," said Caliban, gesturing.

"You just don't want me to have a clear shot at your back," said the assassin, as he followed after the others.

"You are correct," said the paladin, and brought up the rear.

CHAPTER 39

A gnole burrow was, Slate discovered, somewhere between a tent and a badger's den. The outer shell was an abandoned building, but once you stepped inside—and down—you found yourself in a maze of tunnels, winding through old basements and excavations down among the foundations.

The tunnels were divided up by blanket walls hung from the ceiling, making a number of small rooms, like cells in a beehive. Some held beds, some stood empty.

The central hub had an actual fireplace with a chimney that vented outside, and a round table with benches. It seemed like a compromise between the gnole architecture and a safehouse used by artificers. Even the beds in some of the rooms varied between recognizable mattresses and what looked like enormous rat's nests.

Their gear was waiting in the central hub. Slate picked a room with a human-style bed in it and dropped her packs inside the door.

She turned and saw Caliban standing in the hall. He had his own packs in his arms.

"Ah…" he said. "I…ah…if you would prefer…I know…"

He trailed off awkwardly.

"Do you want to sleep here with me?" asked Slate.

"Only if it is what you want."

"That wasn't the question."

He swallowed. "Very, very much."

Slate held the blanket door open like a tent-flap. "You already know that I snore."

He set his gear down inside, caught her up in his arms and kissed her.

They were both a bit mussed by the time they returned to the central room.

"You've got a week or two of grace here," said Ashes. "They'll bring food, too."

"They ought to," muttered Brenner. "We're paying them enough."

"They're good people, the gnoles," said Ashes. "Trustworthy, more or less, by which I mean that if you buy one off, they stay bought. And nobody thinks to ask them questions."

"I suppose we must talk to the grave-gnoles next," said Slate.

"The grave-gnoles don't come into this burrow," said Learned Edmund. "They have their own, I'm told."

"I thought Grimehug wouldn't speak to grave-gnoles," said Caliban.

"The little shy one was in here earlier," said Brenner. "She's agreed to bribe the grave-gnoles. Although I think they're mostly doing it because she asked them to."

"Sweet Lily," said Learned Edmund.

"Oh, Sweet Lily," said Slate, amused. "Does the fact that she's female not bother you, Learned Edmund?"

Learned Edmund glanced up, and she caught a flash of humor in his eyes. "Gnole pronouns are very complicated," he said. "More than I realized at first. All rag-and-bone gnoles are *she*. All job-gnoles are *he*. I don't know what the grave-gnoles are—they either don't get a specific pronoun or the pronoun is *they*, I can't tell."

Slate frowned. "You mean Grimehug's a job-gnole because he's male?"

"No, no." Learned Edmund steepled his fingers. "That's just it. The pronoun's a caste marker. It's the other way around—Grimehug's a he *because* he's a job-gnole."

Everyone tried to work this out in their heads.

Caliban got there first. "You mean's he's…"

"Female. He's borne several litters, apparently."

They stared at the dedicate. Slate began to laugh. "No wonder he wasn't concerned about my modesty!"

"You mean he's a *she?*" said Brenner.

"No!" said Learned Edmund. "Quite the opposite. He's a female gnole, but he's still *he*," Learned Edmund said. "Because *all* job-gnoles are hes. He'll be puzzled if you call him a she. Only rag-and-bone gnoles and hunt-gnoles are she. Job-gnoles are he. Garden-gnoles are 'our gnoles' rather like Brenner says 'our Slate' in that it's an affectionate possessive—"

Brenner draped an arm over Slate's shoulders and beamed. She grumbled at him.

Caliban, who was sitting quite close to her and very carefully not touching her, went absolutely expressionless. Slate felt a flash of mingled pleasure and irritation. Brenner, who missed very little, beamed even harder.

"Oh, and you'll like this, Caliban!" said Learned Edmund, who was completely oblivious. "It's hard to change castes, but possible. But there's another group that isn't casted, and they're the priests and the warriors. They're the same. Their priests are supposed to bite the darkness's tail, they say. They're all he, but it's a different he than a job-gnole. Honored-he, maybe. When he says 'he' about you, he means the honored-he, although you can't tell unless you look at his whiskers."

Slate rubbed her forehead. "Did you write this all down in case we die?"

"Oh yes. I think other people probably know this, some of them. Surely someone's talked to the gnoles before this!"

"People don't even talk to other people much," said Caliban.

"The gnoles *are* people," said Learned Edmund. "Very much so."

"You're right," said Caliban. "Humans, I should have said. I hope some—other human—has talked to them, but just in case, I'd make an extra copy of your notes."

Slate shook her head. "Learned Edmund, do you think we've offended Grimehug with our—err—ignorance?"

The dedicate coughed. "Ah. No. I think...well." He actually looked faintly embarrassed. "I asked, actually. Because...um...well, I fear I have not always been entirely tactful on the subject of female people..."

Slate's lips twitched and Brenner gazed at the ceiling. Caliban became very interested in a nonexistent spot on his gauntlets.

"But he said...ah...no. Well, he said *'humans can't smell.'*"

"He's said that to me, too."

Learned Edmund nodded. "I could be wrong, the Many-Armed God knows, but when I asked him to explain, I think what that means is that he isn't offended because we're...um...not able to tell when we're offending someone. We can't smell that they're insulted. So the gnoles don't take offense because…ah…we can't be expected to know proper manners."

"You mean he thinks we're not smart enough to know better," said Caliban.

Learned Edmund nodded. "I think the gnoles think we're not very bright," he said. "As far as they're concerned, we're very powerful and rather slow." He coughed again. "Grimehug, as near as I can tell, thinks of us as something between a smart horse and a very dim child."

Slate laughed. "Given the way things are going, I can't say he's wrong in that assessment…"

"So why are they helping us?" asked Brenner. "If we're not that smart?"

Learned Edmund shrugged. "I can only tell you what Grimehug says. He says he likes you, Slate. And me."

"I'd have to do a damn sight more than like someone to give them a safehouse and smuggle them into a factory full of clocktaurs," said Brenner.

"Yeah, but you don't actually like anyone," said Slate.

Brenner looked flattered. "Hey now, I always liked *you*."

"Liked," said Slate. "Uh-huh."

Caliban cleared his throat. "Learned Edmund? Your understanding of the gnoles is fascinating, but how are you doing with Brother Amadai's notes?"

The dedicate sighed. "Not well. Or too well, perhaps, but everything I learned is distressing. I will read something that seems like wild speculation, and then I will read something else and realize that it was true. Terrible, but true."

"What sort of things?" asked Slate.

Learned Edmund tapped the page in front of him. "For one thing, I don't think anyone knows how to turn the wonder-engine off."

"Okay," said Brenner. "That thing you just said? That was not a good thing."

"Grimehug will have to confirm for me," said Learned Edmund. "I could be wrong. I hope I am. But I think once they started the wonder-engine back up, they've been producing columns of clocktaurs, over and over, without stopping."

"I could have told you that," said Ashes Magnus. She leaned one heavy forearm on the table and lifted the page that Learned Edmund was studying. "Takes a little over a month for a column and then they send them out. They lost one in the river the first time, I hear—a column, not a clocktaur. Why?"

"And they haven't halted production at any point?" said Learned Edmund.

"Why would they?"

"Because the people who started the war are no longer in power," said Slate. It was falling into place in front of her. Boss Horsehead saying, *Those damn things.* Sparrow saying, *He's not the one in charge of them.*

She stood up and began pacing restlessly back and forth. Caliban scooted his chair in to give her room. "Look...dammit...I can almost see it in my head...the Dowager had a couple of spies here, all in the government, right? And the spies couldn't point to someone to say 'kill that person there.' So the Dowager figures that hey, this must be a really well-kept secret, something run out of the underworld, and so she sends a forger and an assassin to deal with it, right?"

"I'm with you so far," said Caliban.

"And we show up and start poking around and asking a lot of dumb questions and we figure out that the people who started the war aren't even in charge any more. And because we're idiots—"

"Speak for yourself, darlin'."

"—we start thinking 'oh, sure, now they just like having a war.' But what if we're wrong? What if there isn't anyone who really wants to keep the war going? What if they've just got all these damn clocktaurs and they can't shut the damn machine off?"

"Then why bother to attack people with them?" said Caliban. "You don't prolong a war just to use up your war-machines, do you?"

"You might," said Learned Edmund. He looked over at Ashes Magnus. "You might if you were afraid they would turn on you instead."

"Better to have them pointed out than pointed in," said Slate.

Ashes appeared to have stopped listening to them. She slowly set the page down, then pinched the bridge of her nose and closed her eyes.

"He figured it out," she said quietly. "The crazy bastard figured it out."

"Figured what out?" said Brenner. "Look, I'm just a simple murderer for hire, you'll have to explain it to me in small words."

"The point," said Ashes Magnus. "Brother Amadai figured out the point of the wonder-engine."

CHAPTER 40

"To make horrible monsters?" said Slate.

"Yes, but not quite like we thought. They were made to be an army. But we're using it wrong. Or at least differently."

The artificer picked up another sheet of paper and began writing in a swift, blocky hand. "Here. Once we get through the code, this is what we're left with. 'The souls of fallen warriors seek a last chance to serve. This the ancients knew. Give the dying to the engine and they will be reborn into ivory and glory.'"

"What does that mean?" asked Slate.

It was Caliban who spoke up. "It means the ancients took dying soldiers and fed them to the wonder-engine to make clocktaurs."

Slate felt her lips curl back from her teeth, the way Grimehug's did when something disgusted him. "Who the hell would do such a thing?"

The paladin sagged against the wall. "They probably volunteered."

"*What?!*"

Brenner shook his head in disgust.

Caliban stared straight ahead, not looking at any of them. "If you fell on the battlefield, but you knew that you could be put into the body of a clocktaur...a body that could strike a last, terrible blow at the enemy..."

"Should we be stuffing you into a clocktaur to go kill demons, paladin?"

"Shut *up*, Brenner."

"Not me," said Caliban. "I've been an unstoppable killing machine. I don't recommend it." His smile was a horrible, humorless thing to witness. "But I doubt you'd find any shortage of people willing. They don't know. You don't know unless you've been there. And no one listens. They'd tell themselves things about glory and service and they'd crawl into the machine on their knees if you let them."

Grimehug's ears were flat. "*Crazy* people," he said, and Slate suspected that there were nuances there that even Learned Edmund couldn't read.

"But they're not feeding it dying people," said Learned Edmund. "They're feeding it *corpses*."

Ashes Magnus nodded. "That's where I think this other bit comes in that you translated." She shuffled a paper across the table.

"A binding of demons?" The dedicate picked up the paper and frowned. "Well...oh, you're right! If we assume this page goes here, then things make more sense. But what does he want with demons?"

"There are demons in the clocktaurs," said Brenner. "Doesn't it make sense? The one trapped in the hills *said* there were."

"They're binding demons into the clocktaurs in place of souls?"

"Could they *do* that?" asked Slate.

She was watching Caliban and actually saw his lips start to form the word, "No," and then he stopped. He closed his mouth and looked at the ceiling for a minute instead.

He finally said "A year ago, I would have said no. They aren't supposed to inhabit unliving things. They can only enter something with a soul."

"And now?" said Slate.

He lifted his hands and let them drop. "They aren't supposed to die inside someone's soul, either. They aren't supposed to be able to bind each other. So I don't know if I can say, any more, what they're not supposed to do."

Ashes Magnus looked up from the notes spread across the table. "Die inside a soul?"

"It's a long story," said Caliban wearily. "And not a particularly relevant one, I don't think."

"Couldn't you tell if there was a demon inside one?" asked Brenner.

"How?" Caliban shook his head. "It's not like livestock. I don't know how a clocktaur is supposed to act, and I highly doubt any paladins have stood next to one long enough to attempt an exorcism."

Slate remembered the image again of Caliban standing in front of a clocktaur, sword raised, and felt dread wash over her.

"They don't speak in tongues, I don't think," he added. "Do they even have mouths?"

Grimehug shook his head. "Clocktaurs don't eat, big man. Or bite. Just smash."

"Isn't your little…err…friend…bothered by other demons?" pressed Brenner. "You said it was."

"My little *friend's* been laying low," said Caliban.

Ashes looked from one to the other as if she was a spectator at a bout. "Your little friend?"

"I was possessed," said Caliban. "I am now rather less possessed."

Slate knew Caliban well enough now to see the muscles in his jaw tighten as he waited for Ashes to press the matter.

The artificer said "Oh. Huh. Well, it happens," and went back to her notes.

I regret enormously that I did not meet Ashes Magnus before we were going to go off and die in a wonder-engine. I wonder if she teaches classes in how to be unimpressed?

"Mistress Slate," said Learned Edmund, "can you decipher this set of notes? My skill is failing me."

He slid a sheet of vellum across the table. Slate picked it up. It was covered in Brother Amadai's by-now familiar handwriting, the letters run together so tightly that the words looked like single, incomprehensible glyphs. "Oof. What a mess."

Caliban put his hands on her shoulders and began to rub them. Slate started to think that it was worth keeping a paladin around just for that. *If I can break him of acting like an honor guard…no, wait, dammit, going to die very shortly. Damn, damn, damn.*

"Was he trying to write this in code too?" Caliban asked, peering over the top of her head at the page.

"Doubt it," said Slate. She began copying letters down, one at a time, in her own neat hand. "At a guess, he was writing very fast and sloppy because he knew what he meant, and the notes were mostly for himself, to jog his memory later."

"Which would mean he never expected to send these to the temple," said Learned Edmund, a bit sadly.

"He might have planned to transcribe the notes later," said Ashes. She flicked another sheet aside. "These illustrations, though…"

All of them leaned over the table to look.

"Looks painful," drawled Brenner.

A man hung suspended, apparently impaled on long pointed poles. The poles were wrapped in chains. "What do those notes say?" asked Brenner, pointing to a scrawl alongside the drawing.

Slate frowned down at the lines of text. "Gods of scribes and fools have mercy…"

"Bad?" asked Caliban.

"His handwriting? Yes. What it says? Ah…something something the Many-Armed…something…is a…not sure if that's a T or a Y… will see all things through the…that's probably 'eyes'…" She sat back. "That's it. The rest of this page is him wiping his pen to get the ink blobs off."

"What does it mean?" said Caliban.

"How the hell should I know? I'm a forger. Magnus?"

Ashes Magnus shook her head. "I don't even know if this has anything to do with the wonder-engine. It's not up to his usual standards of illustration. It may be an idea he had, or a dream, or just a doodle."

"If only we could ask him…" said Learned Edmund.

Strained silence followed.

"Learned Edmund," said Caliban gently, "I am afraid he must be dead by now."

The dedicate sighed. "I…yes. I know. I had not wanted to believe it, but when we rescued Mistress Slate…" He closed his eyes. "This city. This terrible city. I did not know that life could be held so cheaply."

Caliban and Brenner, who had ended quite a number of lives last night, exchanged a look that Slate couldn't read and didn't want to.

She straightened up, rubbing her back. "Well. I gotta stand up or I'm going to have a permanent hunch." She pushed the chair in and wandered off to find where the gnoles had built the privy.

She was heading back, trying to decipher the twists and turns of the burrow, when Brenner said in her ear: "Bad idea, darlin'."

"What, going to the privy?"

The assassin shook his head. "Don't play dumb. You know perfectly well what I mean."

Slate sighed. She'd hoped, somewhat foolishly, that they could get into the warehouse and thus all probably die horribly *before* she had to have it out with Brenner.

Apparently the assassin was determined to have his say before then. Although at least he'd had the decency to ambush her on the way *back* from using the facilities. The conversation wouldn't have been improved by a full bladder.

"Let's get this over with," she said, stepping into another room of the gnole-warren. It was hard to tell what it was used for—spare bedroom, broom closet, extra dining room. The gnoles liked all rooms to be nearly identical, presumably so they could change their function as needed.

"He's a paladin," said Brenner.

"We've been over this."

Brenner shook his head. "You're gonna break him."

This was not the angle that Slate had expected. She blinked at him. "You've been telling me that he was gonna go berserk and chop me up into pieces! Whose side are you on?"

Brenner grinned, though there wasn't much humor in it. "I'm on my own side, as you ought to know, darlin'. Not yours, not his." He considered. "Well, more yours than his, obviously."

"Thanks. I think."

The assassin leaned against the wall, arms folded. "I'm sayin' this badly. Look, our fine paladin went sniffing around temples, looking for some god to take him, didn't he? And then he stopped. And now he's so wrapped up in you that he'd have gone charging into the Grey Church barehanded if he thought it'd help."

Slate stared at the ceiling.

Brenner drummed his fingers on his bicep. "Some men like to be used. Our paladin more than most, I'd say. He couldn't get a god to do it, fine. He found somebody else."

"You're saying he wants me to be his *god?*"

Brenner smirked. "Someone to worship, anyhow. And he gets to bed you in the bargain, which is a pretty sweet deal, religiously speaking."

Slate threw her hands in the air. "I don't need this right now."

He laughed. "Darlin'. I know you. You're gonna fall off that pedestal before he's got you all the way on. Might break him even worse when you do. Just be careful."

"Oh, and I suppose *you'd* be the safe, sane option? The hired killer?"

Brenner examined his nails.

"Brenner…"

He reached out and tapped her cheek with one finger. "I know what you're like. I may not be pretty, but there's nothing you'll do that'll ever disappoint me."

"We're all gonna die," said Slate, swatting at his hand. "Probably in short order. This is pointless."

"Speak for yourself, darlin'. I've got a trick or two left up my sleeve."

"Then feel free to yell at my corpse about how you warned me," snapped Slate, and stomped off to see if Learned Edmund and Magnus had had any more luck with the translations.

CHAPTER 41

"Sweet Lily reported back. The grave-gnoles will come tomorrow," said Learned Edmund. "Will that be enough time to prepare?"

"Prepare what?" said Slate, leaning against the wall. "I don't have a plan. Does anyone else have a plan?"

"Lots," drawled Brenner. "None of 'em will do any good, but I got 'em."

"I believe that we are, as my lady says, 'winging it,'" said Caliban.

My lady. That's a new one.

Do I like that or is that getting too close to 'my liege' territory?

Brenner raised a derisive eyebrow at her. Slate decided it was worth it, just to spite him.

Learned Edmund was still turning the strange drawing over in his hands. "Mistress Slate?"

"Eh?"

"The cascading code from the journal. What if you apply it here?"

Slate frowned. "There's not enough to work with there, is there?"

"Will you help me try?"

She sat down beside him. "Of course."

It took them twenty or thirty minutes, working letter by letter. Brenner got bored and began rolling cigarettes and lining them up on the table in front of him.

"The other...debris?" said Slate finally. "Delivery?"

"Device," said Learned Edmund. "It must be device. Something about *the other device.*"

"Oh god, not another one," said Ashes, putting her face in her hands.

"Isn't one enough?" asked Caliban.

"I don't understand," said Slate. "These were his own personal notes. Why would he even bother hiding something in code? Even just a fragment?"

Learned Edmund shook his head. "I don't know. I don't even know where this page goes. It was only a guess to apply the code." He chewed on his lower lip. "Could it be an artifact?"

"Like the wonder-engine?"

"No, no, an artifact of the *code*. It's a letter substitution, and we're guessing at some of the letters. We could be making up information that isn't really there."

"It's possible," said Slate. "I'd like to say that I'm better than that, but..." She braced her forehead against her fingers. "Half of a good forgery is knowing what people *want* to see. I won't swear that I'm not wanting to see something here."

"Darlin', if you want another of those wonder-engines lying around, you're even more of a glutton for punishment than the paladin."

Slate made a rude gesture. Caliban put his hand on Slate's thigh under the table.

"Aaand that's all I think I'm good for tonight," said Slate. "If I am seeing things...oh, I don't know. I don't suppose it matters. We're still riding in with the grave-gnoles whether there's one wonder-engine or a dozen."

"I will find some shrouds," said Ashes Magnus. "You'll need those. Otherwise you should all get some sleep." She paused, looked Caliban up and down, and then said "Well, eventually."

Learned Edmund looked baffled. Brenner made a rude noise, not entirely under his breath.

Caliban actually blushed, which, so far as Slate was concerned, was almost worth the price of admission.

"Good night, all." It seemed like a dumb thing to say for her last night on earth, but she couldn't come up with anything better, so she waved.

Caliban followed her down the hallway. For a minute, she was afraid that she was going to have to coax him back into the bedroom again, but he held the blanket door up to let her pass and was stripping out of his armor almost before she turned around.

Good. Good.

It's about damn time something went right.

Slate had wondered any number of times what Caliban would be like in her bed.

The first time probably didn't count. That had been a haze of relief and lust and two people falling into each other's arms because somehow they were not dead.

It was very, very good, don't get me wrong, but when you're starving, any meal is a feast.

What would he be like when he had his choice? Ruthless like Brenner? Careful? God help her, chivalrous? Or perhaps simply a Knight-Champion, used to being serviced like a pedigree stallion when he came back from slaying demons?

Slate was starting to think she'd never find out because it seemed like he was almost frightened to touch her. She stripped off her shirt with no assistance and looked up to see him watching her.

"Well?" she said.

He stroked his fingertips up her arms, barely touching her skin. His eyes were dark and unreadable in the candlelight. He ran a fingertip over her collarbone and she wanted to scream from frustration, but she was a little afraid that he might run out of the room if she did.

"It's all right," she said. "I won't break." *Dear god, if Boss Horsehead didn't break me, you certainly can't...*

He set his lips next to her ear and whispered "I might."

It jolted her harder than his touch had done.

Two words. Two words and I'm ready to go right now. I don't even care if we make it to the bed. God help me. Perhaps it's just as well we haven't been doing this. I'd have been screwing him up against walls every ten minutes.

She shoved him backward toward the bed, determined to make his eyes roll back in his head before she was done.

He yielded to her touch, but only for a moment, and only until she set to work in earnest.

"Careful!" he said, catching her wrists and pulling her hands away. "Much more of that, and we'll both be done before we've started."

"Would that be so bad?"

He chuckled. "If we are possibly going to die tomorrow, at least let me take my time tonight."

Slate raised her eyebrows. *Well, well, well...*

In the end, the answer to how this particular paladin made love seemed to be that he treated her as if she were holy.

This would, under normal circumstances, have been infuriating, not least because it proved Brenner right. Slate did not wish to be worshipped, she wished to be bedded, preferably with skill but failing that, with enthusiasm.

Then he used the voice.

"Let me know you," he said, running his hands over her skin. "Let me see all of you."

"Not much to see," she said, feeling awkward in the face of so much sincerity.

"You're wrong," he said. "Also, beautiful. But wrong."

"But—"

He kissed her.

When a ridiculously handsome man decides he thinks you're beautiful, maybe you should just shut up and enjoy it instead of trying to talk him out of it.

So they left the lamp on, and Caliban mapped out her skin with his fingertips, murmuring words that did not matter nearly so much as the tone in which he said them.

Slate began to think that there was something to be said for being worshipped after all.

He brushed his lips over each scar, even the ugly ones, like the knotted line on her ribs, earned when a rain gutter had given way and dumped her unceremoniously onto the ground. He kissed each of them, ignoring only the one scar that both of them shared, the welt under the tattooed teeth. That one, she was happy enough to leave alone.

He lingered over the blotched acid marks that had left her wedding ring scarred onto her right hand, a brooding line between his eyes.

"It's nothing," she said. "It was a long time ago." Meaning the marriage, as much as the scar.

"Did you burn it off?"

"Good heavens, no. Spilled the acid on it and the ring saved everything underneath. Had to have a jeweler cut it off, though. It was more than time." She shrugged. "It had been over for years. I just…hadn't gotten around to it."

He kissed each scarred knuckle in turn. "You are beautiful," he said again, into her palm, and she believed that he believed.

The only other words she remembered came much later. "There?" he asked, his fingers moving across her flesh, and Slate's own voice sounded very thin and hoarse in her ears as she said "Yes—there—*please*—"

"Shh…" he whispered a moment later, gathering her up in his arms and muffling her cries against his shoulder. "Shhh…"

Later, she'd remember that they were in a gnole burrow and the walls were not so much thin as nonexistent. At the time, she thought nothing of the sort and perhaps would not have cared if she did.

"I need you," she said in his ear, and he nodded and there were no more words.

Probably he meant to take his time there as well. But Slate was in no mood for that any longer. She caught his hips and set a bruising rhythm and after that it went quick and hard and he, too, forgot about the walls.

Slate lay there, feeling warm and sated and a bit sore, feeling Caliban breathing heavily atop her.

Eventually, he propped himself up on his elbows and looked down at her. His eyes were shadowed, but even the shadows were warm and kind.

"Yeah," she said. "Yeah, that'll work."

He started laughing almost soundlessly, which she felt all along her ribcage.

"What? I'm not good at pillow talk!"

"Never change," he said, kissing her forehead.

She thought about telling him that she probably wouldn't live long enough to get a chance, but it seemed like a waste of a perfectly wonderful afterglow, so she didn't. Instead she stretched out alongside him and wondered what, if anything, she should say.

Hey, Brenner says I'm kinda your god now and it's a bad idea.

No. Definitely *not.*

I think I'm in love with you.

Even worse.

Before she could think of anything that made better pillow talk, she drifted off to sleep.

In the morning, the grave-gnoles came to take them away.

CHAPTER 42

"Shrouds," said Ashes. "I'm wrapping live people in shrouds. Of course I am. What a week this has turned out to be."

"You've got to leave my mouth clear," warned Slate, "or I'll be the only corpse in the place having an allergy attack."

"I'll see what I can do," said Ashes. "You allergic to the gnolls?"

"Strangely enough, no." Slate watched the artificer lift a shroud and drape it artfully across her face. She closed her eyes. "Seems like Grimehug's the only thing I'm *not* allergic to."

Learned Edmund made a thoughtful noise. Ashes wound the cloth, leaving a gap over Slate's lips, tucking it tighter across the body. "You, we're going to have to drop under a real werkblight corpse. You're breathing too obviously. Fortunately your grave-gnole buddies brought a couple. Now, I just need to—oh, drat that Edmund boy, where'd he go?"

"He said that he needed to write down a thought," said Caliban.

"Gah. Fine. This isn't blood, incidentally, it's oversteeped tea with beet juice. I don't keep blood just lying around."

"That's a great comfort," said Slate, feeling liquid splatter around her.

"All right, handsome, your girlfriend's ready for the body cart."

"I feel like this is warping our relationship in some fashion," said Slate, as Caliban hefted her in his arms and laid her down in the gnole cart in the courtyard.

He snorted. "I am trying not to think about that, thank you."

"What, our relationship?"

"No, that you're currently wrapped in a burial shroud and I'm about to drop a corpse on top of you."

"Oh, *that.*"

"You're not bothered about having a dead body on you?"

"I'm much more worried about having a tattoo eat me."

"You could catch werkblight."

"My dear paladin, I don't think we're going to live long enough for the werkblight to be an issue."

He sighed, bent down and kissed her. Granted that all Slate could see through the wrapping was light and dark, it looked like a dark blob bending over her, but she figured it out quickly enough when his lips touched hers.

It was a pretty good kiss. His tongue flicked across her lips. She wondered vaguely if he was getting tea with added beet juice on him, and then wondered, much less vaguely, if this was going to be the last kiss they ever had.

"Hey, Caliban?" she said, when they broke apart.

"Yes?"

"If they figure it out and stab us while we're on the body cart, or we get split up or whatever…"

He was very still. Slate had no idea what she had been about to say, except that it seemed like she should say something.

She settled on, "I wish we'd had more time."

His fingers curved against her face. She could feel their warmth even through the cloth.

"We aren't dead yet," he said.

"Yeah, well. Go get your shroud on and let's hope the guards don't realize that."

Slate named the corpse on top of her 'Frederick.' It seemed rude, given that they were becoming increasingly well acquainted, not to think of the body as a person.

Welp, Frederick, guess it's you and me now…

Frederick, of course, had nothing to say. Given her traveling companions of late, that was actually somewhat restful.

Brenner knows how to be quiet, he just doesn't always choose to be. Learned Edmund is…well, Learned Edmund.

Caliban…

It was obviously not fair comparing Frederick to Caliban, although the paladin would probably be the first to admit that Frederick was less likely to say something stupid.

He was heavy, though. In Slate's experience, corpses usually were, so she wasn't sure if Frederick had actually been a weighty individual or if any body thrown on top of her would be equally uncomfortable.

Any body. *Hah. I am hilarious.*

The grave-gnole cart hit a bump and Slate's tailbone bounced off the wooden bottom of the cart. She gritted her teeth over a yelp.

Frederick's not yelping. Be like Frederick.

She concentrated on breathing through her teeth. Frederick had not yet started to smell of death, which was good, but he smelled strongly of Frederick, which in this case was garlic and sweat.

Well, I have no idea how he died. I don't get to judge. Maybe he came out really well, considering.

The grave-gnoles trundled onward, presumably toward the Clockwork District. Slate surreptitiously stretched her foot, which was falling asleep, and hoped that no one was able to see it.

Cover for me, Frederick.

It was probably safe. Nobody stared at body carts for very long, and if things moved, they usually assumed that it was the motion over the cobblestones. Presumably they would stop before reaching the door to the warehouse, and Slate would be exceedingly motionless.

Great-grandmother, if ever you loved me, please don't let your stupid rosemary power go off right now.

Not that rosemary wouldn't be an improvement on garlic, but if she started sneezing, everything was over. Slate did not want the mission to end because of her allergies, and there was no Brenner here to politely strangle her to keep her quiet.

Brenner was, in fact, in the body cart behind her, as far as she knew. Slate thought she and Frederick were in the first one, with Caliban bringing up the rear.

I suppose that means that if I do start sneezing and give away the game, the other two can get away. That's good.

Which likely meant, assuming that the guards didn't kill her outright, yet another daring rescue by the Paladin and Assassin Traveling Road Show.

That would be awkward. Caliban would rescue anyone from anything, of course, but Brenner was bound to get sarcastic about it if it kept happening.

Also, there was the small matter of gratitude. One rescue was probably payment for her having rescued both of them from the rune, but if it kept happening…well. She'd be grateful. Really grateful. She wouldn't even know how to express that kind of gratitude. What did you *do* with all that emotion?

Swear fealty like Caliban had to her, maybe. Brenner would find that *hilarious*.

The cart hit another bump and Frederick slid an inch to one side, compressing her ribcage until she almost couldn't breathe.

Well, I'm not supposed to be breathing anyway.

She was starting to get light-headed. Were the gnoles taking the long way around the city?

Far more of a concern than the sneezing, truly, was that the gnoles might sell them out. They had a longstanding business arrangement with the clocktaur's keepers. Why would they jeopardize that for a few humans?

As near as Slate could tell, the answer was "because Sweet Lily asked them to." And Sweet Lily had asked because Grimehug had asked, and because Sweet Lily liked Learned Edmund.

And Grimehug…well. Grimehug was playing a deep game, that was obvious. But he seemed to be playing it for his people. It would have been very easy indeed for Grimehug to have sold them out at any number of turns. All he had to do was not relay the information about where Slate was being held, and that would have been the end of her.

Bit late to worry about that now, isn't it? You've put yourself entirely in his people's hands. Or paws.

She still didn't fully know what his goals were. She had a sneaking suspicion that the gnoles had decided that the clocktaurs were bad for business and wars between human cities were bad for gnoles. But that was only a guess. Grimehug could have been thinking anything behind his eyes.

Humans can't smell.

At the moment, she was smelling more than she wanted to. Mostly garlic. And a whiff of…

Oh hell.

Rosemary.

We must be getting close. That's it. It's just raising the alarm. Slate's eyes were already closed, but she squeezed them shut under the shroud, concentrating savagely on not sneezing, on lying absolutely quiet…

You've alerted me. I'm alerted. Please don't give me away. Please.

The gnole-cart stopped. The front bumped downward as the grave-gnoles set down their poles.

Slate breathed through her open mouth, tiny sips of air across her tongue. Her lungs screamed for a larger breath. Her nose was dripping and the fact that she could not wipe it was a torture worse than anything Boss Horsehead's professional had done to her.

She heard creaks of wood, a dragging sound on stone. Then the grave-gnoles picked up their poles again and the cart bumped forward.

Was that the gate? Was that all there was to it? Did nobody check?

She could practically hear Caliban in her head yelling—"If these guards were under my command, I would have them up on charges! This is negligence!"

Still, what are they going to do? Get down and poke us? Expose themselves to werkblight just to make sure the dead are really dead?

So it was the werkblight that got you, Frederick. I really am exposed now.

Frederick said nothing, but Slate had to think that lying under a werkblight corpse, even for only half an hour or so, was an excellent way to make sure you were exposed.

Then again… *'No gnoles allowed' the innkeeper had said. 'They carry werkblight'. And Grimehug slept at the foot of my bed for weeks. He'd still be there, except that Caliban's been taking up valuable real estate.*

Well, and we're in a gnole burrow at last. He probably has his real friends and family to dogpile with.

You'd think we'd all have it by now. Or maybe we do, and there's a long time before it manifests.

Now there was a pleasant thought.

Oh well, as long as it holds off until after we get to the bottom of this…
She hadn't lied to Caliban. She just couldn't get too worked up about
potential plague when there were guards, presumably not that far away,
who would fill her full of arrows if they could.

The echoes changed as the grave-gnoles entered a building. Slate
had only an instant of warning before the cart upended and she and
Frederick were dumped unceremoniously onto something lax and
lumpy and…

It's more bodies. I know it's more bodies.

Slate went as bonelessly limp as she could. She couldn't quite
suppress a hiss of air out of her lungs, but hopefully any watchers
would think that was just the sound of bodies settling.

On the one hand, she was now draped over Frederick instead of the
other way around and could breathe.

On the other hand, the other bodies smelled a lot worse than
Frederick.

None of them were in full-on rot, or Slate would have lost her lunch
and secrecy be damned, but there was definitely a scent of heavy decay.

*Thank the gods it's been cool lately instead of hot, or this would be really
bad.*

She waited.

Another gnole-cart entered the room and was dumped out. Brenner's, hopefully, but if so, the assassin was keeping quiet. Slate couldn't
see anything through her shroud and she couldn't tell if the sounds of
breathing were from the grave-gnoles or if there was another guard in
the room as well.

The carts ground away on their creaking wooden wheels. The third
cart was emptied out. Something landed with a clatter of metal.

It's got to be Caliban. Sword and armor and all the rest.

She listened to the gnole-cart being drawn away. A door closed.
Silence.

It seemed like three people listening intently should make a sound,
or perhaps the opposite of a sound. But there was nothing.

Are there any guards?

Are Brenner and Caliban even here? Did we get separated?

Are we all waiting for someone else to speak up?

Slate sneezed.

She got less than a half-second of warning on it, not enough to muffle it. She just sneezed and that meant that she might as well sit up and yank the shroud off her eyes because she was pretty obviously not a corpse.

"Well," drawled Brenner, "I guess that means you made it too, Slate darlin'."

"Are there any guards?" She clawed at the shroud. Ashes had done entirely too good a job wrapping it.

"I'm not seeing any."

"I don't believe there are any in this room," said Caliban softly.

"Looks like we all made it," said Brenner.

Slate finally got her shroud off in time to see Caliban extract himself from a pile of bodies.

The room was large, with two barn-sized doors where the carts entered and left. The floor was packed earth and the bodies lay piled carelessly in a shallow trench that ran in a semi-circle along the back wall. A smaller door was set in the wall behind the trench.

Brenner adjusted his knives. Slate wiped her nose. The paladin signed a benediction over the corpses beside him.

She cleared her throat. It was probably stupid, but…

"Can you do that for this guy, too?"

Brenner snorted. Caliban, though, came and stood beside her. "This one?"

"Yeah." And then, even though he hadn't asked for an explanation: "We, uh, rode over together."

The paladin nodded and signed the Dreaming God's benediction over Frederick.

"Thanks," said Slate.

"If we're all done wasting time, there's only one way farther in," said Brenner, gesturing to the small door. "It's locked." He glanced at Slate. "You or me, darlin'?"

"Me," said Slate. "You just get ready to stab anybody who comes through."

"With pleasure."

The lock was the sort of thing purchased by people who have been ordered to put a lock on a door, and are more concerned about obeying orders than about anyone actually showing up to pick said lock. Slate popped it open in the space of a couple of measured breaths, even though she had to stop and sneeze afterward.

"Rosemary?" asked Caliban, handing her a handkerchief.

"Coming from somewhere inside, I think," said Slate, wiping her nose. "But whether it means something or whether it's because there's clocktaurs or an active wonder-engine, don't ask me."

Brenner eased the door open a fraction and peered through the crack.

"One guard," he murmured. "Down at the end of the hall. We're on a corner here. We can slip out without him seeing us, if somebody can manage not to clank."

"I'll do my best."

The paladin's footfalls sounded incredibly loud to Slate, but somehow the guard didn't turn his head. He didn't look much like a guard at all. Slate couldn't see any weapons. He wore a stained apron and heavy leather gloves.

Now why do I suspect his job is to drag the bodies somewhere, not to make sure the bodies are all dead...?

Brenner was the last one through. He eased the door shut again behind him. His feet made no sound at all.

They crept around the corner, out of sight. Slate made a mental note to teach Caliban how to sneak, if they survived.

Can't do much with the armor, I suppose...although there's a few clinking bits that we could probably trade out for carved wood or muffle with some cloth...at least there's no twigs to step on here. But seriously, I could take this man up on a rooftop and he would sound like a herd of wild horses.

Well, it probably wasn't his fault. You didn't meet that many thieves who specialized in breaking and entering who were six-foot-plus and had shoulders like an ox.

Let's see, I've known…what, two? Gemmy the Wall and Hard Payne. Gemmy was even taller and he sure didn't miss any meals, and he still moved like a dancer. So it can be done…

This train of thought got her down the corridor. The problem with sneaking into places was that it was an excruciating combination of nerve-wracking and incredibly dull.

They slunk along the hallway, listening, moving at a snail's pace. There were drag marks on the floor, a hard, waxy-looking grime that spoke of repeated use and half-hearted cleanings. Some of the drag marks were dark brown and rusty-looking.

She pointed to one that was so obviously blood that it might as well have had a label. Brenner nodded. Caliban looked grim.

Finally, they fetched up against another door. This one wasn't even locked. Slate tried it and rolled her eyes.

"How are people not breaking into here *constantly?*" she whispered to Brenner.

"Maybe there's nothing worth lifting."

"Suppose it's hard to shove a clocktaur under your coat."

They opened the door very quietly and stepped into a vast room, larger even than the Grey Church. Like the Church, it had been excavated downward so that the walls fell away around them.

Catwalks crossed the emptiness and metal grates creaked underfoot, and finally, *finally*, somebody saw them.

CHAPTER 43

Slate's nerves were keyed so tightly that seeing someone turn and gape at them was almost a relief. At least she could stop waiting for it to happen now.

The man who spotted them was also wearing a leather apron. He was sitting on the edge of the metal platform, back to the door. When the metal creaked as they stepped onto it, he turned his head, saying "It isn't time yet, the last one's not gone down—"

And then he stopped and stared at them.

What he thought about the trio facing him, no one would ever find out. Brenner stepped forward, grabbed his hair, hauled his head back, and slit his throat in one cool, professional motion.

Slate winced. There was a lot of blood. There always was when somebody did that.

Brenner glanced over the side of the metal platform, then nodded and pushed the aproned man over. Slate heard the body hit wooden boards, a few scratching sounds…then nothing.

"We might have immobilized him," said Caliban softly. "Tied him up. He did not look like a guard or a soldier."

"You know," said Brenner, "his job was stuffing corpses into *that*. So I'm not feeling a lot of remorse right now." He pointed over the edge of the grate.

She looked over.

On that side of the platform, someone had rigged a crude wooden hopper. The hopper fed into a chute, which fed into a twisted mass of ivory.

It was so large that it took a moment for her eyes to make sense of it. It looked more like a landscape than a face. But once she saw that the hole the chute led to was a mouth, it all snapped into focus. A gaping mouth with teeth like bone stalagmites, eyes screwed up tight. Not a human, this time, but some monstrous hybrid of wolf and sow, muzzle corrugated into a snarl.

It was the wonder-engine, of course.

Its forepaws were stretched forward, its back humped upward. If it had a tail, it was tucked between its legs.

Sheltered underneath the wonder-engine stood a vast mass of ivory and gears.

Clocktaurs.

Three on each side, the ones in front nearly complete, the ones in back looking oddly unfinished. They were not moving, but the crust of ivory gears moved and shifted and ratcheted back and forth, so the impression was of living, squirming motion.

"Dear god," whispered Caliban, swallowing hard. He sounded shaken, and that bothered Slate almost as much as the wonder-engine did. This was an engine fueled by demons and of all of them, Caliban was the one who should have been most able to deal with it.

"It's building them underneath," said Brenner.

Slate grimaced. "It's not building them," she said. "It's nursing them."

She could tell when the assassin and the paladin both saw it too, because they both grunted, one on each side of her, making twin sounds of disgust.

"It's a machine," said Brenner. "How can it nurse anything?"

"How do the clocktaurs walk?" asked Slate. "How does any of it work? It's a damnable abomination from the damnable ancients, that's how."

"I like the ones that turn pears into gold better."

"I don't think they would have sent us to destroy one of those."

They stared at it. It was gigantic, far bigger than the wonder-engine they had seen in the Vagrant Hills. The notion of destroying it seemed laughable. Where would they even start?

What are we going to do? Have Brenner throw knives at it? Tell Caliban to hit it with his sword a few times?

Slate shook her head in disbelief. How had they been so arrogant as to think that they could do anything? The civilization that made this had been vast and terrible, powerful enough to put their dead into machines that could destroy nearly anything. What could three people possibly do against it?

She put out a hand blindly and caught Caliban's forearm. He reached over and squeezed her fingers, carefully since he was wearing gauntlets.

A grip from metal and leather should not have been comforting, but at this point, Slate would take what she could get.

"What do we do now?" she said. "Go home and tell the Dowager it was impossible?"

The tattoo did not like that idea. Slate slapped her bicep irritably. "Would you rather we throw ourselves into the thing one at a time and let them make clocktaurs out of us?"

And now I'm yelling at my own arm. This is not helping.

"There's something up there," said Brenner, pointing.

Slate hadn't looked up since she saw the wonder-engine. Her gaze followed Brenner's arm, past a jumble of catwalks, to a strange shape.

"It looks like a pinecone," she said, frowning. "Or a flower."

"Doubt it's any one of those, darlin', but we might as well take a look."

"It looks like one of Brother Amadai's drawings," rumbled Caliban.

The catwalks ran back and forth like...what had the grave-gnoles called them? Metal spiderwebs?

We were close. They must have seen through the door, but not into the room itself.

They seemed haphazardly placed, as if they had been installed during the excavation and no one had bothered to move them. Fortunately, most of them had railings. The trio climbed up multiple ladders, watching for guards, and yet the whole room was eerily silent except for their footsteps.

Why would they need *guards? What could mere humans possibly do to that?*

What human guards could stand to watch that thing for long?

It took some time to find the sequence of ladders that would lead to the catwalk nearest the strange object. When they reached it at last, it became obvious that of them, Caliban had been the closest to correct.

It was a man.

He hung suspended over the wonder-engine on iron chains, spread-eagled. He seemed to have too many arms, and it took Slate a moment to realize that there were strange ivory spines coming out of his back, the size of elephant tusks, hooked around toward the front so that they rose like arms. Each spine ended in a carved hand. The hands seemed to be the same material as the wonder-engine, which perhaps explained why they had too many fingers, or maybe explained nothing at all.

His eyes were gone. Slate stared into the empty hollows and thought, *He spent too long in the crow cage, they got his eyes,* and had to shake herself to dislodge the thought.

"Poor bastard," she said, looking up at him. He looked as if he had died in pain.

Clockwork was still moving on his back, the restless, ratcheting motion of gears like those on the clocktaurs themselves. Were they doing something? Was it still alive, or was it a living machine, growing pistons and levers the way that an animal might grow scabs and scars?

"Was he controlling the clocktaurs, do you think?" asked Caliban.

Slate spread her hands helplessly. "Brother Amadai labeled this one as 'the other device' but…hell, I don't know."

"If he was, then who's controlling them now?" asked Brenner.

Slate leaned over the edge of the catwalk, trying to see what connected the corpse to the wonder-engine. Had it been severed? Were there others? "I'm really not sure—"

The corpse moved.

It rose in a ratcheting motion, like machinery, the whole clockwork mass rising a few inches, until it was level with the catwalk. The head, impossibly, turned toward Slate.

"Don't…talk about me…as if…I'm not…here…" breathed the man impaled by ivory.

CHAPTER 44

Oh shit oh shit oh shit

Slate flung herself backward in sheer primitive terror. Her back hit Caliban and she stopped there. He caught her with one arm and held the sword across them both, which would have annoyed Slate except that having a sword between her and the godawful spidery corpse thing seemed like a *really good idea.*

"*That's* not good," drawled Brenner.

There was something steadying about how he said it. Assassins were hard people to impress. Brenner sounded as if he had discovered that he was out of cigarettes.

The corpse dangled on the ivory spikes. It ratcheted up on the chains a few more notches and rotated to look eyelessly at Brenner.

Brenner curled his lip back in disgust.

"Did Brother Amadai do this to you?" asked Slate.

It flexed on the end of its chain, turning back and forth as if looking between them.

Then it laughed.

"Oh god," said Slate. She put a hand over her mouth. She knew what was coming next and she wanted very much to be wrong.

The corpse's laughter was airless and gurgling, as if the ivory spikes were forcing its ribcage up, over and over, not caring how it tore the body up inside.

"Amadai...yessss..." The voice came out but the forced, dead laughter didn't stop. "...I know...that name...I am...I *was*...Amadai..."

"There's a demon in him," said Caliban.

"Tell me something I don't know, paladin," said Brenner.

Caliban glanced at him sharply. "How did you know that?"

The assassin waved his hand in Amadai's direction. "Because this is *not* normal human shit!"

"...yeah, okay, that's fair," said Slate.

"Demonsss..." It seemed to consider that. "I have...I am...I control..."

244

It twisted on the chains for a moment longer, perhaps seeking the correct words.

"Are you controlling the clocktaurs?" asked Caliban.

He was using the voice. Slate didn't know what that was costing him and couldn't begin to guess.

"Yesss…." It slowly oriented on Caliban. "I control…them. Yess."

"We found many of your writings, Brother Amadai. It seems that you learned something extraordinary."

"Yes!" The corpse bobbed up and down on the end of the chain. "Yes! The books…my booksss…I could not write down what…I have learned…so much…so much…"

"A scribe could learn much listening to you," suggested Caliban. His voice was soothing and trustworthy. His free hand was closed over Slate's arm so tightly that the gauntlet was leaving red impressions on her skin, but she barely felt it.

"Yesss…."

"Have you bound demons into the clocktaurs in place of souls?"

Again that dead, gutting laughter. "Yess…oh yess…the soulss will not obey…but I was wiser than the ancientss…demons *alwaysss* obey…"

The corpse smiled. Slate watched its lips rictus apart and thought, *Well, if I live through this, my nightmares will be amazing.*

"They trapped demons…" whispered Amadai. "The ancients… They trapped them in thisss…But they had no godsss. They did not use them. I have used them."

"And you put them in the clocktaurs and sent them to fight," said Caliban. He apparently noticed what he was doing to Slate's arm and stepped back from her, eyes wide. "I'm sor—"

She shook her head at him and whispered "It's fine! Keep it talking!"

"But…"

She jerked her chin at the body and gave him a meaningful look.

Fortunately, the creature did not seem to have noticed. "Yess…. wass that not extraordinary…?" Amadai's corpse twisted on the chain. The ivory spines moved up and down like an insect's legs. "Two devic-esss…but I have made them work…together…"

Caliban nodded to her, turning his attention back to Amadai. "Can you call the clocktaurs back?" he asked, in that gentle confessor's voice.

"Whhy....would I...?"

"You could end the war. You could save many lives."

"Mortal...livesss...no longer...concern me..." Amadai smiled more broadly still, and the edges of the corpse's lips split open, revealing pink, bloodless meat beneath. "I am...become...god..."

"Shit," muttered Brenner. "That's it. Once they think they're gods, there's nothing for it but a knife."

Slate was torn between a desire to shush him and an intense desire to agree. She settled for backing away.

"You are *nothing*..." whispered Amadai. "Nothing...you will be mortal dust...unless..."

"Unless?" said Caliban.

The corpse spread its arms wide in an embrace. "...all gods...need servantsss..."

"You want us to serve you?"

"Worsship me..." whispered Brother Amadai.

"I'm gonna stab him."

"Shut up, Brenner!" hissed Slate. As long as Caliban kept him talking, Amadai wasn't...wasn't doing whatever a clockwork corpse did when it was angry.

Please, gods, let me never find out what that is.

Caliban gazed into the eyeless sockets. The echoes rang back and forth "...worssship....worrrshhhip....ip...ip..."

"Yeah?" Brenner growled in Slate's ear. "And what if our fine paladin decides to *do* it? What then?"

She tore her eyes away from Amadai and stared at Brenner.

"I told you he's been looking for a god. You're fine in bed, darlin', but that thing controls clocktaurs. Little more impressive."

"When this is over, I am going to slap you so hard that your *ancestors* will apologize for you."

Caliban ignored them both. So did Amadai. Slate really hoped that the paladin couldn't hear them whispering.

"Worsship me...knight...and I...I will make you...a general...of clocks...and bones..."

"And what would you have me do, as your general?" asked Caliban.

Amadai ratcheted back and forth. It looked almost as if the corpse were excited by the thought.

"The world...the whole world...my servants...will go everywhere...I will see...everything...everything...the bone ones will walk and I will sssseeee...."

Caliban's throat worked. Slate saw him try to form words, his lips curling in disgust.

"What will you see?"

"...everything..." whispered Amadai, swinging back and forth on the chain, the bone arms rising and falling. "Every...mystery...will be...flayed open...my general..."

He can't lie with the voice. Damn, damn, damn. Caliban, you could just not say anything—

"I'd rather die," Caliban said, in the paladin's voice.

—or we'll just go straight to the next idea.

"Ahhhh...." breathed the corpse.

"Can I knife him *now?*" asked Brenner.

"You cannot," said Brother Amadai. "I am become the Many-Armed God. I see...*everything*..."

"Be my guest," said Caliban.

Brenner hefted a knife and threw it directly into Amadai's left eye.

The corpse shot upward toward the ceiling. The knife hilt protruded from the empty socket like an obscene tumor.

Amadai began laughing again.

"This body...isssn't...alive...any more..." it said, clinging near the ceiling like a massive ivory spider.

The three of them stood looking up.

"We must never tell Learned Edmund about this," said Caliban.

"Yeah, well, unless we manage to get that thing down, we might not get a chance." Brenner peered over the edge of the catwalk. "If you haven't noticed...well..."

Slate looked over the railing and started to laugh. *Of course. It wanted only that.*

Four clocktaurs that had been nursing had come detached. Two were obviously unfinished, undersized and missing their forelimbs, but the other two were almost fully formed. Their blunt, eyeless heads had turned upward, toward the catwalk.

As Slate watched, the final two unlatched from the wonder-engine. These had been the closest to the front, and they looked as large and complete as the ones that had been walking through the city.

"They obey…" whispered Amadai, in a voice that filled the whole vast room and sent hissing echoes against the walls. "They obey… *me*…"

"Can you stop laughing, darlin'?" asked Brenner. "Between you and the dead guy, it's gettin' on my nerves."

"Right," said Slate, snapping her mouth shut. It had felt more like a laugh-shaped scream than humor anyway. "Sorry."

"It's fine, darlin'. We're all a little tense."

"Now what?" said Caliban.

They looked down at the clocktaurs and up at the spidery figure of Amadai.

"If we could break those chains he's on…" said Slate, "we might be able to smash the thing."

"The chains are on a pulley up there," said Brenner, tracing the lines with his knife. "But they're anchored down…there. On top of the wonder-engine."

Slate examined the place where the chains appeared to have been bolted. They seemed to protrude from the wonder-engine's neck, attached to what looked like a crude collar.

"That's not part of the original," she said. "Look at it. They bolted it on."

"Maybe they had to keep him out of the way of the clocktaurs," said Brenner.

248

Amadai's choking laughter continued overhead. "Yess...." it said. "One of my servantsss...did not wish to serve...like you..."

"If a demon slipped loose, it could use the clocktaur to smash things up," said Caliban. "Makes sense they'd get him out of the way after that. I'm surprised he lived."

"Maybe he didn't."

"Ah."

One of the clocktaurs, suiting words to action, slammed a massive limb against the wall. The room shuddered.

Slate made her way down the suddenly swaying catwalk and leaned out over the railing. Caliban followed and grabbed the back of her shirt.

"Relax, I'm not going over. Yet." She studied the collar from her new vantage point.

"Yet?"

She sighed. "The chains connect there. It's moving up and down on them through a winch or a pulley or something up above. But they were only able to forge one side to the collar, or they wouldn't have been able to loop him onto it."

"What's holding it in place, then?"

Slate cracked her knuckles. "A very, very large lock."

CHAPTER 45

Both Brenner and Caliban argued with her. Slate let them.

"Slate, you cannot be serious!"

"Darlin', you'll be standing on top of the damn engine."

"You could be killed!"

"Why don't I do it?"

"Why don't you let Brenner do it?"

Slate shook her head. "Because when Brenner goes down there and can't crack the lock, we'll have wasted a whole lot of time. And when the guards come because the clocktaurs are smashing up the joint, I can't shoot them."

Paladin and assassin looked at each other, then back at Slate.

"Besides, if they hammer on the walls long enough, they might take down the catwalks. But I don't think Amadai will let them smash up the wonder-engine."

She stepped up onto the railing. Caliban jumped to grab her around the legs and nearly knocked her over.

"Slate!"

"I appreciate the sentiment," she said, with marvelous patience, "but *stop touching me.*"

He paused for half a heartbeat, then reluctantly stepped back.

She eyed the distance to the chain. Hardly anything, really. She hadn't missed a jump like that in a decade. She took a deep breath. Below, the clocktaur raised its arms for another strike that would shake the catwalk.

Better move quick.

"Caliban, try not to die because I don't want 'stop touching me' to be the last words I say to you."

"I...uh..."

Slate swung out over empty space and grabbed the chain.

He swore behind her. Brenner whistled.

Climbing down the chain was ridiculously easy. It was like a rain gutter with convenient hand and footholds. She could have done it in her sleep.

The only bad moment came when Amadai slid down on his chain. That meant that the links Slate was standing on shot upward and suddenly the corpse was dangling opposite her.

"What…are you…doing…little girl…" whispered the corpse.

"Sightseeing," said Slate, scrambling down the chain.

The corpse sank down and she rose.

Dammit.

Well, sooner or later he'll take up all the slack, I hope.

Amadai tilted his eyeless head. As Slate watched, Brenner's dagger began to work its way loose from the corpse's eye.

He reached out with one ivory arm and Slate swung around the side of the chain in sudden panic.

"Hold…still…"

Two more ivory spines moved toward her from the other side in an insectile embrace. The blade wiggled loose and fell. Slate saw movement inside the corpse's eye socket.

She flung herself down the chain, not even bothering with foot-holds. Her shoulders screamed at her, but she didn't care.

Amadai sank down further, pulling her upward as swiftly as she descended.

"Why…do you…run…"

Ivory tapped the chain. If she hadn't been extremely busy, Slate would have been violently sick. Instead she swayed sideways, away from his touch, setting the chain to spinning.

The warehouse dipped and spun crazily around her as they circled in midair. She heard Caliban shout from above.

Something whistled past her head and a crossbow bolt sprouted from the top of Amadai's head.

"Gaah," she heard Brenner say, sounding disgusted. "There're things inside his skull."

Slate almost started to picture that, slapped the thought down hard, and nearly ran down the chain.

Fortunately, the bolt had distracted Amadai. He spun up again away, toward Brenner, and Slate shot toward the floor as the chain went slack.

She could hear Amadai saying something, but her vision narrowed to the rapidly approaching back of the wonder-engine. If she didn't jump off at the right moment, the chain was going to slap into the ivory machine with her underneath it.

Probably not fatal, but I do like having my ribs intact...

She flexed her feet to make sure neither one was jammed too tightly into the links. If one caught, it was gonna be bad.

Ivory loomed. Slate leapt.

She landed in a sprawl across the wonder-engine's back. Her breath whooshed out of her lungs. Caliban shouted her name.

She lay there for a minute, trying to breathe. The chains rattled behind her. If Amadai came down, it would pull up the slack, but she would have to deal with Amadai. If he went up, the chain would drop on top of her.

Neither option was appealing. She gave up on breathing—*air is overrated anyway*—and scrambled forward, along the wonder-engine's vast back.

She heard the hum of Brenner's crossbow and chain crashed down behind her as Amadai rose toward his attacker.

Slate wanted to yell, "You could wait until I was out of the way!" but she was still dealing with having the wind knocked out of her. She scrambled up into a crouch and crabwalked across the wonder-engine's back to the lock.

She hadn't been entirely truthful about the lock. Brenner could have picked it too. The lock was gigantic, and a lock that big was easy to work with. It was the little tiny ones that gave you trouble. Slate struggled with it mostly because the tumblers were absurdly heavy and her lockpicks were made for smaller things.

God's stripes, I could probably do this with my fingers...

The reason that she had offered to go was because given the choice between working the lock and keeping Amadai occupied, she knew damn well what she would prefer.

The crows took his eyes...

Locks she knew. Fighting corpses, not so much.

It was enormously heavy, though. The padlock was holding the last link of chain to the collar of the wonder-engine, and the bar was nearly as thick as her wrist.

She snapped off her first lockpick and cursed.

She slid another one in and the chain rattled violently as Amadai came down to see what she was doing.

"…ssss…."

"Nothing to see here," muttered Slate.

She risked a look up, saw ivory spines coming at her, and swung out of the way.

How far can that damn thing move? It can't come loose from the spines, can it?

Slate had a sudden image of the corpse pulling itself loose from the chains and chasing her along the back of the wonder-engine.

That was not helpful. Let's not think about that again.

The spines rippled like a centipede's legs, back and forth, as Amadai reached for her again.

"I transcribed some of your journals!" Slate shouted.

"…ohhh….?"

The corpse stilled. Slate jammed the lockpick in, fingers working frantically.

"The cascading code was very good," she said. "We had to get another brother of the Many-Armed God to crack it."

"…yessss…a brother…"

"You'd like him," Slate assured the corpse, feeling a tumbler catch and slide upward. "Very dedicated young man. He said you'd done amazing things. That no one in the order had imagined was possible."

"…ohhh…"

"Two devices!" said Slate. "Two wonder-engine things! Nobody's ever made two work together before, have they?"

"…hhhhheeeehheeee…." The corpse began to swing back and forth in tiny, pleased arcs.

I think it's giggling to itself. I think I made it giddy. Oh gods, gods, any gods, all the gods…

She was working the lock by feel now, her eyes on the corpse. Brenner's crossbow bolt was sticking out of its head and as she watched, a thin bone needle emerged from the back of the skull, moving like a living thing, and began tapping blindly at the arrow shaft.

Slate's mind was nothing but screaming horror, but her hands never faltered on the lock. Another tumbler popped.

The corpse hissed at her. Words. A question?

"I'm sorry," she said, astonished at how automatic the words were. "Can you repeat that?"

The little bone needle bent into segments and wrapped around the arrow shaft. It began to push down. Another needle slid out and joined it, feeding the arrow downward into Amadai's skull.

"….sss…my brothhher…will hhhe tell…thhhe order….of my… achievementsssss…"

"Yes!" Another tumbler fell. *Last one now.* "Monographs. He'll write monographs about it. More than that. Volumes. The whole order will be in awe. He said so."

"Sssss…!"

The point of the crossbow bolt appeared on Amadai's cheek and began to push forward, distending the skin. Slate watched in horrible fascination.

The clocktaurs slammed into the catwalks again, shaking them, and she had to wait for the vibrations to die down. She nearly had it now, she just needed another few seconds…

The skin peeled bloodlessly back from the point of the bolt, sliding along the wicked swallowtail point.

Makes sense, Slate thought. *If you pull Brenner's bolts out, they'll tear you open. You gotta push 'em through. Absolutely sensible. Also I'm going to be sick and I really don't have time to be sick.*

"I can't get a good shot, darlin'," called Brenner. "Not without maybe hitting you."

She didn't dare yell an answer. The corpse cocked his head like a curious dog, watching her, while the ivory needles continued pushing the bolt through Amadai's head.

"…I…know whhhat…you're….doing…." he assured her.

254

"Of course you do," said Slate. "You're very smart." *Come on, last one, just click, just...*

The fletching of Brenner's bolt was slowly emerging from the side of Amadai's face now. The corpse's skin split even farther, a jagged line running up the side of the skull. Another bone needle appeared, tapping at the split, and Slate was probably going completely out of her head now, there was no other explanation, but she would swear that the needle was exasperated by the damage—*Do you see what I have to put up with here? This won't repair itself!*

The lock did not so much click as clank open. The heavy metal bolt groaned loose and Slate hauled down on it and...nothing happened.

The sheer weight of the chain held the bottom link pinned to the top of the metal bar. She'd have to slide the padlock sideways to knock it loose.

She tried to stand up, to get both hands around the lock and pull, and Amadai slashed at her with two sets of arms.

"...not...ssssso...eassssy...isss it?" he breathed, and then burst into another eerie wail of laughter.

Slate nearly fell off the wonder-engine's back, swinging out of the way of the corpse. She clung to the iron collar with both hands while Amadai jittered and twisted above her.

He can't get any farther down. The chain's not long enough. I'm out of his way. I'm safe as long as—

She heard the ponderous footfalls of a clocktaur approaching from behind.

Can it reach me? Oh god, surely it can't reach me?

Do I really want to find out?

"Shoot it!" she screamed at Brenner. "Shoot it!"

"I might hit you!"

"I'll take the chance!"

Caliban would have argued with her. Fortunately, Caliban didn't have the crossbow.

The first bolt went by Amadai's shoulder and tore a line through the corpse's bicep. This interested Amadai enough to swing up a few feet and peer eyelessly at Brenner.

It also missed Slate's face by about three inches.

"Brenner!"

"It didn't hit you!"

"No, I guess not…"

The next bolt went neatly into Amadai's head. The corpse began to swing angrily back and forth.

Slate hauled herself back up on the wonder-engine's back and looked down, to see that the clocktaur was just standing there, doing nothing.

Nothing was good. Nothing was just fine. She would prefer they do nothing, really.

A second clocktaur appeared behind the first and began ponderously climbing atop it.

Slate scrambled backward.

"That's bad," she muttered. "That's really bad. I don't approve of that at all."

The chain slammed down beside her and began to pile up. Links smashed into her thighs with bruising force. She stifled a shriek.

"Slate!"

"I'm fine!" she shouted. That was mostly a lie, but she hadn't felt a bone break, so that was something.

The climbing clocktaur slipped and fell heavily. Bits of gear flew off the bottom one. The clocktaur regained its footing with difficulty and began to climb.

More chain fell. Brenner was clearly distracting it pretty well, or…

She risked a glance up. Great god, Caliban was leaning dangerously far out over the railing, poking at Amadai with his sword. He could almost reach, and it was clearly infuriating Amadai.

Brenner put another bolt in the corpse's face.

Slack. All she needed was a tiny bit of slack. As long as Amadai was up above, slack was what she had.

Slate grabbed one of the links across her legs and dragged it off. She could feel first cloth, then bits of skin catching under the rough metal and snarled in pain.

Doesn't matter. Doesn't matter. If I can get the lock loose, I don't care if my leg comes loose with it.

The clocktaur had gotten both front limbs up on its fellow's back and was working its way forward. They teetered together in a strange, impossible parody of mating.

Slate found the lock and caught it with both hands.

CHAPTER 46

The weight of the slack chain was easily two or three times her own, but she didn't have to lift it all. Just one link and the two or three attached to it, just enough to get the bar of the padlock loose...

Things tore in her back and her wrists, things that would hurt like hell later—if there was a later—but she drove forward, feet braced on the iron collar, and *threw* the padlock off.

It clattered loose and fell to the ground, far below.

The chain began to move. She didn't know if Amadai was descending deliberately or if the weight of the chain was not enough to balance out the weight of the corpse and his device. She decided not to risk it.

"Amadai!" she screamed. "Amadai, you dead shit, I'm talking to you!"

"...whhhat...."

"Nobody's going to write about you! You're an idiot! The order's laughing at you!"

The corpse began to descend. Slow, then faster and faster, and then the loose end of the chain whipped by so close to Slate's face that it nearly took her head off.

Now that would have been ironic...

Amadai slashed at her. An ivory spine slashed across her back, tearing through fabric and scoring a line across her flank. She barely felt it.

At this point, if it doesn't take out my kidneys, I don't care any more.

The corpse realized something was wrong and tried to rise. Slate had the impression of a spider trying to scramble up a line of silk, but it was too late, too late, the lock was breached, the chain was loose...

Brother Amadai smashed into the wonder-engine, shedding gears and bone. The corpse screamed, then bounced off and fell the rest of the way to the floor. Iron sang as it whipped through the pulley overhead and then fell, straight down.

258

Slate threw herself toward the back of the wonder-engine. The machine shook as the chain struck it, then that, too bounced off and slid to the floor.

There was a long and terrible silence.

Caliban thought for a moment that he had gone deaf. Amadai had been screaming as he fell and then it cut off abruptly, without even an echo.

Two clocktaurs, on the far side of the engine, paced toward the fallen man. Without stopping, without pausing, the nearer one stepped on him, trampling the corpse and the bone spines underfoot.

The other drew back one massive, squared-off arm and struck the first one across the back.

Ivory crashed against ivory. The struck clocktaur reared and kicked outward, slamming its attacker against the wonder-engine.

The climbing clocktaur, in the meantime, had stopped climbing and began trying to smash the head off the one beneath it. Its victim reared back, throwing it off onto its side.

"Why are they fighting?" shouted Slate, trying to find something to cling to.

"They're demons!" Caliban shouted back. "Demons hate each other. And they've all come unbound now! All the demons are loose!"

"Yes," breathed Brenner in his ear. "They are."

The assassin was standing much too close, close as a lover. Caliban jerked back, startled. "Brenner? What…"

Brenner smiled, and something else smiled out at Caliban through his eyes, something ancient and terrible and…familiar.

The rune-demon's voice was changed by passing through Brenner's throat, but Caliban would have known it anyway.

"Remember me, shining one?"

"How long?" said Caliban, lifting his sword. And then, answering his own question, "Since you killed the old rune. Of course. You possessed Brenner then, didn't you?"

"So close," purred the demon. "So close, but not quite, Caliban-whose-flaw-is-pride. Did you think that you were the only one worth seducing?"

Caliban remembered kneeling in the darkness inside his mind, with the demon wreathed like smoke around him, trying to get in.

And I never even wondered if it tried to seduce Brenner as well. Because of course I was so much more desirable as a host, why would it even try?

He laughed, almost inaudibly, at himself. At his pride. *Of course.*

That was why my demon has been so quiet, why it stopped coming out when I slept. It's been trying to avoid notice. Even a dead demon is frightened of one that strong.

And he had been foolish enough to be grateful for it. Only rage and terror had dragged it up, and it had fled as quickly as it had come.

Meanwhile, the rune-demon had been curled in Brenner's mind this entire time, alive and waiting. With a willing host, so that it did not need to puppet the assassin's body and risk being found out.

And now, with the Clockwork Boys rendered harmless, it was no longer in danger of the assassin being devoured by the tattoo.

Brenner had a knife.

No. Don't fool yourself. The demon has a knife.

"You could have just walked away," said Caliban. "I would never have known."

"Precisely," purred the demon. "What good is an enemy who doesn't know that he's been defeated?"

Ah. Of course. Perhaps he'd stung its pride a little too.

Caliban swallowed. Could he bind a demon? Could he bind *this* demon?

He had tried, in the rune's nest, and failed. But it had been at full strength then, riding a shaman of ancient power, in a body that it had known for many years.

Brenner had not a drop of magic in his veins, and even though he was certainly not fighting the demon, he was also not putting his full skills at the creature's disposal. Caliban could be reasonably sure of this because, for one thing, he did not currently have a throwing knife sticking out of his head.

He doubted that would last long. As soon as he began to fight back, Brenner was going to realize that one of them could not leave this place alive.

If I do not bind this demon, it will kill me. And then Slate will be left alone with a demon who wears her old lover's face.

Where is Slate?

He risked a quick glance around and saw her down on the lower set of catwalks, looking up at them. She looked puzzled, possibly wondering why they were holding weapons pointed at each other.

He waited until she was gone to reveal the demon. Brenner doesn't want to kill her and the demon's going along with it.

Oh Dreaming God, what will he do to her?

He felt something then, something like terror. He dared not think too much about it. He had seen too many victims when demons got their way.

Brenner feinted with the knife, not a real strike, testing the response. Caliban didn't bother with the sword, slapping the blade aside with his gauntleted hand.

"What the devil are you two doing?"

"Stay down there!" shouted Caliban and Brenner, more or less in unison.

"What?"

Brenner gave him a look, the affectionate, exasperated look they'd shared over Slate once or twice before. With the demon at the bottom of his eyes, it was a sickening mockery.

"Like hell I'm staying down here! Are you two *fighting?*"

"Time to finish this, shining one," said the demon.

Brenner moved forward like an eel. Caliban blocked and blocked again, losing ground with every strike.

Too fast. He's too damn fast.

He swung his sword in a savage arc that should have taken the assassin's head off. Brenner ducked.

Despair was a familiar taste on Caliban's tongue.

But underneath it, something stirred. Something that he thought the demon had driven out forever, something he had long since given up.

For the first time since that long ago exorcism, Caliban felt the presence of his god.

They taught you very early in the temple that the Dreaming God did not make bargains. A demon had a bargain for everything. The Dreaming God did what He deemed necessary.

You accepted His will. It was the only truly important tenet of Caliban's faith.

Caliban had been possessed. He had watched a demon kill the innocent with his body. The temple had turned him out for that crime, and the sin that had engendered it.

It had been the god's will. Caliban had raged against it, wept, even sank into the depths of despair…but in the end, he too had accepted.

Now it seemed that the Dreaming God had returned.

He was a wordless voice in His paladin's mind, a burning star in the darkness.

Caliban had wanted it for so long, and yet now, unaccountably, he fought it.

You abandoned me! You let the demon take me and the temple break me! Why now?

There was no answer to that. There never was. The morality of gods was not the morality of men. You dealt with it or you left the temple.

Brenner sliced at him with a knife and Caliban leapt back.

The wordless voice grew stronger. The god was heat and light and Caliban had grown used to floundering in the dark. His demon gibbered and shrank back, smaller and smaller, but the god was filling up the space where it had been, and yet Caliban was still angry, still fighting to keep it out.

How dare *You come back to me now?*

How dare…how dare…

And then he heard his own thoughts, and almost he laughed at the absurdity of them.

Pride. No matter how many times it trips you up, you are still so proud that you think a god should apologize to you.

Do you apologize to your sword, when you set it aside, then take it up again?

Brenner swung again. Caliban knew perfectly well that the assassin was trying to drive him backward towards the stairs, where one good strike to the legs would end the fight completely.

You are fighting a demon in the body of an assassin, and your god comes to aid you, and all you can do is whine that He did not come soon enough.

The god had come at last. And if Caliban was truly still a servant of his god, then he still had a chance to save Slate.

All he had ever been was a sword in the hand of a god.

He drew in a deep breath, drawn down to the bottom of his lungs, and then he did laugh, because for once, it really was that simple.

He stopped fighting.

Dreaming God...your servant waits.

The demon blinked at him with Brenner's eyes.

What filled Caliban was not power. Power was perhaps the least useful of gifts.

It was grace.

It struck him like a hammer, like a death blow, like falling in love. It filled places that had rung hollow and empty and wrapped him up and made him whole.

The demon took a step back, then two.

The next breath Caliban drew tasted like incense and blood.

Thank you.

And across the catwalk, Slate saw, at last, what it was like when a true Knight-Champion fought a demon.

CHAPTER 47

Why am I going blind? thought Slate, annoyed. It didn't make sense. There was no bright light that she had been staring at, and yet for some reason Caliban was burned into her retinas as if she'd been staring into the sun, and Brenner was warped into a thing of horns and shadows.

Did I take that chain upside the head and not notice?

She'd had to crawl up the blasted wonder-engine to the wooden hopper they were using for the corpses. Every time a clocktaur had attacked the engine, she had to flatten out even farther, clinging to the smooth surface by teeth and toenails, waiting for the vibrations to stop.

The fact that her leg had been savagely bruised and then scraped open in a couple places didn't help at all.

By the time she actually hauled herself over the dead bodies—which should have been disgusting, but by this point was just the sort of day she was having—she had heard steel ringing over the catwalks and had realized that something very bad was going on.

She got to the platform by the door and stared at Caliban and Brenner.

She had seen both men fight any number of times, and her professional opinion was that, in an actual battle between them, Brenner would put two knives in Caliban's eyes and one in his throat within ten seconds. It hadn't happened yet, which had made Slate wonder if Brenner was toying with the paladin, and then something had happened and the air tasted briefly like metal and all of a sudden Brenner wasn't toying with him any more.

The assassin's hand flickered and he threw a knife and Caliban slapped it out the air with his sword and that sort of thing just did *not* happen.

He can't have done that, she thought. *He can't have. He's not fast enough. He fights by just standing there and taking punishment until his opponent drops dead of exhaustion from hammering on him.*

She was going up the ladder like a squirrel when another throwing knife clattered against the railing and fell onto the brawling clocktaurs below.

What the hell is going on?

She wasn't surprised. She was furious and frightened for both of them—but not surprised.

Goddamn men couldn't wait until we were somewhere else to have it out, had to pick right now with a pack of berserk clocktaurs taking down the building...

The clocktaurs in question slammed into a pillar and set the whole catwalk shaking. Slate grabbed for the ladder, hearing bolts shriek as the metal bent.

So not the time. I'm going to yell. Really yell.

The clocktaurs working on the pillar began striking at each other instead. Slate went up the ladder and reached the upper catwalk.

She poked her head up over the edge and said "What the f—"

"Get back!" Caliban sacrificed a second to look at her and took a hit across the ribs. Even through the armor, that had to hurt.

"He's possessed!" shouted the paladin.

"He *what?*"

"Oh, this is better than I'd hoped, shining one..." purred Brenner, in a voice that wasn't Brenner's at all.

Slate froze.

Freezing is stupid. This is stupid. I am stupid.

Brenner's got a demon.

Caliban kills demons.

"Brenner?" she said. Her voice sounded small and uncertain in her own ears. "Are you...are you really..."

He turned his head. There was something wrong with his eyes, and yet he moved toward her and his voice sounded more like Brenner's. "Darlin'. Of course not."

Slate felt the hair on the back of her neck stand up.

She couldn't seem to move, but she could shake her head.

"You're not him."

"Slate, listen to me. Of course I am."

"Don't listen," warned Caliban. "Their voices are tricky. If I can get it bound, it'll stop talking."

"Don't listen to him, darlin'." Brenner was still moving toward Slate, inch by inch. Slate watched this, feeling as if she was a very great distance away. "He's half-mad. You heard what he did to those people at the temple and blamed it on demons."

"Brenner—"

The assassin moved. He tossed his offhand knife at Caliban and lunged for Slate, clearly planning to grab her.

But Caliban did not falter. He swung the sword around, dropped low, and came up inside Brenner's guard.

The pommel cracked across the side of Brenner's head with a crunching sound. The assassin collapsed.

"No!" Slate felt her paralysis break and she lunged forward. Demon or not, it was *Brenner*. "Caliban, *stop!*"

"Get back," said the paladin. He shoved in between them, pushing her away from danger. "It isn't finished."

She wanted to scream that of course it was finished, Brenner was unconscious and possibly worse—and then, impossibly, the assassin rose.

Brenner got up awkwardly, as if he did not know how his joints were supposed to work, setting his weight all wrong. If Slate had only seen him from the back, she would have thought he was a stranger. The lethal assassin's grace was gone. Brenner swayed on his feet, looking less like a killer than like a dead man walking. Blood poured down the side of his head, but he was moving.

"I told you," said Caliban grimly. "They don't go down that easy."

Caliban lifted his sword.

"That's enough! Can't you see he's injured?"

Slate grabbed for Caliban's sword arm, trying to slow him down, to give Brenner the chance to get out of the way. The newly clumsy assassin shuffled sideways, away from the strike.

Caliban turned his head and looked down at Slate. His face was expressionless. He might as well have been carved in marble.

She expected him to say something. Probably to apologize. *It's Caliban, he's always apologizing for something…*

He tossed the hilt of his sword from one hand to the other, picked her up by the scruff of the neck, and dropped her on the ground behind him as if she were a kitten.

He did not apologize. He did not look angry or regretful or even contemptuous. She had been in his way so he had moved her, that was all.

"What the *hell?*" she said, so astonished that she wasn't even angry…at least not at first.

Brenner slashed at him with the knife. He was fast but clumsy, his aim terrible. All Caliban had to do was lean back to avoid the blow.

Caliban began to chant.

Whatever words he was saying seemed to infuriate Brenner—or whatever was inside Brenner now. The assassin shrieked and swung his knives, so badly coordinated that Slate could have disarmed him. Caliban did not even bother with the sword, just grabbed the assassin's wrist with his gauntleted hand and squeezed.

A knife clattered to the catwalk. Caliban's voice never faltered.

Slate stood up. She had to do something. Brenner might be possessed, but this wasn't a fight, this was a *slaughter*. The assassin was moving like he was dead drunk. No, worse. She'd seen Brenner dead drunk, and he could still put a knife in a man's eye across the room.

Brenner screamed. It didn't sound like him. It reminded Slate of the rune somehow, a high-pitched sound like a bird.

He began to rise into the air.

"Holy shit," said Slate, watching the assassin hanging several inches off the catwalk.

Yep, he's possessed all right. No question.

She'd been so blithe about levitating cows. She'd made *jokes* about it. And here was Brenner actually doing it and if Slate hadn't already seen a hundred horrors today, she'd have been violently ill. It was wrong.

Caliban sighed. That was what struck Slate. He actually sighed, as if this was exasperating but not unexpected, and swung his sword up in front of him.

The clocktaurs smashed a ladder loose from the catwalks and Slate stumbled against the railing.

The Knight-Champion held the demonslaying blade in front of him, point up. A ritual gesture, not a defensive one. There was hardly any point in defending against Brenner now. His chanting began to sound strained, but whatever he was doing was working. The assassin began to twist in midair as if the words were arrows striking him.

I should be doing something.

Yeah, and what can you possibly do here? Your friend's possessed and your lover's going to kill him and you are so far out of your depth that the gods themselves couldn't haul you back to shore.

Brenner dropped back to the catwalk. Slate closed her eyes in unutterable relief.

Caliban's voice cracked on the last word and he fell silent.

Brenner stood, swaying. He could not seem to take his eyes off Caliban. Slate was reminded of a bird hypnotized by a snake.

Caliban used the voice then in a language that Slate understood. He said one word, and one word only.

"Kneel."

Brenner—or Brenner's demon—dropped to his knees. Slate felt her own legs twitch. If she had been standing, she might have gone to her knees as well. This was the paladin's voice as she'd never heard it, with the full power of a god behind it, a voice that spoke to the nerves and the skin and the soul as much as the ears.

It no longer said, *Trust me.*

It said, *Obey.*

Brenner knelt at his feet, neck bared, like a sacrifice. The demon no longer spoke. Caliban controlled the demon and the demon controlled Brenner's body. Brenner himself was no longer part of the equation.

How long has the demon been in there? How much of Brenner? No, there was a lot of Brenner, he'd made a joke right before they got wrapped up by the gnoles, he'd called her darlin', surely no demon would ever call her that…

"Caliban—" she said, pushing herself up, nearly choking on horror and the gagging scent of rosemary. "Caliban, can't you—isn't there any way—"

He looked at her. His eyes were like chips of marble.

"No," said Knight-Champion Caliban, paladin of the Dreaming God, and raised his sword like the headsman's axe.

Brenner, or the demon, did not react.

Slate did.

Caliban was moving with the heavy weight of ritual while Slate moved with the speed of desperation. She shot across the catwalk and Caliban froze because there was suddenly a knife blade under his left ear.

"If you kill Brenner," said Slate thickly, "I'll cut your throat."

He was silent for a moment. His sword was still raised, and if he felt any strain from holding it aloft, she couldn't tell.

"Very well," he said finally. Slate nearly sagged with relief, and then tensed again as he continued. "I will command the demon to jump to me. Kill me immediately, and I will bind it to my death."

"No!" Slate wanted to scream and throw the knife across the room. *"No killing!* Can't you exorcise the damn thing? Isn't that what you do?"

"With no temple, and not even a priest to back me?" Caliban finally lowered his sword. "You might recall how I fared last time I tried that!"

"So do it right this time!"

"If I fail, I'll probably run mad and kill you! *No.*"

Slate was ready to sob with frustration and her nose was running so badly that she gave up and wiped it on Caliban's tabard. He twitched as the blade dug in.

"Sorry," muttered Slate. "Nose."

"If you feel a sneeze coming on, I would appreciate it if you moved the knife."

"Look, you can't kill Brenner!" She gritted her teeth. "Order it to jump to me."

"Definitely not."

"Look, I'm not going to make friends with it! And I'm much easier to overpower than Brenner. You two can drag me out and exorcise me."

"I will do no such thing."

"That's an order! As your liege!"

"I respectfully refuse your order, my liege, and will accept any punishment you choose to mete out."

Slate called him names she'd learned growing up in a brothel. He listened politely, the edge of the greatsword still hovering over Brenner's neck.

"If you're quite finished," he said, when she ran out of breath, "it doesn't work like that anyway. Yanking the demon out won't do Brenner any favors, unless you *want* him to become a mindless husk."

Slate swore a bit more.

There was a deep, booming crash. The entire building shook, not just the catwalks. Slate looked over and saw that one of the clocktaurs was determinedly hammering away on the wonder-engine and had managed to smash one of its forelegs. The machine listed to one side. The snarling sow-wolf muzzle was aimed up at an angle, teeth gleaming up at them.

"Slate…" rasped Brenner.

They both jumped. Slate forgot that she was supposed to be holding a knife on Caliban and went to her knees next to the assassin. "Brenner, you goddamn idiot, *why?*"

"Ah, darlin'…" he croaked, as she caught his face in her hands. "You know…never could resist…a trick…"

"Brenner!"

"Figured…it'd keep…the rune…from killing me…outright. Heh. Was right…too…" He swallowed thickly.

"We'll find a way. We'll make Caliban exorcise you."

He shook his head almost imperceptibly. The stubble on his cheeks rasped against Slate's fingers. "Know how they do…that…darlin'?"

"Uh…no?"

"We drown them," said Caliban. "And pull them out, as many times as it takes for the demon to decide to leave, or until the victim dies and their death can be used to bind it."

Slate, still holding Brenner, turned and stared at him. *"What?!"*

"I thought you knew."

"No water here. Sword's…quicker…anyway. Don't have much… time…" He rolled his eyes up to look at Caliban, still standing over both of them like a carving of a vengeful god. "Hey, Caliban… How many demons can you fit…in one soul…?"

Caliban frowned. "They're territorial, but if they're already bound…?"

It struck Slate first. "Brenner, no!"

Below the platform, the clocktaurs smashed into each other and the walls, filling the room with crashing echoes.

"Think…you can fit…six…in here?"

Slate stared at him, then looked down at the rampaging clocktaurs. Already they were leaving great holes in the masonry. It was far too easy to imagine them loose in the city, to remember what they had done to villages along the trade road.

Perhaps the Dowager would have preferred it if they let the clocktaurs destroy Anuket City, but the Dowager's hold was gone. Now it was simply an ugly tattoo.

Caliban lowered his sword. In Brenner's eyes, the demon raged, but it was bound and Brenner was, temporarily, the stronger.

"I don't know," the Knight-Champion admitted. "Let's find out."

CHAPTER 48

He had to walk down on the wonder-engine itself. Slate was extremely unhappy about that.

"There's no handholds except the collar," she said. "And if that clocktaur gets it taken down, you'll fall."

"Then I will bind that one first," he said, as calm as ever, and slid down the ladder to the platform with the hopper.

A guard skidded into the room from the door they had entered, face white.

"Took you long enough," said Slate acidly. She picked up Brenner's crossbow and shot him in the head.

"What was that?" called Caliban.

"Nothing important."

"Not...bad...darlin'..."

"Yeah, well, I'll never get the damn thing cocked again, so we better hope he didn't have friends."

"I c'd...cock it...for...no!" He swallowed as if it pained him. "Don't...listen. Be...stupid to...give me...a weapon."

"Damn you, Brenner."

"Bit...late..."

She heard chanting from below. She dragged herself to the rail and looked down.

Caliban had crawled practically into the wonder-engine's jaws and hooked his feet around the fangs. His sword was held upright and he was speaking to the clocktaur below him.

The thing seemed to have gone berserk. It was smashing at the wonder-engine and itself with equal fury. Whatever Caliban was saying, the clocktaur hated it.

Oh gods, it's so close... She watched the giant limbs striking barely a foot below the engine's head. If the wonder-engine settled any farther to the side, it was going to put Caliban in range of its blows.

"How's...he doin'....?"

"Hell if I know. Not dead."

Brenner nodded. Sweat was pouring off him now. It had the stale scent of illness to it.

Even if I got him out of here, that thing is chewing him up inside. Would he even live?

Caliban's chant stopped. Slate gripped the railing so tightly that her nails began to split.

The clocktaur froze with its arms upraised.

The paladin leaned far out and placed his hand on the thing's blunt ivory head. Slate's nerves screamed.

It lowered its arms and turned away. She watched it walk over to one of the other clocktaurs and slam into it.

"Caliban? Are you all right?"

"I'm fine." His voice was clipped and raspy.

The clocktaur he'd bound didn't waste time hitting its fellow. It just put its chest against the other one and began to push. Slate watched it shove the second clocktaur toward the wonder-engine, leaving great furrows in the dirt floor.

When it was within range, Caliban began chanting again.

This one seemed to go faster, or perhaps it only seemed that way because it wasn't attacking the wonder-engine and Caliban. The first clocktaur took a beating in the process, but Slate didn't particularly care about it.

Once bound, the two of them went together, like a pair of sheep-dogs, and herded the next clocktaur toward the paladin.

His voice was definitely suffering now. Slate winced to hear it.

"What's happening?" squeaked a voice from the doorway. Slate looked over and saw a young man wearing a stained apron. *One of the people feeding the bodies into the hopper. Not a guard.*

Slate stood up and yelled, "They've gone berserk! They're attacking everything! *Run!*"

The youngster gaped at her, backed away, and ran.

"It's impossible to get good help these days," she told Brenner.

His eyes were closed. He gave a weak huff of laughter, but that was all.

Slate knelt down and reached into the assassin's shirt. He opened his eyes and managed a smile. "Getting…one last…feel?"

"Getting you a cigarette, you ass."

"...Saint...among women...darlin'...."

She found the little tin and lit the cigarette with shaking hands. She had to hold it to his lips. Brenner breathed out smoke and shuddered.

"Damn," she whispered. "Damn, damn, damn. Brenner, what would you have done?"

"Made a deal," he rasped, inhaling. The tobacco seemed to give him strength. "Him for you. She likes to bargain."

Boots clattered on the catwalk. Slate looked up, going for her knife. If the guards had come, all she could do was try to slow them up until Caliban finished.

It was the paladin.

"It's done," he said.

When he spoke, she barely recognized his voice. He looked nearly as unhealthy as Brenner.

"You sound like ten miles of hard road," she said.

He laughed hoarsely. He was trembling. She dropped the assassin's cigarette and leaped to help prop him up.

"Great god," she said. "I can't carry you both out of here."

"You won't have to. It's keeping them all separate that's killing me. Once I give them the command to jump to Brenner, it'll be much easier."

Slate winced. "What are you waiting for?"

He pointed.

Slate craned her neck, not wanting to drop him. The clocktaurs were hammering on the wonder-engine now, focusing on the underbelly and the mechanisms.

As she watched, a huge crack appeared in the ivory. The front half of the wonder-engine calved off and fell.

The catwalk nearly upended itself. Brenner fell over on his side. Slate kept Caliban upright mostly by force of will. Her bruised leg screamed at her.

Caliban lifted his head and shouted *"Stop,"* in a voice that made Slate's throat ache in sympathy.

The clocktaurs froze in place, their arms lifted high. Silence fell around them.

"Get me to the rail," he ordered. "It'll be...easier..."

Nothing about this was easy. She walked him to the edge of the catwalk. She had to pull his sword off his back and push it into his fingers.

If he knew how much weight he's putting on me, he'd be mortified. I just hope he stays conscious long enough to deal with these damn things before the guards realize that the banging has stopped and decide to become brave.

The paladin's eyes were closed. He croaked out his commands, one by one.

The clocktaurs began to batter themselves apart.

One by one, they collapsed into heaps of broken ivory. As each one fell, Caliban spoke a word, and then another, and then he took a deep breath and stood on his own.

"That's better," he said, sounding far more like himself. "Dreaming God have mercy. They were very weak, but six at once..." He shook his head.

"Where are they now?" asked Slate, although she already knew the answer.

The paladin sighed and pointed.

Lying sprawled across the catwalk, Brenner twitched and jerked as if in agony.

Slate got the assassin up onto his knees. Caliban looked disapproving but he didn't say anything, which was good because Slate would have taken him apart if he had.

And right now, I could do it, too...

Then Brenner tried to talk, and it reclaimed all her attention.

"Hard...t'talk..." he whispered. "Lot of...lot of..." His eyes rolled back in his head for a moment. Slate cradled his head against her shoulder. He swallowed a few times. "Lot of voices...in here..."

"Brenner," said Slate miserably. "Brenner, you stupid bastard. You were supposed to have a trick up your sleeve. It wasn't supposed to go like this."

She heard the scrape of steel as Caliban slowly drew his sword.

"It's done," he said quietly. "They're all in there. All the ones that are left."

He looked as unhealthy as Brenner. Thin skeins of blood had dried on the sides of his face where the wonder-engine's teeth had cut him.

"No," said Slate, looking at the sword. "No. Not yet!"

She held out one hand, as if that would really stop a slash from the demonslaying sword.

Caliban shook his head. Brenner laughed weakly into Slate's shoulder. "Time…"

"Brenner, I can't let him kill you!"

The assassin's smile was a shadow of its old self. "Darlin'," he said.

It was the last word he spoke that she could be sure was Brenner. The next words were a demon's voice—*"Nngaa! Hai! Ha!"*

The difference between a living and dead demon was extraordinary. When Caliban's demon spoke, it sounded like inhuman words from a human tongue. This sounded like nothing human at all. Slate didn't know how those sounds could even come from Brenner without shredding his throat to ribbons.

She had too much experience with demons now to panic. She took a deep breath and kissed Brenner's forehead. He smelled like sweat and tobacco and blood.

The demon began to laugh, high and terrible.

"Kneel," ordered Caliban, and the demons pulled the assassin's body upright and away from Slate and knelt him at the paladin's feet.

She rose and stepped back.

"Don't look," said Caliban.

"I owe him," said Slate. "He's saved my life so many times. I *owe* him."

"He wouldn't want you to see this."

Slate closed her eyes, but not for long enough. She opened them when the demon stopped laughing, and she saw too much anyway.

The first blow had killed him. It was a heavy sword and Caliban knew how to use it. He grabbed Brenner's shoulder as blood washed over his gauntlets, and he spoke words in the paladin's voice, in that language that Slate did not know, the same words he'd spoken over the old rune woman.

Words of exorcism. Words to bind the demons to Brenner's death.

Words that could not change the fact that her strange, maddening, dark-souled friend was dead.

He saved me from assassins. He kept me from giving us away on the road. He came after me when Boss Horsehead captured me. We were in the Grey Market together...we worked together...

Caliban released the assassin's body and it fell over onto the walkway, boneless and lifeless, with neither demon nor man left inside it. Slate heard herself cry out: a short, ugly sound of surprise. It had all happened too fast. It could not be over so quickly. Brenner could not be gone. Caliban could not have killed him.

The paladin turned to her, bloody sword in his hand.

"Come on," he said. "Brenner bought us some time. Let's go."

CHAPTER 49

It was easier to get out than it had any right to be. Possibly because no one was expecting to try to keep anyone from leaving the compound, but more likely, Slate thought, because there had been a rampaging clocktaur there until just a moment ago.

"You drove one out here before you exorcised it," said Slate.

"Yes. I was having the others destroy the wonder-engine. It seemed a shame to waste them."

There were guards around that clocktaur now, bashing it with any weapons they could bring to hand. It wasn't moving, but Slate knew how much courage that must have taken, just to walk up to it at all.

All the gates were open. People were running away. No one noticed two more people running. The clocktaurs had broken down order as easily as they had broken down the walls.

One guard near the gate did look at them and Caliban snapped, "The building's on fire! Form a bucket brigade!"

The guard saluted and ran off. Slate shook her head in weary disgust.

"How...?"

"People want someone to tell them what to do in a crisis," said Caliban tiredly.

Shadows leapt behind them. Maybe there was a fire, or maybe it was people bringing lanterns to see what was going on and how much damage there had been.

The paladin seemed to be recovering strength with every step away from the bound demons. Slate hated him a little for that. Her bruised leg had stiffened up and she was limping.

She was careful not to touch him.

They went through the gate. Slate's shoulderblades itched, expecting a crossbow bolt at any moment, but none came. No one was worried about mere humans, when ivory monsters might go rampaging through the city at any moment.

"What about the other ones?" she asked.

"The ones already on the road?" He grimaced. "Nothing we can do. I expect a lot of them will attack each other, or smash themselves up. It lets the demons out, but I suppose it can't be helped. The temple will be cleaning up after that for a long time."

And then, just like that, they were walking through the streets of the poor part of the city, sliding through alleyways where rain gurgled in the gutters. The warehouse and the clocktaurs and Brenner were very far away. They might have been two people out for an evening stroll.

"This is your territory, not mine," said Caliban. "Can you find us a way back that avoids pursuit?"

"I'll try," said Slate. Thinking *Brenner could have* and then *Brenner is dead and there was a demon in him* and then she thought she might have to scream so she stopped thinking about it.

It would be just her luck to get out of the clocktaur's warehouse and get picked up by Boss Horsehead's people. She focused on a winding route, doubling back, going into a tenement building and out the back door, while Caliban walked behind her.

She could see gnoles, out of the corner of her eye. A few looked directly at her. *Friends*, she thought. *I hope you're really on our side, Grimehug.*

And then finally, they were in the Gnole Quarter, and the gnoles closed ranks around them. Sweet Lily appeared and Slate started crying with relief.

"Is all right," said Sweet Lily, in her high voice. "Is all right, Crazy Slate."

"No," whispered Slate, shaking her head. "No. It'll never be all right again."

The gnole didn't try to argue. Instead she led them onward, deeper into the quarter, and at last into the safehouse.

"You're here," said Learned Edmund. "Were you not able to enter the district?"

Slate blinked at him, and then thought, *It has only been about four hours. The whole world has changed and it has barely been four hours.*

How is that possible? It should have been years…decades…we should have died of old age instead of on each other's swords…

"We destroyed it," said Slate. "The wonder-engine. The Clockwork District is on fire."

"What?"

Learned Edmund sounded astonished. He could not have been more astonished than Slate felt.

Is it over? Is it really over? Did we do it?

God, she was so tired.

Learned Edmund cried out. Slate started to recoil, until she realized that it was with joy.

"I knew you'd do it. I knew it! I prayed and I thought—I hoped—" The dedicate flung his arms around her and Slate thought, in a night full of terrible surprises, that at least here was one positive one.

"Yeah," she said. Her voice sounded like it belonged to someone else. "Yeah."

Learned Edmund looked over her shoulder. "Sir Caliban! And..."

Slate didn't know if he looked for Brenner and didn't find him, or if something in Caliban's expression told him.

"No..." he whispered. "No, oh no." He pulled away from Slate and signed a benediction. Slate had a mad urge to laugh, thinking what Brenner would have said at that, but if she started laughing, she would start crying.

She was going to start anyway, very soon. She didn't know how much longer she could keep walking and talking like a normal human being.

"I'm very tired," she said. "I need to sleep. Later. Tomorrow. Something. Please."

"Of course, yes, of course..." He dashed tears from his eyes. "You did it. You succeeded. But the cost...oh, by the Many-Armed One..."

Slate patted his arm. It was all the comfort she had left in her, and she spent it on Learned Edmund without a second thought.

He stepped out of her way. She walked into the gnole-burrow and went to the kitchen. She found that she was very thirsty.

She poured a mug of water and stared into it, her mind absolutely empty. If she felt anything at all, it would all come crashing down around her.

She thought, *I am very tired,* and the thought lay in isolation in her mind, words without context.

She turned away, the mug still in her hand, and Caliban was standing behind her.

"Slate—"

She looked up at his face, streaked with soot and blood. Sweat had left snail tracks through the soot. Under the layer of grime, his face was a mask of anguish.

He reached for her and she leapt backward.

He froze. His arm was still outstretched, and they both stared at it, at the blood that had dried in stiff black patterns on the bracer and left thick black lines in the gauntlet's joints.

Brenner's blood.

It was hard to tell which of them was more horrified in that moment. Slate shook her head, backing away, and Caliban dropped his hand and said, "I'm sorry."

She fled to her room. Which had been their room. His clothes were still neatly folded in one corner, his pack beside it.

The pack flung very satisfactorily out the door, but there was something about folded clothes. Her mother's training, probably. She had to set them outside the blanket door, still in their folds.

When she looked up, he was standing at the end of the corridor, watching her.

Her vision blurred with tears. She wasn't sure if they were from rage or sorrow or both.

She couldn't slam a blanket behind her. She wished that she could. But she stalked into her room with all the dignity she could muster and then she fell down on the bed and sobbed as if her grief were an ocean and she were drowning in it.

Caliban stood in the hallway, listening to Slate weep.

He had no idea what to do next. Paladins were chosen partly for their endurance but he was so tired he could hardly think. The Dreaming God was a bar of molten iron in his soul, but the flesh that held that soul was exhausted.

He had never commanded more than one demon at a time. The ones that had inhabited the clocktaurs had been small, weak things, already bound by the wonder-engine's power, but there had been so many of them…and the rune demon had been anything but weak…

Slate sounded as if her heart were breaking. He made a fist against the post that held up the door and leaned his forehead against it.

He wanted to go to her. He wanted to hold her and comfort her and say words that would fix things.

And what words would those be? She watched me bind the demon and cut Brenner practically in half. Am I supposed to touch her with hands that were covered in her close friend's blood?

Am I supposed to say her name in a voice that can make demons kneel?

He bent down slowly and picked up his gear. She'd made her wishes clear. All that was left for him to do was obey.

He went to the kitchen and drank water until his bruised throat felt a fraction less dry. Then he walked down the hallway, past the room that had been Brenner's, into the first unused one. The bed on the floor was a gnole-style nest, too small for a human's comfort, but it hardly mattered now. There was no power under heaven that could have enticed him to sleep in the dead man's bed.

He shed his armor, piece by piece. He was so tired that his hands seemed to be moving automatically. He cleaned his sword because you did not rest while your sword was still bloody, no matter how tired you were.

Had Slate been in love with Brenner after all?

Disgust nearly gagged him. *How dare he even think such a thing? As if she wouldn't have mourned for a friend. As if I have any right to ask.*

As if it matters now.

The sword was clean. His armor was a bloody ruin, but that he could clean in the morning.

He fell over into the bed.

The blankets were cold but the Dreaming God burned inside him. It was the thing he had wanted most, to be centered again, to know with a core of certainty that he stood on the side of angels.

He would have knelt but he no longer thought his legs would hold him up. It didn't matter. The god was there. The god remembered his name.

Thank you, he prayed. *Thank you. Thank you for coming back to me. Thank you for using me to stop the clocktaurs. Thank you for letting me be your sword.*

Thank you for letting me save Slate.

And then, a terrible prayer he knew he could never make aloud, *Thank you for letting it be Brenner, and not her.*

CHAPTER 50

Slate sat in the largest room of the gnole warren, the one that they had used as a meeting room. Grimehug had brought her food.

"I'm not hungry," she said.

"Doesn't matter, Crazy Slate," the gnole said. "Body's hungry. Body ought to be hungry." He pushed the plate toward her. It was bread with some kind of jam on it. Slate took a bite mechanically, then another, then had to stop and put her face in her hands for a bit, waiting for things to settle.

"It's all right," she said to Grimehug. "It's not...I'm not sick. I'm just..."

The gnole leaned against her. There was something undemanding about the gnole's presence, something that required no words. Slate passed him the plate and he finished off the rest of the bread.

"Sorry," she said.

Grimehug smiled with his sharp little teeth. "Used your money to pay for it."

"Heh."

"Tomorrow will be easier, Crazy Slate."

"God, I hope so!" Her voice cracked when she laughed and she let out a sob. "Because I can't handle another one like yesterday."

"None of us can," said Caliban from the doorway.

She stiffened.

He looked like hell. He had washed, of course. Probably a dozen times over, probably in a bath hot enough to broil. He still looked like hell.

It was a grim sort of comfort.

He was careful not to touch her as he passed. He took the kettle from the hearth and poured it into a mug for himself, then poured more for her. She resented that, even though her tea had gotten cold and the warmth in her hands was welcome.

They sat there in cold silence for what seemed like hours, until the knight finally broke it.

"Slate, taking the demon yourself wouldn't have saved Brenner."

She set the mug down. It seemed that they were not even going to make a pretense of normalcy.

Might as well get it all out now. Might as well drag all the ugly bits up and throw them out into plain sight.

"It wouldn't?"

Caliban sighed. "No. Because when a demon leaves a soul, it doesn't do it gently. I could have ordered the rune-demon to possess someone else, yes…and it would have torn Brenner's mind in half on the way out. A demon is like a barbed arrow. You can't pull it out. You have to push it through instead. If they're bound in a body when it dies, they follow the death back into the demon realm."

Slate grimaced. This was not what she wanted to hear, and yet already her mind was working at it, pulling it apart, looking for angles. "So you can't just order them to jump to…I don't know, to a chicken or a mouse or something?"

The paladin shook his head. "Not unless you want to destroy the current host's mind."

"You said the exorcism is *drowning?*"

Caliban nodded. "If you drown someone, you have the best chance of having them die—at least briefly—without actually killing them. Someone worked it out a long time ago."

She stared at him.

"It's fast," said Caliban grimly. "And it can be brutal. If we can get anything into them beforehand, there's a drink the priests make so they're not really conscious when it happens. The demon won't always let that happen, though."

There was something about the way he paused over the last words that made Slate think he spoke from grim experience. She did not want to think about it. It made her skull and her heart ache.

"Why didn't you tell me that *then?*"

"We were a little busy and you had a knife at my throat. I didn't think you were in the mood for a lecture on demonology."

She grunted.

After a minute, something occurred to her. "Wait…*you've* exorcised people."

"I have."

"Lots of people."

"Enough of them."

"And paladins on temple duty are exempt from murder charges."

Caliban sighed. "If you are working up to asking how many possessed individuals I have personally exorcised, eleven. Not including the one who was bound in the infant as bait for its mother's trap. Six of them survived the experience. I offered each one the choice of the sword, and each one chose the water instead."

Slate's mouth had fallen open and she closed it with a click.

"Our survival rate is higher than surgeons taking off diseased limbs," he said. "If you can get to a temple, the odds are better still. No worse than childbirth, say. But in the field, paladins have to do the best we can with what we have available. It is much like field surgery, in that regard, and the results are much the same."

"Still a lower bodycount than Brenner," she said, swallowing. Was she making a joke? It didn't sound like a joke to her. Probably not to him either.

"I tried my best," he said. "If I could have gone into the water myself, instead of the victims, I would have." His expression was set, gazing straight ahead. Perhaps only Slate would have noticed that his jaw was tightly clenched.

She didn't doubt him. It was exactly the sort of thing that he would say, and do, and be.

"I thought you knew," he said finally. "It is not a thing that the temple conceals, although they do not go out of their way to advertise it, either."

"I can see why not!"

They both stared into their tea. Caliban got up and went to the fire, jabbing it with the poker.

"He chose to work with the demon willingly," said Caliban at last.

Slate rounded on him, baring her teeth. "Shut up!"

"Listen to me. I know you don't want to hear it—"

"Stop using that voice!" snarled Slate. "Stop it! I don't want to talk to—to a paladin right now, do you hear me? Stop sounding like a

goddamn knight and sound like somebody who just killed their friend!"

He blinked at her.

Slate thought, for a minute, that she'd asked something impossible. Perhaps she had.

But then his shoulders sagged and he sat down next to her on the bench. Not touching. Touch was too dangerously charged now. Instead he stared at the ground between his feet.

When he spoke again, he sounded like a man who was tired and strained almost to the breaking point.

"It's the only way they can hide what they are," he said, dragging his hand over his face. "They have to let the person run the body. Otherwise it's obvious. We'd all have known, if he was fighting the demon. He had to have agreed to it."

Slate swallowed. "He could have killed either of us. A bunch of times. And Learned Edmund, too."

"I think the demon wanted the clocktaurs destroyed," said Caliban. "It was very angry about their presence in its territory. Well, there were demons bound inside them, that would explain it. And possibly it was afraid that the tattoo would eat Brenner's body if he went too far afield. It knew that it could not jump here, without being sucked into the wonder-engine. So it waited until it had all that it wanted, and then it struck."

Slate knew that he was right. She did not know if she could forgive him for it.

"When you said 'Kneel,' I almost did," she said abruptly. "How much can you actually do?"

He shook his head. "Not that. Unless you're a demon, which I doubt. It's reflex. Like ducking when someone yells, 'Duck!'"

"I don't *reflexively* kneel."

He said nothing.

"If I had ordered you to let him go—" she said, in a high voice.

"Does it matter what I say now?"

"It matters to *me*."

"No," he said. He had slipped back into the voice again, the one that couldn't lie. The temple paladin's voice. "I will not let a demon live. Not even for you."

The next question was in her throat—*what if it had been me the demon took?*—and she swallowed it down.

It was not Brenner she was thinking of. It was the moment when she had grabbed his arm and Caliban had tossed her aside, neither cruel nor kind, simply an obstacle to be moved out of the way so that he could reach his target.

She got up and walked away and left him sitting on the bench alone, and he did not try to follow her.

CHAPTER 51

Caliban sat on the bench and wondered if Slate would ever forgive him. It seemed unlikely.

"Stupid," said Grimehug. Caliban had forgotten that the gnole was there. *Well. It only lacked public humiliation to make things complete.* "Being stupid, big man." He grimaced, showing all his fangs. "One of mine, a gnole would wonder if you had worms."

"I am fairly certain I don't have worms," said Caliban. He considered this. "On the other hand, I've been wrong about everything else lately, so I'm probably wrong about this, too."

"Should go after her, big man."

"Sometimes women want to be left alone."

"Yeah. Not this time, probably. Humans can't smell." He shook his head.

Caliban sighed. It was entirely possible that Grimehug was right, but on the other hand, humans didn't understand other humans most of the time, so how could a gnole be expected to?

She pitched my belongings out of her room. I don't think she's looking for me to come back.

Even under the best of circumstances, it was rare for a dalliance in the temple to last past one's lover witnessing an exorcism. It was not a gentle act.

And it is one thing to know that the one in your bed is fundamentally a machine for killing demons, and another to watch them do that for which they were made.

Some Knight-Champions limited their liaisons to others of the order, for just such a reason. Caliban could understand why.

Awfully late for that now, isn't it? That's the sort of thought you should have had before *you fell in love with a woman and then had to kill her former lover in front of her eyes.*

He put his face in his hands and wondered what the hell to do now.

"Stupid. Rather twist your own whiskers than bite the back of her neck."

"I doubt she'd appreciate that right now," said Caliban, bleakly amused.

"Stupid," said Grimehug, almost affectionately. He patted Caliban's arm. "Stupid's a good mate for crazy, though, maybe."

"I think stupid blew its chance there," said Caliban.

Slate slept and woke and wept and slept again. She did not know how many hours it took. Someone left a pitcher of water by her bed, and she chose to believe that it was one of the gnoles.

"Mistress Slate!" said Learned Edmund, when she finally came back to the kitchen. "I am so glad—I must tell someone—"

She looked at him blearily. Her skull pounded, probably from hunger. She poured out some tea into a mug and tore off a chunk of bread from the loaf.

Let's see if I can get this down and if I feel any better afterward...

"Mistress Slate?"

Even half dead and sick with grief, the dedicate's hopeful expression cut through her haze. Slate raised her eyebrows. "Mmm?"

"I think—I believe—I've found the cause of werkblight! And it was your doing!"

Slate frowned at him. The words all made sense, but not in the order he was using them. "What? Say that again, slowly."

He said it again, slowly.

"You *know* what causes werkblight?"

"Yes!"

"...I gotta sit down."

She sat. She ate the bread while Learned Edmund vibrated like a hummingbird in front of her.

"All right," she said. "Talk."

"It's an *allergy!*" he said. "To gnoles!"

Slate attempted to arrange the words in a way that made sense and failed.

"I read up on allergic reactions," said the dedicate. "In severe cases, it causes skin reactions—hives, itching, even lesions, correct?"

"Yeah," said Slate.

"If an allergic reaction were severe enough, it would be fatal, yes?"

"Oh gods, yes," said Slate, remembering a few times when she had nearly coughed herself to death. "Easy."

"There you go!" Learned Edmund sat back, beaming. "The skin lesions associated with werkblight are much like those that develop when one handles the leaves of certain plants. Yet others can handle those same plants without fear, because they do not react. We are all walking around here unharmed, but for a few, the presence of the gnoles provokes a fatal reaction."

Slate rubbed her face. "It's an interesting theory. But what does it have to do with me?"

"You said it!" said Learned Edmund, practically bouncing in his chair. "When Mistress Magnus was wrapping you in the shroud. You said that the gnoles were about the only thing you weren't allergic to!"

Had she said that? Slate honestly couldn't remember. "It does sound like the sort of thing I'd say," she admitted. "But okay, assuming it's true, then…err…what now?"

Learned Edmund considered. "There are palliatives that healers can make for allergies," he said. "Have you not found this?"

"I guess," said Slate. "I mean, they make up a couple concoctions for spring that keep me from choking myself to death. One makes me want to sleep all day, so I don't use it much, and the other one makes my heart hammer and that's really unpleasant so I don't use it at all."

"Compared to the werkblight, though?"

Slate thought of the corpses covered in their huge sores. "Well, it'd be better than *that*, that's for sure."

"I don't know which one would work," said Learned Edmund. "But if we could get this information in the hands of healers, they could try that as a treatment."

Slate frowned, running her finger over the rim of her mug. "What about that town we passed? The blighted one? The villager said they *all* had it."

Learned Edmund nodded. "The body in the well," he said. "That man said that it wasn't human. What if it was a gnole?"

"Some kind of animal…" said Slate slowly. "If you didn't know what a gnole was…yes, all right, I can see that. But they all caught blight."

"They drank water that was effectively infused with…well…gnole," said Learned Edmund. "A concentrated dose delivered internally. I suspect many perished from throat lesions, and even those who would not normally react would do so when faced with such concentrations."

Slate rubbed her forehead. "Learned Edmund, you can't just tell the healers it's gnoles."

"Why not?" He looked puzzled. "We could save lives."

"And end them. People already kill gnoles because they think they carry werkblight. If they know they're the actual cause? They'll kill every gnole they see. They'll torch the Quarter." She gestured aimlessly at the walls around them.

Learned Edmund gaped at her. She watched the color drain out of his face.

"But it's not their fault! Surely…surely no one would…"

"Ask Grimehug," said Slate. "Ask Sweet Lily what she thinks would happen."

The dedicate put his head in his hands.

"I don't have to ask," he said. "Although I will, because there are things that a human will not have thought of. But…*no*…"

Nineteen, thought Slate wearily. *Nineteen and realizing that you don't have all the answers and sometimes there aren't any good answers at all.*

Nineteen, and given a choice to save lives or end them.

She wondered how old Caliban had been, when the temple had taught him the only way they knew to save the damned.

Slate stared into her mug.

"I can tell no one, then," said Learned Edmund. "Not at the cost of the gnoles. The werkblight will go on. I will destroy my notes."

"You will do no such thing!" snapped Slate.

From under the table, Grimehug said, "God's scat. Humans can't smell."

Slate crouched down and looked at her gnole friend. "Are we being stupid again, Grimehug?"

He sat up and flicked his ears at her. "Crazy Slate. Book man." He took a deep breath, and Slate had the impression that the gnole was picking his words very carefully. "You tell a human what werkblight is. You don't tell a human *why*."

"You mean we shouldn't tell them the cause?" said Learned Edmund.

"Humans can't *smell*," said Grimehug. "Won't know unless you tell them. Maybe a human figures it out. Maybe a human doesn't. Human gets treated. Gnole gets blamed, well, gnole already gets blamed sometimes."

"To deliberately conceal knowledge goes against the teachings of the Many-Armed God," said Learned Edmund.

"So does genocide, I'm guessing," said Slate. "You'll save a lot of lives. Just…keep your notes."

He bowed his head.

She felt a smile tug unwillingly at her lips. "You might even consider putting them in code."

CHAPTER 52

The better part of a week passed, and Slate had to acknowledge that she was spending most of her time conscious. Her body had apparently decided that her brain was not a reliable ally and had begun feeling things like hunger and thirst again.

As for grief…well. She had run through all of her coping skills and had finally taken refuge in drinking heavily. It didn't help, but Brenner wasn't going to get a funeral. *A one-woman wake, that's me…*

Caliban came up the hallway. She knew it was him, even though her back was to the door. She could feel his presence like heat on her skin.

He stood in the doorway with his hands clasped behind his back. "Madam," he said.

Madam. Well. Here we are, back where we started.

Slate wanted to throw something at his head, but there was nothing within arm's reach except her mug. The alcohol inside was fairly terrible, the sort of thing an artificer would make if they had a lot of time on their hands and no guidelines beyond *shouldn't make the drinker go blind.*

Still, waste not, want not.

"What?" she growled.

"Learned Edmund has requested immediate escort to the Temple of the Many-Armed God," he said. "I believe that it might be for the best. The knowledge of the werkblight's source should be spread as widely and as quickly as possible."

"Good," she said. He was leaving. That was what she wanted. There was no reason why she should feel as if her stomach had dropped through the floor. "Have fun."

"Of course, this is dependent on you being willing to make the detour," said Caliban.

"It's got nothing to do with me," Slate said, not looking at him. "Go wherever you want."

"You're still my liege," said Caliban.

"The hell I am!" she snapped. Goddammit, he was not going to let *anything* lie, was he? "You don't need me anymore. I was a convenient substitute for your god, apparently, since you can't go five minutes without being told what to do—which is pretty damn funny, since it's not like you listen to me anyway. What use is all this fealty garbage, if you're going to do whatever you damn well please?"

"Very little, I expect," he said. He sounded so damn calm about it. She started to reconsider throwing things at his head. "But I will see you back to the capitol, at least. If you do not wish to go with Learned Edmund, then so be it."

She turned and glared at him. "I don't need you to get home."

"You are the most wanted woman in the city," he said. "You can barely ride a horse. How do you propose to make your way to the capitol alone?"

"I did it once without your help. Horsehead wanted me dead back then, too. I can do it again."

"Very well," he said. "Then if you will not think of yourself, think of your gnole friends, and Ashes Magnus. Anyone who aids you on the road will be putting themselves in grave danger."

Her breath hissed between her teeth.

"If we travel together, then the only other life you will be risking will be mine." His tone was so dry that Slate thought she might choke on it. "And as my life is of little value to you at the moment, that should not trouble you overmuch."

Slate bared her teeth at him. "If Brenner was alive—"

"Then I would let you go."

There were whole layers of meaning wrapped up in that sentence. Slate hated them all.

"It gives me no pleasure to continue to inflict my presence on you," Caliban said, sounding as cold and distant as a star. "If I could hire a bodyguard and trust they weren't working for Horsehead, I would. But the city is in turmoil and people are fleeing in droves now that word has come that the clocktaurs have stopped working. They expect reprisals from the Dowager's City. We must go soon. Let me travel with you."

"Ha!" Slate laughed, because otherwise she was going to swear. "*Let* you. What if I *don't* let you?"

"Then I will follow behind you to the capitol to see that you arrive safely. And then I shall take myself out of your life and trouble you no more."

Slate rubbed her forehead. "I hate you," she said conversationally.

"I'm aware." He shrugged. "It will be easier if we travel together. You do not need to speak to me on the road, beyond the bare minimum. And you need not fear my advances. I am aware that that part of our relationship is over."

"So long as we are clear," said Slate, and drained the mug dry.

It was harder to part from Grimehug than she expected. Slate would have sworn that she had no tears left in her, but she shed a few anyway, down on her knees with her arms around the gnole.

"Crazy Slate," he said affectionately, and licked her forehead. "Crazy Slate. Twisting your whiskers again."

"Everything's terrible," she said. "I'll miss you, Grimehug."

He shrugged. "Maybe a gnole comes to the capitol some time, eh? Maybe a human and a gnole meet somewhere else. Maybe a gnole goes to a temple to read what book man writes about gnoles."

She pressed her forehead against his. "Maybe. Yes. If a gnole ever needs a crazy human…"

"Dangerous promise, Crazy Slate. A gnole might take a human up on that."

She wiped at her tears. "Please do. We owe you everything."

Grimehug looked over her shoulder at Caliban.

"Anything," said the paladin. "Anything the gnoles need, you have only to ask."

"God's scat," muttered Grimehug. "Humans and dangerous promises. Go on. Dead humans no use to any gnole."

He pushed Slate forward, toward her horse. The last Slate saw of him was a gleam of stripes vanishing into the shadows.

They left the city not under cover of darkness, but in mid-afternoon, with a crowd streaming out of the gates after the market. There was no mistaking Caliban for anything but a knight, so he rode in front, wearing the emblem of the Forge God, while Learned Edmund rode beside him.

Slate had cut her hair brutally short, bound her breasts, and was trying to look like a squire or a temple novice. She wasn't sure if she succeeded, but anyway, no one shot at her. She rode behind the other two, on a horse with a mouth like iron and a gait to match.

The guards might have looked twice, but a half-dozen gnoles dragged a body cart through the entryway and the crowd parted like a whiplash. The guards hastened to clear the way, yelling at people to move their oxen and get the hell out of the way…and then they were out on the road, with Anuket City behind them.

Slate hadn't expected to leave the city alive. She didn't know how to feel.

Angry. Angry seems good. Yes.

They rode away, the mass of people seeming to push them from behind. Ox-drovers prodded at their charges with goads and messengers on fleet horses passed them, throwing up clouds of dust. They passed a group of pilgrims heading to a shrine, and one rode up to Caliban and asked for a blessing. Caliban placed his hand on the woman's forehead and told her to walk with the gods.

Slate had no problem being angry at him. The sudden stab of jealousy made no sense at all, but hell with it. It could be part of the anger.

I wonder if those people know what paladins do…no, they think he's with the Forge God. Forge God blesses blacksmiths, He doesn't mess around drowning people.

She'd stolen the tabard herself. It was too short, but she didn't have Brenner's eye for fit.

Neither did Brenner any more.

Tears prickled at her eyes and she fought them back.

She hadn't even *liked* Brenner, dammit.

Learned Edmund said something to the Knight-Champion and he nodded gravely. Slate rode behind them, a fuming novice on an unimpressive horse.

She stared at Caliban's back and remembered a kiss.

It hadn't been a passionate one. He probably had no memory of it at all. He'd been curled up around her, chest against her back, and he had bent his head just a little and kissed her shoulderblade. A very small kiss saying, *I'm here.*

Not ownership, not passion, just…presence.

God's stripes, as Grimehug would say! I'm mooning over what a kiss meant that he's almost certainly forgotten. And Brenner's still dead and Caliban killed him.

Funny, you knew he'd murdered a pack of novices while possessed, and you were still perfectly happy to hop in his bed. But when it's someone you knew, now you care?

Shut up.

Even her own mind was against her. How nice.

Well, it hardly mattered now, did it? His god had come back to him. Caliban would be the first to tell her that being a servant of the gods was all he was good for.

Certainly not wandering around after some muddled little forger with a price on her head. It's over now. He's a real paladin again. He doesn't need a liege and I never wanted a knight anyway.

He killed Brenner.

Brenner was possessed. He had to do it. I know *he had to do it.*

So why am I so goddamn angry?

They rode away from Anuket City and the crowd thinned and still Slate couldn't find an answer.

CHAPTER 53

They spent that night camped off the trade road. There was a traveler's rest not too far away, with running water and a man selling firewood and hay. Presumably Horsehead had people watching it. Learned Edmund went to purchase some, as he was the only one probably *not* wanted by the crime lord.

Slate and Caliban said nothing to each other. Slate made a fire. Caliban tended to the horses. Slate boiled water, because she couldn't think of much else to do, and made tea.

He poured hot water for himself and then retired to his side of the campfire. He did not say anything. He so obviously did not say anything that Slate wanted to scream and throw the hot water on him, but she didn't because he would forgive her immediately and what the hell was she supposed to do about that?

Learned Edmund came back. He chatted cheerfully with both of them, either oblivious to the tension or pretending to be. It was hard to tell with Learned Edmund.

They ate. They rolled out their bedrolls. They climbed into them and went to sleep.

Well, the two men went to sleep. Slate tossed and turned, thinking that she hated sleeping on the ground, that her back was not as young as it used to be, and finally that it was too damn cold. She'd gotten used to having Grimehug wrapped around her feet.

She rolled over again, trying to find a comfortable place, or at least a warm one.

Caliban was on the other side of the dying fire, curled up neatly on his side. Slate could picture, very clearly, sliding out of her bedroll (hopefully without catching her feet on the blankets and falling over) and sliding into his. He would be very warm against her back, and she would fall asleep with his arm wrapped over her.

And in the morning, Learned Edmund would pretend to be oblivious again.

And Brenner would still be dead.

She stared into the dark. The sky was deep blue and the tree branches made black outlines against it. Insects sang in the woods.

She didn't get up and eventually she fell asleep, still cold and irritated and wishing she wasn't alone.

"What will you do now?" asked Learned Edmund, the second night on the road.

Caliban, to whom the question had been directed, was feeding branches to the fire. The orange light lay kindly on his skin, or perhaps Slate was simply mooning after the unobtainable again.

She wrapped herself tighter in her blanket and brooded.

"My god has taken me back," said Caliban. "But the temple has not, and I do not think they will. I was too dramatic a failure." His lips twisted. "So I will serve Him as best I can, outside the temple. There are always demons to kill somewhere. Perhaps He has need of a paladin who is not chained to the politics of His order."

"It seems that we of the Many-Armed God are not immune to demons," said Learned Edmund. "If you find yourself at loose ends, I am certain that our order would welcome a visit. You could still accompany me, of course, if you wish."

Caliban met Slate's eyes over the fire. Slate didn't look away.

Neither did he.

"My first responsibility is to see Mistress Slate back to her home safely," he said. "After that is done, perhaps I will."

She didn't say, *I can get home myself.* It would be far more difficult now. She would have to find a group of travelers going her way, and she had a horse to deal with. Horses were hard.

"You'd be welcome too, Mistress," said Learned Edmund.

Slate had to laugh. "Learned Edmund…you know as well as I do what would happen if I showed up on your doorstep with my feminine exhalations."

The dedicate blinked at her. "Oh," he said. "Oh…right. I had forgotten. I…" She saw his throat work as he swallowed. "I'm sorry. My order is wrong in this. I know that now. I will have to…have to do something…or…or…" He looked at Caliban. "I don't know if I have your strength, Sir Caliban. To leave my order."

He looked so young and so guilty that Slate felt ancient by comparison. "You're curing werkblight," she said gently, "and writing a book about gnoles. You need your order for that. It's all right to change them from the inside."

"I will," he promised her. "I will."

When Learned Edmund left them, a few days later, Slate found that she was both glad and sorry to see him go.

She wanted nothing more than to sink into a deep pit of despair, and he had been cheerful and chatty. It was exhausting. She couldn't even bring herself to snap at him to just *shut up.*

It's not his fault. He's young. He's excited. And I know he feels bad about Brenner. But he's nineteen and he's going to change the world and dear sweet gods I'm old.

But when he waved for the last time and rode off, the mules slouching along in his wake, Slate felt a stab of loss.

May the gods look after you, Learned Edmund. Better than they have for the rest of us.

Caliban turned his horse toward the Dowager's city. In silence, Slate followed.

They rode through the ruins of a village that the Clockwork Boys had reached. There were people there, digging out buildings. Everywhere, Slate heard saws and shouts and sounds of industry.

"They're rebuilding," said Caliban, so quietly that Slate thought he was probably talking to himself.

"What else can they do?" she snapped. "Lie down in the dust and die?"

He looked over at her and she flushed. She hoped he couldn't see it and suspected that he probably knew the subtle signs by now.

I don't want to lie down in the dust and die. I want to lie down in the dust and swear a lot, and then drink heavily. It's different.

That night, she lay in the blankets in the dust and heard Caliban breathing on the other side of the fire and knew that neither one of them were sleeping.

"Your demon's not yelling at night," said Slate the next morning, almost accusingly.

They were the first words she'd spoken to him since they broke camp. Without Learned Edmund's presence, the silence grew between them like a wall.

He answered easily enough, though: "That is good to know. It is a gift from the god, perhaps. Or merely a by-product of the god's return." He smiled ruefully. "I find that I would prefer to think that it was a gift, all things considered."

"Pity your god didn't come back a lot sooner."

Caliban shrugged. "Perhaps He had some reason. Perhaps His attention was simply elsewhere. I am only one man, after all. If gods were all-present and all-powerful, they would not need us to do their work for them."

"That's it, then?" said Slate in disbelief. "He hangs you out to dry like a prison snitch and comes back just in time to slaughter Brenner, and you're just 'oh well, these things happen'? *Seriously?*"

"I'm a paladin," he said mildly. "Does a sword get angry when it is set aside, and then refuse to be drawn again?"

"Swords can't think!"

"To hear you tell it, neither can paladins. At least, not very well."

Slate cursed in sheer frustration and kicked her horse forward. The horse, appalled, managed about five steps at a trot, then settled back into a walk.

Caliban did not comment on this, which was good, because otherwise she was going to get off the horse and punch him as high up as she could reach.

After a little while, while she breathed through her mouth and tried not to sneeze at the dust, he said, "I was angry at first."

"Good!"

"I was angry He didn't kill me."

"Are you *serious?*" She didn't try to make the horse move, because that was clearly pointless. She thought about getting off and just bashing her head into a tree for awhile.

"If He had struck me down when I was first possessed, I would not have killed those people." Caliban shook his head. "I was angry about that for…well, a long time."

Slate looked around for a suitably bashable tree.

"But not killing me meant that I was available when He needed me again."

"So, what then? The ends justify the means? A pack of nuns and novices for a pack of clocktaurs?"

Caliban shook his head. "I doubt that the God saw so far, or so coldly. I think… well. The gods walk among us, using what tools they must. They see a little farther than we do, but They are not all-knowing. I suspect—I *know*—that the Dreaming God has many tools. But it seems that I, as broken as I am, was the closest He had to hand."

"He couldn't have sent someone else?" said Slate bitterly.

"How? There were no demons in Anuket City, so far as anyone knew. What was He to do, appear in a blaze of light? Hope that some other paladin caught a whiff of demon before a clocktaur flattened them, and managed to let the temple know?"

"He's a god! He should have done better!"

Caliban raised an eyebrow at her. "This is the sort of argument that one has in the second year at temple," he said. "I was never any good at them. It's a shame that Learned Edmund is gone. I suspect he could recite chapter and verse about free will and humanity."

"I could really get to hate the gods," said Slate.

"That's all right," said Caliban. "I'm pretty sure They're used to it."

CHAPTER 54

"Caliban?"

He was briefly silent, perhaps surprised that she had initiated a conversation at all. "Yes?"

They were five or six days on the road now, she'd lost count. They had passed villages that were being rebuilt and villages that had been abandoned completely. There were definitely looters about, but they looked at Caliban and the sword and they looked for easier prey.

The silence between them was going to drive her mad soon. The hoofbeats of the horses were part of a rhythm that echoed in her head, over and over, like unspoken words. She'd run the words through her head a dozen times, in a dozen variations, before she finally spoke them aloud.

"What happens after an exorcism?"

Caliban glanced over at her, his eyes unreadable. "If the demon's gone? The victim stays in the temple for a time. Even if you get it out early, even if they haven't hurt anyone, the demon's presence clings to you like...filth..."

Slate stopped even pretending they were speaking in the abstract.

Caliban cleared his throat. "The nuns take care of them. The unlucky ones will get a demon that doesn't know how humans work, and they'll have done things...eating rocks or mud because they're hungry, staring at the sun because they don't understand, walking on all fours and tearing up their hands. They need healers. And even the ones who had demons that don't damage their bodies need...kindness. Someone to remind them that they are not responsible for what the demon did, or the thoughts it made them have."

Slate stared at the reins gathered over her fingers and thought dark thoughts.

"Some of them never leave the temple again," Caliban continued, when it became obvious she had nothing to add. "They become nuns or monks themselves. It is easier to be with other people who understand."

"They exorcised you," said Slate.

"They did."

She had to work the thought around in her mind before she could say it. Caliban rode beside her in silence while she did.

"That means they drowned you."

"Four times," said Caliban, with no trace of emotion. "My demon was...tenacious."

"Four!"

"I was very strong," he said. Not bragging. "And I knew what was happening. That was perhaps the key. I knew that there was a good chance that I would survive, and thus the demon knew it as well. It refused to leave." He gave a hoarse little laugh, one of the worst sounds that Slate had ever heard. "Which should not be possible, but I kept *not* dying."

Slate stared at him in horror.

He caught her eye, gave a shrug, and looked down at the reins. "The third time, they say I begged for the sword. I don't remember, but I suspect it's true. They couldn't get the draught into me, to make it easier. And they were all priests. They didn't dare have another paladin present, you understand, in case it found a way to jump. All they knew was that this demon could take a paladin, and they were afraid. The last time, I think they actually did try to kill me. I was dead for...well, for quite a long time, to hear them tell it. And the demon could not jump and would not flee. They cannot live in dead flesh, so it died. And then I woke up." He arranged the reins very neatly over the saddlebow, watching his own hands, not looking up.

"...shit," said Slate, with feeling.

One corner of his mouth crooked up. "Waking up wasn't so bad. I was cold, that was all. I've never been quite so cold in my life. Then I realized what was happening, and...well."

"You're always taking hot baths! I'd think water would...you know..."

He looked embarrassed that she'd noticed. "If you tried to hold me under, I expect I'd panic quickly enough. You've never seen me put my face in the water, and you never will."

For no apparent reason, she remembered Brenner, what seemed like an eternity ago—*"I offered to shave him, since he doesn't have a mirror. Acted like a hot towel was a murder weapon."*

"They use the coldest water they can," said Caliban. "You're more likely to survive. Someone figured that out…a long time ago."

"Good to know!"

"But you wake up cold. Very cold." He shrugged. "Hot water's different. It helps the cold. And it helps me think. Or stop thinking. These days, that's mostly what I prefer."

Slate found that she was filled with rage again, not *at* Caliban this time but *for* him. *He gave them his entire life! He went out every damn day slaughtering demons! And a demon finally gets him and they just threw him away! Nobody helped* him *afterward!*

She was going to go to the capitol and tear down the Dreaming God's temple with her own two hands if she had to.

"But they threw you in a cell afterward! They tried you for murder!"

"Can you blame them?"

"Yes!"

"I don't. I was their great failure, after all."

Slate found that she was, in fact, capable of being mad at him and for him simultaneously.

It took her a few moments to work up to the next question. It had been in her head since Brenner died, but it was an ugly thing to drag out into the light.

She couldn't stop herself.

"If I were possessed, would you kill me?"

"Not if I could exorcise you."

Slate's breath hissed through her teeth. "You'd let someone *drown* me?"

"What would you have me do?" he shot back. Actually raising his voice, which astonished her on some level, since Caliban *never* raised his voice. "Let the demon walk off with you trapped inside? Let you ride around behind your eyes while a demon uses your body to slaughter everything in range, or worse? They don't much care how they use you, you know. You're there the whole time, whatever horrible disgusting thing they decide to try while they're wearing your skin."

Slate stared at him, speechless.

"But no," he said. He gave a bark of humorless laughter. "No, after everything, I *wouldn't* let someone drown you. I'd hold you under water myself. Because exorcism is hard and things go wrong. And if they go far enough wrong, you're left with a demon rotting inside your soul, and how the *hell* could I let that happen to someone I loved?"

He spurred his horse forward. Slate tried to kick her animal after him and it managed another brief, useless trot.

"Wait—*wait!*"

Caliban vanished around a bend in the road and Slate thought, *That was it. That was the end. That was the point where I strained it all too far and it broke.*

Which was stupid, because it had broken days before, it had broken the moment Caliban had tossed her aside without a thought to get to Brenner. There was no reason she should be sitting on this stupid horse in the middle of the road, crying. No reason at all.

CHAPTER 55

"Please send this package to the temple of the Forge God," said Caliban to the innkeeper.

He's returning the tabard. Gods. I stole that damn thing myself, and he's returning it. I…yes, of course he is. Why would I think any differently?

The wall of silence was between them again. Slate had plodded along the road for what felt like an hour and then Caliban had simply ridden up beside her. She couldn't think of what to say that would bridge the growing rift between them, so she didn't say anything.

Someone I loved.

She worried at the words like a scab inside her head.

Someone I loved.

Someone I loved.

Eventually they had argued about staying at an inn, or at least, Slate had tried to start an argument about it. Caliban had said, "It will be safer to avoid people."

Slate said, "I need a mattress or somebody dies."

And damn him, he had opened his mouth and she could see him about to say, "But it isn't safe," and then he closed his mouth again and nodded and said, "As you wish."

Bastard.

The inn had one room free. Caliban went down to the stable. Slate sat in the room, staring fixedly at a glass of wine.

He'd killed Brenner.

He'd drowned—what was it? Eleven people? And saved some of them in the process.

We have a better survival rate than a surgeon taking off a diseased limb.

Slate had stood by and watched Brenner kill a lot more than that, for much less pure motives.

How many people had Caliban handed over to the temple to exorcise? Even he didn't know.

If I could have gone into the water myself, instead of the victims, I would have.

Four times, they'd drowned him. Until he was dead enough to kill a demon, too, until it rotted in the back of his head.

Did the scales balance out? Did anything ever balance out? Brenner had saved an enormous portion of the city. Did that make up for lives he'd been paid to take?

Did a kiss on the shoulder in the dark make up for not giving her an argument when she damn well wanted one?

Slate pushed her glass aside.

She went down to the stable, stopping briefly at the bar to place a request, and found Caliban in the stableyard, praying.

"Get up," she said. She didn't care if she interrupted him. The Dreaming God was the one person in this whole mess that she was utterly unwilling to forgive.

Caliban rose to his feet. "Is there a problem?"

"They're filling a tub in my room with hot water," she said.

He looked at her levelly.

"It's for you."

It seemed like everything that could happen was balanced on what Caliban said next. Slate was very aware of the sound of the horses moving in their stalls and the smell of straw and dung.

This is ridiculous. We saved Anuket City and the Dowager's City, we put a stop to the Clockwork Boys, we even figured out the damned werk-blight. I had a tattoo eating me and I stood over a wonder-engine and people died and all I care about is what a man standing in a stableyard says next.

What he said next was, "I would like that very much."

"Come on, then."

They climbed the stairs together. Slate opened the door to her room and gestured him inside.

The servants had indeed filled the tub with hot water, as she'd requested at the bar. It was still steaming.

Caliban looked at it, then at her, with his hands on his belt.

He waited for her to leave. She sat down instead.

"Don't mind me," she said. "I've seen it all already."

"So you have."

"I'll turn my back, if you're feeling modest."

"You're too kind, madam."

Slate turned her chair around and dedicated her attention firmly to her wine.

She heard the clatter of metal hitting the floor behind her and the rustle of clothing being folded. Then footsteps and the gurgle of water and a sigh verging on a moan.

She stared into the bottom of her wineglass, listening to quiet splashing sounds. It was completely a trick of her mind that she could feel his presence against the back of her neck, like sun on raw skin.

"You could stay here tonight," she said abruptly.

The splashing sounds halted.

"If you wanted. It's not—" Slate grimaced "—an order or anything like that."

I am a master of seduction. Truly.

The silence went on for long enough that she felt embarrassment start to heat up her cheeks. She wanted to tell him to forget she'd said anything.

"Is this pity?"

It was so completely unexpected a question that Slate wheeled around to look at him.

He was half-lying in the tub with his arms hanging over the sides and the back of his head against the rim. With his knees pulled up, he had as much of himself submerged as he could manage in a tub that size.

He turned his head enough to look at her. "Well?"

"Pity?" she said, baffled.

"My exorcism," he said. "If you're pitying me because I was drowned a few times last year, don't. I was unconscious for most of it. Being possessed was much worse. I remember *all* of that."

Slate let out a squawk of laughter. "Pity! You look like a damn god, you kill demons for a living, you and Brenner saved the damn city a week ago while I stood around wringing my hands, and you worry *I'm* pitying *you?*"

He closed his eyes and let out a groan that had nothing to do with the hot water. "We are doing this very badly."

"Tell me about it," said Slate, with feeling.

"Grimehug told me I was stupid before we left. Said I was twisting my whiskers instead of biting the back of your neck."

Slate snorted.

"Then he told me that stupid was a good mate for crazy, maybe."

She couldn't think of anything much to say to that.

"Slate…at this moment, I am willing to take you to the capitol. I will make my report to the Dowager's people. I will do everything in my power to see that you are settled safely there. And then, if it is what you want, I will leave again."

She still felt as if her stomach were dropping out from under her when he said it. She nodded.

"But to do all that, I have to sleep in the stables. I *cannot* spend another night in your bed and then walk away." He had opened his eyes again, but seemed to be staring at the ceiling.

"You said—earlier—someone you loved—" Slate found that she was steeling herself for something. *He loves me, he loves me not, and which would be worse, I wonder?*

"I am hopelessly in love with you and the only thing that is keeping me from following you around like a stray dog for the rest of my life is the fact that it would make you hate me even more." He considered this for a moment. "Also, pride. My sins haven't been quite beaten out of me yet, I suppose."

"You could have said something earlier," said Slate.

"Did I not mention it?"

"First I've heard of it."

"I was afraid if I told you outright, you'd run screaming. But I thought that it was blindingly obvious."

"Obvious? Gah!" Slate clutched the back of the chair.

"Ah." He nodded slowly. "Grimehug may have been on to something."

"Possibly."

He returned his gaze to the ceiling. "It doesn't matter, though. If you're sick of the sight of me, how I feel is somewhat immaterial, isn't it?"

She got up, not sure if she was going to pounce on him or try to drown him in the bathtub. "Do they *train* you to be martyrs, or does it just come naturally?"

"Most paladins do have some natural aptitude in that direction…"

Slate took a deep breath. She was going to tell him exactly what she thought of him, whatever that was. She was going to yell. She was going to say things so cutting that he'd wake up in the middle of the night bleeding. She was…she was…

Apparently she was going to sneeze.

"Auuhh….auuhh…*gnnnrghghkk*!…bugger…"

She pinched the bridge of her nose and tilted her head back, trying not to drown in the sudden wave of rosemary. Was she in danger? Had a clocktaur gotten into the room somehow?

A distant part of her mind registered splashing and squelching and then Caliban pressed a handkerchief into her hand.

She took it grimly, blew her nose, wiped the back of her wrist across her eyes, and looked up at him.

He was standing very close. He was still damp. She watched a droplet of water meander down his chest and thought angrily that no one should be allowed to be that pretty in the middle of a fight. Certainly not while her eyes were red and she was trying violently not to sneeze.

She didn't look down. She had standards. Somewhere.

Still.

"The bath was pity," she admitted. Her eyes seemed to have gotten stuck somewhere around his throat. Stupid paladins. Idiots, the lot of them.

"I figured as much."

This one was probably stupider than most.

On the other hand, a smart man would never get involved with a forger from the capitol. Certainly not one with a price on her head in Anuket City.

Of course, he had a price on his head there, too. So at least they had that much in common.

"Love, huh?" she said.

"Utterly. Profoundly. Would you like to send me off to kill a dragon or something to prove it, like in a ballad?"

"What the hell would that prove?"

"I suppose it would prove that I could kill a dragon. I'm not sure why that would be a good thing. They never cover that bit in ballads."

"What would I even *do* with a dead dragon?"

"I'm open to other suggestions."

"What would I do with a live paladin, for that matter?"

He considered this at some length. She decided to lean her head against his chest while she waited.

"Well," he said, "You've had a paladin for awhile, and I don't think you've been terribly impressed. But if you keep me around, I will make sure I always have a handkerchief."

He put his arms around her. One of his hands wrapped around her bicep, where the tattoo lay ugly and inert. You were never supposed to get matching tattoos, they said in the brothel. It pretty much guaranteed he'd run off with the first bit of fluff that came his way.

Somehow she didn't think that would be much of a problem with Caliban. Still…

"I warn you, I'm the jealous type."

"I can't imagine you'll ever have cause to be jealous."

"Are you kidding? You wander around in that armor looking noble and half the city would probably fall into your arms! Men *and* women!"

"Sounds exhausting," he said. "I will clearly be much safer with you to fend them off."

"You know what I do for a living," she warned. "I'm not going to give up my profession to become respectable."

"Dreaming God forbid. I shall simply have to guard you against any angry clients." He rested his chin on top of her head. "I fear that I may be prone to going off and killing demons."

She shuddered. "That's going to make me crazy."

"And I will be a wreck every time you break into a building to raid the filing cabinet. Do you think we can make do?"

"Can you stick to the ones that are possessing cows and things?"

"I make no promises, but I will try. After the last month, a levitating cow would be positively restful."

Slate let out a huff of laughter.

"As the temple is not going to take me back, it may be a moot point anyway. Though the Dreaming God seems to have no such qualms. But really, most of my job always did involve possessed livestock."

"Mmm."

"Beyond that, I had been thinking that perhaps the gnoles could make use of a human knight. And that they might very well need someone who could forge letters of safe conduct and so forth. Useful when dealing with other humans."

Slate recognized a peace offering when it was standing in front of her, dripping.

"It's possible we know someone like that," she admitted.

"Well, then."

"I'm still pissed at your god," she warned.

"I know."

"That doesn't bother you?"

She felt the muscle under her cheek move as he shrugged. "I doubt it bothers Him. And I am…touched…that you care enough to be angry on my behalf."

Slate's cheek was getting damp. She was either going to have to get him a towel or strip off her own clothes. She knew which one she'd prefer.

"Well," she said, heaving a sigh that seemed to come from the soles of her feet. "If only for the handkerchiefs."

"Naturally."

"And clearly I must be in love with you, to even be considering this. Despite my better judgment!"

His arms tightened around her. "I'm extremely relieved to hear it… my liege."

She swore at him but he stopped the torrent of obscenities with a kiss. Slate grumbled against his lips and put her arms around his neck, and didn't even mind the faint, lingering scent of rosemary.

Acknowledgments

AKA

I Can't Believe That's Finally Over

It is 2018 and I am finally finished writing the Clocktaur War.

I have been working on what is not, when you get down to it, a terribly long pair of books—165K and some change, all told—for almost twelve years. Caliban and Slate and Brenner and crew have been living in my head for over a decade now. If I do the math (never do the math) that is literally half of my adult life.

It is very strange to close the book on a project that's lasted that long. I've done it before—my webcomic Digger took up an even greater percentage of my existence—but it still doesn't get any less strange to shuffle the whole crew out of the section of my mind labelled "Characters" and into the section labelled "Characters Emeritus."

I can't swear it's the end for everybody, of course. Learned Edmund is very young and needs some adventures of his own, and I can't swear that future books in this universe won't have a good-natured paladin and a disgruntled forger show up somewhere in the background. Still.

(Yes, of course there will be future books in this universe. There's a trilogy in the works right now that I keep telling myself will be novellas.)

Well! Acknowledgements! To my faithful proofreaders and copy-editors, without whom this would be even more flawed than usual. To my patient editor, K.B. Spangler, who had a LOT to say and eventually just started sending me pictures of Deadpool whenever Brenner did something more than usually diabolical.

To my husband Kevin, who would probably make a very good paladin.

And to all my fans who read stuff and stuck with me until Book Two. I could not have done it without you, and I hope it was worth the wait.

T. Kingfisher (Ursula Vernon)

North Carolina

2018

CPSIA information can be obtained
at www.ICGtesting.com
Printed in the USA
LVOW13*0156090718

583121LV00005B/24/P